DATE DUE		
MAR 0 1 2002			
AUG 0 3 2002			

THE TRAIL OF THE
LONESOME PINE

"KEEP IT SAFE, OLD PINE..AND BLESS HIM, DEAR GOD, AND GUARD HIM EVERMORE."

John Fox, Jr.

The Trail
of the
Lonesome Pine

Illustrated by F.C. Yohn

Buccaneer Books
Cutchogue, New York

10-00 Bt 35.95

To
F. S.

THE TRAIL OF THE LONESOME PINE

I

SHE sat at the base of the big tree—her little sunbonnet pushed back, her arms locked about her knees, her bare feet gathered under her crimson gown and her deep eyes fixed on the smoke in the valley below. Her breath was still coming fast between her parted lips. There were tiny drops along the roots of her shining hair, for the climb had been steep, and now the shadow of disappointment darkened her eyes. The mountains ran in limitless blue waves towards the mounting sun—but at birth her eyes had opened on them as on the white mists trailing up the steeps below her. Beyond them was a gap in the next mountain chain and down in the little valley, just visible through it, were trailing blue mists as well, and she knew that they were smoke. Where was the great glare of yellow light that the "circuit rider" had told about—and the leaping tongues of fire? Where was the shrieking monster that ran without horses like the wind and tossed back rolling black plumes all streaked with fire ? For many days now she had heard stories of the "furriners" who had come into those hills and were doing strange things down there, and so at last she had climbed up through the dewy morning from the cove on the other side to see the wonders for herself. She had never been up there before. She had no business there now, and, if she were found out when she got back, she would get a scolding and maybe something worse from her step-mother—and all that trouble and risk for nothing but smoke. So, she lay back and rested—her little mouth tightening fiercely. It was a big world, though, that was spread before her and a vague awe of it seized her straightway and held her motionless and dreaming. Beyond those white mists trailing up the hills, beyond the blue smoke drifting in the valley, those limitless blue waves must run under the sun on and on to the end of the world! Her dead sister had gone into that far silence and had brought back wonderful stories of that outer world: and she began to wonder more than ever before whether she would ever go into it and see for herself what was there. With the thought, she rose slowly to her feet, moved slowly to the cliff that dropped sheer ten feet aside from the trail, and stood there like a great scarlet flower in still air. There was the way at her feet—that path that coiled under the cliff and ran down loop by loop through ma-

jestic oak and poplar and masses of rhododendron.
She drew a long breath and stirred uneasily—she'd
better go home now—but the path had a snake-
like charm for her and still she stood, following it
as far down as she could with her eyes. Down it
went, writhing this way and that to a spur that
had been swept bare by forest fires. Along this
spur it travelled straight for a while and, as her
eyes eagerly followed it to where it sank sharply
into a covert of maples, the little creature dropped
of a sudden to the ground and, like something wild,
lay flat.

A human figure had filled the leafy mouth that
swallowed up the trail and it was coming towards
her. With a thumping heart she pushed slowly
forward through the brush until her face, fox-like
with cunning and screened by a blueberry bush,
hung just over the edge of the cliff, and there she
lay, like a crouched panther-cub, looking down.
For a moment, all that was human seemed gone
from her eyes, but, as she watched, all that was
lost came back to them, and something more.
She had seen that it was a man, but she had
dropped so quickly that she did not see the big,
black horse that, unled, was following him. Now
both man and horse had stopped. The stranger
had taken off his gray slouched hat and he was
wiping his face with something white. Something
blue was tied loosely about his throat. She had
never seen a man like that before. His face was

3

smooth and looked different, as did his throat and his hands. His breeches were tight and on his feet were strange boots that were the colour of his saddle, which was deep in seat, high both in front and behind and had strange long-hooded stirrups. Starting to mount, the man stopped with one foot in the stirrup and raised his eyes towards her so suddenly that she shrank back again with a quicker throbbing at her heart and pressed closer to the earth. Still, seen or not seen, flight was easy for her, so she could not forbear to look again. Apparently, he had seen nothing—only that the next turn of the trail was too steep to ride, and so he started walking again, and his walk, as he strode along the path, was new to her, as was the erect way with which he held his head and his shoulders.

In her wonder over him, she almost forgot herself, forgot to wonder where he was going and why he was coming into those lonely hills until, as his horse turned a bend of the trail, she saw hanging from the other side of the saddle something that looked like a gun. He was a "raider"—that man: so, cautiously and swiftly then, she pushed herself back from the edge of the cliff, sprang to her feet, dashed past the big tree and, winged with fear, sped down the mountain—leaving in a spot of sunlight at the base of the pine the print of one bare foot in the black earth.

4

II

HE had seen the big pine when he first came
to those hills—one morning, at daybreak,
when the valley was a sea of mist that threw soft
clinging spray to the very mountain tops: for even
above the mists, that morning, its mighty head
arose—sole visible proof that the earth still slept
beneath. Straightway, he wondered how it had
ever got there, so far above the few of its kind that
haunted the green dark ravines far below. Some
whirlwind, doubtless, had sent a tiny cone circling
heavenward and dropped it there. It had sent
others, too, no doubt, but how had this tree faced
wind and storm alone and alone lived to defy both
so proudly? Some day he would learn. Thereafter, he had seen it, at noon—but little less majestic among the oaks that stood about it; had seen
it catching the last light at sunset, clean-cut against
the after-glow, and like a dark, silent, mysterious
sentinel guarding the mountain pass under the
moon. He had seen it giving place with sombre
dignity to the passing burst of spring—had seen
it green among dying autumn leaves, green in the
gray of winter trees and still green in a shroud of
snow—a changeless promise that the earth must

wake to life again. The Lonesome Pine, the mountaineers called it, and the Lonesome Pine it always looked to be. From the beginning it had a curious fascination for him, and straightway within him—half exile that he was—there sprang up a sympathy for it as for something that was human and a brother. And now he was on the trail of it at last. From every point that morning it had seemed almost to nod down to him as he climbed and, when he reached the ledge that gave him sight of it from base to crown, the winds murmured among its needles like a welcoming voice. At once, he saw the secret of its life. On each side rose a cliff that had sheltered it from storms until its trunk had shot upwards so far and so straight and so strong that its green crown could lift itself on and on and bend—blow what might—as proudly and securely as a lily on its stalk in a morning breeze. Dropping his bridle rein he put one hand against it as though on the shoulder of a friend.

"Old Man," he said, "You must be pretty lonesome up here, and I'm glad to meet you."

For a while he sat against it—resting. He had no particular purpose that day—no particular destination. His saddle-bags were across the cantle of his cow-boy saddle. His fishing rod was tied under one flap. He was young and his own master. Time was hanging heavy on his hands that day and he loved the woods and the nooks and crannies of them where his own kind rarely made its way. Beyond, the cove looked dark, forbidding, mysterious, and what was beyond he did not know. So down there he would go. As he bent his head forward to rise, his eye caught the spot of sunlight, and he leaned over it with a smile. In the black earth was a human foot-print—too small and slender for the foot of a man, a boy or a woman. Beyond, the same prints were visible—wider apart—and he smiled again. A girl had been there. She was the crimson flash that he saw as he started up the steep and mistook for a flaming bush of sumach. She had seen him coming and she had fled. Still smiling, he rose to his feet.

III

ON one side he had left the earth yellow with
the coming noon, but it was still morning as
he went down on the other side. The laurel and
rhododendron still reeked with dew in the deep,
ever-shaded ravine. The ferns drenched his stirrups, as he brushed through them, and each dripping tree-top broke the sunlight and let it drop in
tent-like beams through the shimmering under-
mist. A bird flashed here and there through the
green gloom, but there was no sound in the air but
the footfalls of his horse and the easy creaking of
leather under him, the drip of dew overhead and
the running of water below. Now and then he
could see the same slender foot-prints in the rich
loam and he saw them in the sand where the first
tiny brook tinkled across the path from a gloomy
ravine. There the little creature had taken a flying leap across it and, beyond, he could see the
prints no more. He little guessed that while he
halted to let his horse drink, the girl lay on a rock
above him, looking down. She was nearer home
now and was less afraid; so she had slipped from
the trail and climbed above it there to watch him
pass. As he went on, she slid from her perch and

8

with cat-footed quiet followed him. When he reached the river she saw him pull in his horse and eagerly bend forward, looking into a pool just below the crossing. There was a bass down there in the clear water—a big one—and the man whistled cheerily and dismounted, tying his horse to a sassafras bush and unbuckling a tin bucket and a curious looking net from his saddle. With the net in one hand and the bucket in the other, he turned back up the creek and passed so close to where she had slipped aside into the bushes that she came near shrieking, but his eyes were fixed on a pool of the creek above and, to her wonder, he strolled straight into the water, with his boots on, pushing the net in front of him.

He was a "raider" sure, she thought now, and he was looking for a "moonshine" still, and the wild little thing in the bushes smiled cunningly— there was no still up that creek—and as he had left his horse below and his gun, she waited for him to come back, which he did, by and by, dripping and soaked to his knees. Then she saw him untie the queer "gun" on his saddle, pull it out of a case and—her eyes got big with wonder—take it to pieces and make it into a long limber rod. In a moment he had cast a minnow into the pool and waded out into the water up to his hips. She had never seen so queer a fishing-pole—so queer a fisherman. How could he get a fish out with that little switch, she thought contemptuously? By and by

9

something hummed queerly, the man gave a slight jerk and a shining fish flopped two feet into the air. It was surely very queer, for the man didn't put his rod over his shoulder and walk ashore, as did the mountaineers, but stood still, winding something with one hand, and again the fish would flash into the air and then that humming would start again while the fisherman would stand quiet and waiting for a while—and then he would begin to wind again. In her wonder, she rose unconsciously to her feet and a stone rolled down to the ledge below her. The fisherman turned his head and she started to run, but without a word he turned again to the fish he was playing. Moreover, he was too far out in the water to catch her, so she advanced slowly—even to the edge of the stream, watching the fish cut half circles about the man. If he saw her, he gave no notice, and it was well that he did not. He was pulling the bass to and fro now through the water, tiring him out—drowning him—stepping backward at the same time, and, a moment later, the fish slid easily out of the edge of the water, gasping along the edge of a low sand-bank, and the fisherman reaching down with one hand caught him in the gills. Then he looked up and smiled—and she had seen no smile like that before.

"Howdye, Little Girl?"

One bare toe went burrowing suddenly into the sand, one finger went to her red mouth—and that was all. She merely stared him straight in the eye and he smiled again.

"Cat got your tongue?"

Her eyes fell at the ancient banter, but she lifted them straightway and stared again.

"You live around here?"

She stared on.

"Where?"

No answer.

"What's your name, little girl?"

And still she stared.

"Oh, well, of course, you can't talk, if the cat's got your tongue."

The steady eyes leaped angrily, but there was still no answer, and he bent to take the fish off his hook, put on a fresh minnow, turned his back and tossed it into the pool.

"Hit hain't!"

He looked up again. She surely was a pretty little thing—and more, now that she was angry.

"I should say not," he said teasingly. "What did you say your name was?"

"What's *yo'* name?"

The fisherman laughed. He was just becoming accustomed to the mountain etiquette that commands a stranger to divulge himself first.

"My name's—Jack."

"An' mine's—Jill." She laughed now, and it was his time for surprise—where could she have heard of Jack and Jill?

His line rang suddenly.

"Jack," she cried, "you got a bite!"

He pulled, missed the strike, and wound in. The minnow was all right, so he tossed it back again.

"That isn't your name," he said.

"If 'tain't, then that ain't your'n?"

"Yes 'tis," he said, shaking his head affirmatively.

A long cry came down the ravine:

"J-u-n-e! eh—oh—J-u-n-e!" That was a queer name for the mountains, and the fisherman wondered if he had heard aright—June.

The little girl gave a shrill answering cry, but she did not move.

"Thar now!" she said.

"Who's that—your Mammy?"

"No, 'tain't—hit's my step-mammy. I'm a goin' to ketch hell now." Her innocent eyes turned sullen and her baby mouth tightened.

"Good Lord!" said the fisherman, startled, and then he stopped—the words were as innocent on her lips as a benediction.

"Have you got a father?" Like a flash, her whole face changed.

"I reckon I have."

"Where is he?"

"Hyeh he is!" drawled a voice from the bushes, and it had a tone that made the fisherman whirl suddenly. A giant mountaineer stood on the

12

bank above him, with a Winchester in the hollow of his arm.

"How are you?" The giant's heavy eyes lifted quickly, but he spoke to the girl.

"You go on home—what you doin' hyeh gassin' with furriners!"

The girl shrank to the bushes, but she cried sharply back:

"Don't you hurt him now, Dad. He ain't even got a pistol. He ain't no——"

"Shet up!" The little creature vanished and the mountaineer turned to the fisherman, who had just put on a fresh minnow and tossed it into the river.

"Purty well, thank you," he said shortly. "How are you?"

"Fine!" was the nonchalant answer. For a moment there was silence and a puzzled frown gathered on the mountaineer's face.

"That's a bright little girl of yours— What did she mean by telling you not to hurt me?"

"You haven't been long in these mountains, have ye?"

"No—not in *these* mountains—why?" The fisherman looked around and was almost startled by the fierce gaze of his questioner.

"Stop that, please," he said, with a humourous smile. "You make me nervous."

The mountaineer's bushy brows came together across the bridge of his nose and his voice rumbled like distant thunder.

13

"What's yo' name, stranger, an' what's yo' business over hyeh?"

"Dear me, there you go! You can see I'm fishing, but why does everybody in these mountains want to know my name?"

"You heerd me!"

"Yes." The fisherman turned again and saw the giant's rugged face stern and pale with open anger now, and he, too, grew suddenly serious.

"Suppose I don't tell you," he said gravely. "What——"

"Git!" said the mountaineer, with a move of one huge hairy hand up the mountain. "An' git quick!"

The fisherman never moved and there was the click of a shell thrown into place in the Winchester and a guttural oath from the mountaineer's beard.

"Damn ye," he said hoarsely, raising the rifle. "I'll give ye——"

"Don't, Dad!" shrieked a voice from the bushes. "I know his name, hit's Jack ——" the rest of the name was unintelligible. The mountaineer dropped the butt of his gun to the ground and laughed.

"Oh, air *you* the engineer?"

The fisherman was angry now. He had not moved hand or foot and he said nothing, but his mouth was set hard and his bewildered blue eyes had a glint in them that the mountaineer did not

14

at the moment see. He was leaning with one arm on the muzzle of his Winchester, his face had suddenly become suave and shrewd and now he laughed again:

"So you're Jack Hale, air ye?"

The fisherman spoke. "*John* Hale, except to my friends." He looked hard at the old man.

"Do you know that's a pretty dangerous joke of yours, my friend—I might have a gun myself sometimes. Did you think you could scare me?" The mountaineer stared in genuine surprise.

"Twusn't no joke," he said shortly. "An' I don't waste time skeering folks. I reckon you don't know who I be?"

"I don't care who you are." Again the mountaineer stared.

"No use gittin' mad, young feller," he said coolly. "I mistaken ye fer somebody else an' I axe yer pardon. When you git through fishin' come up to the house right up the creek thar an' I'll give ye a dram."

"Thank you," said the fisherman stiffly, and the mountaineer turned silently away. At the edge of the bushes, he looked back; the stranger was still fishing, and the old man went on with a shake of his head.

"He'll come," he said to himself. "Oh, he'll come!"

That very point Hale was debating with himself as he unavailingly cast his minnow into the swift water and slowly wound it in again. How did that old man know his name? And would the old savage really have hurt him had he not found out who he was? The little girl was a wonder: evidently she had muffled his last name on purpose—not knowing it herself—and it was a quick and cunning ruse. He owed her something for that—why did she try to protect him? Wonderful eyes, too, the little thing had—deep and dark—and how the flame did dart from them when she got angry! He smiled, remembering—he liked that. And her hair—it was exactly like the gold-bronze on the wing of a wild turkey that he had shot the day before. Well, it was noon now, the fish had stopped biting after the wayward fashion of bass, he was hungry and thirsty and he would go up and see the little girl and the giant again and get that promised dram. Once more, however, he let his minnow float down into the shadow of a big rock, and while he was winding in, he looked up to see in the road two people on a gray horse, a man with a woman behind him—both old and spectacled—all three motionless on the bank and looking at him: and he wondered if all three had stopped to ask his name and his business. No, they had just come down to the creek and both they must know already.

"Ketching any?" called out the old man, cheerily.

"Only one," answered Hale with equal cheer.

16

The old woman pushed back her bonnet as he waded through the water towards them and he saw that she was puffing a clay pipe. She looked at the fisherman and his tackle with the naïve wonder of a child, and then she said in a commanding undertone.

"Go on, Billy."

"Now, ole Hon, I wish ye'd jes' wait a minute." Hale smiled. He loved old people, and two kinder faces he had never seen—two gentler voices he had never heard.

"I reckon you got the only green pyerch up hyeh," said the old man, chuckling, "but thar's a sight of 'em down thar below my old mill." Quietly the old woman hit the horse with a stripped branch of elm and the old gray, with a switch of his tail, started.

"Wait a minute, Hon," he said again, appealingly, "won't ye?" but calmly she hit the horse again and the old man called back over his shoulder:

"You come on down to the mill an' I'll show ye whar you can ketch a mess."

"All right," shouted Hale, holding back his laughter, and on they went, the old man remonstrating in the kindliest way—the old woman silently puffing her pipe and making no answer except to flay gently the rump of the lazy old gray.

Hesitating hardly a moment, Hale unjointed his pole, left his minnow bucket where it was, mounted his horse and rode up the path. About him, the beech leaves gave back the gold of the autumn sunlight, and a little ravine, high under the crest of the mottled mountain, was on fire with the scarlet of maple. Not even yet had the morning chill left the densely shaded path. When he got to the bare crest of a little rise, he could see up the creek a spiral of blue rising swiftly from a stone chimney. Geese and ducks were hunting crawfish in the little creek that ran from a milk-house of logs, half hidden by willows at the edge of the forest, and a turn in the path brought into view a log-cabin well chinked with stones and plaster, and with a well-built porch. A fence ran around the yard and there was a meat house near a little orchard of apple-trees, under which were many hives of bee-gums. This man had things "hung up" and was well-to-do. Down the rise and through a thicket he went, and as he approached the creek that came down past the cabin there was a shrill cry ahead of him.

"Whoa thar, Buck! Gee-haw, I tell ye!" An ox-wagon evidently was coming on, and the road was so narrow that he turned his horse into the bushes to let it pass.

"Whoa—Haw!—Gee—Gee—Buck, Gee, I tell ye! I'll knock yo' fool head off the fust thing you know!"

Still there was no sound of ox or wagon and the voice sounded like a child's. So he went on at a

"DON'T, DAD!" SHRIEKED A VOICE FROM THE BUSHES. "I KNOW HIS NAME."

walk in the thick sand, and when he turned the bushes he pulled up again with a low laugh. In the road across the creek was a chubby, tow-haired boy with a long switch in his right hand, and a pine dagger and a string in his left. Attached to the string and tied by one hind leg was a frog. The boy was using the switch as a goad and driving the frog as an ox, and he was as earnest as though both were real.

"I give ye a little rest now, Buck," he said, shaking his head earnestly. "Hit's a purty hard pull hyeh, but I know, by Gum, you can make hit —if you hain't too durn lazy. Now, git up, Buck!" he yelled suddenly, flaying the sand with his switch. "Git up—Whoa—Haw—Gee, Gee!" The frog hopped several times.

"Whoa, now!" said the little fellow, panting in sympathy. "I knowed you could do it." Then he looked up. For an instant he seemed terrified but he did not run. Instead he stealthily shifted the pine dagger over to his right hand and the string to his left.

"Here, boy," said the fisherman with affected sternness: "What are you doing with that dagger?"

The boy's breast heaved and his dirty fingers clenched tight around the whittled stick.

"Don't you talk to me that-a-way," he said with an ominous shake of his head. "I'll gut ye!"

The fisherman threw back his head, and his

peal of laughter did what his sternness failed to do. The little fellow wheeled suddenly, and his feet spurned the sand around the bushes for home —the astonished frog dragged bumping after him. "Well!" said the fisherman.

IV

EVEN the geese in the creek seemed to know that he was a stranger and to distrust him, for they cackled and, spreading their wings, fled cackling up the stream. As he neared the house, the little girl ran around the stone chimney, stopped short, shaded her eyes with one hand for a moment and ran excitedly into the house. A moment later, the bearded giant slouched out, stooping his head as he came through the door.

"Hitch that 'ar post to yo' hoss and come right in," he thundered cheerily. "I'm waitin' fer ye."

The little girl came to the door, pushed one brown slender hand through her tangled hair, caught one bare foot behind a deer-like ankle and stood motionless. Behind her was the boy—his dagger still in hand.

"Come right in!" said the old man, "we are purty pore folks, but you're welcome to what we have."

The fisherman, too, had to stoop as he came in, for he, too, was tall. The interior was dark, in spite of the wood fire in the big stone fireplace. Strings of herbs and red-pepper pods and twisted tobacco hung from the ceiling and down the wall on either side of the fire; and in one corner, near the two beds in the room, hand-made quilts of many colours were piled several feet high. On wooden pegs above the door where ten years before would have been buck antlers and an old-fashioned rifle, lay a Winchester; on either side of the door were auger holes through the logs (he did not understand that they were port-holes) and another Winchester stood in the corner. From the mantel the butt of a big 44-Colt's revolver protruded ominously. On one of the beds in the corner he could see the outlines of a figure lying under a brilliantly figured quilt, and at the foot of it the boy with the pine dagger had retreated for refuge. From the moment he stooped at the door something in the room had made him vaguely uneasy, and when his eyes in swift survey came back to the fire, they passed the blaze swiftly and met on the edge of the light another pair of eyes burning on him.

"Howdye!" said Hale.

"Howdye!" was the low, unpropitiating answer.

The owner of the eyes was nothing but a boy, in spite of his length: so much of a boy that a slight crack in his voice showed that it was just past the throes of "changing," but those black eyes burned on without swerving—except once when they flashed at the little girl who, with her chin in her hand and one foot on the top rung of her chair, was gazing at the stranger with equal steadiness. She saw the boy's glance, she shifted her knees impatiently and her little face grew sullen. Hale smiled inwardly, for he thought he could already see the lay of the land, and he wondered that, at such an age, such fierceness could be: so every now and then he looked at the boy, and every time he looked, the black eyes were on him. The mountain youth must have been almost six feet tall, young as he was, and while he was lanky in limb he was well knit. His jean trousers were stuffed in the top of his boots and were tight over his knees which were well-moulded, and that is rare with a mountaineer. A loop of black hair curved over his forehead, down almost to his left eye. His nose was straight and almost delicate and his mouth was small, but extraordinarily resolute. Somewhere he had seen that face before, and he turned suddenly, but he did not startle the lad with his abruptness, nor make him turn his gaze.

"Why, haven't I—?" he said. And then he suddenly remembered. He had seen that boy not long since on the other side of the mountains, riding his horse at a gallop down the county road with his reins in his teeth, and shooting a pistol alternately at the sun and the earth with either hand. Perhaps it was as well not to recall the incident. He turned to the old mountaineer.

"Do you mean to tell me that a man can't go through these mountains without telling everybody who asks him what his name is?"

The effect of his question was singular. The old man spat into the fire and put his hand to his beard. The boy crossed his legs suddenly and shoved his muscular fingers deep into his pockets. The figure shifted position on the bed and the infant at the foot of it seemed to clench his toy-dagger a little more tightly. Only the little girl was motionless—she still looked at him, unwinking. What sort of wild animals had he fallen among?

"No, he can't—an' keep healthy." The giant spoke shortly.

"Why not?"

"Well, if a man hain't up to some devilment, what reason's he got fer not tellin' his name?"

"That's his business."

"Tain't over hyeh. Hit's mine. Ef a man don't want to tell his name over hyeh, he's a spy or a raider or an officer looking fer somebody or," he added carelessly, but with a quick covert look at his visitor—"he's got some kind o' business that he don't want nobody to know about."

"Well, I came over here—just to—well, I hardly know why I did come."

"Jess so," said the old man dryly. "An' if ye ain't looking fer trouble, you'd better tell your name in these mountains, whenever you're axed. Ef enough people air backin' a custom anywhar hit goes, don't hit?"

His logic was good—and Hale said nothing.

Presently the old man rose with a smile on his face that looked cynical, picked up a black lump and threw it into the fire. It caught fire, crackled, blazed, almost oozed with oil, and Hale leaned forward and leaned back.

"Pretty good coal!"

"Hain't it, though?" The old man picked up a sliver that had flown to the hearth and held a match to it. The piece blazed and burned in his hand.

"I never seed no coal in these mountains like that—did you?"

"Not often—find it around here?"

"Right hyeh on this farm—about five feet thick!"

"What?"

"An' no partin'."

"No partin'"—it was not often that he found a mountaineer who knew what a parting in a coal bed was.

"A friend o' mine on t'other side,"—a light dawned for the engineer.

"Oh," he said quickly. "That's how you knew my name."

"Right you air, stranger. He tol' me you was a—expert."

The old man laughed loudly. "An' that's why you come over hyeh."

"No, it isn't."

"Co'se not,"—the old fellow laughed again. Hale shifted the talk.

"Well, now that you know my name, suppose you tell me what yours is?"

"Tolliver—Judd Tolliver." Hale started.

"Not Devil Judd!"

"That's what some evil folks calls me." Again he spoke shortly. The mountaineers do not like to talk about their feuds. Hale knew this—and the subject was dropped. But he watched the huge mountaineer with interest. There was no more famous character in all those hills than the giant before him—yet his face was kind and was good-humoured, but the nose and eyes were the beak and eyes of some bird of prey. The little girl had disappeared for a moment. She came back with a blue-backed spelling-book, a second reader and a worn copy of "Mother Goose," and she opened first one and then the other until the attention of the visitor was caught—the black-haired youth watching her meanwhile with lowering brows.

"Where did you learn to read?" Hale asked. The old man answered:

"A preacher come by our house over on the Nawth Fork 'bout three year ago, and afore I knowed it he made me promise to send her sister Sally to some school up thar on the edge of the settlements. And after she come home, Sal larned that little gal to read and spell. Sal died 'bout a year ago."

Hale reached over and got the spelling-book,

and the old man grinned at the quick, unerring responses of the little girl, and the engineer looked surprised. She read, too, with unusual facility, and her pronunciation was very precise and not at all like her speech.

"You ought to send her to the same place," he said, but the old fellow shook his head.

"I couldn't git along without her."

The little girl's eyes began to dance suddenly, and, without opening "Mother Goose," she began:

"Jack and Jill went up a hill," and then she broke into a laugh and Hale laughed with her.

Abruptly, the boy opposite rose to his great length.

"I reckon I better be goin'." That was all he said as he caught up a Winchester, which stood unseen by his side, and out he stalked. There was not a word of good-by, not a glance at anybody. A few minutes later Hale heard the creak of a barn door on wooden hinges, a cursing command to a horse, and four feet going in a gallop down the path, and he knew there went an enemy.

"That's a good-looking boy—who is he?"

The old man spat into the fire. It seemed that he was not going to answer and the little girl broke in:

"Hit's my cousin Dave—he lives over on the Nawth Fork."

That was the seat of the Tolliver-Falin feud. Of that feud, too, Hale had heard, and so no more along that line of inquiry. He, too, soon rose to go.

"Why, ain't ye goin' to have something to eat?"

"Oh, no, I've got something in my saddle-bags and I must be getting back to the Gap."

"Well, I reckon you ain't. You're jes' goin' to take a snack right here." Hale hesitated, but the little girl was looking at him with such unconscious eagerness in her dark eyes that he sat down again.

"All right, I will, thank you." At once she ran to the kitchen and the old man rose and pulled a bottle of white liquid from under the quilts.

"I reckon I can trust ye," he said. The liquor burned Hale like fire, and the old man, with a laugh at the face the stranger made, tossed off a tumblerful.

"Gracious!" said Hale, "can you do that often?"

"Afore breakfast, dinner and supper," said the old man—"but I don't." Hale felt a plucking at his sleeve. It was the boy with the dagger at his elbow.

"Less see you laugh that-a-way agin," said Bub with such deadly seriousness that Hale unconsciously broke into the same peal.

"Now," said Bub, unwinking, "I ain't afeard o' you no more."

28

V

AWAITING dinner, the mountaineer and the "furriner" sat on the porch while Bub carved away at another pine dagger on the stoop. As Hale passed out the door, a querulous voice said "Howdye" from the bed in the corner and he knew it was the step-mother from whom the little girl expected some nether-world punishment for an offence of which he was ignorant. He had heard of the feud that had been going on between the red Falins and the black Tollivers for a quarter of a century, and this was Devil Judd, who had earned his nickname when he was the leader of his clan by his terrible strength, his marksmanship, his cunning and his courage. Some years since the old man had retired from the leadership, because he was tired of fighting or because he had quarrelled with his brother Dave and his foster-brother, Bad Rufe—known as the terror of the Tollivers—or from some unknown reason, and in consequence there had been peace for a long time—the Falins fearing that Devil Judd would be led into the feud again, the Tollivers wary of starting hostilities without his aid. After the last trouble, Bad Rufe Tolliver had gone West and old Judd had moved his family as far away as possible. Hale looked around him: this, then, was the home of Devil Judd Tolliver; the little creature inside was his daughter and her name was June. All around the cabin the wooded mountains towered except where, straight before his eyes, Lonesome Creek slipped through them to the river, and the old man had certainly picked out the very heart of silence for his home. There was no neighbour within two leagues, Judd said, except old Squire Billy Beams, who ran a mill a mile down the river. No wonder the spot was called Lonesome Cove.

"You must ha' seed Uncle Billy and ole Hon passin'," he said.

"I did." Devil Judd laughed and Hale made out that "Hon" was short for Honey.

"Uncle Billy used to drink right smart. Ole Hon broke him. She followed him down to the grocery one day and walked in. 'Come on, boys —let's have a drink'; and she set 'em up an' set 'em up until Uncle Billy most went crazy. He had hard work gittin' her home, an' Uncle Billy hain't teched a drap since." And the old mountaineer chuckled again.

All the time Hale could hear noises from the kitchen inside. The old step-mother was abed, he had seen no other woman about the house and he wondered if the child could be cooking dinner. Her flushed face answered when she opened the kitchen door and called them in. She had not only cooked but now she served as well, and when he thanked her, as he did every time she passed something to him, she would colour faintly. Once or twice her hand seemed to tremble, and he never looked at her but her questioning dark eyes were full upon him, and always she kept one hand busy pushing her thick hair back from her forehead. He had not asked her if it was her footprints he had seen coming down the mountain for fear that he might betray her, but apparently she had told on herself, for Bub, after a while, burst out suddenly:

"June, thar, thought you was a raider." The little girl flushed and the old man laughed.

"So'd you, pap," she said quietly.

"That's right," he said. "So'd anybody. I reckon you're the first man that ever come over hyeh jus' to go a-fishin'," and he laughed again. The stress on the last words showed that he believed no man had yet come just for that purpose, and Hale merely laughed with him. The old fellow gulped his food, pushed his chair back, and when Hale was through, he wasted no more time.

"Want to see that coal?"

"Yes, I do," said Hale.

"All right, I'll be ready in a minute."

The little girl followed Hale out on the porch and stood with her back against the railing.

"Did you catch it?" he asked. She nodded, unsmiling.

31

"I'm sorry. What were you doing up there?"
She showed no surprise that he knew that she had
been up there, and while she answered his question, he could see that she was thinking of something else.

"I'd heerd so much about what you furriners
was a-doin' over thar."

"You must have heard about a place farther
over—but it's coming over there, too, some day."
And still she looked an unspoken question.

The fish that Hale had caught was lying where he
had left it on the edge of the porch.

"That's for you, June," he said, pointing to it,
and the name as he spoke it was sweet to his ears.

"I'm much obleeged," she said, shyly. "I'd
'a' cooked hit fer ye if I'd 'a' knowed you wasn't
goin' to take hit home."

"That's the reason I didn't give it to you at
first—I was afraid you'd do that. I wanted you
to have it."

"Much obleeged," she said again, still unsmiling, and then she suddenly looked up at him—the
deeps of her dark eyes troubled.

"Air ye ever comin' back agin, Jack?" Hale
was not accustomed to the familiar form of address common in the mountains, independent of
sex or age—and he would have been staggered
had not her face been so serious. And then few
women had ever called him by his first name, and
this time his own name was good to his ears.

"Yes, June," he said soberly. "Not for some time, maybe—but I'm coming back again, sure." She smiled then with both lips and eyes—radiantly.

"I'll be lookin' fer ye," she said simply.

VI

THE old man went with him up the creek and, passing the milk house, turned up a brush-bordered little branch in which the engineer saw signs of coal. Up the creek the mountaineer led him some thirty yards above the water level and stopped. An entry had been driven through the rich earth and ten feet within was a shining bed of coal. There was no parting except two inches of mother-of-coal—midway, which would make it but easier to mine. Who had taught that old man to open coal in such a way—to make such a facing? It looked as though the old fellow were in some scheme with another to get him interested. As he drew closer, he saw radiations of some twelve inches, all over the face of the coal, star-shaped, and he almost gasped. It was not only cannel coal—it was "bird's-eye" cannel. Heavens, what a find! Instantly he was the cautious man of business, alert, cold, uncommunicative.

"That looks like a pretty good—" he drawled the last two words—"vein of coal. I'd like to take a sample over to the Gap and analyze it." His hammer, which he always carried—was in his saddle pockets, but he did not have to go down to his horse. There were pieces on the ground that would suit his purpose, left there, no doubt, by his predecessor.

"Now I reckon you know that I know why you came over hyeh."

Hale started to answer, but he saw it was no use.

"Yes—and I'm coming again—for the same reason."

"Shore—come agin and come often."

The little girl was standing on the porch as he rode past the milk house. He waved his hand to her, but she did not move nor answer. What a life for a child—for that keen-eyed, sweet-faced child! But that coal, cannel, rich as oil, above water, five feet in thickness, easy to mine, with a solid roof and perhaps self-drainage, if he could judge from the dip of the vein: and a market everywhere—England, Spain, Italy, Brazil. The coal, to be sure, might not be persistent—thirty yards within it might change in quality to ordinary bituminous coal, but he could settle that only with a steam drill. A steam drill! He would as well ask for the wagon that he had long ago hitched to a star; and then there might be a fault in the formation. But why bother now? The coal would stay there, and now he had other plans that made even that find insignificant. And yet if he bought that coal now—what a bargain! It was not that the ideals of his college days were tarnished, but he was a man of business now, and if he would take the old man's land for a song—it was because others of his kind would do the same! But why bother, he asked himself again, when his brain was in a ferment with a colossal scheme that would make dizzy the magnates who would some day drive their roadways of steel into those wild hills. So he shook himself free of the question, which passed from his mind only with a transient wonder as to who it was that had told of him to the old mountaineer, and had so paved his way for an investigation—and then he wheeled suddenly in his saddle. The bushes had rustled gently behind him and out from them stepped an extraordinary human shape—wearing a coon-skin cap, belted with two rows of big cartridges, carrying a big Winchester over one shoulder and a circular tube of brass in his left hand. With his right leg straight, his left thigh drawn into the hollow of his saddle and his left hand on the rump of his horse, Hale simply stared, his eyes dropping by and by from the pale-blue eyes and stubbly red beard of the stranger, down past the cartridge-belts to the man's feet, on which were moccasins—with the heels forward! Into what sort of a world had he dropped!

"So nary a soul can tell which way I'm going," said the red-haired stranger, with a grin that loosed a hollow chuckle far behind it.

"Would you mind telling me what difference it

can make to me which way you are going?"
Every moment he was expecting the stranger to
ask his name, but again that chuckle came.

"It makes a mighty sight o' difference to some
folks."

"But none to me."

"I hain't wearin' 'em fer you. I know *you*."

"Oh, you do." The stranger suddenly lowered
his Winchester and turned his face, with his ear
cocked like an animal. There was some noise on
the spur above.

"Nothin' but a hickory nut," said the chuckle
again. But Hale had been studying that strange
face. One side of it was calm, kindly, philosophic,
benevolent; but, when the other was turned, a
curious twitch of the muscles at the left side of the
mouth showed the teeth and made a snarl there
that was wolfish.

"Yes, and I know you," he said slowly. Self-
satisfaction, straightway, was ardent in the face.

"I knowed you would git to know me in time,
if you didn't now."

This was the Red Fox of the mountains, of
whom he had heard so much—"yarb" doctor
and Swedenborgian preacher; revenue officer and,
some said, cold-blooded murderer. He would
walk twenty miles to preach, or would start at any
hour of the day or night to minister to the sick,
and would charge for neither service. At other
hours he would be searching for moonshine stills,

37

or watching his enemies in the valley from some mountain top, with that huge spy-glass—Hale could see now that the brass tube was a telescope —that he might slip down and unawares take a pot-shot at them. The Red Fox communicated with spirits, had visions and superhuman powers of locomotion—stepping mysteriously from the bushes, people said, to walk at the traveller's side and as mysteriously disappearing into them again, to be heard of in a few hours an incredible distance away.

"I've been watchin' ye from up thar," he said with a wave of his hand. "I seed ye go up the creek, and then the bushes hid ye. I know what you was after—but did you see any signs up thar of anything you wasn't looking fer?"

Hale laughed.

"Well, I've been in these mountains long enough not to tell you, if I had."

The Red Fox chuckled.

"I wasn't sure you had—" Hale coughed and spat to the other side of his horse. When he looked around, the Red Fox was gone, and he had heard no sound of his going.

"Well, I be—" Hale clucked to his horse and as he climbed the last steep and drew near the Big Pine he again heard a noise out in the woods and he knew this time it was the fall of a human foot and not of a hickory nut. He was right, and, as he rode by the Pine, saw again at its

base the print of the little girl's foot—wondering
afresh at the reason that led her up there—and
dropped down through the afternoon shadows
towards the smoke and steam and bustle and
greed of the Twentieth Century. A long, lean,
black-eyed boy, with a wave of black hair over his
forehead, was pushing his horse the other way
along the Big Black and dropping down through
the dusk into the Middle Ages—both all but
touching on either side the outstretched hands of
the wild little creature left in the shadows of Lonesome Cove.

VII

PAST the Big Pine, swerving with a smile his horse aside that he might not obliterate the foot-print in the black earth, and down the mountain, his brain busy with his big purpose, went John Hale, by instinct, inheritance, blood and tradition—pioneer.

One of his forefathers had been with Washington on the Father's first historic expedition into the wilds of Virginia. His great-grandfather had accompanied Boone when that hunter first penetrated the "Dark and Bloody Ground," had gone back to Virginia and come again with a surveyor's chain and compass to help wrest it from the red men, among whom there had been an immemorial conflict for possession and a never-recognized claim of ownership. That compass and that chain his grandfather had fallen heir to and with that compass and chain his father had earned his livelihood amid the wrecks of the Civil War. Hale went to the old Transylvania University at Lexington, the first seat of learning planted beyond the Alleghanies. He was fond of history, of the sciences and literature, was unusually adept in Latin and Greek, and had a passion for mathematics. He was graduated with honours, he taught two years and got his degree of Master of Arts, but the pioneer spirit in his blood would still out, and his polite learning he then threw to the winds.

Other young Kentuckians had gone West in shoals, but he kept his eye on his own State, and one autumn he added a pick to the old compass and the ancestral chain, struck the Old Wilderness Trail that his grandfather had travelled, to look for his own fortune in a land which that old gentleman had passed over as worthless. At the Cumberland River he took a canoe and drifted down the river into the wild coal-swollen hills. Through the winter he froze, starved and prospected, and a year later he was opening up a region that became famous after his trust and inexperience had let others worm out of him an interest that would have made him easy for life.

With the vision of a seer, he was as innocent as Boone. Stripped clean, he got out his map, such geological reports as he could find and went into a studious trance for a month, emerging mentally with the freshness of a snake that has shed its skin. What had happened in Pennsylvania must happen all along the great Alleghany chain in the mountains of Virginia, West Virginia, Kentucky, Alabama, Tennessee. Some day the avalanche must sweep south, it must—it must. That he might be a quarter of a century too soon in his calculations never crossed his mind. Some day it must come.

Now there was not an ounce of coal immediately south-east of the Cumberland Mountains—not an ounce of iron ore immediately north-east; all the coal lay to the north-east; all of the iron ore to the south-east. So said Geology. For three hundred miles there were only four gaps through that mighty mountain chain—three at water level, and one at historic Cumberland Gap which was not at water level and would have to be tunnelled. So said Geography.

All railroads, to east and to west, would have to pass through those gaps; through them the coal must be brought to the iron ore, or the ore to the coal. Through three gaps water flowed between ore and coal and the very hills between were limestone. Was there any such juxtaposition of the four raw materials for the making of iron in the known world? When he got that far in his logic, the sweat broke from his brows; he felt dizzy and he got up and walked into the open air. As the vastness and certainty of the scheme—what fool could not see it?—rushed through him full force, he could scarcely get his breath. There must be a town in one of those gaps—but in which? No matter—he would buy all of them—all of them, he repeated over and over again; for some day there must be a town in one, and some day a town in all, and from all he would reap his harvest. He

optioned those four gaps at a low purchase price
that was absurd. He went back to the Bluegrass;
he went to New York; in some way he managed
to get to England. It had never crossed his mind
that other eyes could not see what he so clearly
saw and yet everywhere he was pronounced crazy.
He failed and his options ran out, but he was undaunted. He picked his choice of the four gaps
and gave up the other three. This favourite gap
he had just finished optioning again, and now
again he meant to keep at his old quest. That gap
he was entering now from the north side and the
North Fork of the river was hurrying to enter too.
On his left was a great gray rock, projecting edge-
wise, covered with laurel and rhododendron, and
under it was the first big pool from which the
stream poured faster still. There had been a terrible convulsion in that gap when the earth was
young; the strata had been tossed upright and
planted almost vertical for all time, and, a little farther, one mighty ledge, moss-grown, bush-covered,
sentinelled with grim pines, their bases unseen,
seemed to be making a heavy flight toward the
clouds.
    Big bowlders began to pop up in the river-bed
and against them the water dashed and whirled
and eddied backward in deep pools, while above
him the song of a cataract dropped down a tree-
choked ravine. Just there the drop came, and for
a long space he could see the river lashing rock and

43

cliff with increasing fury as though it were seeking shelter from some relentless pursuer in the dark thicket where it disappeared. Straight in front of him another ledge lifted itself. Beyond that loomed a mountain which stopped in mid-air and dropped sheer to the eye. Its crown was bare and Hale knew that up there was a mountain farm, the refuge of a man who had been involved in that terrible feud beyond Black Mountain behind him. Five minutes later he was at the yawning mouth of the gap and there lay before him a beautiful valley shut in tightly, for all the eye could see, with mighty hills. It was the heaven-born site for the unborn city of his dreams, and his eyes swept every curve of the valley lovingly. The two forks of the river ran around it—he could follow their course by the trees that lined the banks of each— curving within a stone's throw of each other across the valley and then looping away as from the neck of an ancient lute and, like its framework, coming together again down the valley, where they surged together, slipped through the hills and sped on with the song of a sweeping river. Up that river could come the track of commerce, out the South Fork, too, it could go, though it had to turn east- ward: back through that gap it could be traced north and west; and so none could come as her- alds into those hills but their footprints could be traced through that wild, rocky, water-worn chasm. Hale drew breath and raised in his stirrups.

"It's a cinch," he said aloud. "It's a shame to take the money."

Yet nothing was in sight now but a valley farm-house above the ford where he must cross the river and one log cabin on the hill beyond. Still on the the other river was the only woollen mill in miles around; farther up was the only grist mill, and near by was the only store, the only black-smith shop and the only hotel. That much of a start the gap had had for three-quarters of a century—only from the south now a railroad was already coming; from the east another was trav-elling like a wounded snake and from the north still another creeped to meet them. Every road must run through the gap and several had already run through it lines of survey. The coal was at one end of the gap, and the iron ore at the other, the cliffs between were limestone, and the other elements to make it the iron centre of the world flowed through it like a torrent.

"Selah! It's a shame to take the money."

He splashed into the creek and his big black horse thrust his nose into the clear running water. Minnows were playing about him. A hog-fish flew for shelter under a rock, and below the ripples a two-pound bass shot like an arrow into deep water.

Above and below him the stream was arched with beech, poplar and water maple, and the banks were thick with laurel and rhododendron. His eye had never rested on a lovelier stream, and on the other side of the town site, which nature had kindly lifted twenty feet above the water level, the other fork was of equal clearness, swiftness and beauty.

"Such a drainage," murmured his engineering instinct. "Such a drainage!" It was Saturday. Even if he had forgotten he would have known that it must be Saturday when he climbed the bank on the other side. Many horses were hitched under the trees, and here and there was a farm-wagon with fragments of paper, bits of food and an empty bottle or two lying around. It was the hour when the alcoholic spirits of the day were usually most high. Evidently they were running quite high that day and something distinctly was going on "up town." A few yells—the high, clear, penetrating yell of a fox-hunter—rent the air, a chorus of pistol shots rang out, and the thunder of horses' hoofs started beyond the little slope he was climbing. When he reached the top, a merry youth, with a red, hatless head was splitting the dirt road toward him, his reins in his teeth, and a pistol in each hand, which he was letting off alternately into the inoffensive earth and toward the unrebuking heavens—that seemed a favourite way in those mountains of defying God and the devil—and behind him galloped a dozen horsemen to the music of throat, pistol and iron hoof.

The fiery-headed youth's horse swerved and shot by. Hale hardly knew that the rider even saw him, but the coming ones saw him afar and they seemed to be charging him in close array. Hale stopped his horse a little to the right of the centre of the road, and being equally helpless against an inherited passion for maintaining his own rights and a similar disinclination to get out of anybody's way—he sat motionless. Two of the coming horsemen, side by side, were a little in advance.

"Git out o' the road!" they yelled. Had he made the motion of an arm, they might have ridden or shot him down, but the simple quietness of him as he sat with hands crossed on the pommel of his saddle, face calm and set, eyes unwavering and fearless, had the effect that nothing else he could have done would have brought about—and they swerved on either side of him, while the rest swerved, too, like sheep, one stirrup brushing his, as they swept by. Hale rode slowly on. He could hear the mountaineers yelling on top of the hill, but he did not look back. Several bullets sang over his head. Most likely they were simply "bantering" him, but no matter—he rode on.

The blacksmith, the storekeeper and one passing drummer were coming in from the woods when he reached the hotel.

"A gang o' those Falins," said the storekeeper, "they come over lookin' for young Dave Tolliver. They didn't find him, so they thought they'd have some fun"; and he pointed to the hotel sign which was punctuated with pistol-bullet periods. Hale's eyes flashed once but he said nothing. He turned his horse over to a stable boy and went across to the little frame cottage that served as office and home for him. While he sat on the veranda that almost hung over the mill-pond of the other stream three of the Falins came riding back. One of them had left something at the hotel, and while he was gone in for it, another put a bullet through the sign, and seeing Hale rode over to him. Hale's blue eye looked anything than friendly.

"Don't ye like it?" asked the horseman.

"I do not," said Hale calmly. The horseman seemed amused.

"Well, whut you goin' to do about it?"

"Nothing—at least not now."

"All right—whenever you git ready. You ain't ready now?"

"No," said Hale, "not now." The fellow laughed.

"Hit's a damned good thing for you that you ain't."

Hale looked long after the three as they galloped down the road. "When I start to build this town," he thought gravely and without humour, "I'll put a stop to all that."

VIII

ON a spur of Black Mountain, beyond the Kentucky line, a lean horse was tied to a sassafras bush, and in a clump of rhododendron ten yards away, a lean black-haired boy sat with a Winchester between his stomach and thighs—waiting for the dusk to drop. His chin was in both hands, the brim of his slouch hat was curved crescent-wise over his forehead, and his eyes were on the sweeping bend of the river below him. That was the "Bad Bend" down there, peopled with ancestral enemies and the head-quarters of their leader for the last ten years. Though they had been at peace for some time now, it had been Saturday in the county town ten miles down the river as well, and nobody ever knew what a Saturday might bring forth between his people and them. So he would not risk riding through that bend by the light of day.

All the long way up spur after spur and along ridge after ridge, all along the still, tree-crested top of the Big Black, he had been thinking of the man—the "furriner" whom he had seen at his uncle's cabin in Lonesome Cove. He was thinking of him still, as he sat there waiting for darkness to come, and the two vertical little lines in his forehead, that had hardly relaxed once during his climb, got deeper and deeper, as his brain puzzled into the problem that was worrying it: who the stranger was, what his business was over in the Cove and his business with the Red Fox with whom the boy had seen him talking.

He had heard of the coming of the "furriners" on the Virginia side. He had seen some of them, he was suspicious of all of them, he disliked them all—but this man he hated straightway. He hated his boots and his clothes; the way he sat and talked, as though he owned the earth, and the lad snorted contemptuously under his breath:

"He called pants 'trousers.'" It was a fearful indictment, and he snorted again: "Trousers!"

The "furriner" might be a spy or a revenue officer, but deep down in the boy's heart the suspicion had been working that he had gone over there to see his little cousin—the girl whom, boy that he was, he had marked, when she was even more of a child than she was now, for his own. His people understood it as did her father, and, child though she was, she, too, understood it. The difference between her and the "furriner"—difference in age, condition, way of life, education—meant nothing to him, and as his suspicion deepened, his hands dropped and gripped his Winchester, and through his gritting teeth came vaguely:

"By God, if he does—if he just does!"

Away down at the lower end of the river's curving sweep, the dirt road was visible for a hundred yards or more, and even while he was cursing to himself, a group of horsemen rode into sight. All seemed to be carrying something across their saddle bows, and as the boy's eyes caught them, he sank sidewise out of sight and stood upright, peering through a bush of rhododendron. Something had happened in town that day—for the horsemen carried Winchesters, and every foreign thought in his brain passed like breath from a window pane, while his dark, thin face whitened a little with anxiety and wonder. Swiftly he stepped backward, keeping the bushes between him and his far-away enemies. Another knot he gave the reins around the sassafras bush and then, Winchester in hand, he dropped noiseless as an Indian, from rock to rock, tree to tree, down the sheer spur on the other side. Twenty minutes later, he lay behind a bush that was sheltered by the top boulder of the rocky point under which the road ran. His enemies were in their own country; they would probably be talking over the happenings in town that day, and from them he would learn what was going on.

So long he lay that he got tired and out of patience, and he was about to creep around the boulder, when the clink of a horseshoe against a stone told him they were coming, and he flattened to the earth and closed his eyes that his ears might be more keen. The Falins were riding silently, but as the first two passed under him, one said:

"I'd like to know who the hell warned 'em!"

"Whar's the Red Fox?" was the significant answer.

The boy's heart leaped. There had been deviltry abroad, but his kinsmen had escaped. No one uttered a word as they rode two by two, under him, but one voice came back to him as they turned the point.

"I wonder if the other boys ketched young Dave?" He could not catch the answer to that— only the oath that was in it, and when the sound of the horses' hoofs died away, he turned over on his back and stared up at the sky. Some trouble had come and through his own caution, and the mercy of Providence that had kept him away from the Gap, he had had his escape from death that day. He would tempt that Providence no more, even by climbing back to his horse in the waning light, and it was not until dusk had fallen that he was leading the beast down the spur and into a ravine that sank to the road. There he waited an hour, and when another horseman passed he still waited a while. Cautiously then, with ears alert, eyes straining through the darkness and Winchester ready, he went down the road at a slow walk. There was a light in the first house, but the front door was closed and the road was deep with sand, as he knew; so he passed noiselessly. At the second house, light streamed through the open door; he could hear talking on the porch and he halted. He could neither cross the river nor get around the house by the rear—the ridge was too steep—so he drew off into the bushes, where he had to wait another hour before the talking ceased. There was only one more house now between him and the mouth of the creek, where he would be safe, and he made up his mind to dash by it. That house, too, was lighted and the sound of fiddling struck his ears. He would give them a surprise; so he gathered his reins and Winchester in his left hand, drew his revolver with his right, and within thirty yards started his horse into a run, yelling like an Indian and firing his pistol in the air. As he swept by, two or three figures dashed pell-mell indoors, and he shouted derisively:

"Run, damn ye, run!" They were running for their guns, he knew, but the taunt would hurt and he was pleased. As he swept by the edge of a cornfield, there was a flash of light from the base of a cliff straight across, and a bullet sang over him, then another and another, but he sped on, cursing and yelling and shooting his own Winchester up in the air—all harmless, useless, but just to hurl defiance and taunt them with his safety. His father's house was not far away, there was no sound of pursuit, and when he reached the river he drew down to a walk and stopped short in a shadow. Something had clicked in the bushes above him and he bent over his saddle and lay close to his horse's neck. The moon was rising behind him and its light was creeping toward him through the bushes. In a moment he would be full in its yellow light, and he was slipping from his horse to dart aside into the bushes, when a voice ahead of him called sharply:

"That you, Dave?"

It was his father, and the boy's answer was a loud laugh. Several men stepped from the bushes —they had heard firing and, fearing that young Dave was the cause of it, they had run to his help.

"What the hell you mean, boy, kickin' up such a racket?"

"Oh, I knowed somethin'd happened an' I wanted to skeer 'em a leetle."

"Yes, an' you never thought o' the trouble you might be causin' us."

"Don't you bother about me. I can take keer o' myself."

Old Dave Tolliver grunted—though at heart he was deeply pleased.

"Well, you come on home!"

All went silently—the boy getting meagre monosyllabic answers to his eager questions but, by the time they reached home, he had gathered the story of what had happened in town that day. There were more men in the porch of the house and all were armed. The women of the house moved about noiselessly and with drawn faces. There were no lights lit, and nobody stood long even in the light of the fire where he could be seen through a window; and doors were opened and passed through quickly. The Falins had opened the feud that day, for the boy's foster-uncle, Bad Rufe Tolliver, contrary to the terms of the last truce, had come home from the West, and one of his kinsmen had been wounded. The boy told what he had heard while he lay over the road along which some of his enemies had passed and his father nodded. The Falins had learned in some way that the lad was going to the Gap that day and had sent men after him. Who was the spy?

"You *told* me you was a-goin' to the Gap," said old Dave. "Whar was ye?"

"I didn't git that far," said the boy.

The old man and Loretta, young Dave's sister, laughed, and quiet smiles passed between the others.

"Well, you'd better be keerful 'bout gittin' even as far as you did git—wherever that was—from now on."

"I ain't afeered," the boy said sullenly, and he turned into the kitchen. Still sullen, he ate his supper in silence and his mother asked him no questions. He was worried that Bad Rufe had come back to the mountains, for Rufe was always teasing June and there was something in his bold, black eyes that made the lad furious, even when the foster-uncle was looking at Loretta or the little girl in Lonesome Cove. And yet that was nothing to his new trouble, for his mind hung persistently to the stranger and to the way June had behaved in the cabin in Lonesome Cove. Before he went to bed, he slipped out to the old well behind the house and sat on the water-trough in gloomy unrest, looking now and then at the stars that hung over the Cove and over the Gap beyond, where the stranger was bound. It would have pleased him a good deal could he have known that the stranger was pushing his big black horse on his way, under those stars, toward the outer world.

IX

IT was court day at the county seat across the Kentucky line. Hale had risen early, as everyone must if he would get his breakfast in the mountains, even in the hotels in the county seats, and he sat with his feet on the railing of the hotel porch which fronted the main street of the town. He had had his heart-breaking failures since the autumn before, but he was in good cheer now, for his feverish enthusiasm had at last clutched a man who would take up not only his options on the great Gap beyond Black Mountain but on the cannel-coal lands of Devil Judd Tolliver as well. He was riding across from the Bluegrass to meet this man at the railroad in Virginia, nearly two hundred miles away; he had stopped to examine some titles at the county seat and he meant to go on that day by way of Lonesome Cove. Opposite was the brick Court House—every window lacking at least one pane, the steps yellow with dirt and tobacco juice, the doorway and the bricks about the upper windows bullet-dented and eloquent with memories of the feud which had long embroiled the whole county. Not that everybody took part in it but, on the matter, everybody, as

57

an old woman told him, "had feelin's." It had begun, so he learned, just after the war. Two boys were playing marbles in the road along the Cumberland River, and one had a patch on the seat of his trousers. The other boy made fun of it and the boy with the patch went home and told his father. As a result there had already been thirty years of local war. In the last race for legislature, political issues were submerged and the feud was the sole issue. And a Tolliver had carried that boy's trouser-patch like a flag to victory and was sitting in the lower House at that time helping to make laws for the rest of the State. Now Bad Rufe Tolliver was in the hills again and the end was not yet. Already people were pouring in, men, women and children—the men slouch-hatted and stalking through the mud in the rain, or filing in on horseback—riding double sometimes—two men or two women, or a man with his wife or daughter behind him, or a woman with a baby in her lap and two more children behind—all dressed in homespun or store-clothes, and the paint from artificial flowers on her hat streaking the face of every girl who had unwisely scanned the heavens that morning. Soon the square was filled with hitched horses, and an auctioneer was bidding off cattle, sheep, hogs and horses to the crowd of mountaineers about him, while the women sold eggs and butter and bought things for use at home. Now and then, an open feudsman with a Winchester passed and many a man was belted with cartridges for the big pistol dangling at his hip. When court opened, the rain ceased, the sun came out and Hale made his way through the crowd to the battered temple of justice. On one corner of the square he could see the chief store of the town marked "Buck Falin—General Merchandise," and the big man in the door with the bushy redhead, he guessed, was the leader of the Falin clan. Outside the door stood a smaller replica of the same figure, whom he recognized as the leader of the band that had nearly ridden him down at the Gap when they were looking for young Dave Tolliver, the autumn before. That, doubtless, was young Buck. For a moment he stood at the door of the court-room. A Falin was on trial and the grizzled judge was speaking angrily:

"This is the third time you've had this trial postponed because you hain't got no lawyer. I ain't goin' to put it off. Have you got you a lawyer now?"

"Yes, jedge," said the defendant.

"Well, whar is he?"

"Over thar on the jury."

The judge looked at the man on the jury.

"Well, I reckon you better leave him whar he is. He'll do you more good thar than any whar else."

Hale laughed aloud—the judge glared at him and he turned quickly upstairs to his work in the deed-room. Till noon he worked and yet there was no trouble. After dinner he went back and in two hours his work was done. An atmospheric difference he felt as soon as he reached the door. The crowd had melted from the square. There were no women in sight, but eight armed men were in front of the door and two of them, a red Falin and a black Tolliver—Bad Rufe it was— were quarrelling. In every doorway stood a man cautiously looking on, and in a hotel window he saw a woman's frightened face. It was so still that it seemed impossible that a tragedy could be imminent, and yet, while he was trying to take the conditions in, one of the quarrelling men—Bad Rufe Tolliver—whipped out his revolver and before he could level it, a Falin struck the muzzle of a pistol into his back. Another Tolliver flashed his weapon on the Falin. This Tolliver was covered by another Falin and in so many flashes of lightning the eight men in front of him were covering each other—every man afraid to be the first to shoot, since he knew that the flash of his own pistol meant instantaneous death for him. As Hale shrank back, he pushed against somebody who thrust him aside. It was the judge:

"Why don't somebody shoot?" he asked sarcastically. "You're a purty set o' fools, ain't you? I want you all to stop this damned foolishness. Now when I give the word I want you, Jim Falin and Rufe Tolliver thar, to drap yer guns."

Already Rufe was grinning like a devil over the absurdity of the situation.

"Now!" said the judge, and the two guns were dropped.

"Put 'em in yo' pockets."

They did.

"Drap!" All dropped and, with those two, all put up their guns—each man, however, watching now the man who had just been covering him. It is not wise for the stranger to show too much interest in the personal affairs of mountain men, and Hale left the judge berating them and went to the hotel to get ready for the Gap, little dreaming how fixed the faces of some of those men were in his brain and how, later, they were to rise in his memory again. His horse was lame—but he must go on: so he hired a "yaller" mule from the landlord, and when the beast was brought around, he overheard two men talking at the end of the porch.

"You don't mean to say they've made peace?"

"Yes, Rufe's going away agin and they shuk hands—all of 'em." The other laughed.

"Rufe ain't gone yit!"

The Cumberland River was rain-swollen. The home-going people were helping each other across it and, as Hale approached the ford of a creek half a mile beyond the river, a black-haired girl was standing on a boulder looking helplessly at the yellow water, and two boys were on the ground below her. One of them looked up at Hale:

"I wish ye'd help this lady 'cross."

"Certainly," said Hale, and the girl giggled when he laboriously turned his old mule up to the boulder. Not accustomed to have ladies ride behind him, Hale had turned the wrong side. Again he laboriously wheeled about and then into the yellow torrent he went with the girl behind him, the old beast stumbling over the stones, whereat the girl, unafraid, made sounds of much merriment. Across, Hale stopped and said courteously:

"If you are going up this way, you are quite welcome to ride on."

"Well, I wasn't crossin' that crick jes' exactly fer fun," said the girl demurely, and then she murmured something about her cousins and looked back. They had gone down to a shallower ford, and when they, too, had waded across, they said nothing and the girl said nothing—so Hale started on, the two boys following. The mule was slow and, being in a hurry, Hale urged him with his whip. Every time he struck, the beast would kick up and once the girl came near going off.

"You must watch out, when I hit him," said Hale.

"I don't know when you're goin' to hit him," she drawled unconcernedly.

"Well, I'll let you know," said Hale laughing. "Now!" And, as he whacked the beast again, the girl laughed and they were better acquainted. Presently they passed two boys. Hale was wearing riding-boots and tight breeches, and one of the boys ran his eyes up boot and leg and if they were lifted higher, Hale could not tell.

"Whar'd you git him?" he squeaked.

The girl turned her head as the mule broke into a trot.

"Ain't got time to tell. They are my cousins," explained the girl.

"What is your name?" asked Hale.

"Loretty Tolliver." Hale turned in his saddle.

"Are you the daughter of Dave Tolliver?"

"Yes."

"Then you've got a brother named Dave?"

"Yes." This, then, was the sister of the black-haired boy he had seen in the Lonesome Cove.

"Haven't you got some kinfolks over the mountain?"

"Yes, I got an uncle livin' over thar. Devil Judd, folks calls him," said the girl simply. This girl was cousin to little June in Lonesome Cove. Every now and then she would look behind them, and when Hale turned again inquiringly she explained:

"I'm worried about my cousins back thar. I'm afeered somethin' mought happen to 'em."

"Shall we wait for them?"

"Oh, no—I reckon not."

Soon they overtook two men on horseback, and after they passed and were fifty yards ahead of them, one of the men lifted his voice jestingly:

"Is that your woman, stranger, or have you just borrowed her?" Hale shouted back:

"No, I'm sorry to say, I've just borrowed her," and he turned to see how she would take this answering pleasantry. She was looking down shyly and she did not seem much pleased.

"They are kinfolks o' mine, too," she said, and whether it was in explanation or as a rebuke, Hale could not determine.

"You must be kin to everybody around here?"

"Most everybody," she said simply.

By and by they came to a creek.

"I have to turn up here," said Hale.

"So do I," she said, smiling now directly at him.

"Good!" he said, and they went on—Hale asking more questions. She was going to school at the county seat the coming winter and she was fifteen years old.

"That's right. The trouble in the mountains is that you girls marry so early that you don't have time to get an education." She wasn't going to marry early, she said, but Hale learned now that she had a sweetheart who had been in town that day and apparently the two had had a quarrel. Who it was, she would not tell, and Hale would have been amazed had he known the sweetheart was none other than young Buck Falin and that the quarrel between the lovers had sprung from the opening quarrel that day between the clans.

Once again she came near going off the mule, and Hale observed that she was holding to the cantel of his saddle.

"Look here," he said suddenly, "hadn't you better catch hold of me?" She shook her head vigorously and made two not-to-be-rendered sounds that meant:

"No, indeed."

"Well, if this were your sweetheart you'd take hold of him, wouldn't you?"

Again she gave a vigorous shake of the head.

"Well, if he saw you riding behind me, he wouldn't like it, would he?"

"She didn't keer," she said, but Hale did; and when he heard the galloping of horses behind him, saw two men coming, and heard one of them shouting—"Hyeh, you man on that yaller mule, stop thar"—he shifted his revolver, pulled in and waited with some uneasiness. They came up, reeling in their saddles—neither one the girl's sweetheart, as he saw at once from her face—and began to ask what the girl characterized afterward as "unnecessary questions": who he was, who she was, and where they were going. Hale answered so shortly that the girl thought there was going to be a fight, and she was on the point of slipping from the mule.

"Sit still," said Hale, quietly. "There's not going to be a fight so long as you are here."

"Thar hain't!" said one of the men. "Well"

—then he looked sharply at the girl and turned his horse—"Come on, Bill—that's ole Dave Tolliver's gal." The girl's face was on fire.

"Them mean Falins!" she said contemptuously, and somehow the mere fact that Hale had been even for the moment antagonistic to the other faction seemed to put him in the girl's mind at once on her side, and straightway she talked freely of the feud. Devil Judd had taken no active part in it for a long time, she said, except to keep it down—especially since he and her father had had a "fallin' out" and the two families did not visit much—though she and her cousin June sometimes spent the night with each other.

"You won't be able to git over thar till long atter dark," she said, and she caught her breath so suddenly and so sharply that Hale turned to see what the matter was. She searched his face with her black eyes, which were like June's without the depths of June's.

"I was just a-wonderin' if mebbe you wasn't the same feller that was over in Lonesome last fall."

"Maybe I am—my name's Hale." The girl laughed. "Well, if this ain't the beatenest! I've heerd June talk about you. My brother Dave don't like you overmuch," she added frankly. "I reckon we'll see Dave purty soon. If this ain't the beatenest!" she repeated, and she laughed again, as she always did laugh, it seemed to Hale,

66

when there was any prospect of getting him into trouble.

"You can't git over thar till long atter dark," she said again presently.

"Is there any place on the way where I can get to stay all night?"

"You can stay all night with the Red Fox on top of the mountain."

"The Red Fox," repeated Hale.

"Yes, he lives right on top of the mountain. You can't miss his house."

"Oh, yes, I remember him. I saw him talking to one of the Falins in town to-day, behind the barn, when I went to get my horse."

"You—seed—him—a-talkin'—to a Falin *afore* the trouble come up?" the girl asked slowly and with such significance that Hale turned to look at her. He felt straightway that he ought not to have said that, and the day was to come when he would remember it to his cost. He knew how foolish it was for the stranger to show sympathy with, or interest in, one faction or another in a mountain feud, but to give any kind of information of one to the other—that was unwise indeed. Ahead of them now, a little stream ran from a ravine across the road. Beyond was a cabin; in the doorway were several faces, and sitting on a horse at the gate was young Dave Tolliver.

"Well, I git down here," said the girl, and before his mule stopped she slid from behind him and made for the gate without a word of thanks or good-by.

"Howdye!" said Hale, taking in the group with his glance, but leaving his eyes on young Dave. The rest nodded, but the boy was too surprised for speech, and the spirit of deviltry took the girl when she saw her brother's face, and at the gate she turned:

"Much obleeged," she said. "Tell June I'm a-comin' over to see her next Sunday."

"I will," said Hale, and he rode on. To his surprise, when he had gone a hundred yards, he heard the boy spurring after him and he looked around inquiringly as young Dave drew alongside; but the boy said nothing and Hale, amused, kept still, wondering when the lad would open speech. At the mouth of another little creek the boy stopped his horse as though he was to turn up that way.

"You've come back agin," he said, searching Hale's face with his black eyes.

"Yes," said Hale, "I've come back again."

"You goin' over to Lonesome Cove?"

"Yes."

The boy hesitated, and a sudden change of mind was plain to Hale in his face.

"I wish you'd tell Uncle Judd about the trouble in town to-day," he said, still looking fixedly at Hale.

"Certainly."

"Did you tell the Red Fox that day you seed him when you was goin' over to the Gap last fall that you seed me at Uncle Judd's?"

"No," said Hale. "But how did you know that I saw the Red Fox that day?" The boy laughed unpleasantly.

"So long," he said. "See you agin some day."

The way was steep and the sun was down and darkness gathering before Hale reached the top of the mountain—so he hallooed at the yard fence of the Red Fox, who peered cautiously out of the door and asked his name before he came to the gate. And there, with a grin on his curious mismatched face, he repeated young Dave's words:

"You've come back agin." And Hale repeated his:

"Yes, I've come back again."

"You goin' over to Lonesome Cove?"

"Yes," said Hale impatiently, "I'm going over to Lonesome Cove. Can I stay here all night?"

"Shore!" said the old man hospitably. "That's a fine hoss you got thar," he added with a chuckle. "Been swappin'?" Hale had to laugh as he climbed down from the bony ear-flopping beast.

"I left my horse in town—he's lame."

"Yes, I seed you thar." Hale could not resist:

"Yes, and I seed you." The old man almost turned.

"Whar?" Again the temptation was too great.

"Talking to the Falin who started the row." This time the Red Fox wheeled sharply and his pale-blue eyes filled with suspicion.

"I keeps friends with both sides," he said. "Ain't many folks can do that."

"I reckon not," said Hale calmly, but in the pale eyes he still saw suspicion.

When they entered the cabin, a little old woman in black, dumb and noiseless, was cooking supper. The children of the two, he learned, had scattered, and they lived there alone. On the mantel were two pistols and in one corner was the big Winchester he remembered and behind it was the big brass telescope. On the table was a Bible and a volume of Swedenborg, and among the usual strings of pepper-pods and beans and twisted long green tobacco were drying herbs and roots of all kinds, and about the fireplace were bottles of liquids that had been stewed from them. The little old woman served, and opened her lips not at all. Supper was eaten with no further reference to the doings in town that day, and no word was said about their meeting when Hale first went to Lonesome Cove until they were smoking on the porch.

"I heerd you found some mighty fine coal over in Lonesome Cove."

"Yes."

"Young Dave Tolliver thinks you found somethin' else thar, too," chuckled the Red Fox.

"I did," said Hale coolly, and the old man chuckled again.

"She's a purty leetle gal—shore."

"Who is?" asked Hale, looking calmly at his questioner, and the Red Fox lapsed into baffled silence.

The moon was brilliant and the night was still. Suddenly the Red Fox cocked his ear like a hound, and without a word slipped swiftly within the cabin. A moment later Hale heard the galloping of a horse and from out the dark woods loped a horseman with a Winchester across his saddle bow. He pulled in at the gate, but before he could shout "Hello" the Red Fox had stepped from the porch into the moonlight and was going to meet him. Hale had never seen a more easy, graceful, daring figure on horseback, and in the bright light he could make out the reckless face of the man who had been the first to flash his pistol in town that day—Bad Rufe Tolliver. For ten minutes the two talked in whispers—Rufe bent forward with one elbow on the withers of his horse but lifting his eyes every now and then to the stranger seated in the porch—and then the horseman turned with an oath and galloped into the darkness whence he came, while the Red Fox slouched back to the porch and dropped silently into his seat.

"Who was that?" asked Hale.

"Bad Rufe Tolliver."

"I've heard of him."

"Most everybody in these mountains has. He's the feller that's always causin' trouble. Him and Joe Falin agreed to go West last fall to end the war. Joe was killed out thar, and now Rufe claims Joe don't count now an' he's got the right to come back. Soon's he comes back, things git frolicksome agin. He swore he wouldn't go back unless another Falin goes too. Wirt Falin agreed, and that's how they made peace to-day. Now Rufe says he won't go at all—truce or no truce. My wife in thar is a Tolliver, but both sides comes to me and I keeps peace with both of 'em."

No doubt he did, Hale thought, keep peace or mischief with or against anybody with that face of his. That was a common type of the bad man, that horseman who had galloped away from the gate—but this old man with his dual face, who preached the Word on Sundays and on other days was a walking arsenal; who dreamed dreams and had visions and slipped through the hills in his mysterious moccasins on errands of mercy or chasing men from vanity, personal enmity or for fun, and still appeared so sane—he was a type that confounded. No wonder for these reasons and as a tribute to his infernal shrewdness he was known far and wide as the Red Fox of the Mountains. But Hale was too tired for further speculation and presently he yawned.

"Want to lay down?" asked the old man quickly.

"I think I do," said Hale, and they went inside.

The little old woman had her face to the wall in a bed in one corner and the Red Fox pointed to a bed in the other:

"Thar's yo' bed." Again Hale's eyes fell on the big Winchester.

"I reckon thar hain't more'n two others like it in all these mountains."

"What's the calibre?"

"Biggest made," was the answer, "a 50 x 75."

"Centre fire?"

"Rim," said the Red Fox.

"Gracious," laughed Hale, "what do you want such a big one for?"

"Man cannot live by bread alone—in these mountains," said the Red Fox grimly.

When Hale lay down he could hear the old man quavering out a hymn or two on the porch outside: and when, worn out with the day, he went to sleep, the Red Fox was reading his Bible by the light of a tallow dip. It is fatefully strange when people, whose lives tragically intersect, look back to their first meetings with one another, and Hale never forgot that night in the cabin of the Red Fox. For had Bad Rufe Tolliver, while he whispered at the gate, known the part the quiet young man silently seated in the porch would play in his life, he would have shot him where he sat: and could the Red Fox have known the part his sleeping guest was to play in his, the old man would have knifed him where he lay.

73

X

HALE opened his eyes next morning on the little old woman in black, moving ghost-like through the dim interior to the kitchen. A wood-thrush was singing when he stepped out on the porch and its cool notes had the liquid freshness of the morning. Breakfast over, he concluded to leave the yellow mule with the Red Fox to be taken back to the county town, and to walk down the mountain, but before he got away the land-lord's son turned up with his own horse, still lame, but well enough to limp along without doing himself harm. So, leading the black horse, Hale started down.

The sun was rising over still seas of white mist and wave after wave of blue Virginia hills. In the shadows below, it smote the mists into tatters; leaf and bush glittered as though after a heavy rain, and down Hale went under a trembling dew-drenched world and along a tumbling series of water-falls that flashed through tall ferns, blos-soming laurel and shining leaves of rhododendron. Once he heard something move below him and then the crackling of brush sounded far to one side of the road. He knew it was a man who would be watching him from a covert and, straightway, to prove his innocence of any hostile or secret purpose, he began to whistle. Farther below, two men with Winchesters rose from the bushes and asked his name and his business. He told both readily. Everybody, it seemed, was prepared for hostilities and, though the news of the patched-up peace had spread, it was plain that the factions were still suspicious and on guard. Then the loneliness almost of Lonesome Cove itself set in. For miles he saw nothing alive but an occasional bird and heard no sound but of running water or rustling leaf. At the mouth of the creek his horse's lameness had grown so much better that he mounted him and rode slowly up the river. Within an hour he could see the still crest of the Lonesome Pine. At the mouth of a creek a mile farther on was an old gristmill with its water-wheel asleep, and whittling at the door outside was the old miller, Uncle Billy Beams, who, when he heard the coming of the black horse's feet, looked up and showed no surprise at all when he saw Hale.

"I heard you was comin'," he shouted, hailing him cheerily by name. "Ain't fishin' this time!"

"No," said Hale, "not this time."

"Well, git down and rest a spell. June'll be here in a minute an' you can ride back with her. I reckon you air goin' that a-way."

"June!"

"Shore! My, but she'll be glad to see ye!

75

She's always talkin' about ye. You told her you was comin' back an' ever'body told her you wasn't: but that leetle gal al'ays said she *knowed* you was, because you *said* you was. She's growed some—an' if she ain't purty, well I'd tell a man! You jes' tie yo' hoss up thar behind the mill so she can't see it, an' git inside the mill when she comes round that bend thar. My, but hit'll be a surprise fer her."

The old man chuckled so cheerily that Hale, to humour him, hitched his horse to a sapling, came back and sat in the door of the mill. The old man knew all about the trouble in town the day before.

"I want to give ye a leetle advice. Keep yo' mouth plum' shut about this here war. I'm Jestice of the Peace, but that's the only way I've kept outen of it fer thirty years; an' hit's the only way you can keep outen it."

"Thank you, I mean to keep my mouth shut, but would you mind——"

"Git in!" interrupted the old man eagerly. "Hyeh she comes." His kind old face creased into a welcoming smile, and between the logs of the mill Hale, inside, could see an old sorrel horse slowly coming through the lights and shadows down the road. On its back was a sack of corn and perched on the sack was a little girl with her bare feet in the hollows behind the old nag's withers. She was looking sidewise, quite hidden by a scarlet poke-bonnet, and at the old man's shout

76

she turned the smiling face of little June. With an answering cry, she struck the old nag with a switch and before the old man could rise to help her down, slipped lightly to the ground.

"Why, honey," he said, "I don't know whut I'm goin' to do 'bout yo' corn. Shaft's broke an' I can't do no grindin' till to-morrow."

"Well, Uncle Billy, we ain't got a pint o' meal in the house," she said. "You jes' got to *lend* me some."

"All right, honey," said the old man, and he cleared his throat as a signal for Hale.

The little girl was pushing her bonnet back when Hale stepped into sight and, unstartled, unsmiling, unspeaking, she looked steadily at him—one hand motionless for a moment on her bronze heap of hair and then slipping down past her cheek to clench the other tightly. Uncle Billy was bewildered.

"Why, June, hit's Mr. Hale—why——"

"Howdye, June!" said Hale, who was no less puzzled—and still she gave no sign that she had ever seen him before except reluctantly to give him her hand. Then she turned sullenly away and sat down in the door of the mill with her elbows on her knees and her chin in her hands.

Dumfounded, the old miller pulled the sack of corn from the horse and leaned it against the mill. Then he took out his pipe, filled and lighted it slowly and turned his perplexed eyes to the sun.

"Well, honey," he said, as though he were doing the best he could with a difficult situation, "I'll have to git you that meal at the house. 'Bout dinner time now. You an' Mr. Hale thar come on and git somethin' to eat afore ye go back."

"I got to get on back home," said June, rising.

"No you ain't—I bet you got dinner fer yo' step-mammy afore you left, an' I jes' know you was aimin' to take a snack with me an' ole Hon." The little girl hesitated—she had no denial—and the old fellow smiled kindly.

"Come on, now."

Little June walked on the other side of the miller from Hale back to the old man's cabin, two hundred yards up the road, answering his questions but not Hale's and never meeting the latter's eyes with her own. "Ole Hon," the portly old woman whom Hale remembered, with brass-rimmed spectacles and a clay pipe in her mouth, came out on the porch and welcomed them heartily under the honeysuckle vines. Her mouth and face were alive with humour when she saw Hale, and her eyes took in both him and the little girl keenly. The miller and Hale leaned chairs against the wall while the girl sat at the entrance of the porch. Suddenly Hale went out to his horse and took out a package from his saddle-pockets.

"I've got some candy in here for you," he said smiling.

"I don't want no candy," she said, still not looking at him and with a little movement of her knees away from him.

"Why, honey," said Uncle Billy again, "whut *is* the matter with ye? I thought ye was great friends." The little girl rose hastily.

"No, we ain't, nuther," she said, and she whisked herself indoors. Hale put the package back with some embarrassment and the old miller laughed.

"Well, well—she's a quar little critter; mebbe she's mad because you stayed away so long."

At the table June wanted to help ole Hon and wait to eat with her, but Uncle Billy made her sit down with him and Hale, and so shy was she that she hardly ate anything. Once only did she look up from her plate and that was when Uncle Billy, with a shake of his head, said:

"He's a bad un." He was speaking of Rufe Tolliver, and at the mention of his name there was a frightened look in the little girl's eyes, when she quickly raised them, that made Hale wonder.

An hour later they were riding side by side— Hale and June—on through the lights and shadows toward Lonesome Cove. Uncle Billy turned back from the gate to the porch.

"He ain't come back hyeh jes' fer coal," said ole Hon.

"Shucks!" said Uncle Billy; "you women-folks can't think 'bout nothin' 'cept one thing. He's too old fer her."

79

"She'll git ole enough fer *him*—an' you men-folks don't think less—you jes' talk less." And she went back into the kitchen, and on the porch the old miller puffed on a new idea in his pipe.

For a few minutes the two rode in silence and not yet had June lifted her eyes to him.

"You've forgotten me, June."

"No, I hain't, nuther."

"You said you'd be waiting for me." June's lashes went lower still.

"I was."

"Well, what's the matter? I'm mighty sorry I couldn't get back sooner."

"Huh!" said June scornfully, and he knew Uncle Billy in his guess as to the trouble was far afield, and so he tried another tack.

"I've been over to the county seat and I saw lots of your kinfolks over there." She showed no curiosity, no surprise, and still she did not look up at him.

"I met your cousin, Loretta, over there and I carried her home behind me on an old mule"—Hale paused, smiling at the remembrance—and still she betrayed no interest.

"She's a mighty pretty girl, and whenever I'd hit that old——"

"She hain't!"—the words were so shrieked out that Hale was bewildered, and then he guessed that the falling out between the fathers was more serious than he had supposed.

"But she isn't as nice as you are," he added quickly, and the girl's quivering mouth steadied. the tears stopped in her vexed dark eyes and she lifted them to him at last.

"She ain't?"

"No, indeed, she ain't."

For a while they rode along again in silence. June no longer avoided his eyes now, and the unspoken question in her own presently came out:

"You won't let Uncle Rufe bother me no more, will ye?"

"No, indeed, I won't," said Hale heartily. "What does he do to you?"

"Nothin'—'cept he's always a-teasin' me, an'—an' I'm afeered o' him."

"Well, I'll take care of Uncle Rufe."

"I knowed you'd say that," she said. "Pap and Dave always laughs at me," and she shook her head as though she were already threatening her bad uncle with what Hale would do to him, and she was so serious and trustful that Hale was curiously touched. By and by he lifted one flap of his saddle-pockets again.

"I've got some candy here for a nice little girl," he said, as though the subject had not been mentioned before. "It's for you. Won't you have some?"

"I reckon I will," she said with a happy smile.

Hale watched her while she munched a striped

stick of peppermint. Her crimson bonnet had fallen from her sunlit hair and straight down from it to her bare little foot with its stubbed toe just darkening with dried blood, a sculptor would have loved the rounded slenderness in the curving long lines that shaped her brown throat, her arms and her hands, which were prettily shaped but so very dirty as to the nails, and her dangling bare leg. Her teeth were even and white, and most of them flashed when her red lips smiled. Her lashes were long and gave a touching softness to her eyes even when she was looking quietly at him, but there were times, as he had noticed already, when a brooding look stole over them, and then they were the lair for the mysterious loneliness that was the very spirit of Lonesome Cove. Some day that little nose would be long enough, and some day, he thought, she would be very beautiful.

"Your cousin, Loretta, said she was coming over to see you."

June's teeth snapped viciously through the stick of candy and then she turned on him and behind the long lashes and deep down in the depth of those wonderful eyes he saw an ageless something that bewildered him more than her words.

"I hate her," she said fiercely.

"Why, little girl?" he said gently.

"I don't know—" she said—and then the tears came in earnest and she turned her head, sobbing. Hale helplessly reached over and patted her on the shoulder, but she shrank away from him.

"Go away!" she said, digging her fist into her eyes until her face was calm again.

They had reached the spot on the river where he had seen her first, and beyond, the smoke of the cabin was rising above the undergrowth.

"Lordy!" she said, "but I do git lonesome over hyeh."

"Wouldn't you like to go over to the Gap with me sometimes?"

Straightway her face was a ray of sunlight.

"Would—I like—to—go—over——"

She stopped suddenly and pulled in her horse, but Hale had heard nothing.

"Hello!" shouted a voice from the bushes, and Devil Judd Tolliver issued from them with an axe on his shoulder. "I heerd you'd come back an' I'm glad to see ye." He came down to the road and shook Hale's hand heartily.

"Whut you been cryin' about?" he added, turning his hawk-like eyes on the little girl.

"Nothin'," she said sullenly.

"Did she git mad with ye 'bout somethin'?" said the old man to Hale. "She never cries 'cept when she's mad." Hale laughed.

"You jes' hush up—both of ye," said the girl with a sharp kick of her right foot.

"I reckon you can't stamp the ground that fer away from it," said the old man dryly. "If you

83

don't git the better of that all-fired temper o' yourn hit's goin' to git the better of you, an' then I'll have to spank you agin."

"I reckon you ain't goin' to whoop me no more, pap. I'm a-gittin' too big."

The old man opened eyes and mouth with an indulgent roar of laughter.

"Come on up to the house," he said to Hale, turning to lead the way, the little girl following him. The old step-mother was again a-bed; small Bub, the brother, still unafraid, sat down beside Hale and the old man brought out a bottle of moonshine.

"I reckon I can still trust ye," he said.

"I reckon you can," laughed Hale.

The liquor was as fiery as ever, but it was grateful, and again the old man took nearly a tumbler full plying Hale, meanwhile, about the happenings in town the day before—but Hale could tell him nothing that he seemed not already to know.

"It was quar," the old mountaineer said. "I've seed two men with the drap on each other and both afeerd to shoot, but I never heerd of sech a ring-around-the-rosy as eight fellers with bead on one another and not a shoot shot. I'm glad I wasn't thar."

He frowned when Hale spoke of the Red Fox.

"You can't never tell whether that ole devil is fer ye or agin ye, but I've been plum' sick o' these doin's a long time now and sometimes I think I'll just pull up stakes and go West and git out of hit —altogether."

"How did you learn so much about yesterday—so soon?"

"Oh, we hears things purty quick in these mountains. Little Dave Tolliver come over here last night."

"Yes," broke in Bub, "and he tol' us how you carried Loretty from town on a mule behind ye, and she jest a-sassin' you, an' as how she said she was a-goin' to git you fer *her* sweetheart."

Hale glanced by chance at the little girl. Her face was scarlet, and a light dawned.

"An' sis, thar, said he was a-tellin' lies—an' when she growed up she said she was a-goin' to marry——"

Something snapped like a toy-pistol and Bub howled. A little brown hand had whacked him across the mouth, and the girl flashed indoors without a word. Bub got to his feet howling with pain and rage and started after her, but the old man caught him:

"Set down, boy! Sarved you right fer blabbin' things that hain't yo' business." He shook with laughter.

Jealousy! Great heavens—Hale thought—in that child, and for him!

"I knowed she was cryin' 'bout something like

that. She sets a great store by you, an' she's studied them books you sent her plum' to pieces while you was away. She ain't nothin' but a baby, but in sartain ways she's as old as her mother was when she died." The amazing secret was out, and the little girl appeared no more until supper time, when she waited on the table, but at no time would she look at Hale or speak to him again. For a while the two men sat on the porch talking of the feud and the Gap and the coal on the old man's place, and Hale had no trouble getting an option for a year on the old man's land. Just as dusk was setting he got his horse.

"You'd better stay all night."

"No, I'll have to get along."

The little girl did not appear to tell him good-by, and when he went to his horse at the gate, he called:

"Tell June to come down here. I've got something for her."

"Go on, baby," the old man said, and the little girl came shyly down to the gate. Hale took a brown-paper parcel from his saddle-bags, unwrapped it and betrayed the usual blue-eyed, flaxen-haired, rosy-cheeked doll. Only June did not know the like of it was in all the world. And as she caught it to her breast there were tears once more in her uplifted eyes.

"How about going over to the Gap with me, little girl—some day?"

86

He never guessed it, but there were a child and a woman before him now and both answered:

"I'll go with ye anywhar."

.   .   .   .

Hale stopped a while to rest his horse at the base of the big pine. He was practically alone in the world. The little girl back there was born for something else than slow death in that God-forsaken cove, and whatever it was—why not help her to it if he could? With this thought in his brain, he rode down from the luminous upper world of the moon and stars toward the nether world of drifting mists and black ravines. She belonged to just such a night—that little girl— she was a part of its mists, its lights and shadows, its fresh wild beauty and its mystery. Only once did his mind shift from her to his great purpose, and that was when the roar of the water through the rocky chasm of the Gap made him think of the roar of iron wheels, that, rushing through, some day, would drown it into silence. At the mouth of the Gap he saw the white valley lying at peace in the moonlight and straightway from it sprang again, as always, his castle in the air; but before he fell asleep in his cottage on the edge of the millpond that night he heard quite plainly again:

"I'll go with ye—anywhar."

XI

SPRING was coming: and, meanwhile, that late autumn and short winter, things went merrily on at the gap in some ways, and in some ways—not.

Within eight miles of the place, for instance, the man fell ill—the man who was to take up Hale's options—and he had to be taken home. Still Hale was undaunted: here he was and here he would stay—and he would try again. Two other young men, Bluegrass Kentuckians, Logan and Macfarlan, had settled at the gap—both lawyers and both of pioneer, Indian-fighting blood. The report of the State geologist had been spread broadcast. A famous magazine writer had come through on horseback and had gone home and given a fervid account of the riches and the beauty of the region. Helmeted Englishmen began to prowl prospectively around the gap sixty miles to the southwest. New surveying parties were directing lines for the rocky gateway between the iron ore and the coal. Engineers and coal experts passed in and out. There were rumours of a furnace and a steel plant when the railroad should reach the place. Capital had flowed in from the East, and already a Pennsylvanian was starting a main entry into a ten-foot vein of coal up through the gap and was coking it. His report was that his own was better than the Connellsville coke, which was the standard: it was higher in carbon and lower in ash. The Ludlow brothers, from Eastern Virginia, had started a general store. Two of the Berkley brothers had come over from Bluegrass Kentucky and their family was coming in the spring. The bearded Senator up the valley, who was also a preacher, had got his Methodist brethren interested—and the community was further enriched by the coming of the Hon. Samuel Budd, lawyer and budding statesman. As a recreation, the Hon. Sam was an anthropologist: he knew the mountaineers from Virginia to Alabama and they were his pet illustrations of his pet theories of the effect of a mountain environment on human life and character. Hale took a great fancy to him from the first moment he saw his smooth, ageless, kindly face, surmounted by a huge pair of spectacles that were hooked behind two large ears, above which his pale yellow hair, parted in the middle, was drawn back with plaster-like precision. A mayor and a constable had been appointed, and the Hon. Sam had just finished his first case—Squire Morton and the Widow Crane, who ran a boarding-house, each having laid claim to three pigs that obstructed traffic in the town. The Hon. Sam was sitting by the stove, deep in thought, when Hale came into the hotel and he lifted his

great glaring lenses and waited for no intro-
duction:

"Brother," he said, "do you know twelve reliable
witnesses come on the stand and *swore* them pigs belonged to the squire's sow, and twelve equally reliable
witnesses *swore* them pigs belonged to the Widow
Crane's sow? I shorely was a heap perplexed."

"That was curious." The Hon. Sam laughed:

"Well, sir, them intelligent pigs used both them
sows as mothers, and may be they had another
mother somewhere else. They would breakfast
with the Widow Crane's sow and take supper with
the squire's sow. And so them witnesses, too, was
naturally perplexed."

Hale waited while the Hon. Sam puffed his pipe
into a glow:

"Believin', as I do, that the most important
principle in law is mutually forgivin' and a square
division o' spoils, I suggested a compromise. The
widow said the squire was an old rascal an' thief
and he'd never sink a tooth into one of them
shoats, but that her lawyer was a gentleman—
meanin' me—and the squire said the widow had
been blackguardin' him all over town and he'd see
her in heaven before she got one, but that *his* lawyer was a prince of the realm: so the other lawyer
took one and I got the other."

"What became of the third?"

The Hon. Sam was an ardent disciple of Sir
Walter Scott:

"Well, just now the mayor is a-playin' Gurth to that little runt for costs."

Outside, the wheels of the stage rattled, and as half a dozen strangers trooped in, the Hon. Sam waved his hand: "Things is comin'."

Things were coming. The following week "the booming editor" brought in a printing-press and started a paper. An enterprising Hoosier soon established a brick-plant. A geologist—Hale's predecessor in Lonesome Cove—made the Gap his headquarters, and one by one the vanguard of engineers, surveyors, speculators and coalmen drifted in. The wings of progress began to sprout, but the new town-constable soon tendered his resignation with informality and violence. He had arrested a Falin, whose companions straightway took him from custody and set him free. Straightway the constable threw his pistol and badge of office to the ground.

"I've fit an' I've hollered fer help," he shouted, almost crying with rage, "an' I've fit agin. Now this town can go to hell": and he picked up his pistol but left his symbol of law and order in the dust. Next morning there was a new constable, and only that afternoon when Hale stepped into the Ludlow Brothers' store he found the constable already busy. A line of men with revolver or knife in sight was drawn up inside with their backs to Hale, and beyond them he could see the new constable with a man under arrest. Hale had not forgotten his promise to himself and he began now:

"Come on," he called quietly, and when the men turned at the sound of his voice, the constable, who was of sterner stuff than his predecessor, pushed through them, dragging his man after him.

"Look here, boys," said Hale calmly. "Let's not have any row. Let him go to the mayor's office. If he isn't guilty, the mayor will let him go. If he is, the mayor will give him bond. I'll go on it myself. But let's not have a row."

Now, to the mountain eye, Hale appeared no more than the ordinary man, and even a close observer would have seen no more than that his face was clean-cut and thoughtful, that his eye was blue and singularly clear and fearless, and that he was calm with a calmness that might come from anything else than stolidity of temperament —and that, by the way, is the self-control which counts most against the unruly passions of other men—but anybody near Hale, at a time when excitement was high and a crisis was imminent, would have felt the resultant of forces emanating from him that were beyond analysis. And so it was now—the curious power he instinctively had over rough men had its way.

"Go on," he continued quietly, and the constable went on with his prisoner, his friends following, still swearing and with their weapons in their hands. When constable and prisoner passed into the mayor's office, Hale stepped quickly after them and turned on the threshold with his arm across the door.

"Hold on, boys," he said, still good-naturedly. "The mayor can attend to this. If you boys want to fight anybody, fight me. I'm unarmed and you can whip me easily enough," he added with a laugh, "but you mustn't come in here," he concluded, as though the matter was settled beyond further discussion. For one instant—the crucial one, of course—the men hesitated, for the reason that so often makes superior numbers of no avail among the lawless—the lack of a leader of nerve— and without another word Hale held the door. But the frightened mayor inside let the prisoner out at once on bond and Hale, combining law and diplomacy, went on the bond.

Only a day or two later the mountaineers, who worked at the brick-plant with pistols buckled around them, went on a strike and, that night, shot out the lights and punctured the chromos in their boarding-house. Then, armed with sticks, knives, clubs and pistols, they took a triumphant march through town. That night two knives and two pistols were whipped out by two of them in the same store. One of the Ludlows promptly blew out the light and astutely got under the counter. When the combatants scrambled outside, he locked the door and crawled out the back window.

Next morning the brick-yard malcontents marched triumphantly again and Hale called for volunteers to arrest them. To his disgust only Logan, Macfarlan, the Hon. Sam Budd, and two or three others seemed willing to go, but when the few who would go started, Hale, leading them, looked back and the whole town seemed to be strung out after him. Below the hill, he saw the mountaineers drawn up in two bodies for battle and, as he led his followers towards them, the Hoosier owner of the plant rode out at a gallop, waving his hands and apparently beside himself with anxiety and terror.

"Don't," he shouted; "somebody'll get killed. Wait—they'll give up." So Hale halted and the Hoosier rode back. After a short parley he came back to Hale to say that the strikers would give up, but when Logan started again, they broke and ran, and only three or four were captured. The Hoosier was delirious over his troubles and straightway closed his plant.

"See," said Hale in disgust. "We've got to do something now."

"We have," said the lawyers, and that night on Hale's porch, the three, with the Hon. Sam Budd, pondered the problem. They could not build a town without law and order—they could not have law and order without taking part themselves, and even then they plainly would have their hands full. And so, that night, on the tiny porch of the

94

little cottage that was Hale's sleeping-room and office, with the creaking of the one wheel of their one industry—the old grist-mill—making patient music through the rhododendron-darkness that hid the steep bank of the stream, the three pioneers forged their plan. There had been gentlemen-regulators a plenty, vigilance committees of gentlemen, and the Ku-Klux clan had been originally composed of gentlemen, as they all knew, but they meant to hew to the strict line of town-ordinance and common law and do the rough every-day work of the common policeman. So volunteer policemen they would be and, in order to extend their authority as much as possible, as county policemen they would be enrolled. Each man would purchase his own Winchester, pistol, billy, badge and a whistle—to call for help—and they would begin drilling and target-shooting at once. The Hon. Sam shook his head dubiously:

"The natives won't understand."

"We can't help that," said Hale.

"I know—I'm with you."

Hale was made captain, Logan first lieutenant, Macfarlan second, and the Hon. Sam third. Two rules, Logan, who, too, knew the mountaineer well, suggested as inflexible. One was never to draw a pistol at all unless necessary, never to pretend to draw as a threat or to intimidate, and never to draw unless one meant to shoot, if need be.

"And the other," added Logan, "always go in

force to make an arrest—never alone unless necessary." The Hon. Sam moved his head up and
down in hearty approval.

"Why is that?" asked Hale.

"To save bloodshed," he said. "These fellows
we will have to deal with have a pride that is morbid. A mountaineer doesn't like to go home and
have to say that one man put him in the calaboose
—but he doesn't mind telling that it took several
to arrest him. Moreover, he will give in to two
or three men, when he would look on the coming
of one man as a personal issue and to be met as
such."

Hale nodded.

"Oh, there'll be plenty of chances," Logan
added with a smile, "for everyone to go it alone."
Again the Hon. Sam nodded grimly. It was plain
to him that they would have all they could do,
but no one of them dreamed of the far-reaching
effect that night's work would bring.

They were the vanguard of civilization—"cru-
saders of the nineteenth century against the be-
nighted of the Middle Ages," said the Hon. Sam,
and when Logan and Macfarlan left, he lingered
and lit his pipe.

"The trouble will be," he said slowly, "that
they won't understand our purpose or our meth-
ods. They will look on us as a lot of meddlesome
'furriners' who have come in to run their country
as we please, when they have been running it as

THE TRAIL OF THE LONESOME PINE

they please for more than a hundred years. You see, you mustn't judge them by the standards of to-day—you must go back to the standards of the Revolution. Practically, they are the pioneers of that day and hardly a bit have they advanced. They are our contemporary ancestors." And then the Hon. Sam, having dropped his vernacular, lounged ponderously into what he was pleased to call his anthropological drool.

"You see, mountains isolate people and the effect of isolation on human life is to crystallize it. Those people over the line have had no navigable rivers, no lakes, no wagon roads, except often the beds of streams. They have been cut off from all communication with the outside world. They are a perfect example of an arrested civilization and they are the closest link we have with the Old World. They were Unionists because of the Revolution, as they were Americans in the beginning because of the spirit of the Covenanter. They live like the pioneers; the axe and the rifle are still their weapons and they still have the same fight with nature. This feud business is a matter of clan-loyalty that goes back to Scotland. They argue this way: You are my friend or my kinsman, your quarrel is my quarrel, and whoever hits you hits me. If you are in trouble, I must not testify against you. If you are an officer, you must not arrest me; you must send me a kindly request to come into court. If I'm innocent and it's perfectly convenient—why, maybe I'll come. Yes, we're the vanguard of civilization, all right, all right—but I opine we're goin' to have a hell of a merry time."

Hale laughed, but he was to remember those words of the Hon. Samuel Budd. Other members of that vanguard began to drift in now by twos and threes from the bluegrass region of Kentucky and from the tide-water country of Virginia and from New England—strong, bold young men with the spirit of the pioneer and the birth, breeding and education of gentlemen, and the war between civilization and a lawlessness that was the result of isolation, and consequent ignorance and idleness started in earnest.

"A remarkable array," murmured the Hon. Sam, when he took an inventory one night with Hale. "I'm proud to be among 'em."

Many times Hale went over to Lonesome Cove and with every visit his interest grew steadily in the little girl and in the curious people over there, until he actually began to believe in the Hon. Sam Budd's anthropological theories. In the cabin on Lonesome Cove was a crane swinging in the big stone fireplace, and he saw the old step-mother and June putting the spinning wheel and the loom to actual use. Sometimes he found a cabin of unhewn logs with a puncheon floor, clapboards for shingles and wooden pin and auger holes for nails; a batten wooden shutter, the logs filled with

98

mud and stones and holes in the roof for the wind and the rain. Over a pair of buck antlers sometimes lay the long heavy home-made rifle of the backwoodsman—sometimes even with a flintlock and called by some pet feminine name. Once he saw the hominy block that the mountaineers had borrowed from the Indians, and once a handmill like the one from which the one woman was taken and the other left in biblical days. He struck communities where the medium of exchange was still barter, and he found mountaineers drinking metheglin still as well as moonshine. Moreover, there were still log-rollings, house-warmings, corn-shuckings, and quilting parties, and sports were the same as in pioneer days—wrestling, racing, jumping, and lifting barrels. Often he saw a cradle of bee-gum, and old Judd had in his house a fox-horn made of hickory bark which even June could blow. He ran across old-world superstitions, too, and met one seventh son of a seventh son who cured children of rash by blowing into their mouths. And he got June to singing transatlantic songs, after old Judd said one day that she knowed the "miserablest song he'd ever heerd"—meaning the most sorrowful. And, thereupon, with quaint simplicity, June put her heels on the rung of her chair, and with her elbows on her knees, and her chin on both bent thumbs, sang him the oldest version of "Barbara Allen" in a voice that startled Hale by its power and sweetness. She knew lots

99

more "song-ballets," she said shyly, and the old man had her sing some songs that were rather rude, but were as innocent as hymns from her lips.

Everywhere he found unlimited hospitality.

"Take out, stranger," said one old fellow, when there was nothing on the table but some bread and a few potatoes, "have a tater. Take two of 'em—take damn nigh *all* of 'em."

Moreover, their pride was morbid, and they were very religious. Indeed, they used religion to cloak their deviltry, as honestly as it was ever used in history. He had heard old Judd say once, when he was speaking of the feud:

"Well, I've al'ays laid out my enemies. The Lord's been on my side an' I gits a better Christian every year."

Always Hale took some children's book for June when he went to Lonesome Cove, and she rarely failed to know it almost by heart when he went again. She was so intelligent that he began to wonder if, in her case, at least, another of the Hon. Sam's theories might not be true—that the mountaineers were of the same class as the other westward-sweeping emigrants of more than a century before, that they had simply lain dormant in the hills and—a century counting for nothing in the matter of inheritance—that their possibilities were little changed, and that the children of that day would, if given the chance, wipe out the handi-

cap of a century in one generation and take their
place abreast with children of the outside world.
The Tollivers were of good blood; they had come
from Eastern Virginia, and the original Tolliver
had been a slave-owner. The very name was, un-
doubtedly, a corruption of Tagliaferro. So, when
the Widow Crane began to build a brick house for
her boarders that winter, and the foundations of a
school-house were laid at the Gap, Hale began to
plead with old Judd to allow June to go over to
the Gap and go to school, but the old man was firm
in refusal:

"He couldn't git along without her," he said;
"he was afeerd he'd lose her, an' he reckoned June
was a-larnin' enough without goin' to school—she
was a-studyin' them leetle books o' hers so hard."
But as his confidence in Hale grew and as Hale
stated his intention to take an option on the old
man's coal lands, he could see that Devil Judd,
though his answer never varied, was considering
the question seriously.

Through the winter, then, Hale made occasional
trips to Lonesome Cove and bided his time. Often
he met young Dave Tolliver there, but the boy
usually left when Hale came, and if Hale was already there, he kept outside the house, until the
engineer was gone.

Knowing nothing of the ethics of courtship in
the mountains—how, when two men meet at the
same girl's house, "they makes the gal say which

one she likes best and t'other one gits"—Hale little dreamed that the first time Dave stalked out of the room, he threw his hat in the grass behind the big chimney and executed a war-dance on it, cursing the blankety-blank "furriner" within from Dan to Beersheba.

Indeed, he never suspected the fierce depths of the boy's jealousy at all, and he would have laughed incredulously, if he had been told how, time after time as he climbed the mountain homeward, the boy's black eyes burned from the bushes on him, while his hand twitched at his pistol-butt and his lips worked with noiseless threats. For Dave had to keep his heart-burnings to himself or he would have been laughed at through all the mountains, and not only by his own family, but by June's; so he, too, bided his time.

In late February, old Buck Falin and old Dave Tolliver shot each other down in the road and the Red Fox, who hated both and whom each thought was his friend, dressed the wounds of both with equal care. The temporary lull of peace that Bad Rufe's absence in the West had brought about, gave way to a threatening storm then, and then it was that old Judd gave his consent: when the roads got better, June could go to the Gap to school. A month later the old man sent word that he did not want June in the mountains while the trouble was going on, and that Hale could come over for her when he pleased: and Hale sent word back that within three days he would meet the father and the little girl at the big Pine. That last day at home June passed in a dream. She went through her daily tasks in a dream and she hardly noticed young Dave when he came in at mid-day, and Dave, when he heard the news, left in sullen silence. In the afternoon she went down to the mill to tell Uncle Billy and ole Hon good-by and the three sat in the porch a long time and with few words. Ole Hon had been to the Gap once, but there was "so much bustle over thar it made her head ache." Uncle Billy shook his head doubtfully over June's going, and the two old people stood at the gate looking long after the little girl when she went homeward up the road. Before supper June slipped up to her little hiding-place at the pool and sat on the old log saying good-by to the comforting spirit that always brooded for her there, and, when she stood on the porch at sunset, a new spirit was coming on the wings of the South wind. Hale felt it as he stepped into the soft night air; he heard it in the piping of frogs—"Marsh-birds," as he always called them; he could almost see it in the flying clouds and the moonlight and even the bare trees seemed tremulously expectant. An indefinable happiness seemed to pervade the whole earth and Hale stretched his arms lazily. Over in Lonesome Cove little June felt it more keenly than ever in her life before. She did not want to go to bed that night, and when the others were asleep she slipped out to the porch and sat on the steps, her eyes luminous and her face wistful—looking towards the big Pine which pointed the way towards the far silence into which she was going at last.

XII

JUNE did not have to be awakened that morning. At the first clarion call of the old rooster behind the cabin, her eyes opened wide and a happy thrill tingled her from head to foot—why, she didn't at first quite realize—and then she stretched her slender round arms to full length above her head and with a little squeal of joy bounded out of the bed, dressed as she was when she went into it, and with no changes to make except to push back her tangled hair. Her father was out feeding the stock and she could hear her step-mother in the kitchen. Bub still slept soundly, and she shook him by the shoulder.

"Git up, Bub."

"Go 'way," said Bub fretfully. Again she started to shake him but stopped—Bub wasn't going to the Gap, so she let him sleep. For a little while she looked down at him—at his round rosy face and his frowsy hair from under which protruded one dirty fist. She was going to leave him, and a fresh tenderness for him made her breast heave, but she did not kiss him, for sisterly kisses are hardly known in the hills. Then she went out into the kitchen to help her step-mother.

"Gittin' mighty busy, all of a sudden, ain't ye," said the sour old woman, "now that ye air goin' away."

"'Tain't costin' you nothin'," answered June quietly, and she picked up a pail and went out into the frosty, shivering daybreak to the old well. The chain froze her fingers, the cold water splashed her feet, and when she had tugged her heavy burden back to the kitchen, she held her red, chapped hands to the fire.

"I reckon you'll be mighty glad to git shet o' me." The old woman sniffled, and June looked around with a start.

"Pears like I'm goin' to miss ye right smart," she quavered, and June's face coloured with a new feeling towards her step-mother.

"I'm goin' ter have a hard time doin' all the work and me so poorly."

"Lorrety is a-comin' over to he'p ye, if ye git sick," said June, hardening again. "Or, I'll come back myself." She got out the dishes and set them on the table.

"You an' me don't git along very well together," she went on placidly. "I never heerd o' no step-mother and children as did, an' I reckon you'll be might glad to git shet o' me."

"Pears like I'm going to miss ye a right smart," repeated the old woman weakly.

June went out to the stable with the milking pail. Her father had spread fodder for the cow and she could hear the rasping of the ears of corn against each other as he tumbled them into the trough for the old sorrel. She put her head against the cow's soft flank and under her sinewy fingers two streams of milk struck the bottom of the tin pail with such thumping loudness that she did not hear her father's step; but when she rose to make the beast put back her right leg, she saw him looking at her.

"Who's goin' ter milk, pap, atter I'm gone?"

"This the fust time you thought o' that?" June put her flushed cheek back to the flank of the cow. It was not the first time she had thought of that—her step-mother would milk and if she were ill, her father or Loretta. She had not meant to ask that question—she was wondering when they would start. That was what she meant to ask and she was glad that she had swerved. Breakfast was eaten in the usual silence by the boy and the man—June and the step-mother serving it, and waiting on the lord that was and the lord that was to be—and then the two females sat down.

"Hurry up, June," said the old man, wiping his mouth and beard with the back of his hand. "Clear away the dishes an' git ready. Hale said he would meet us at the Pine an' hour by sun, fer I told him I had to git back to work. Hurry up, now!"

June hurried up. She was too excited to eat anything, so she began to wash the dishes while her step-mother ate. Then she went into the living-room to pack her things and it didn't take long. She wrapped the doll Hale had given her in an extra petticoat, wound one pair of yarn stockings around a pair of coarse shoes, tied them up into one bundle and she was ready. Her father appeared with the sorrel horse, caught up his saddle from the porch, threw it on and stretched the blanket behind it as a pillion for June to ride on.

"Let's go!" he said. There is little or no demonstrativeness in the domestic relations of mountaineers. The kiss of courtship is the only one known. There were no good-bys—only that short "Let's go!"

June sprang behind her father from the porch. The step-mother handed her the bundle which she clutched in her lap, and they simply rode away, the step-mother and Bub silently gazing after them. But June saw the boy's mouth working, and when she turned the thicket at the creek, she looked back at the two quiet figures, and a keen pain cut her heart. She shut her mouth closely, gripped her bundle more tightly and the tears streamed down her face, but the man did not know. They climbed in silence. Sometimes her father dismounted where the path was steep, but June sat on the horse to hold the bundle and thus they mounted through the mist and chill of the morning. A shout greeted them from the top of the little spur whence the big Pine was visible, and up there they found Hale waiting. He had reached the Pine earlier than they and was coming down to meet them.

"Hello, little girl," called Hale cheerily, "you didn't fail me, did you?"

June shook her head and smiled. Her face was blue and her little legs, dangling under the bundle, were shrinking from the cold. Her bonnet had fallen to the back of her neck, and he saw that her hair was parted and gathered in a Psyche knot at the back of her head, giving her a quaint old look when she stood on the ground in her crimson gown. Hale had not forgotten a pillion and there the transfer was made. Hale lifted her behind his saddle and handed up her bundle.

"I'll take good care of her," he said.

"All right," said the old man.

"And I'm coming over soon to fix up that coal matter, and I'll let you know how she's getting on."

"All right."

"Good-by," said Hale.

"I wish ye well," said the mountaineer. "Be a good girl, Juny, and do what Mr. Hale thar tells ye."

"All right, pap." And thus they parted. June felt the power of Hale's big black horse with exultation the moment he started.

"Now we're off," said Hale gayly, and he patted the little hand that was about his waist, "Give me that bundle."

109

"I can carry it."

"No, you can't—not with me," and when he reached around for it and put it on the cantle of his saddle, June thrust her left hand into his overcoat pocket and Hale laughed.

"Loretta wouldn't ride with me this way."

"Loretty ain't got much sense," drawled June complacently. "'Tain't no harm. But don't you tell me! I don't want to hear nothin' 'bout Loretty noway." Again Hale laughed and June laughed, too. Imp that she was, she was just pretending to be jealous now. She could see the big Pine over his shoulder.

"I've knowed that tree since I was a little girl—since I was a baby," she said, and the tone of her voice was new to Hale. "Sister Sally uster tell me lots about that ole tree." Hale waited, but she stopped again.

"What did she tell you?"

"She used to say hit was curious that hit should be 'way up here all alone—that she reckollected it ever since *she* was a baby, and she used to come up here and talk to it, and she said sometimes she could hear it jus' a whisperin' to her when she was down home in the cove."

"What did she say it said?"

"She said it was always a-whisperin' 'come—come—come!'" June crooned the words, "an' atter she died, I heerd the folks sayin' as how she riz up in bed with her eyes right wide an' sayin'

'I hears it! It's a-whisperin'—I hears it—come—come—come'!" And still Hale kept quiet when she stopped again.

"The Red Fox said hit was the sperits, but I knowed when they told me that she was a thinkin' o' that ole tree thar. But I never let on. I reckon that's *one* reason made me come here that day." They were close to the big tree now and Hale dismounted to fix his girth for the descent.

"Well, I'm mighty glad you came, little girl. I might never have seen you."

"That's so," said June.

"I saw the print of your foot in the mud right there."

"Did ye?"

"And if I hadn't, I might never have gone down into Lonesome Cove." June laughed.

"You ran from me," Hale went on.

"Yes, I did: an' that's why you follered me." Hale looked up quickly. Her face was demure, but her eyes danced. She was an aged little thing.

"Why did you run?"

"I thought yo' fishin' pole was a rifle-gun an' that you was a raider." Hale laughed—"I see."

"'Member when you let yo' horse drink?" Hale nodded. "Well, I was on a rock above the creek, lookin' down at ye. An' I seed ye catchin' minners an' thought you was goin' up the crick lookin' fer a still."

"Weren't you afraid of me then?"

"Huh!" she said contemptuously. "I wasn't afeared of you at all, 'cept fer what you mought find out. You couldn't do no harm to nobody without a gun, and I knowed thar wasn't no still up that crick. I know—I knowed whar it was." Hale noticed the quick change of tense.

"Won't you take me to see it some time?"

"No!" she said shortly, and Hale knew he had made a mistake. It was too steep for both to ride now, so he tied the bundle to the cantle with leathern strings and started leading the horse. June pointed to the edge of the cliff.

"I was a-layin' flat right thar and I seed you comin' down thar. My, but you looked funny to me! You don't now," she added hastily. "You look mighty nice to me now——!"

"You're a little rascal," said Hale, "that's what you are." The little girl bubbled with laughter and then she grew mock-serious.

"No, I ain't."

"Yes, you are," he repeated, shaking his head, and both were silent for a while. June was going to begin her education now and it was just as well for him to begin with it now. So he started vaguely when he was mounted again:

"June, you thought my clothes were funny when you first saw them—didn't you?"

"Uh, huh!" said June.

"But you like them now?"

"Uh, huh!" she crooned again.

112

"Well, some people who weren't used to clothes that people wear over in the mountains might think *them* funny for the same reason—mightn't they?" June was silent for a moment.

"Well, mebbe, I like your clothes better, because I like you better," she said, and Hale laughed.

"Well, it's just the same—the way people in the mountains dress and talk is different from the way people outside dress and talk. It doesn't make much difference about clothes, though, I guess you will want to be as much like people over here as you can——"

"I don't know," interrupted the little girl shortly, "I ain't seed 'em yit."

"Well," laughed Hale, "you will want to talk like them anyhow, because everybody who is learning tries to talk the same way." June was silent, and Hale plunged unconsciously on.

"Up at the Pine now you said, 'I *seed* you when I was *a-layin'* on the edge of the cliff'; now you ought to have said, 'I *saw* you when I was *lying*——'"

"I wasn't," she said sharply, "I don't tell lies—" her hand shot from his waist and she slid suddenly to the ground. He pulled in his horse and turned a bewildered face. She had lighted on her feet and was poised back above him like an enraged eaglet—her thin nostrils quivering, her mouth as tight as a bow-string, and her eyes two points of fire.

"Why—June!"

"Ef you don't like my clothes an' the way I talk, I reckon I'd better go back home." With a groan Hale tumbled from his horse. Fool that he was, he had forgotten the sensitive pride of the mountaineer, even while he was thinking of that pride. He knew that fun might be made of her speech and her garb by her schoolmates over at the Gap, and he was trying to prepare her—to save her mortification, to make her understand.

"Why, June, little girl, I didn't mean to hurt your feelings. You don't understand—you can't now, but you will. Trust me, won't you? *I* like you just as you are. I *love* the way you talk. But other people—forgive me, won't you?" he pleaded. "I'm sorry. I wouldn't hurt you for the world."

She didn't understand—she hardly heard what he said, but she did know his distress was genuine and his sorrow: and his voice melted her fierce little heart. The tears began to come, while she looked, and when he put his arms about her, she put her face on his breast and sobbed.

"There now!" he said soothingly. "It's all right now. I'm so sorry—so very sorry," and he patted her on the shoulder and laid his hand across her temple and hair, and pressed her head tight to his breast. Almost as suddenly she stopped sobbing and loosening herself turned away from him.

"I'm a fool—that's what I am," she said hotly.

"No, you aren't! Come on, little girl! We're friends again, aren't we?" June was digging at her eyes with both hands.

"Aren't we?"

"Yes," she said with an angry little catch of her breath, and she turned submissively to let him lift her to her seat. Then she looked down into his face.

"Jack," she said, and he started again at the frank address, "I ain't *never goin' to do that no more.*"

"Yes, you are, little girl," he said soberly but cheerily. "You're goin' to do it whenever I'm wrong or whenever you think I'm wrong." She shook her head seriously.

"No, Jack."

In a few minutes they were at the foot of the mountain and on a level road.

"Hold tight!" Hale shouted, "I'm going to let him out now." At the touch of his spur, the big black horse sprang into a gallop, faster and faster, until he was pounding the hard road in a swift run like thunder. At the creek Hale pulled in and looked around. June's bonnet was down, her hair was tossed, her eyes were sparkling fearlessly, and her face was flushed with joy.

"Like it, June?"

"I never did know nothing like it."

"You weren't scared?"

"Skeered o' what?" she asked, and Hale wondered if there was anything of which she would be afraid.

They were entering the Gap now and June's eyes got big with wonder over the mighty up-shooting peaks and the rushing torrent.

"See that big rock yonder, June?" June craned her neck to follow with her eyes his outstretched finger.

"Uh, huh."

"Well, that's called Bee Rock, because it's covered with flowers—purple rhododendrons and laurel—and bears used to go there for wild honey. They say that once on a time folks around here put whiskey in the honey and the bears got so drunk that people came and knocked 'em in the head with clubs."

"Well, what do you think o' that!" said June wonderingly.

Before them a big mountain loomed, and a few minutes later, at the mouth of the Gap, Hale stopped and turned his horse sidewise.

"There we are, June," he said.

June saw the lovely little valley rimmed with big mountains. She could follow the course of the two rivers that encircled it by the trees that fringed their banks, and she saw smoke rising here and there and that was all. She was a little disappointed.

"It's mighty purty," she said, "I never seed" —she paused, but went on without correcting herself—"so much level land in all my life."

The morning mail had just come in as they rode by the post-office and several men hailed her escort, and all stared with some wonder at her. Hale smiled to himself, drew up for none and put on a face of utter unconsciousness that he was doing anything unusual. June felt vaguely uncomfortable. Ahead of them, when they turned the corner of the street, her eyes fell on a strange tall red house with yellow trimmings, that was not built of wood and had two sets of windows one above the other, and before that Hale drew up.

"Here we are. Get down, little girl."

"Good-morning!" said a voice. Hale looked around and flushed, and June looked around and stared—transfixed as by a vision from another world—at the dainty figure behind them in a walking suit, a short skirt that showed two little feet in laced tan boots and a cap with a plume, under which was a pair of wide blue eyes with long lashes, and a mouth that suggested active mischief and gentle mockery.

"Oh, good-morning," said Hale, and he added gently, "Get down, June!"

The little girl slipped to the ground and began pulling her bonnet on with both hands—but the newcomer had caught sight of the Psyche knot that made June look like a little old woman strangely young, and the mockery at her lips was gently accentuated by a smile. Hale swung from his saddle.

"This is the little girl I told you about, Miss Anne," he said. "She's come over to go to school." Instantly, almost, Miss Anne had been melted by the forlorn looking little creature who stood before her, shy for the moment and dumb, and she came forward with her gloved hand outstretched. But June had seen that smile. She gave her hand, and Miss Anne straightway was no little surprised; there was no more shyness in the dark eyes that blazed from the recesses of the sunbonnet, and Miss Anne was so startled when she looked into them that all she could say was: "Dear me!" A portly woman with a kind face appeared at the door of the red brick house and came to the gate.

"Here she is, Mrs. Crane," called Hale.

"Howdye, June!" said the Widow Crane kindly. "Come right in!" In her June knew straightway she had a friend and she picked up her bundle and followed upstairs—the first real stairs she had ever seen—and into a room on the floor of which was a rag carpet. There was a bed in one corner with a white counterpane and a washstand with a bowl and pitcher, which, too, she had never seen before.

"Make yourself at home right now," said the Widow Crane, pulling open a drawer under a big looking-glass—"and put your things here. That's your bed," and out she went.

How clean it was! There were some flowers in

a glass vase on the mantel. There were white curtains at the big window and a bed to herself— her own bed. She went over to the window. There was a steep bank, lined with rhododendrons, right under it. There was a mill-dam below and down the stream she could hear the creaking of a water-wheel, and she could see it dripping and shining in the sun—a gristmill! She thought of Uncle Billy and ole Hon, and in spite of a little pang of home-sickness she felt no loneliness at all.

"I *knew* she would be pretty," said Miss Anne at the gate outside.

"I *told* you she was pretty," said Hale.

"But not so pretty as *that*," said Miss Anne. "We will be great friends."

"I hope so—for her sake," said Hale.

. . . .

Hale waited till noon-recess was nearly over, and then he went to take June to the school-house. He was told that she was in her room and he went up and knocked at the door. There was no an-swer—for one does not knock on doors for en-trance in the mountains, and, thinking he had made a mistake, he was about to try another room, when June opened the door to see what the matter was. She gave him a glad smile.

"Come on," he said, and when she went for her bonnet, he stepped into the room.

"How do you like it?" June nodded toward the window and Hale went to it.

"Thar's Uncle Billy's mill out thar."

"Why, so it is," said Hale smiling. "That's fine."

The school-house, to June's wonder, had shingles on the *outside* around all the walls from roof to foundation, and a big bell hung on top of it under a little shingled roof of its own. A pale little man with spectacles and pale blue eyes met them at the door and he gave June a pale, slender hand and cleared his throat before he spoke to her.

"She's never been to school," said Hale; "she can read and spell, but she's not very strong on arithmetic."

"Very well, I'll turn her over to the primary." The school-bell sounded; Hale left with a parting prophecy—"You'll be proud of her some day"— at which June blushed and then, with a beating heart, she followed the little man into his office. A few minutes later, the assistant came in, and she was none other than the wonderful young woman whom Hale had called Miss Anne. There were a few instructions in a halting voice and with much clearing of the throat from the pale little man; and a moment later June walked the gauntlet of the eyes of her schoolmates, every one of whom looked up from his book or hers to watch her as she went to her seat. Miss Anne pointed out the arithmetic lesson and, without lifting her eyes, June bent with a flushed face to her task. It reddened with shame when she was called to the class, for she sat on the bench, taller by a head and more than any of the boys and girls thereon, except one awkward youth who caught her eye and grinned with unashamed companionship. The teacher noticed her look and understood with a sudden keen sympathy, and naturally she was struck by the fact that the new pupil was the only one who never missed an answer.

"She won't be there long," Miss Anne thought, and she gave June a smile for which the little girl was almost grateful. June spoke to no one, but walked through her schoolmates homeward, when school was over, like a haughty young queen. Miss Anne had gone ahead and was standing at the gate talking with Mrs. Crane, and the young woman spoke to June most kindly.

"Mr. Hale has been called away on business," she said, and June's heart sank—"and I'm going to take care of you until he comes back."

"I'm much obleeged," she said, and while she was not ungracious, her manner indicated her belief that she could take care of herself. And Miss Anne felt uncomfortably that this extraordinary young person was steadily measuring her from head to foot. June saw the smart close-fitting gown, the dainty little boots, and the carefully brushed hair. She noticed how white her teeth were and her hands, and she saw that the nails looked polished and that the tips of them were like little white crescents; and she could still see every detail when she sat at her window, looking down at the old mill. She *saw* Mr. Hale when he left, the young lady had said; and she had a headache now and was going home to *lie* down. She understood now what Hale meant, on the mountainside when she was so angry with him. She was learning fast, and most from the two persons who were not conscious what they were teaching her. And she would learn in the school, too, for the slumbering ambition in her suddenly became passionately definite now. She went to the mirror and looked at her hair—she would learn how to plait that in two braids down her back, as the other school-girls did. She looked at her hands and straightway she fell to scrubbing them with soap as she had never scrubbed them before. As she worked, she heard her name called and she opened the door.

"Yes, mam!" she answered, for already she had picked that up in the school-room.

"Come on, June, and go down the street with me."

"Yes, mam," she repeated, and she wiped her hands and hurried down. Mrs. Crane had looked through the girl's pathetic wardrobe, while she was at school that afternoon, had told Hale before he left and she had a surprise for little June. Together they went down the street and into the chief store in town and, to June's amazement, Mrs. Crane began ordering things for "this little girl."

"Who's a-goin' to pay fer all these things?" whispered June, aghast.

"Don't you bother, honey. Mr. Hale said he would fix all that with your pappy. It's some coal deal or something—don't you bother!" And June in a quiver of happiness didn't bother. Stockings, petticoats, some soft stuff for a new dress and *tan* shoes that looked like the ones that wonderful young woman wore and then some long white things.

"What's them fer?" she whispered, but the clerk heard her and laughed, whereat Mrs. Crane gave him such a glance that he retired quickly.

"Night-gowns, honey."

"You *sleep* in 'em?" said June in an awed voice.

"That's just what you do," said the good old woman, hardly less pleased than June.

"My, but you've got pretty feet."

"I wish they were half as purty as——"

"Well, they are," interrupted Mrs. Crane a little snappishly; apparently she did not like Miss Anne.

"Wrap 'em up and Mr. Hale will attend to the bill."

"All right," said the clerk looking much mystified.

Outside the door, June looked up into the beaming goggles of the Hon. Samuel Budd.

"Is *this* the little girl? Howdye, June," he

said, and June put her hand in the Hon. Sam's with a sudden trust in his voice.

"I'm going to help take care of you, too," said Mr. Budd, and June smiled at him with shy gratitude. How kind everybody was!

"I'm much obleeged," she said, and she and Mrs. Crane went on back with their bundles.

June's hands so trembled when she found herself alone with her treasures that she could hardly unpack them. When she had folded and laid them away, she had to unfold them to look at them again. She hurried to bed that night merely that she might put on one of those wonderful night-gowns, and again she had to look all her treasures over. She was glad that she had brought the doll because *he* had given it to her, but she said to herself "I'm a-gittin' too big now fer dolls!" and she put it away. Then she set the lamp on the mantel-piece so that she could see herself in her wonderful night-gown. She let her shining hair fall like molten gold around her shoulders, and she wondered whether she could ever look like the dainty creature that just now was the model she so passionately wanted to be like. Then she blew out the lamp and sat a while by the window, looking down through the rhododendrons, at the shining water and at the old water-wheel sleepily at rest in the moonlight. She knelt down then at her bedside to say her prayers—as her dead sister had taught her to do—and she asked

God to bless Jack—wondering as she prayed that she had heard nobody else call him Jack—and then she lay down with her breast heaving. She had told him she would never do that again, but she couldn't help it now—the tears came and from happiness she cried herself softly to sleep.

XIII

HALE rode that night under a brilliant moon to the worm of a railroad that had been creeping for many years toward the Gap. The head of it was just protruding from the Natural Tunnel twenty miles away. There he sent his horse back, slept in a shanty till morning, and then the train crawled through a towering bench of rock. The mouth of it on the other side opened into a mighty amphitheatre with solid rock walls shooting vertically hundreds of feet upward. Vertically, he thought—with the back of his head between his shoulders as he looked up—they were more than vertical—they were actually concave. The Almighty had not only stored riches immeasurable in the hills behind him—He had driven this passage Himself to help puny man to reach them, and yet the wretched road was going toward them like a snail. On the fifth night, thereafter he was back there at the tunnel again from New York—with a grim mouth and a happy eye. He had brought success with him this time and there was no sleep for him that night. He had been delayed by a wreck, it was two o'clock in the morning, and not a horse was available; so he started those twenty miles afoot, and day was breaking when he looked down on the little valley shrouded in mist and just wakening from sleep.

Things had been moving while he was away, as he quickly learned. The English were buying lands right and left at the gap sixty miles southwest. Two companies had purchased most of the town-site where he was—*his* town-site—and were going to pool their holdings and form an improvement company. But a good deal was left, and straightway Hale got a map from his office and with it in his hand walked down the curve of the river and over Poplar Hill and beyond. Early breakfast was ready when he got back to the hotel. He swallowed a cup of coffee so hastily that it burned him, and June, when she passed his window on her way to school, saw him busy over his desk. She started to shout to him, but he looked so haggard and grim that she was afraid, and went on, vaguely hurt by a preoccupation that seemed quite to have excluded her. For two hours then, Hale haggled and bargained, and at ten o'clock he went to the telegraph office. The operator who was speculating in a small way himself smiled when he read the telegram.

"A thousand an acre?" he repeated with a whistle. "You could have got that at twenty-five per—three months ago."

"I know," said Hale, "there's time enough yet." Then he went to his room, pulled the blinds down and went to sleep, while rumour played with his name through the town.

It was nearly the closing hour of school when, dressed and freshly shaven, he stepped out into the pale afternoon and walked up toward the schoolhouse. The children were pouring out of the doors. At the gate there was a sudden commotion, he saw a crimson figure flash into the group that had stopped there, and flash out, and then June came swiftly toward him followed closely by a tall boy with a cap on his head. That far away he could see that she was angry and he hurried toward her. Her face was white with rage, her mouth was tight and her dark eyes were aflame. Then from the group another tall boy darted out and behind him ran a smaller one, bellowing. Hale heard the boy with the cap call kindly:

"Hold on, little girl! I won't let 'em touch you." June stopped with him and Hale ran to them.

"Here," he called, "what's the matter?"

June burst into crying when she saw him and leaned over the fence sobbing. The tall lad with the cap had his back to Hale, and he waited till the other two boys came up. Then he pointed to the smaller one and spoke to Hale without looking around.

"Why, that little skate there was teasing this little girl and——"

"She slapped him," said Hale grimly. The lad with the cap turned. His eyes were dancing and the shock of curly hair that stuck from his absurd little cap shook with his laughter.

"Slapped him! She knocked him as flat as a pancake."

"Yes, an' you said you'd stand fer her," said the other tall boy who was plainly a mountain lad. He was near bursting with rage.

"You bet I will," said the boy with the cap heartily, "right now!" and he dropped his books to the ground.

"Hold on!" said Hale, jumping between them. "You ought to be ashamed of yourself," he said to the mountain boy.

"I wasn't atter the gal," he said indignantly. "I was comin' fer him."

The boy with the cap tried to get away from Hale's grasp.

"No use, sir," he said coolly. "You'd better let us settle it now. We'll have to do it some time. I know the breed. He'll fight all right and there's no use puttin' it off. It's got to come."

"You bet it's got to come," said the mountain lad. "You can't call my brother names."

"Well, he *is* a skate," said the boy with the cap, with no heat at all in spite of his indignation, and Hale wondered at his aged calm.

"Every one of you little tads," he went on coolly, waving his hand at the gathered group, "is a skate who teases this little girl. And you older boys are skates for letting the little ones do it, the whole pack of you—and I'm going to spank any little tadpole who does it hereafter, and I'm going to punch the head off any big one who allows it. It's got to stop *now!*" And as Hale dragged him off he added to the mountain boy, "and I'm going to begin with you whenever you say the word." Hale was laughing now.

"You don't seem to understand," he said, "this is my affair."

"I beg your pardon, sir, I don't understand."

"Why, I'm taking care of this little girl."

"Oh, well, you see I didn't know that. I've only been here two days. But"—his frank, generous face broke into a winning smile—"you don't go to school. You'll let me watch out for her there?"

"Sure! I'll be very grateful."

"Not at all, sir—not at all. It was a great pleasure and I think I'll have lots of fun." He looked at June, whose grateful eyes had hardly left his face.

"So don't you soil your little fist any more with any of 'em, but just tell me—er—er——"

"June," she said, and a shy smile came through her tears.

"June," he finished with a boyish laugh. "Good-by, sir."

"You haven't told me your name."

"I suppose you know my brothers, sir, the Berkleys."

"I should say so," and Hale held out his hand.
"You're Bob?"

"Yes, sir."

"I knew you were coming, and I'm mighty glad
to see you. I hope you and June will be good
friends and I'll be very glad to have you watch
over her when I'm away."

"I'd like nothing better, sir," he said cheer-
fully, and quite impersonally as far as June was
concerned. Then his eyes lighted up.

"My brothers don't seem to want me to join
the Police Guard. Won't you say a word for me?"

"I certainly will."

"Thank you, sir."

That "sir" no longer bothered Hale. At first
he had thought it a mark of respect to his superior
age, and he was not particularly pleased, but when
he knew now that the lad was another son of the
old gentleman whom he saw riding up the valley
every morning on a gray horse, with several dogs
trailing after him—he knew the word was merely
a family characteristic of old-fashioned courtesy.

"Isn't he nice, June?"

"Yes," she said.

"Have you missed me, June?"

June slid her hand into his. "I'm so glad you
come back." They were approaching the gate
now.

"June, you said you weren't going to cry any
more." June's head drooped.

"I know, but I jes' can't help it when I git mad," she said seriously. "I'd bust if I didn't."

"All right," said Hale kindly.

"I've cried twice," she said.

"What were you mad about the other time?"

"I wasn't mad."

"Then why did you cry, June?"

Her dark eyes looked full at him a moment and then her long lashes hid them.

"Cause you was so good to me."

Hale choked suddenly and patted her on the shoulder.

"Go in, now, little girl, and study. Then you must take a walk. I've got some work to do. I'll see you at supper time."

"All right," said June. She turned at the gate to watch Hale enter the hotel, and as she started indoors, she heard a horse coming at a gallop and she turned again to see her cousin, Dave Tolliver, pull up in front of the house. She ran back to the gate and then she saw that he was swaying in his saddle.

"Hello, June!" he called thickly.

Her face grew hard and she made no answer.

"I've come over to take ye back home."

She only stared at him rebukingly, and he straightened in his saddle with an effort at self-control—but his eyes got darker and he looked ugly.

"D'you hear me? I've come over to take ye home."

"You oughter be ashamed o' yourself," she said hotly, and she turned to go back into the house.

"Oh, you ain't ready now. Well, git ready an' we'll start in the mornin'. I'll be aroun' fer ye 'bout the break o' day."

He whirled his horse with an oath—June was gone. She saw him ride swaying down the street and she ran across to the hotel and found Hale sitting in the office with another man. Hale saw her entering the door swiftly, he knew something was wrong and he rose to meet her.

"Dave's here," she whispered hurriedly, "an' he says he's come to take me home."

"Well," said Hale, "he won't do it, will he?" June shook her head and then she said significantly:

"Dave's drinkin'."

Hale's brow clouded. Straightway he foresaw trouble—but he said cheerily:

"All right. You go back and keep in the house and I'll be over by and by and we'll talk it over." And, without another word, she went. She had meant to put on her new dress and her new shoes and stockings that night that Hale might see her —but she was in doubt about doing it when she got to her room. She tried to study her lessons for the next day, but she couldn't fix her mind on them. She wondered if Dave might not get into a fight or, perhaps, he would get so drunk that he would go to sleep somewhere—she knew that men

133

did that after drinking very much—and, anyhow, he would not bother her until next morning, and then he would be sober and would go quietly back home. She was so comforted that she got to thinking about the hair of the girl who sat in front of her at school. It was plaited and she had studied just how it was done and she began to wonder whether she could fix her own that way. So she got in front of the mirror and loosened hers in a mass about her shoulders—the mass that was to Hale like the golden bronze of a wild turkey's wing. The other girl's plaits were the same size, so that the hair had to be equally divided— thus she argued to herself—but how did that girl manage to plait it behind her back? She did it in front, of course, so June divided the bronze heap behind her and pulled one half of it in front of her and then for a moment she was helpless. Then she laughed—it must be done like the grass-blades and strings she had plaited for Bub, of course, so, dividing that half into three parts, she did the plaiting swiftly and easily. When it was finished she looked at the braid, much pleased— for it hung below her waist and was much longer than any of the other girls' at school. The transition was easy now, so interested had she become. She got out her tan shoes and stockings and the pretty white dress and put them on. The mill-pond was dark with shadows now, and she went down the stairs and out to the gate just as Dave again pulled up in front of it. He stared at the vision wonderingly and long, and then he began to laugh with the scorn of soberness and the silliness of drink.

"*You* ain't June, air ye?" The girl never moved. As if by a preconcerted signal three men moved toward the boy, and one of them said sternly:

"Drop that pistol. You are under arrest." The boy glared like a wild thing trapped, from one to another of the three—a pistol gleamed in the hand of each—and slowly thrust his own weapon into his pocket.

"Get off that horse," added the stern voice. Just then Hale rushed across the street and the mountain youth saw him.

"Ketch his pistol," cried June, in terror for Hale—for she knew what was coming, and one of the men caught with both hands the wrist of Dave's arm as it shot behind him.

"Take him to the calaboose!"

At that June opened the gate—that disgrace she could never stand—but Hale spoke.

"I know him, boys. He doesn't mean any harm. He doesn't know the regulations yet. Suppose we let him go home."

"All right," said Logan. "The calaboose or home. Will you go home?"

In the moment, the mountain boy had apparently forgotten his captors—he was staring at

135

June with wonder, amazement, incredulity struggling through the fumes in his brain to his flushed face. She—a Tolliver—had warned a stranger against her own blood-cousin.

"Will you go home?" repeated Logan sternly.

The boy looked around at the words, as though he were half dazed, and his baffled face turned sick and white.

"Lemme loose!" he said sullenly. "I'll go home." And he rode silently away, after giving Hale a vindictive look that told him plainer than words that more was yet to come. Hale had heard June's warning cry, but now when he looked for her she was gone. He went in to supper and sat down at the table and still she did not come.

"She's got a surprise for you," said Mrs. Crane, smiling mysteriously. "She's been fixing for you for an hour. My! but she's pretty in them new clothes—why, June!"

June was coming in—she wore her homespun, her scarlet homespun and the Psyche knot. She did not seem to have heard Mrs. Crane's note of wonder, and she sat quietly down in her seat. Her face was pale and she did not look at Hale. Nothing was said of Dave—in fact, June said nothing at all, and Hale, too, vaguely understanding, kept quiet. Only when he went out, Hale called her to the gate and put one hand on her head.

"I'm sorry, little girl."

The girl lifted her great troubled eyes to him, but no word passed her lips, and Hale helplessly left her.

June did not cry that night. She sat by the window—wretched and tearless. She had taken sides with "furriners" against her own people. That was why, instinctively, she had put on her old homespun with a vague purpose of reparation to them. She knew the story Dave would take back home—the bitter anger that his people and hers would feel at the outrage done him—anger against the town, the Guard, against Hale because he was a part of both and even against her. Dave was merely drunk, he had simply shot off his pistol— that was no harm in the hills. And yet everybody had dashed toward him as though he had stolen something—even Hale. Yes, even that boy with the cap who had stood up for her at school that afternoon—he had rushed up, his face aflame with excitement, eager to take part should Dave resist. She had cried out impulsively to save Hale, but Dave would not understand. No, in his eyes she had been false to family and friends—to the clan—she had sided with "furriners." What would her father say? Perhaps she'd better go home next day—perhaps for good—for there was a deep unrest within her that she could not fathom, a premonition that she was at the parting of the ways, a vague fear of the shadows that hung about the strange new path on which her feet were set. The old mill creaked in the moonlight below her. Sometimes, when the wind blew up Lonesome Cove, she could hear Uncle Billy's wheel creaking just that way. A sudden pang of homesickness choked her, but she did not cry. Yes, she would go home next day. She blew out the light and undressed in the dark as she did at home and went to bed. And that night the little night-gown lay apart from her in the drawer—unfolded and untouched.

XIV

BUT June did not go home. Hale anticipated that resolution of hers and forestalled it by being on hand for breakfast and taking June over to the porch of his little office. There he tried to explain to her that they were trying to build a town and must have law and order; that they must have no personal feeling for or against anybody and must treat everybody exactly alike—no other course was fair—and though June could not quite understand, she trusted him and she said she would keep on at school until her father came for her.

"Do you think he will come, June?"

The little girl hesitated.

"I'm afeerd he will," she said, and Hale smiled.

"Well, I'll try to persuade him to let you stay, if he does come."

June was quite right. She had seen the matter the night before just as it was. For just at that hour young Dave, sobered, but still on the verge of tears from anger and humiliation, was telling the story of the day in her father's cabin. The old man's brows drew together and his eyes grew fierce and sullen, both at the insult to a Tolliver

139

and at the thought of a certain moonshine still up
a ravine not far away and the indirect danger to it
in any finicky growth of law and order. Still he
had a keen sense of justice, and he knew that
Dave had not told all the story, and from him
Dave, to his wonder, got scant comfort—for another reason as well: with a deal pending for the
sale of his lands, the shrewd old man would not
risk giving offence to Hale—not until that matter
was settled, anyway. And so June was safer from
interference just then than she knew. But Dave
carried the story far and wide, and it spread as a
story can only in the hills. So that the two people
most talked about among the Tollivers and,
through Loretta, among the Falins as well, were
June and Hale, and at the Gap similar talk would
come. Already Hale's name was on every tongue
in the town, and there, because of his recent pur-
chases of town-site land, he was already, aside
from his personal influence, a man of mysterious
power.

Meanwhile, the prescient shadow of the coming
"boom" had stolen over the hills and the work of
the Guard had grown rapidly.

Every Saturday there had been local lawlessness to deal with. The spirit of personal liberty
that characterized the spot was traditional. Here
for half a century the people of Wise County and
of Lee, whose border was but a few miles down
the river, came to get their wool carded, their grist

ground and farming utensils mended. Here, too, elections were held *viva voce* under the beeches, at the foot of the wooded spur now known as Imboden Hill. Here were the muster-days of wartime. Here on Saturdays the people had come together during half a century for sport and horse-trading and to talk politics. Here they drank apple-jack and hard cider, chaffed and quarrelled and fought fist and skull. Here the bullies of the two counties would come together to decide who was the "best man." Here was naturally engendered the hostility between the hill-dwellers of Wise and the valley people of Lee, and here was fought a famous battle between a famous bully of Wise and a famous bully of Lee. On election days the country people would bring in gingercakes made of cane-molasses, bread homemade of Burr flour and moonshine and apple-jack which the candidates would buy and distribute through the crowd. And always during the afternoon there were men who would try to prove themselves the best Democrats in the State of Virginia by resort to tooth, fist and eye-gouging thumb. Then to these elections sometimes would come the Kentuckians from over the border to stir up the hostility between state and state, which makes that border bristle with enmity to this day. For half a century, then, all wild oats from elsewhere usually sprouted at the Gap. And thus the Gap had been the shrine of personal freedom—the place where any one individual had the right to do his pleasure with bottle and cards and politics and any other the right to prove him wrong if he were strong enough. Very soon, as the Hon. Sam Budd predicted, they had the hostility of Lee concentrated on them as siding with the county of Wise, and they would gain, in addition now, the general hostility of the Kentuckians, because as a crowd of meddlesome "furriners" they would be siding with the Virginians in the general enmity already alive. Moreover, now that the feud threatened activity over in Kentucky, more trouble must come, too, from that source, as the talk that came through the Gap, after young Dave Tolliver's arrest, plainly indicated.

Town ordinances had been passed. The wild centaurs were no longer allowed to ride up and down the plank walks of Saturdays with their reins in their teeth and firing a pistol into the ground with either hand; they could punctuate the hotel sign no more; they could not ride at a fast gallop through the streets of the town, and, Lost Spirit of American Liberty!—they could not even yell. But the lawlessness of the town itself and its close environment was naturally the first objective point, and the first problem involved was moonshine and its faithful ally "the blind tiger." The "tiger" is a little shanty with an ever-open mouth—a hole in the door like a post-office window. You place your money on the sill and, at the ring of the coin, a mysterious arm emerges from the hole, sweeps the money away and leaves a bottle of white whiskey. Thus you see nobody's face; the owner of the beast is safe, and so are you— which you might not be, if you saw and told. In every little hollow about the Gap a tiger had his lair, and these were all bearded at once by a petition to the county judge for high license saloons, which was granted. This measure drove the tigers out of business, and concentrated moonshine in the heart of the town, where its devotees were under easy guard. One "tiger" only indeed was left, run by a round-shouldered crouching creature whom Bob Berkley—now at Hale's solicitation a policeman and known as the Infant of the Guard—dubbed Caliban. His shanty stood midway in the Gap, high from the road, set against a dark clump of pines and roared at by the river beneath. Everybody knew he sold whiskey, but he was too shrewd to be caught, until, late one afternoon, two days after young Dave's arrest, Hale coming through the Gap into town glimpsed a skulking figure with a hand-barrel as it slipped from the dark pines into Caliban's cabin. He pulled in his horse, dismounted and deliberated. If he went on down the road now, they would see him and suspect. Moreover, the patrons of the tiger would not appear until after dark, and he wanted a prisoner or two. So Hale led his horse up into the bushes and came back to a covert by the roadside to watch and wait. As he sat there, a merry whistle sounded down the road, and Hale smiled. Soon the Infant of the Guard came along, his hands in his pockets, his cap on the back of his head, his pistol bumping his hip in manly fashion and making the ravines echo with his pursed lips. He stopped in front of Hale, looked toward the river, drew his revolver and aimed it at a floating piece of wood. The revolver cracked, the piece of wood skidded on the surface of the water and there was no splash.

"That was a pretty good shot," said Hale in a low voice. The boy whirled and saw him.

"Well—what are you——?"

"Easy—easy!" cautioned Hale. "Listen! I've just seen a moonshiner go into Caliban's cabin." The boy's eager eyes sparkled.

"Let's go after him."

"No, you go on back. If you don't, they'll be suspicious. Get another man"—Hale almost laughed at the disappointment in the lad's face at his first words, and the joy that came after it—"and climb high above the shanty and come back here to me. Then after dark we'll dash in and cinch Caliban and his customers."

"Yes, sir," said the lad. "Shall I whistle going back?" Hale nodded approval.

"Just the same." And off Bob went, whistling like a calliope and not even turning his head to look at the cabin. In half an hour Hale thought

144

he heard something crashing through the bushes high on the mountain side, and, a little while afterward, the boy crawled through the bushes to him alone. His cap was gone, there was a bloody scratch across his face and he was streaming with perspiration.

"You'll have to excuse me, sir," he panted, "I didn't see anybody but one of my brothers, and if I had told him, he wouldn't have let *me* come. And I hurried back for fear—for fear something would happen."

"Well, suppose I don't let you go."

"Excuse me, sir, but I don't see how you can very well help. You aren't my brother and you can't go alone."

"I was," said Hale.

"Yes, sir, but not now."

Hale was worried, but there was nothing else to be done.

"All right. I'll let you go if you stop saying 'sir' to me. It makes me feel so old."

"Certainly, sir," said the lad quite unconsciously, and when Hale smothered a laugh, he looked around to see what had amused him. Darkness fell quickly, and in the gathering gloom they saw two more figures skulk into the cabin.

"We'll go now—for we want the fellow who's selling the moonshine."

Again Hale was beset with doubts about the boy and his own responsibility to the boy's brothers. The lad's eyes were shining, but his face was more eager than excited and his hand was as steady as Hale's own.

"You slip around and station yourself behind that pine-tree just behind the cabin"—the boy looked crestfallen—"and if anybody tries to get out of the back door—you halt him."

"Is there a back door?"

"I don't know," Hale said rather shortly. "You obey orders. I'm not your brother, but I'm your captain."

"I beg your pardon, sir. Shall I go now?"

"Yes, you'll hear me at the front door. They won't make any resistance." The lad stepped away with nimble caution high above the cabin, and he even took his shoes off before he slid lightly down to his place behind the pine. There was no back door, only a window, and his disappointment was bitter. Still, when he heard Hale at the front door, he meant to make a break for that window, and he waited in the still gloom. He could hear the rough talk and laughter within and now and then the clink of a tin cup. By and by there was a faint noise in front of the cabin, and he steadied his nerves and his beating heart. Then he heard the door pushed violently in and Hale's cry:

"Surrender!"

Hale stood on the threshold with his pistol outstretched in his right hand. The door had struck something soft and he said sharply again:

"Come out from behind that door—hands up!"

At the same moment, the back window flew open with a bang and Bob's pistol covered the edge of the opened door. "Caliban" had rolled from his box like a stupid animal. Two of his patrons sat dazed and staring from Hale to the boy's face at the window. A mountaineer stood in one corner with twitching fingers and shifting eyes like a caged wild thing and forth issued from behind the door, quivering with anger—young Dave Tolliver. Hale stared at him amazed, and when Dave saw Hale, such a wave of fury surged over his face that Bob thought it best to attract his attention again; which he did by gently motioning at him with the barrel of his pistol.

"Hold on, there," he said quietly, and young Dave stood still.

"Climb through that window, Bob, and collect the batteries," said Hale.

"Sure, sir," said the lad, and with his pistol still prominently in the foreground he threw his left leg over the sill and as he climbed in he quoted with a grunt: "Always go in force to make an arrest." Grim and serious as it was, with June's cousin glowering at him, Hale could not help smiling.

"You didn't go home, after all," said Hale to young Dave, who clenched his hands and his lips but answered nothing; "or, if you did,

147

you got back pretty quick." And still Dave was silent.

"Get 'em all, Bob?" In answer the boy went the rounds—feeling the pocket of each man's right hip and his left breast.

"Yes, sir."

"Unload 'em!"

The lad "broke" each of the four pistols, picked up a piece of twine and strung them together through each trigger-guard.

"Close that window and stand here at the door."

With the boy at the door, Hale rolled the hand-barrel to the threshold and the white liquor gurgled joyously on the steps.

"All right, come along," he said to the captives, and at last young Dave spoke:

"Whut you takin' me fer?"

Hale pointed to the empty hand-barrel and Dave's answer was a look of scorn.

"I nuvver brought that hyeh."

"You were drinking illegal liquor in a blind tiger, and if you didn't bring it you can prove that later: Anyhow, we'll want you as a witness," and Hale looked at the other mountaineer, who had turned his eyes quickly to Dave. Caliban led the way with young Dave, and Hale walked side by side with them while Bob was escort for the other two. The road ran along a high bank, and as Bob was adjusting the jangling weapons on his left arm, the strange mountaineer darted behind him and leaped headlong into the tops of thick rhododendron. Before Hale knew what had happened the lad's pistol flashed.

"Stop, boy!" he cried, horrified. "Don't shoot!" and he had to catch the lad to keep him from leaping after the runaway. The shot had missed; they heard the runaway splash into the river and go stumbling across it and then there was silence. Young Dave laughed:

"Uncle Judd'll be over hyeh to-morrow to see about this." Hale said nothing and they went on. At the door of the calaboose Dave balked and had to be pushed in by main force. They left him weeping and cursing with rage.

"Go to bed, Bob," said Hale.

"Yes, sir," said Bob; "just as soon as I get my lessons."

Hale did not go to the boarding-house that night—he feared to face June. Instead he went to the hotel to scraps of a late supper and then to bed. He had hardly touched the pillow, it seemed, when somebody shook him by the shoulder. It was Macfarlan, and daylight was streaming through the window.

"A gang of those Falins are here," Macfarlan said, "and they're after young Dave Tolliver— about a dozen of 'em. Young Buck is with them, and the sheriff. They say he shot a man over the mountains yesterday."

Hale sprang for his clothes—here was a quandary.

"If we turn him over to them—they'll kill him." Macfarlan nodded.

"Of course, and if we leave him in that weak old calaboose, they'll get more help and take him out to-night."

"Then we'll take him to the county jail."

"They'll take him away from us."

"No, they won't. You go out and get as many shotguns as you can find and load them with buckshot."

Macfarlan nodded approvingly and disappeared. Hale plunged his face in a basin of cold water, soaked his hair and, as he was mopping his face with a towel, there was a ponderous tread on the porch, the door opened without the formality of a knock, and Devil Judd Tolliver, with his hat on and belted with two huge pistols, stepped stooping within. His eyes, red with anger and loss of sleep, were glaring, and his heavy moustache and beard showed the twitching of his mouth.

"Whar's Dave?" he said shortly.

"In the calaboose."

"Did you put him in?"

"Yes," said Hale calmly.

"Well, by God," the old man said with repressed fury, "you can't git him out too soon if you want to save trouble."

"Look here, Judd," said Hale seriously. "You

are one of the last men in the world I want to have
trouble with for many reasons; but I'm an officer
over here and I'm no more afraid of you"—Hale
paused to let that fact sink in and it did—"than
you are of me. Dave's been selling liquor."

"He hain't," interrupted the old mountaineer.
"He didn't bring that liquor over hyeh. I know
who done it."

"All right," said Hale; "I'll take your word for
it and I'll let him out, if you say so, but——"

"Right now," thundered old Judd.

"Do you know that young Buck Falin and a
dozen of his gang are over here after him?" The
old man looked stunned.

"Whut—now?"

"They're over there in the woods across the
river *now* and they want me to give him up to
them. They say they have the sheriff with them
and they want him for shooting a man on Leather-
wood Creek, day before yesterday."

"It's all a lie," burst out old Judd. "They
want to kill him."

"Of course—and I was going to take him up to
the county jail right away for safe-keeping."

"D'ye mean to say you'd throw that boy into
jail and then fight them Falins to pertect him?"
the old man asked slowly and incredulously.
Hale pointed to a two-store building through
his window.

"If you get in the back part of that store at a

window, you can see whether I will or not. I can summon you to help, and if a fight comes up you can do your share from the window."

The old man's eyes lighted up like a leaping flame.

"Will you let Dave out and give him a Winchester and help us fight 'em?" he said eagerly. "We three can whip 'em all."

"No," said Hale shortly. "I'd try to keep both sides from fighting, and I'd arrest Dave or you as quickly as I would a Falin."

The average mountaineer has little conception of duty in the abstract, but old Judd belonged to the better class—and there are many of them—that does. He looked into Hale's eyes long and steadily.

"All right."

Macfarlan came in hurriedly and stopped short—seeing the hatted, bearded giant.

"This is Mr. Tolliver—an uncle of Dave's—Judd Tolliver," said Hale. "Go ahead."

"I've got everything fixed—but I couldn't get but five of the fellows—two of the Berkley boys. They wouldn't let me tell Bob."

"All right. Can I summon Mr. Tolliver here?"

"Yes," said Macfarlan doubtfully, "but you know——"

"He won't be seen," interrupted Hale, understandingly. "He'll be at a window in the back of that store and he won't take part unless a fight begins, and if it does, we'll need him."

An hour later Devil Judd Tolliver was in the store Hale pointed out and peering cautiously around the edge of an open window at the wooden gate of the ramshackle calaboose. Several Falins were there—led by young Buck, whom Hale recognized as the red-headed youth at the head of the tearing horsemen who had swept by him that late afternoon when he was coming back from his first trip to Lonesome Cove. The old man gritted his teeth as he looked and he put one of his huge pistols on a table within easy reach and kept the other clenched in his right fist. From down the street came five horsemen, led by John Hale. Every man carried a double-barrelled shotgun, and the old man smiled and his respect for Hale rose higher, high as it already was, for nobody—mountaineer or not—has love for a hostile shotgun. The Falins, armed only with pistols, drew near.

"Keep back!" he heard Hale say calmly, and they stopped—young Buck alone going on.

"We want that feller," said young Buck.

"Well, you don't get him," said Hale quietly. "He's our prisoner. Keep back!" he repeated, motioning with the barrel of his shotgun—and young Buck moved backward to his own men. The old man saw Hale and another man—the sergeant—go inside the heavy gate of the stockade. He saw a boy in a cap, with a pistol in one hand

and a strapped set of books in the other, come running up to the men with the shotguns and he heard one of them say angrily:

"I told you not to come."

"I know you did," said the boy imperturbably.

"You go on to school," said another of the men, but the boy with the cap shook his head and dropped his books to the ground. The big gate opened just then and out came Hale and the sergeant, and between them young Dave—his eyes blinking in the sunlight.

"Damn ye," he heard Dave say to Hale. "I'll get even with you fer this some day"—and then the prisoner's eyes caught the horses and shotguns and turned to the group of Falins and he shrank back utterly dazed. There was a movement among the Falins and Devil Judd caught up his other pistol and with a grim smile got ready. Young Buck had turned to his crowd:

"Men," he said, "you know I never back down"—Devil Judd knew that, too, and he was amazed by the words that followed—"an' if you say so, we'll have him or die; but we ain't in our own state now. They've got the law and the shotguns on us, an' I reckon we'd better go slow."

The rest seemed quite willing to go slow, and, as they put their pistols up, Devil Judd laughed in his beard. Hale put young Dave on a horse and the little shotgun cavalcade quietly moved away toward the county-seat.

The crestfallen Falins dispersed the other way
after they had taken a parting shot at the Hon.
Samuel Budd, who, too, had a pistol in his hand.
Young Buck looked long at him—and then he
laughed:

"You, too, Sam Budd," he said. "We folks'll
rickollect this on election day." The Hon. Sam
deigned no answer.

And up in the store Devil Judd lighted his pipe
and sat down to think out the strange code of ethics that governed that police-guard. Hale had
told him to wait there, and it was almost noon before the boy with the cap came to tell him that
the Falins had all left town. The old man looked
at him kindly.

"Air you the little feller whut fit fer June?"

"Not yet," said Bob; "but it's coming."

"Well, you'll whoop him."

"I'll do my best."

"Whar is she?"

"She's waiting for you over at the boarding-
house."

"Does she know about this trouble?"

"Not a thing; she thinks you've come to take
her home. The old man made no answer, and
Bob led him back toward Hale's office. June
was waiting at the gate, and the boy, lifting his
cap, passed on. June's eyes were dark with
anxiety.

"You come to take me home, dad?"

"I been thinkin' 'bout it," he said, with a doubtful shake of his head.

June took him upstairs to her room and pointed out the old water-wheel through the window and her new clothes (she had put on her old homespun again when she heard he was in town), and the old man shook his head.

"I'm afeerd 'bout all these fixin's—you won't never be satisfied agin in Lonesome Cove."

"Why, dad," she said reprovingly. "Jack says I can go over whenever I please, as soon as the weather gits warmer and the roads gits good."

"I don't know," said the old man, still shaking his head.

All through dinner she was worried. Devil Judd hardly ate anything, so embarrassed was he by the presence of so many "furriners" and by the white cloth and table-ware, and so fearful was he that he would be guilty of some breach of manners. Resolutely he refused butter, and at the third urging by Mrs. Crane he said firmly, but with a shrewd twinkle in his eye:

"No, thank ye. I never eats butter in town. I've kept store myself," and he was no little pleased with the laugh that went around the table. The fact was he was generally pleased with June's environment and, after dinner, he stopped teasing June.

"No, honey, I ain't goin' to take you away. I want ye to stay right where ye air. Be a good girl

156

now and do whatever Jack Hale tells ye and tell that boy with all that hair to come over and see me." June grew almost tearful with gratitude, for never had he called her "honey" before that she could remember, and never had he talked so much to her, nor with so much kindness.

"Air ye comin' over soon?"

"Mighty soon, dad."

"Well, take keer o' yourself."

"I will, dad," she said, and tenderly she watched his great figure slouch out of sight.

An hour after dark, as old Judd sat on the porch of the cabin in Lonesome Cove, young Dave Tolliver rode up to the gate on a strange horse. He was in a surly mood.

"He lemme go at the head of the valley and give me this hoss to git here," the boy grudgingly explained. "I'm goin' over to git mine termorrer."

"Seems like you'd better keep away from that Gap," said the old man dryly, and Dave reddened angrily.

"Yes, and fust thing you know he'll be over hyeh atter *you*." The old man turned on him sternly

"Jack Hale knows that liquer was mine. He knows I've got a still over hyeh as well as you do —an' he's never axed a question nor peeped an eye. I reckon he would come if he thought he oughter—but I'm on this side of the state-line. If I was on his side, mebbe I'd stop."

Young Dave stared, for things were surely coming to a pretty pass in Lonesome Cove.

"An' I reckon," the old man went on, "hit 'ud be better grace in you to stop sayin' things agin' him; fer if it hadn't been fer him, you'd be laid out by them Falins by this time."

It was true, and Dave, silenced, was forced into another channel.

"I wonder," he said presently, "how them Falins always know when I go over thar."

"I've been studyin' about that myself," said Devil Judd. Inside, the old step-mother had heard Dave's query.

"I seed the Red Fox this afternoon," she quavered at the door.

"Whut was he doin' over hyeh?" asked Dave.

"Nothin'," she said, "jus' a-sneakin' aroun' the way he's al'ays a-doin'. Seemed like he was mighty pertickuler to find out when you was comin' back."

Both men started slightly.

"We're all Tollivers now all right," said the Hon. Samuel Budd that night while he sat with Hale on the porch overlooking the mill-pond—and then he groaned a little.

"Them Falins have got kinsfolks to burn on the

Virginia side and they'd fight me tooth and toe-nail for this a hundred years hence!"

He puffed his pipe, but Hale said nothing.

"Yes, sir," he added cheerily, "we're in for a hell of a merry time *now*. The mountaineer hates as long as he remembers and—he never forgets."

XV

HAND in hand, Hale and June followed the footsteps of spring from the time June met him at the school-house gate for their first walk into the woods. Hale pointed to some boys playing marbles.

"That's the first sign," he said, and with quick understanding June smiled.

The birdlike piping of hylas came from a marshy strip of woodland that ran through the centre of the town and a toad was croaking at the foot of Imboden Hill.

"And they come next."

They crossed the swinging foot-bridge, which was a miracle to June, and took the foot-path along the clear stream of South Fork, under the laurel which June called "ivy," and the rhodendendron which was "laurel" in her speech, and Hale pointed out catkins greening on alders in one swampy place and willows just blushing into life along the banks of a little creek. A few yards aside from the path he found, under a patch of snow and dead leaves, the pink-and-white blossoms and the waxy green leaves of the trailing arbutus, that fragrant harbinger of the old Mother's awakening, and June breathed in from it the very breath of spring. Near by were turkey peas, which she had hunted and eaten many times.

"You can't put that arbutus in a garden," said Hale, "it's as wild as a hawk."

Presently he had the little girl listen to a pewee twittering in a thorn-bush and the lusty call of a robin from an apple-tree. A bluebird flew overhead with a merry chirp—its wistful note of autumn long since forgotten. These were the first birds and flowers, he said, and June, knowing them only by sight, must know the name of each and the reason for that name. So that Hale found himself walking the woods with an interrogation point, and that he might not be confounded he had, later, to dip up much forgotten lore. For every walk became a lesson in botany for June, such a passion did she betray at once for flowers, and he rarely had to tell her the same thing twice, since her memory was like a vise—for everything, as he learned in time.

Her eyes were quicker than his, too, and now she pointed to a snowy blossom with a deeply lobed leaf.

"Whut's that?"

"Bloodroot," said Hale, and he scratched the stem and forth issued scarlet drops. "The Indians used to put it on their faces and tomahawks" —she knew that word and nodded—"and I used to make red ink of it when I was a little boy."

"No!" said June. With the next look she found a tiny bunch of fuzzy hepaticas.

"Liver-leaf."

"Whut's liver?"

Hale, looking at her glowing face and eyes and her perfect little body, imagined that she would never know unless told that she had one, and so he waved one hand vaguely at his chest:

"It's an organ—and that herb is supposed to be good for it."

"Organ? Whut's that?"

"Oh, something inside of you."

June made the same gesture that Hale had.

"Me?"

"Yes," and then helplessly, "but not there exactly."

June's eyes had caught something else now and she ran for it:

"Oh! Oh!" It was a bunch of delicate anemones of intermediate shades between white and red—yellow, pink and purple-blue.

"Those are anemones."

"A-nem-o-nes," repeated June.

"Wind-flowers—because the wind is supposed to open them." And, almost unconsciously, Hale lapsed into a quotation:

"'And where a tear has dropped, a wind-flower blows.'"

"Whut's that?" said June quickly.

"That's poetry."

162

"Whut's po-e-try?" Hale threw up both hands.

"I don't know, but I'll read you some—some day."

By that time she was gurgling with delight over a bunch of spring beauties that came up, root, stalk and all, when she reached for them.

"Well, ain't they purty?" While they lay in her hand and she looked, the rose-veined petals began to close, the leaves to droop and the stem got limp.

"Ah-h!" crooned June. "I won't pull up no more o' *them*."

"'These little dream-flowers found in the spring.' More poetry, June."

A little later he heard her repeating that line to herself. It was an easy step to poetry from flowers, and evidently June was groping for it.

A few days later the service-berry swung out white stars on the low hill-sides, but Hale could tell her nothing that she did not know about the "sarvice-berry." Soon, the dogwood swept in snowy gusts along the mountains, and from a bank of it one morning a red-bird flamed and sang: "What cheer! What cheer! What cheer!" And like its scarlet coat the red-bud had burst into bloom. June knew the red-bud, but she had never heard it called the Judas tree.

"You see, the red-bud was supposed to be poisonous. It shakes in the wind and says to the

163

bees, 'Come on, little fellows—here's your nice fresh honey,' and when they come, it betrays and poisons them.''

"Well, what do you think o' that!" said June indignantly, and Hale had to hedge a bit.

"Well, I don't know whether it *really* does, but that's what they *say*." A little farther on the white stars of the trillium gleamed at them from the border of the woods and near by June stooped over some lovely sky-blue blossoms with yellow eyes.

"Forget-me-nots," said Hale. June stooped to gather them with a radiant face.

"Oh," she said, "is that what you call 'em?"

"They aren't the real ones—they're false for-get-me-nots."

"Then I don't want 'em," said June. But they were beautiful and fragrant and she added gently:

"'Tain't their fault. I'm agoin' to call 'em jus' forget-me-nots, an' I'm givin' 'em to you," she said—"so that you won't."

"Thank you," said Hale gravely. "I won't."

They found larkspur, too——

"'Blue as the heaven it gazes at,'" quoted Hale.

"Whut's 'gazes'?"

"Looks." June looked up at the sky and down at the flower.

"'Tain't," she said, "hit's bluer."

When they discovered something Hale did not know he would say that it was one of those——

"'Wan flowers without a name.'"

"My!" said June at last, "seems like them wan flowers is a mighty big fambly."

"They are," laughed Hale, "for a bachelor like me."

"Huh!" said June.

Later, they ran upon yellow adder's tongues in a hollow, each blossom guarded by a pair of ear-like leaves, Dutchman's breeches and wild bleeding hearts—a name that appealed greatly to the fancy of the romantic little lady, and thus together they followed the footsteps of that spring. And while she studied the flowers Hale was studying the loveliest flower of them all—little June. About ferns, plants and trees as well, he told her all he knew, and there seemed nothing in the skies, the green world of the leaves or the under world at her feet to which she was not magically responsive. Indeed, Hale had never seen a man, woman or child so eager to learn, and one day, when she had apparently reached the limit of inquiry, she grew very thoughtful and he watched her in silence a long while.

"What's the matter, June?" he asked finally.

"I'm just wonderin' *why* I'm always axin' why," said little June.

She was learning in school, too, and she was happier there now, for there had been no more open teasing of the new pupil. Bob's championship saved her from that, and, thereafter, school changed straightway for June. Before that day she had kept apart from her school-fellows at recess-times as well as in the school-room. Two or three of the girls had made friendly advances to her, but she had shyly repelled them—why she hardly knew—and it was her lonely custom at recess-times to build a play-house at the foot of a great beech with moss, broken bits of bottles and stones. Once she found it torn to pieces and from the look on the face of the tall mountain boy, Cal Heaton, who had grinned at her when she went up for her first lesson, and who was now Bob's arch-enemy, she knew that he was the guilty one. Again a day or two later it was destroyed, and when she came down from the woods almost in tears, Bob happened to meet her in the road and made her tell the trouble she was in. Straightway he charged the trespasser with the deed and was lied to for his pains. So after school that day he slipped up on the hill with the little girl and helped her rebuild again.

"Now I'll lay for him," said Bob, "and catch him at it."

"All right," said June, and she looked both her worry and her gratitude so that Bob understood both; and he answered both with a nonchalant wave of one hand.

"Never you mind—and don't you tell Mr. Hale," and June in dumb acquiescence crossed heart and body. But the mountain boy was wary, and for two or three days the play-house was undisturbed and so Bob himself laid a trap. He mounted his horse immediately after school, rode past the mountain lad, who was on his way home, crossed the river, made a wide détour at a gallop and, hitching his horse in the woods, came to the play-house from the other side of the hill. And half an hour later, when the pale little teacher came out of the school-house, he heard grunts and blows and scuffling up in the woods, and when he ran toward the sounds, the bodies of two of his pupils rolled into sight clenched fiercely, with torn clothes and bleeding faces—Bob on top with the mountain boy's thumb in his mouth and his own fingers gripped about his antagonist's throat. Neither paid any attention to the school-master, who pulled at Bob's coat unavailingly and with horror at his ferocity. Bob turned his head, shook it as well as the thumb in his mouth would let him, and went on gripping the throat under him and pushing the head that belonged to it into the ground. The mountain boy's tongue showed and his eyes bulged.

"'Nough!" he yelled. Bob rose then and told his story and the school-master from New England gave them a short lecture on gentleness and Christian charity and fixed on each the awful penalty of "staying in" after school for an hour every day for a week. Bob grinned:

"All right, professor—it was worth it," he said, but the mountain lad shuffled silently away.

An hour later Hale saw the boy with a swollen
lip, one eye black and the other as merry as ever—
but after that there was no more trouble for June.
Bob had made his promise good and gradually
she came into the games with her fellows thereafter, while Bob stood or sat aside, encouraging
but taking no part—for was he not a member of
the Police Force? Indeed he was already known
far and wide as the Infant of the Guard, and always he carried a whistle and usually, outside the
school-house, a pistol bumped his hip, while a
Winchester stood in one corner of his room and a
billy dangled by his mantel-piece.

The games were new to June, and often Hale
would stroll up to the school-house to watch them
—Prisoner's Base, Skipping the Rope, Antny
Over, Cracking the Whip and Lifting the Gate;
and it pleased him to see how lithe and active his
little protégé was and more than a match in
strength even for the boys who were near her size.
June had to take the penalty of her greenness, too,
when she was "introduced to the King and
Queen" and bumped the ground between the
make-believe sovereigns, or got a cup of water in
her face when she was trying to see stars through
a pipe. And the boys pinned her dress to the
bench through a crack and once she walked into
school with a placard on her back which read:
"June-Bug." But she was so good-natured that
she fast became a favourite. Indeed it was no-

ticeable to Hale as well as Bob that Cal Heaton, the mountain boy, seemed always to get next to June in the Tugs of War, and one morning June found an apple on her desk. She swept the room with a glance and met Cal's guilty flush, and though she ate the apple, she gave him no thanks —in word, look or manner. It was curious to Hale, moreover, to observe how June's instinct deftly led her to avoid the mistakes in dress that characterized the gropings of other girls who, like her, were in a stage of transition. They wore gaudy combs and green skirts with red waists, their clothes bunched at the hips, and to their shoes and hands they paid no attention at all. None of these things for June—and Hale did not know that the little girl had leaped her fellows with one bound, had taken Miss Anne Saunders as her model and was climbing upon the pedestal where that lady justly stood. The two had not become friends as Hale hoped. June was always silent and reserved when the older girl was around, but there was never a move of the latter's hand or foot or lip or eye that the new pupil failed to see. Miss Anne rallied Hale no little about her, but he laughed good-naturedly, and asked why *she* could not make friends with June.

"She's jealous," said Miss Saunders, and Hale ridiculed the idea, for not one sign since she came to the Gap had she shown him. It was the jealousy of a child she had once betrayed 'and that

169

she had outgrown, he thought; but he never knew how June stood behind the curtains of her window, with a hungry suffering in her face and eyes, to watch Hale and Miss Anne ride by and he never guessed that concealment was but a sign of the dawn of womanhood that was breaking within her. And she gave no hint of that breaking dawn until one day early in May, when she heard a woodthrush for the first time with Hale: for it was the bird she loved best, and always its silver fluting would stop her in her tracks and send her into dreamland. Hale had just broken a crimson flower from its stem and held it out to her.

"Here's another of the 'wan ones,' June. Do you know what that is?"

"Hit's"—she paused for correction with her lips drawn severely in for precision—"*it's* a mountain poppy. Pap says it kills goslings"— her eyes danced, for she was in a merry mood that day, and she put both hands behind her—"if you air any kin to a goose, you better drap it."

"That's a good one," laughed Hale, "but it's so lovely I'll take the risk. I won't drop it."

"Drop it," caught June with a quick upward look, and then to fix the word in her memory she repeated—"drop it, drop it, *drop* it!"

"Got it now, June?"

"Uh-huh."

It was then that a woodthrush voiced the

crowning joy of spring, and with slowly filling eyes she asked its name.

"That bird," she said slowly and with a breaking voice, "sung just that-a-way the mornin' my sister died."

She turned to him with a wondering smile.

"Somehow it don't make me so miserable, like it useter." Her smile passed while she looked, she caught both hands to her heaving breast and a wild intensity burned suddenly in her eyes.

"Why, June!"

"'Tain't nothin'," she choked out, and she turned hurriedly ahead of him down the path. Startled, Hale had dropped the crimson flower to his feet. He saw it and he let it lie.

Meanwhile, rumours were brought in that the Falins were coming over from Kentucky to wipe out the Guard, and so straight were they sometimes that the Guard was kept perpetually on watch. Once while the members were at target practice, the shout arose:

"The Kentuckians are coming! The Kentuckians are coming!" And, at double quick, the Guard rushed back to find it a false alarm and to see men laughing at them in the street. The truth was that, while the Falins had a general hostility against the Guard, their particular enmity was concentrated on John Hale, as he discovered when June was to take her first trip home one Friday afternoon. Hale meant to carry her over, but the morning they were to leave, old Judd Tolliver came to the Gap himself. He did not want June to come home at that time, and he didn't think it was safe over there for Hale just then. Some of the Falins had been seen hanging around Lonesome Cove for the purpose, Judd believed, of getting a shot at the man who had kept young Dave from falling into their hands, and Hale saw that by that act he had, as Budd said, arrayed himself with the Tollivers in the feud. In other words, he was a Tolliver himself now, and as such the Falins meant to treat him. Hale rebelled against the restriction, for he had started some work in Lonesome Cove and was preparing a surprise over there for June, but old Judd said:

"Just wait a while," and he said it so seriously that Hale for a while took his advice.

So June stayed on at the Gap—with little disappointment, apparently, that she could not visit home. And as spring passed and the summer came on, the little girl budded and opened like a rose. To the pretty school-teacher she was a source of endless interest and wonder, for while the little girl was reticent and aloof, Miss Saunders felt herself watched and studied in and out of school, and Hale often had to smile at June's unconscious imitation of her teacher in speech, manners and dress. And all the time her hero-worship of Hale went on, fed by the talk of the boarding-

house, her fellow pupils and of the town at large—
and it fairly thrilled her to know that to the Falins
he was now a Tolliver himself.

Sometimes Hale would get her a saddle, and
then June would usurp Miss Anne's place on a
horseback-ride up through the gap to see the
first blooms of the purple rhododendron on Bee
Rock, or up to Morris's farm on Powell's mountain, from which, with a glass, they could see the
Lonesome Pine. And all the time she worked at
her studies tirelessly—and when she was done
with her lessons, she read the fairy books that Hale
got for her—read them until "Paul and Virginia"
fell into her hands, and then there were no more
fairy stories for little June. Often, late at night,
Hale, from the porch of his cottage, could see the
light of her lamp sending its beam across the dark
water of the mill-pond, and finally he got worried
by the paleness of her face and sent her to the doctor. She went unwillingly, and when she came
back she reported placidly that "organatically she
was all right, the doctor said," but Hale was glad
that vacation would soon come. At the beginning of the last week of school he brought a little
present for her from New York—a slender necklace of gold with a little reddish stone-pendant
that was the shape of a cross. Hale pulled the
trinket from his pocket as they were walking down
the river-bank at sunset and the little girl quivered
like an aspen-leaf in a sudden puff of wind.

173

"Hit's a fairy-stone," she cried excitedly.

"Why, where on earth did you——"

"Why, sister Sally told me about 'em. She said folks found 'em somewhere over here in Virginny, an' all her life she was a-wishin' fer one an' she never could git it"—her eyes filled—"seems like ever'thing she wanted is a-comin' to me."

"Do you know the story of it, too?" asked Hale.

June shook her head. "Sister Sally said it was a luck-piece. Nothin' could happen to ye when ye was carryin' it, but it was awful bad luck if you lost it." Hale put it around her neck and fastened the clasp and June kept hold of the little cross with one hand.

"Well, you mustn't lose it," he said.

"No—no—no," she repeated breathlessly, and Hale told her the pretty story of the stone as they strolled back to supper. The little crosses were to be found only in a certain valley in Virginia, so perfect in shape that they seemed to have been chiselled by hand, and they were a great mystery to the men who knew all about rocks—the geologists.

"The ge-ol-o-gists," repeated June.

These men said there was no crystallization— nothing like them, amended Hale—elsewhere in the world, and that just as crosses were of different shapes—Roman, Maltese and St. Andrew's—so, too, these crosses were found in all these different shapes. And the myth—the story—was that this little valley was once inhabited by fairies—June's eyes lighted, for it was a fairy story after all—and that when a strange messenger brought them the news of Christ's crucifixion, they wept, and their tears, as they fell to the ground, were turned into tiny crosses of stone. Even the Indians had some queer feeling about them, and for a long, long time people who found them had used them as charms to bring good luck and ward off harm.

"And that's for you," he said, "because you've been such a good little girl and have studied so hard. School's most over now and I reckon you'll be right glad to get home again."

June made no answer, but at the gate she looked suddenly up at him.

"Have you got one, too?" she asked, and she seemed much disturbed when Hale shook his head.

"Well, *I'll* git—*get*—you one—some day."

"All right," laughed Hale.

There was again something strange in her manner as she turned suddenly from him, and what it meant he was soon to learn. It was the last week of school and Hale had just come down from the woods behind the school-house at "little recess-time" in the afternoon. The children were playing games outside the gate, and Bob and Miss Anne and the little Professor were leaning on the fence watching them. The little man

175

raised his hand to halt Hale on the plank side-walk.

"I've been wanting to see you," he said in his dreamy, abstracted way. "You prophesied, you know, that I should be proud of your little pro-tégé some day, and I am indeed. She is the most remarkable pupil I've yet seen here, and I have about come to the conclusion that there is no quicker native intelligence in our country than you shall find in the children of these mountain-eers and——"

Miss Anne was gazing at the children with an expression that turned Hale's eyes that way, and the Professor checked his harangue. Something had happened. They had been playing "Ring Around the Rosy" and June had been caught. She stood scarlet and tense and the cry was:

"Who's your beau—who's your beau?"

And still she stood with tight lips—flushing.

"You got to tell—you got to tell!"

The mountain boy, Cal Heaton, was grinning with fatuous consciousness, and even Bob put his hands in his pockets and took on an uneasy smile.

"Who's your beau?" came the chorus again.

The lips opened almost in a whisper, but all could hear:

"Jack!"

"Jack who?" But June looked around and saw the four at the gate. Almost staggering, she broke from the crowd and, with one forearm across her scarlet face, rushed past them into the school-house. Miss Anne looked at Hale's amazed face and she did not smile. Bob turned respectfully away, ignoring it all, and the little Professor, whose life-purpose was psychology, murmured in his ignorance:

"Very remarkable—very remarkable!"

Through that afternoon June kept her hot face close to her books. Bob never so much as glanced her way—little gentleman that he was—but the one time she lifted her eyes, she met the mountain lad's bent in a stupor-like gaze upon her. In spite of her apparent studiousness, however, she missed her lesson and, automatically, the little Professor told her to stay in after school and recite to Miss Saunders. And so June and Miss Anne sat in the school-room alone—the teacher reading a book, and the pupil—her tears unshed—with her sullen face bent over her lesson. In a few moments the door opened and the little Professor thrust in his head. The girl had looked so hurt and tired when he spoke to her that some strange sympathy moved him, mystified though he was, to say gently now and with a smile that was rare with him:

"You might excuse June, I think, Miss Saunders, and let her recite some time to-morrow," and gently he closed the door. Miss Anne rose:

"Very well, June," she said quietly.

June rose, too, gathering up her books, and as

she passed the teacher's platform she stopped and looked her full in the face. She said not a word, and the tragedy between the woman and the girl was played in silence, for the woman knew from the searching gaze of the girl and the black defiance in her eyes, as she stalked out of the room, that her own flush had betrayed her secret as plainly as the girl's words had told hers.

Through his office window, a few minutes later, Hale saw June pass swiftly into the house. In a few minutes she came swiftly out again and went back swiftly toward the school-house. He was so worried by the tense look in her face that he could work no more, and in a few minutes he threw his papers down and followed her. When he turned the corner, Bob was coming down the street with his cap on the back of his head and swinging his books by a strap, and the boy looked a little conscious when he saw Hale coming.

"Have you seen June?" Hale asked.

"No, sir," said Bob, immensely relieved.

"Did she come up this way?"

"I don't know, but—" Bob turned and pointed to the green dome of a big beech.

"I think you'll find her at the foot of that tree," he said. "That's where her play-house is and that's where she goes when she's—that's where she usually goes."

"Oh, yes," said Hale—"her play-house. Thank you."

"Not at all, sir."

Hale went on, turned from the path and climbed noiselessly. When he caught sight of the beech he stopped still. June stood against it like a wood-nymph just emerged from its sun-dappled trunk —stood stretched to her full height, her hands behind her, her hair tossed, her throat tense under the dangling little cross, her face uplifted. At her feet, the play-house was scattered to pieces. She seemed listening to the love-calls of a woodthrush that came faintly through the still woods, and then he saw that she heard nothing, saw nothing—that she was in a dream as deep as sleep. Hale's heart throbbed as he looked.

"June!" he called softly. She did not hear him, and when he called again, she turned her face—unstartled—and moving her posture not at all. Hale pointed to the scattered play-house.

"I done it!" she said fiercely—"I done it myself." Her eyes burned steadily into his, even while she lifted her hands to her hair as though she were only vaguely conscious that it was all undone.

"*You* heerd me?" she cried, and before he could answer—"*She* heerd me," and again, not waiting for a word from him, she cried still more fiercely:

"I don't keer! I don't keer *who* knows."

Her hands were trembling, she was biting her quivering lip to keep back the starting tears, and Hale rushed toward her and took her in his arms.

"June! June!" he said brokenly. "You mustn't, little girl. I'm proud—proud—why little sweetheart—" She was clinging to him and looking up into his eyes and he bent his head slowly. Their lips met and the man was startled. He knew now it was no child that answered him.

Hale walked long that night in the moonlit woods up and around Imboden Hill, along a shadow-haunted path, between silvery beech-trunks, past the big hole in the earth from which dead trees tossed out their crooked arms as if in torment, and to the top of the ridge under which the valley slept and above which the dark bulk of Powell's Mountain rose. It was absurd, but he found himself strangely stirred. She was a child, he kept repeating to himself, in spite of the fact that he knew she was no child among her own people, and that mountain girls were even wives who were younger still. Still, she did not know what she felt—how could she?—and she would get over it, and then came the sharp stab of a doubt—would he want her to get over it? Frankly and with wonder he confessed to himself that he did not know—he did not know. But again, why bother? He had meant to educate her, anyhow. That was the first step—no matter what happened. June must go out into the world to school. He would have plenty of money. Her father would not object, and June need never know. He could include for her an interest in her own father's coal lands that he meant to buy, and she could think that it was her own money that she was using. So, with a sudden rush of gladness from his brain to his heart, he recklessly yoked himself, then and there, under all responsibility for that young life and the eager, sensitive soul that already lighted it so radiantly.

And June? Her nature had opened precisely as had bud and flower that spring. The Mother of Magicians had touched her as impartially as she had touched them with fairy wand, and as unconsciously the little girl had answered as a young dove to any cooing mate. With this Hale did not reckon, and this June could not know. For a while, that night, she lay in a delicious tremor, listening to the bird-like chorus of the little frogs in the marsh, the booming of the big ones in the mill-pond, the water pouring over the dam with the sound of a low wind, and, as had all the sleeping things of the earth about her, she, too, sank to happy sleep.

XVI

THE in-sweep of the outside world was broadening its current now. The improvement company had been formed to encourage the growth of the town. A safe was put in the back part of a furniture store behind a wooden partition and a bank was started. Up through the Gap and toward Kentucky, more entries were driven into the coal, and on the Virginia side were signs of stripping for iron ore. A furnace was coming in just as soon as the railroad could bring it in, and the railroad was pushing ahead with genuine vigor. Speculators were trooping in and the town had been divided off into lots—a few of which had already changed hands. One agent had brought in a big steel safe and a tent and was buying coal lands right and left. More young men drifted in from all points of the compass. A tent-hotel was put at the foot of Imboden Hill, and of nights there were under it much poker and song. The lilt of a definite optimism was in every man's step and the light of hope was in every man's eye.

And the Guard went to its work in earnest. Every man now had his Winchester, his revolver, his billy and his whistle. Drilling and target-shooting became a daily practice. Bob, who had been a year in a military school, was drill-master for the recruits, and very gravely he performed his duties and put them through the skirmishers' drill—advancing in rushes, throwing themselves in the new grass, and very gravely he commended one enthusiast—none other than the Hon. Samuel Budd—who, rather than lose his position in line, threw himself into a pool of water: all to the surprise, scorn and anger of the mountain onlookers, who dwelled about the town. Many were the comments the members of the Guard heard from them, even while they were at drill.

"I'd like to see one o' them fellers hit me with one of them locust posts."

"Huh! I could take two good men an' run the whole batch out o' the county."

"Look at them dudes and furriners. They come into our country and air tryin' to larn us how to run it."

"Our boys air only tryin' to have their little fun. They don't mean nothin', but someday some fool young guard'll hurt somebody and then thar'll be hell to pay."

Hale could not help feeling considerable sympathy for their point of view—particularly when he saw the mountaineers watching the Guard at target-practice—each volunteer policeman with his back to the target, and at the word of command wheeling and firing six shots in rapid succession—and he did not wonder at their snorts of scorn at such bad shooting and their open anger that the Guard was practising for *them*. But sometimes he got an unexpected recruit. One bully, who had been conspicuous in the brickyard trouble, after watching a drill went up to him with a grin:

"Hell," he said cheerily, "I believe you fellers air goin' to have more fun than we air, an' danged if I don't jine you, if you'll let me."

"Sure," said Hale. And others, who might have been bad men, became members and, thus getting a vent for their energies, were as enthusiastic for the law as they might have been against it.

Of course, the antagonistic element in the town lost no opportunity to plague and harass the Guard, and after the destruction of the "blind tigers," mischief was naturally concentrated in the high-license saloons—particularly in the one run by Jack Woods, whose local power for evil and cackling laugh seemed to mean nothing else than close personal communion with old Nick himself. Passing the door of his saloon one day, Bob saw one of Jack's customers trying to play pool with a Winchester in one hand and an open knife between his teeth, and the boy stepped in and halted. The man had no weapon concealed and was making no disturbance, and Bob did not

know whether or not he had the legal right to
arrest him, so he turned, and, while he was standing in the door, Jack winked at his customer, who,
with a grin, put the back of his knife-blade between Bob's shoulders and, pushing, closed it.
The boy looked over his shoulder without moving
a muscle, but the Hon. Samuel Budd, who came
in at that moment, pinioned the fellow's arms from
behind and Bob took his weapon away.

"Hell," said the mountaineer, "I didn't aim to
hurt the little feller. I jes' wanted to see if I
could skeer him."

"Well, brother, 'tis scarce a merry jest," quoth
the Hon. Sam, and he looked sharply at Jack
through his big spectacles as the two led the man
off to the calaboose: for he suspected that the
saloon-keeper was at the bottom of the trick.
Jack's time came only the next day. He had re-
garded it as the limit of indignity when an ordinance was up that nobody should blow a whistle
except a member of the Guard, and it was great
fun for him to have some drunken customer blow
a whistle and then stand in his door and laugh at
the policemen running in from all directions.
That day Jack tried the whistle himself and Hale
ran down.

"Who did that?" he asked. Jack felt bold
that morning.

"I blowed it."

Hale thought for a moment. The ordinance

against blowing a whistle had not yet been passed, but he made up his mind that, under the circumstances, Jack's blowing was a breach of the peace, since the Guard had adopted that signal. So he said:

"You mustn't do that again."

Jack had doubtless been going through precisely the same mental process, and, on the nice legal point involved, he seemed to differ.

"I'll blow it when I damn please," he said.

"Blow it again and I'll arrest you," said Hale.

Jack blew. He had his right shoulder against the corner of his door at the time, and, when he raised the whistle to his lips, Hale drew and covered him before he could make another move. Woods backed slowly into his saloon to get behind his counter. Hale saw his purpose, and he closed in, taking great risk, as he always did, to avoid bloodshed, and there was a struggle. Jack managed to get his pistol out; but Hale caught him by the wrist and held the weapon away so that it was harmless as far as he was concerned; but a crowd was gathering at the door toward which the saloon-keeper's pistol was pointed, and he feared that somebody out there might be shot; so he called out:

"Drop that pistol!"

The order was not obeyed, and Hale raised his right hand high above Jack's head and dropped the butt of his weapon on Jack's skull—hard.

Jack's head dropped back between his shoulders, his eyes closed and his pistol clicked on the floor.

Hale knew how serious a thing a blow was in that part of the world, and what excitement it would create, and he was uneasy at Jack's trial, for fear that the saloon-keeper's friends would take the matter up; but they didn't, and, to the surprise of everybody, Jack quietly paid his fine, and thereafter the Guard had little active trouble from the town itself, for it was quite plain there, at least, that the Guard meant business.

Across Black Mountain old Dave Tolliver and old Buck Falin had got well of their wounds by this time, and though each swore to have vengeance against the other as soon as he was able to handle a Winchester, both factions seemed waiting for that time to come. Moreover, the Falins, because of a rumour that Bad Rufe Tolliver might come back, and because of Devil Judd's anger at their attempt to capture young Dave, grew wary and rather pacificatory: and so, beyond a little quarrelling, a little threatening and the exchange of a harmless shot or two, sometimes in banter, sometimes in earnest, nothing had been done. Sternly, however, though the Falins did not know the fact, Devil Judd continued to hold aloof in spite of the pleadings of young Dave, and so confident was the old man in the balance of power that lay with him that he sent June word that he was coming to take her home. And, in truth, with

Hale going away again on a business trip and Bob, too, gone back home to the Bluegrass, and school closed, the little girl was glad to go, and she waited for her father's coming eagerly. Miss Anne was still there, to be sure, and if she, too, had gone, June would have been more content. The quiet smile of that astute young woman had told Hale plainly, and somewhat to his embarrassment, that she knew something had happened between the two, but that smile she never gave to June. Indeed, she never encountered aught else than the same silent searching gaze from the strangely mature little creature's eyes, and when those eyes met the teacher's, always June's hand would wander unconsciously to the little cross at her throat as though to invoke its aid against anything that could come between her and its giver.

The purple rhododendrons on Bee Rock had come and gone and the pink-flecked laurels were in bloom when June fared forth one sunny morning of her own birth-month behind old Judd Tolliver—home. Back up through the wild Gap they rode in silence, past Bee Rock, out of the chasm and up the little valley toward the Trail of the Lonesome Pine, into which the father's old sorrel nag, with a switch of her sunburnt tail, turned leftward. June leaned forward a little, and there was the crest of the big tree motionless in the blue high above, and sheltered by one big white cloud. It was the first time she had seen the

188

pine since she had first left it, and little tremblings went through her from her bare feet to her bonneted head. Thus was she unclad, for Hale had told her that, to avoid criticism, she must go home clothed just as she was when she left Lonesome Cove. She did not quite understand that, and she carried her new clothes in a bundle in her lap, but she took Hale's word unquestioned. So she wore her crimson homespun and her bonnet, with her bronze-gold hair gathered under it in the same old Psyche knot. She must wear her shoes, she told Hale, until she got out of town, else someone might see her, but Hale had said she would be leaving too early for that: and so she had gone from the Gap as she had come into it, with unmittened hands and bare feet. The soft wind was very good to those dangling feet, and she itched to have them on the green grass or in the cool waters through which the old horse splashed. Yes, she was going home again, the same June as far as mountain eyes could see, though she had grown perceptibly, and her little face had blossomed from her heart almost into a woman's, but she knew that while her clothes were the same, they covered quite another girl. Time wings slowly for the young, and when the sensations are many and the experiences are new, slowly even for all—and thus there was a double reason why it seemed an age to June since her eyes had last rested on the big Pine.

Here was the place where Hale had put his big black horse into a dead run, and as vivid a thrill of it came back to her now as had been the thrill of the race. Then they began to climb laboriously up the rocky creek—the water singing a joyous welcome to her along the path, ferns and flowers nodding to her from dead leaves and rich mould and peeping at her from crevices between the rocks on the creek-banks as high up as the level of her eyes—up under bending branches full-leafed, with the warm sunshine darting down through them upon her as she passed, and making a playfellow of her sunny hair. Here was the place where she had got angry with Hale, had slid from his horse and stormed with tears. What a little fool she had been when Hale had meant only to be kind! He was never anything but kind— Jack was—dear, dear Jack! That wouldn't happen *no* more, she thought, and straightway she corrected that thought.

"It won't happen *any* more," she said aloud.

"Whut'd you say, June?"

The old man lifted his bushy beard from his chest and turned his head.

"Nothin', dad," she said, and old Judd, himself in a deep study, dropped back into it again. How often she had said that to herself—that it would happen no more—she had stopped saying it to Hale, because he laughed and forgave her, and seemed to love her mood, whether she cried from joy or anger—and yet she kept on doing both just the same.

Several times Devil Judd stopped to let his horse rest, and each time, of course, the wooded slopes of the mountains stretched downward in longer sweeps of summer green, and across the widening valley the tops of the mountains beyond dropped nearer to the straight level of her eyes, while beyond them vaster blue bulks became visible and ran on and on, as they always seemed, to the farthest limits of the world. Even out there, Hale had told her, she would go some day. The last curving up-sweep came finally, and there stood the big Pine, majestic, unchanged and murmuring in the wind like the undertone of a far-off sea. As they passed the base of it, she reached out her hand and let the tips of her fingers brush caressingly across its trunk, turned quickly for a last look at the sunlit valley and the hills of the outer world and then the two passed into a green gloom of shadow and thick leaves that shut her heart in as suddenly as though some human hand had clutched it. She was going home—to see Bub and Loretta and Uncle Billy and "old Hon" and her step-mother and Dave, and yet she felt vaguely troubled. The valley on the other side was in dazzling sunshine—she had seen that. The sun must still be shining over there—it must be shining above her over here, for here and there shot a sunbeam message from that outer world down through the leaves, and yet it seemed that black night had suddenly fallen about her, and helplessly she wondered about it all, with her hands gripped tight and her eyes wide. But the mood was gone when they emerged at the "deadening" on the last spur and she saw Lonesome Cove and the roof of her little home peacefully asleep in the same sun that shone on the valley over the mountain. Colour came to her face and her heart beat faster. At the foot of the spur the road had been widened and showed signs of heavy hauling. There was sawdust in the mouth of the creek and, from coal-dust, the water was black. The ring of axes and the shouts of ox-drivers came from the mountain side. Up the creek above her father's cabin three or four houses were being built of fresh boards, and there in front of her was a new store. To a fence one side of it two horses were hitched and on one horse was a side-saddle. Before the door stood the Red Fox and Uncle Billy, the miller, who peered at her for a moment through his big spectacles and gave her a wondering shout of welcome that brought her cousin Loretta to the door, where she stopped a moment, anchored with surprise. Over her shoulder peered her cousin Dave, and June saw his face darken while she looked.

"Why, Honey," said the old miller, "have ye really come home agin?" While Loretta simply said:

"My Lord!" and came out and stood with her hands on her hips looking at June.

"Why, ye ain't a bit changed! I knowed ye wasn't goin' to put on no airs like Dave thar said" —she turned on Dave, who, with a surly shrug, wheeled and went back into the store. Uncle Billy was going home.

"Come down to see us right away now," he called back. "Ole Hon's might nigh crazy to git her eyes on ye."

"All right, Uncle Billy," said June, "early ter-morrer." The Red Fox did not open his lips, but his pale eyes searched the girl from head to foot.

"Git down, June," said Loretta, "and I'll walk up to the house with ye."

June slid down, Devil Judd started the old horse, and as the two girls, with their arms about each other's waists, followed, the wolfish side of the Red Fox's face lifted in an ironical snarl. Bub was standing at the gate, and when he saw his father riding home alone, his wistful eyes filled and his cry of disappointment brought the step-mother to the door.

"Whar's June?" he cried, and June heard him, and loosening herself from Loretta, she ran round the horse and had Bub in her arms. Then she looked up into the eyes of her step-mother. The old woman's face looked kind—so kind that for the first time in her life June did what her father could never get her to do: she called her

"Mammy," and then she gave that old woman the surprise of her life—she kissed her. Right away she must see everything, and Bub, in ecstasy, wanted to pilot her around to see the new calf and the new pigs and the new chickens, but dumbly June looked to a miracle that had come to pass to the left of the cabin—a flower-garden, the like of which she had seen only in her dreams.

XVII

TWICE her lips opened soundlessly and, dazed, she could only point dumbly. The old step-mother laughed:

"Jack Hale done that. He pestered yo' pap to let him do it fer ye, an' anything Jack Hale wants from yo' pap, he gits. I thought hit was plum' foolishness, but he's got things to eat planted thar, too, an' I declar hit's right purty."

That wonderful garden! June started for it on a run. There was a broad grass-walk down through the middle of it and there were narrow grass-walks running sidewise, just as they did in the gardens which Hale told her he had seen in the outer world. The flowers were planted in raised beds, and all the ones that she had learned to know and love at the Gap were there, and many more besides. The hollyhocks, bachelor's buttons and marigolds she had known all her life. The lilacs, touch-me-nots, tulips and narcissus she had learned to know in gardens at the Gap. Two rose-bushes were in bloom, and there were strange grasses and plants and flowers that Jack would tell her about when he came. One side was sentinelled by sun-flowers and another side by transplanted laurel and rhododendron shrubs;

and hidden in the plant-and-flower-bordered squares were the vegetables that won her step-mother's tolerance of Hale's plan. Through and through June walked, her dark eyes flashing joyously here and there when they were not a little dimmed with tears, with Loretta following her, unsympathetic in appreciation, wondering that June should be making such a fuss about a lot of flowers, but envious withal when she half guessed the reason, and impatient Bub eager to show her other births and changes. And, over and over all the while, June was whispering to herself:

"My garden—*my* garden!"

When she came back to the porch, after a tour through all that was new or had changed, Dave had brought his horse and Loretta's to the gate. No, he wouldn't come in and "rest a spell"— "they must be gittin' along home," he said shortly. But old Judd Tolliver insisted that he should stay to dinner, and Dave tied the horses to the fence and walked to the porch, not lifting his eyes to June. Straightway the girl went into the house to help her step-mother with dinner, but the old woman told her she "reckoned she needn't start in yit"—adding in the querulous tone June knew so well:

"I've been mighty po'ly, an' thar'll be a mighty lot fer you to do now." So with this direful proph-ecy in her ears the girl hesitated. The old woman looked at her closely.

"Ye ain't a bit changed," she said.

They were the words Loretta had used, and in the voice of each was the same strange tone of disappointment. June wondered: were they sorry she had not come back putting on airs and fussed up with ribbons and feathers that they might hear her picked to pieces and perhaps do some of the picking themselves? Not Loretta, surely—but the old step-mother! June left the kitchen and sat down just inside the door. The Red Fox and two other men had sauntered up from the store and all were listening to his quavering chat:

"I seed a vision last night, and thar's trouble a-comin' in these mountains. The Lord told me so straight from the clouds. These railroads and coal-mines is a-goin' to raise taxes, so that a pore man'll have to sell his hogs and his corn to pay 'em an' have nothin' left to keep him from starvin' to death. Them police-fellers over thar at the Gap is a-stirrin' up strife and a-runnin' things over thar as though the earth was made fer 'em, an' the citizens ain't goin' to stand it. An' this war's a-comin' on an' thar'll be shootin' an' killin' over thar an' over hyeh. I seed all this devilment in a vision last night, as shore as I'm settin' hyeh."

Old Judd grunted, shifted his huge shoulders, parted his mustache and beard with two fingers and spat through them.

"Well, I reckon you didn't see no devilment, Red, that you won't take a hand in, if it comes."

197

The other men laughed, but the Red Fox looked meek and lowly.

"I'm a servant of the Lord. He says do this, an' I does it the best I know how. I goes about a-preachin' the word in the wilderness an' a-healin' the sick with soothin' yarbs and sech."

"An' a-makin' compacts with the devil," said old Judd shortly, "when the eye of man is a-lookin' t'other way." The left side of the Red Fox's face twitched into the faintest shadow of a snarl, but, shaking his head, he kept still.

"Well," said Sam Barth, who was thin and long and sandy, "I don't keer what them fellers do on t'other side o' the mountain, but what air they a-comin' over here fer?"

Old Judd spoke again.

"To give you a job, if you wasn't too durned lazy to work."

"Yes," said the other man, who was dark, swarthy and whose black eyebrows met across the bridge of his nose—"and that damned Hale, who's a-tearin' up Hellfire here in the cove." The old man lifted his eyes. Young Dave's face wore a sudden malignant sympathy which made June clench her hands a little more tightly.

"What about him? You must have been over to the Gap lately—like Dave thar—did you git board in the calaboose?" It was a random thrust, but it was accurate and it went home, and there was silence for a while. Presently old Judd went on:

"Taxes hain't goin' to be raised, and if they are, folks will be better able to pay 'em. Them police-fellers at the Gap don't bother nobody if he behaves himself. This war will start when it does start, an' as for Hale, he's as square an' clever a feller as I've ever seed. His word is just as good as his bond. I'm a-goin' to sell him this land. It'll be his'n, an' he can do what he wants to with it. I'm his friend, and I'm goin' to stay his friend as long as he goes on as he's goin' now, an' I'm not goin' to see him bothered as long as he tends to his own business."

The words fell slowly and the weight of them rested heavily on all except on June. Her fingers loosened and she smiled.

The Red Fox rose, shaking his head.

"All right, Judd Tolliver," he said warningly.

"Come in and git something to eat, Red."

"No," he said, "I'll be gittin' along"—and he went, still shaking his head.

The table was covered with an oil-cloth spotted with drippings from a candle. The plates and cups were thick and the spoons were of pewter. The bread was soggy and the bacon was thick and floating in grease. The men ate and the women served, as in ancient days. They gobbled their food like wolves, and when they drank their coffee, the noise they made was painful to June's ears. There were no napkins and when her father pushed his chair back, he wiped his dripping mouth with the back of his sleeve. And Loretta and the step-mother—they, too, ate with their knives and used their fingers. Poor June quivered with a vague newborn disgust. Ah, had she not changed—in ways they could not see!

June helped clear away the dishes—the old woman did not object to that—listening to the gossip of the mountains—courtships, marriages, births, deaths, the growing hostility in the feud, the random killing of this man or that—Hale's doings in Lonesome Cove.

"He's comin' over hyeh agin next Saturday," said the old woman.

"Is he?" said Loretta in a way that made June turn sharply from her dishes toward her. She knew Hale was not coming, but she said nothing. The old woman was lighting her pipe.

"Yes—you better be over hyeh in yo' best bib and tucker."

"Pshaw," said Loretta, but June saw two bright spots come into her pretty cheeks, and she herself burned inwardly. The old woman was looking at her.

"'Pears like you air mighty quiet, June."

"That's so," said Loretta, looking at her, too.

June, still silent, turned back to her dishes. They were beginning to take notice after all, for the girl hardly knew that she had not opened her lips.

Once only Dave spoke to her, and that was

when Loretta said she must go. June was out in the porch looking at the already beloved garden, and hearing his step she turned. He looked her steadily in the eyes. She saw his gaze drop to the fairy-stone at her throat, and a faint sneer appeared at his set mouth—a sneer for June's folly and what he thought was uppishness in "furriners" like Hale.

"So you ain't good enough fer him jest as ye air—air ye?" he said slowly. He's got to make ye all over agin—so's you'll be fitten fer him."

He turned away without looking to see how deep his barbed shaft went and, startled, June flushed to her hair. In a few minutes they were gone—Dave without the exchange of another word with June, and Loretta with a parting cry that she would come back on Saturday. The old man went to the cornfield high above the cabin, the old woman, groaning with pains real and fancied, lay down on a creaking bed, and June, with Dave's wound rankling, went out with Bub to see the new doings in Lonesome Cove. The geese cackled before her, the hog-fish darted like submarine arrows from rock to rock and the willows bent in the same wistful way toward their shadows in the little stream, but its crystal depths were there no longer—floating sawdust whirled in eddies on the surface and the water was black as soot. Here and there the white belly of a fish lay up-turned to the sun, for the cruel, deadly work of civilization had already begun. Farther up the creek was a buzzing monster that, creaking and snorting, sent a flashing disk, rimmed with sharp teeth, biting a savage way through a log, that screamed with pain as the brutal thing tore through its vitals, and gave up its life each time with a ghost-like cry of agony. Farther on little houses were being built of fresh boards, and farther on the water of the creek got blacker still. June suddenly clutched Bud's arms. Two demons had appeared on a pile of fresh dirt above them—sooty, begrimed, with black faces and black hands, and in the cap of each was a smoking little lamp.

"Huh," said Bub, "that ain't nothin'! Hello, Bill," he called bravely.

"Hello, Bub," answered one of the two demons, and both stared at the lovely little apparition who was staring with such naïve horror at them. It was all very wonderful, though, and it was all happening in Lonesome Cove, but Jack Hale was doing it all and, therefore, it was all right, thought June—no matter what Dave said. Moreover, the ugly spot on the great, beautiful breast of the Mother was such a little one after all and June had no idea how it must spread. Above the opening for the mines, the creek was crystal-clear as ever, the great hills were the same, and the sky and the clouds, and the cabin and the fields of corn. Nothing could happen to them, but if even they were wiped out by Hale's hand she would have made no complaint. A wood-thrush flitted from a ravine as she and Bub went back down the creek—and she stopped with uplifted face to listen. All her life she had loved its song, and this was the first time she had heard it in Lonesome Cove since she had learned its name from Hale. She had never heard it thereafter without thinking of him, and she thought of him now while it was breathing out the very spirit of the hills, and she drew a long sigh for already she was lonely and hungering for him. The song ceased and a long wavering cry came from the cabin.

"So-o-o-cow! S-o-o-kee! S-o-o-kee!"

The old mother was calling the cows. It was near milking-time, and with a vague uneasiness she hurried Bub home. She saw her father coming down from the cornfield. She saw the two cows come from the woods into the path that led to the barn, switching their tails and snatching mouthfuls from the bushes as they swung down the hill and, when she reached the gate, her step-mother was standing on the porch with one hand on her hip and the other shading her eyes from the slanting sun—waiting for her. Already kindness and consideration were gone.

"Whar you been, June? Hurry up, now. You've had a long restin'-spell while I've been a-workin' myself to death."

It was the old tone, and the old fierce rebellion

rose within June, but Hale had told her to be patient. She could not check the flash from her eyes, but she shut her lips tight on the answer that sprang to them, and without a word she went to the kitchen for the milking-pails. The cows had forgotten her. They eyed her with suspicion and were restive. The first one kicked at her when she put her beautiful head against its soft flank. Her muscles had been in disuse and her hands were cramped and her forearms ached before she was through—but she kept doggedly at her task. When she finished, her father had fed the horses and was standing behind her.

"Hit's mighty good to have you back agin, little gal."

It was not often that he smiled or showed tenderness, much less spoke it thus openly, and June was doubly glad that she had held her tongue. Then she helped her step-mother get supper. The fire scorched her face, that had grown unaccustomed to such heat, and she burned one hand, but she did not let her step-mother see even that. Again she noticed with aversion the heavy thick dishes and the pewter spoons and the candle-grease on the oil-cloth, and she put the dishes down and, while the old woman was out of the room, attacked the spots viciously. Again she saw her father and Bub ravenously gobbling their coarse food while she and her step-mother served and waited, and she began to wonder. The women

sat at the table with the men over in the Gap—
why not here? Then her father went silently to
his pipe and Bub to playing with the kitten at the
kitchen-door, while she and her mother ate with
never a word. Something began to stifle her, but
she choked it down. There were the dishes to
be cleared away and washed, and the pans and
kettles to be cleaned. Her back ached, her arms
were tired to the shoulders and her burned hand
quivered with pain when all was done. The old
woman had left her to do the last few little things
alone and had gone to her pipe. Both she and her
father were sitting in silence on the porch when
June went out there. Neither spoke to each other,
nor to her, and both seemed to be part of the
awful stillness that engulfed the world. Bub fell
asleep in the soft air, and June sat and sat and sat.
That was all except for the stars that came out
over the mountains and were slowly being sprayed
over the sky, and the pipings of frogs from the
little creek. Once the wind came with a sudden
sweep up the river and she thought she could hear
the creak of Uncle Billy's water-wheel. It smote
her with sudden gladness, not so much because it
was a relief and because she loved the old miller,
but—such is the power of association—because
she now loved the mill more, loved it because the
mill over in the Gap had made her think more of
the mill at the mouth of Lonesome Cove. A tapping vibrated through the railing of the porch on

205

which her cheek lay. Her father was knocking the ashes from his pipe. A similar tapping sounded inside at the fireplace. The old woman had gone and Bub was in bed, and she had heard neither move. The old man rose with a yawn.

"Time to lay down, June."

The girl rose. They all slept in one room. She did not dare to put on her night-gown—her mother would see it in the morning. So she slipped off her dress, as she had done all her life, and crawled into bed with Bub, who lay in the middle of it and who grunted peevishly when she pushed him with some difficulty over to his side. There were no sheets—not even one—and the coarse blankets, which had a close acrid odour that she had never noticed before, seemed almost to scratch her flesh. She had hardly been to bed that early since she had left home, and she lay sleepless, watching the firelight play hide and seek with the shadows among the aged, smoky rafters and flicker over the strings of dried things that hung from the ceiling. In the other corner her father and step-mother snored heartily, and Bub, beside her, was in a nerveless slumber that would not come to her that night—tired and aching as she was. So, quietly, by and by, she slipped out of bed and out the door to the porch. The moon was rising and the radiant sheen of it had dropped down over the mountain side like a golden veil and was lighting up the white rising mists that trailed the curves of the river. It sank below the still crests of the pines beyond the garden and dropped on until it illumined, one by one, the dewy heads of the flowers. She rose and walked down the grassy path in her bare feet through the silent fragrant emblems of the planter's thought of her—touching this flower and that with the tips of her fingers. And when she went back, she bent to kiss one lovely rose and, as she lifted her head with a start of fear, the dew from it shining on her lips made her red mouth as flower-like and no less beautiful. A yell had shattered the quiet of the world—not the high fox-hunting yell of the mountains, but something new and strange. Up the creek were strange lights. A loud laugh shattered the succeeding stillness—a laugh she had never heard before in Lonesome Cove. Swiftly she ran back to the porch. Surely strange things were happening there. A strange spirit pervaded the Cove and the very air throbbed with premonitions. What was the matter with everything—what was the matter with her? She knew that she was lonely and that she wanted Hale—but what else was it? She shivered—and not alone from the chill night-air—and puzzled and wondering and stricken at heart, she crept back to bed.

XVIII

PAUSING at the Pine to let his big black horse blow a while, Hale mounted and rode slowly down the green-and-gold gloom of the ravine. In his pocket was a quaint little letter from June to "John Hail"; thanking him for the beautiful garden, saying she was lonely, and wanting him to come soon. From the low flank of the mountain he stopped, looking down on the cabin in Lonesome Cove. It was a dreaming summer day. Trees, air, blue sky and white cloud were all in a dream, and even the smoke lazing from the chimney seemed drifting away like the spirit of something human that cared little whither it might be borne. Something crimson emerged from the door and stopped in indecision on the steps of the porch. It moved again, stopped at the corner of the house, and then, moving on with a purpose, stopped once more and began to flicker slowly to and fro like a flame. June was working in her garden. Hale thought he would halloo to her, and then he decided to surprise her, and he went on down, hitched his horse and stole up to the garden fence. On the way he pulled up a bunch of weeds by the roots and with them in his arms he noiselessly climbed the fence. June neither heard nor saw him. Her underlip was clenched tight between her teeth, the little cross swung violently at her throat and she was so savagely wielding the light hoe he had given her that he thought at first she must be killing a snake; but she was only fighting to death every weed that dared to show its head. Her feet and her head were bare, her face was moist and flushed and her hair was a tumbled heap of what was to him the rarest gold under the sun. The wind was still, the leaves were heavy with the richness of full growth, bees were busy about June's head and not another soul was in sight

"Good morning, little girl!" he called cheerily.

The hoe was arrested at the height of a vicious stroke and the little girl whirled without a cry, but the blood from her pumping heart crimsoned her face and made her eyes shine with gladness. Her eyes went to her feet and her hands to her hair.

"You oughtn't to slip up an' s-startle a lady that-a-way," she said with grave rebuke, and Hale looked humbled. "Now you just set there and wait till I come back."

"No—no—I want you to stay just as you are."

"Honest?"

Hale gravely crossed heart and body and June gave out a happy little laugh—for he had caught that gesture—a favourite one—from her. Then suddenly:

"How long?" She was thinking of what **Dave** said, but the subtle twist in her meaning passed Hale by. He raised his eyes to the sun and June shook her head.

"You got to go home 'fore sundown."

She dropped her hoe and came over toward him.

"Whut you doin' with them—those weeds?"

"Going to plant 'em in our garden." Hale had got a theory from a garden-book that the humble burdock, pig-weed and other lowly plants were good for ornamental effect, and he wanted to experiment, but June gave a shrill whoop and fell to scornful laughter. Then she snatched the weeds from him and threw them over the fence.

"Why, June!"

"Not in *my* garden. Them's stagger-weeds— they kill cows," and she went off again.

"I reckon you better c-consult me 'bout weeds next time. I don't know much 'bout flowers, but I've knowed all my life 'bout *weeds*." She laid so much emphasis on the word that Hale wondered for the moment if her words had a deeper meaning—but she went on:

"Ever' spring I have to watch the cows fer two weeks to keep 'em from eatin'—those weeds." Her self-corrections were always made gravely now, and Hale consciously ignored them except when he had something to tell her that she ought to know. Everything, it seemed, she wanted to know.

"Do they really kill cows?"

June snapped her fingers: "Like that. But you just come on here," she added with pretty imperiousness. "I want to axe—ask you some things—what's that?"

"Scarlet sage."

"Scarlet sage," repeated June. "An' that?"

"Nasturtium, and that's Oriental grass."

"Nas-tur-tium, Oriental. An' what's that vine?"

"That comes from North Africa—they call it 'matrimonial vine.'"

"Whut fer?" asked June quickly.

"Because it clings so." Hale smiled, but June saw none of his humour—the married people she knew clung till the finger of death unclasped them. She pointed to a bunch of tall tropical-looking plants with great spreading leaves and big green-white stalks.

"They're called Palmæ Christi."

"Whut?"

"That's Latin. It means 'Hands of Christ,'" said Hale with reverence. "You see how the leaves are spread out—don't they look like hands?"

"Not much," said June frankly. "What's Latin?"

"Oh, that's a dead language that some people used a long, long time ago."

"What do folks use it nowadays fer? Why don't they just say 'Hands o' Christ'?"

"I don't know," he said helplessly, "but maybe you'll study Latin some of these days." June shook her head.

"Gettin' *your* language is a big enough job fer me," she said with such quaint seriousness that Hale could not laugh. She looked up suddenly. "You been a long time git-gettin' over here."

"Yes, and now you want to send me home before sundown."

"I'm afeer—I'm afraid for you. Have you got a gun?" Hale tapped his breast-pocket.

"Always. What are you afraid of?"

"The Falins." She clenched her hands.

"I'd like to *see* one o' them Falins tech ye," she added fiercely, and then she gave a quick look at the sun.

"You better go now, Jack. I'm afraid fer you. Where's your horse?" Hale waved his hand.

"Down there. All right, little girl," he said. "I ought to go, anyway." And, to humour her, he started for the gate. There he bent to kiss her, but she drew back.

"I'm afraid of Dave," she said, but she leaned on the gate and looked long at him with wistful eyes.

"Jack," she said, and her eyes swam suddenly, "it'll most kill me—but I reckon you better not come over here much." Hale made light of it all.

"Nonsense, I'm coming just as often as I can." June smiled then.

"All right. I'll watch out fer ye."

He went down the path, her eyes following him, and when he looked back from the spur he saw her sitting in the porch and watching that she might wave him farewell.

Hale could not go over to Lonesome Cove much that summer, for he was away from the mountains a good part of the time, and it was a weary, racking summer for June when he was not there. The step-mother was a stern taskmistress, and the girl worked hard, but no night passed that she did not spend an hour or more on her books, and by degrees she bribed and stormed Bub into learning his A, B, C's and digging at a blue-back spelling book. But all through the day there were times when she could play with the boy in the garden, and every afternoon, when it was not raining, she would slip away to a little ravine behind the cabin, where a log had fallen across a little brook, and there in the cool, sun-pierced shadows she would study, read and dream—with the water bubbling underneath and wood-thrushes singing overhead. For Hale kept her well supplied with books. He had given her children's books at first, but she outgrew them when the first love-story fell into her hands, and then he gave her novels—good, old ones and the best of the new ones, and they were to her what water is to a thing athirst. But the happy days were when Hale was there. She had a thousand questions for him to answer, whenever he came, about birds, trees and flowers and the things she read in her books. The words she could not understand in them she marked, so that she could ask their meaning, and it was amazing how her vocabulary increased. Moreover, she was always trying to use the new words she learned, and her speech was thus a quaint mixture of vernacular, self-corrections and unexpected words. Happening once to have a volume of Keats in his pocket, he read some of it to her, and while she could not understand, the music of the lines fascinated her and she had him leave that with her, too. She never tired hearing him tell of the places where he had been and the people he knew and the music and plays he had heard and seen. And when he told her that she, too, should see all those wonderful things some day, her deep eyes took fire and she dropped her head far back between her shoulders and looked long at the stars that held but little more wonder for her than the world of which he told. But each time he was there she grew noticeably shyer with him and never once was the love-theme between them taken up in open words. Hale was reluctant, if only because she was still such a child, and if he took her hand or put his own on her wonderful head or his arm around her as they stood in the garden under the stars—he did it as to a child, though the leap in her eyes and the quickening of his own heart told him the lie that he was acting, rightly, to her and

to himself. And no more now were there any
breaking-downs within her—there was only a
calm faith that staggered him and gave him an
ever-mounting sense of his responsibility for whatever might, through the part he had taken in
moulding her life, be in store for her.

When he was not there, life grew a little easier
for her in time, because of her dreams, the patience that was built from them and Hale's kindly
words, the comfort of her garden and her books,
and the blessed force of habit. For as time went
on, she got consciously used to the rough life, the
coarse food and the rude ways of her own people
and her own home. And though she relaxed not
a bit in her own dainty cleanliness, the shrinking
that she felt when she first arrived home, came to
her at longer and longer intervals. Once a week
she went down to Uncle Billy's, where she watched
the water-wheel dripping sun-jewels into the sluice,
the kingfisher darting like a blue bolt upon his
prey, and listening to the lullaby that the water
played to the sleepy old mill—and stopping, both
ways, to gossip with old Hon in her porch under
the honeysuckle vines. Uncle Billy saw the change
in her and he grew vaguely uneasy about her—
she dreamed so much, she was at times so restless,
she asked so many questions he could not answer,
and she failed to ask so many that were on the tip
of her tongue. He saw that while her body was at
home, her thoughts rarely were; and it all haunted

him with a vague sense that he was losing her. But old Hon laughed at him and told him he was an old fool and to "git another pair o' specs" and maybe he could see that the "little gal" was in love. This startled Uncle Billy, for he was so like a father to June that he was as slow as a father in recognizing that his child has grown to such absurd maturity. But looking back to the beginning—how the little girl had talked of the "furriner" who had come into Lonesome Cove all during the six months he was gone; how gladly she had gone away to the Gap to school, how anxious she was to go still farther away again, and, remembering all the strange questions she asked him about things in the outside world of which he knew nothing—Uncle Billy shook his head in confirmation of his own conclusion, and with all his soul he wondered about Hale—what kind of a man he was and what his purpose was with June—and of every man who passed his mill he never failed to ask if he knew "that ar man Hale" and what he knew. All he had heard had been in Hale's favour, except from young Dave Tolliver, the Red Fox or from any Falin of the crowd, which Hale had prevented from capturing Dave. Their statements bothered him—especially the Red Fox's evil hints and insinuations about Hale's purposes one day at the mill. The miller thought of them all the afternoon and all the way home, and when he sat down at his fire his eyes very naturally and simply rose to his old rifle over the door—and then he laughed to himself so loudly that old Hon heard him.

"Air you goin' crazy, Billy?" she asked. "Whut you studyin' 'bout?"

"Nothin'; I was jest a-thinkin' Devil Judd wouldn't leave a grease-spot of him."

"You *air* goin' crazy—who's him?"

"Uh—nobody," said Uncle Billy, and old Hon turned with a shrug of her shoulders—she was tired of all this talk about the feud.

All that summer young Dave Tolliver hung around Lonesome Cove. He would sit for hours in Devil Judd's cabin, rarely saying anything to June or to anybody, though the girl felt that she hardly made a move that he did not see, and while he disappeared when Hale came, after a surly grunt of acknowledgment to Hale's cheerful greeting, his perpetual espionage began to anger June. Never, however, did he put himself into words until Hale's last visit, when the summer had waned and it was nearly time for June to go away again to school. As usual, Dave had left the house when Hale came, and an hour after Hale was gone she went to the little ravine with a book in her hand, and there the boy was sitting on her log, his elbows dug into his legs midway between thigh and knee, his chin in his hands, his slouched hat over his black eyes—every line of him picturing angry, sullen dejection. She would have slipped away, but he heard her and lifted his head and stared at her without speaking. Then he slowly got off the log and sat down on a moss-covered stone.

"'Scuse me," he said with elaborate sarcasm. "This bein' yo' school-house over hyeh, an' me not bein' a scholar, I reckon I'm in your way."

"How do you happen to know hit's my school-house?" asked June quietly.

"I've seed you hyeh."

"Jus' as I s'posed."

"You an' *him*."

"Jus' as I s'posed," she repeated, and a spot of red came into each cheek. "But we didn't see *you*." Young Dave laughed.

"Well, everybody don't always see me when I'm seein' them."

"No," she said unsteadily. "So, you've been sneakin' around through the woods a-spyin' on me—*sneakin' an' spyin'*," she repeated so searingly that Dave looked at the ground suddenly, picked up a pebble confusedly and shot it in the water.

"I had a mighty good reason," he said doggedly. "Ef he'd been up to some of his furrin tricks——" June stamped the ground.

"Don't you think I kin take keer o' myself?"

"No, I don't. I never seed a gal that could—with one o' them furriners."

"Huh!" she said scornfully. "You seem to set

218

a mighty big store by the decency of yo' own kin."
Dave was silent. "He ain't up to no tricks. An'
whut do you reckon Dad 'ud be doin' while you
was pertecting me?"

"Air ye goin' away to school?" he asked suddenly. June hesitated.

"Well, seein' as hit's none o' yo' business—I am."

"Air ye goin' to marry him?"

"He ain't axed me." The boy's face turned
red as a flame.

"Ye air honest with me, an' now I'm goin' to
be honest with you. You hain't never goin' to
marry him."

"Mebbe you think I'm goin' to marry *you.*"
A mist of rage swept before the lad's eyes so that
he could hardly see, but he repeated steadily:

"You hain't goin' to marry *him.*" June looked
at the boy long and steadily, but his black eyes
never wavered—she knew what he meant.

"An' he kept the Falins from killin' you," she
said, quivering with indignation at the shame of
him, but Dave went on unheeding:

"You pore little fool! Do ye reckon as how
he's *ever* goin' to axe ye to marry him? Whut's
he sendin' you away fer? Because you hain't
good enough fer him! Whar's yo' pride? You
hain't good enough fer him," he repeated scath-
ingly. June had grown calm now.

"I know it," she said quietly, "but I'm goin'
to try to be."

Dave rose then in impotent fury and pointed one finger at her. His black eyes gleamed like a demon's and his voice was hoarse with resolution and rage, but it was Tolliver against Tolliver now, and June answered him with contemptuous fearlessness.

"*You hain't never goin' to marry him.*"

"An' he kept the Falins from killin' ye."

"Yes," he retorted savagely at last, "an' I kept the Falins from killin' *him*," and he stalked away, leaving June blanched and wondering.

It was true. Only an hour before, as Hale turned up the mountain that very afternoon at the mouth of Lonesome Cove, young Dave had called to him from the bushes and stepped into the road.

"You air goin' to court Monday?" he said.

"Yes," said Hale.

"Well, you better take another road this time," he said quietly. "Three o' the Falins will be waitin' in the lorrel somewhar on the road to lay-way ye."

Hale was dumfounded, but he knew the boy spoke the truth.

"Look here," he said impulsively, "I've got nothing against you, and I hope you've got nothing against me. I'm much obliged—let's shake hands!"

The boy turned sullenly away with a dogged shake of his head.

"I was beholden to you," he said with dignity,

"an' I warned you 'bout them Falins to git even with you. We're quits now."

Hale started to speak—to say that the lad was not beholden to him—that he would as quickly have protected a Falin, but it would have only made matters worse. Moreover, he knew precisely what Dave had against him, and that, too, was no matter for discussion. So he said simply and sincerely:

"I'm sorry we can't be friends."

"No," Dave gritted out, "not this side o' Heaven—or Hell."

XIX

AND still farther into that far silence about which she used to dream at the base of the big Pine, went little June. At dusk, weary and travel-stained, she sat in the parlours of a hotel— a great gray columned structure of stone. She was confused and bewildered and her head ached. The journey had been long and tiresome. The swift motion of the train had made her dizzy and faint. The dust and smoke had almost stifled her, and even now the dismal parlours, rich and wonderful as they were to her unaccustomed eyes, oppressed her deeply. If she could have one more breath of mountain air!

The day had been too full of wonders. Impressions had crowded on her sensitive brain so thick and fast that the recollection of them was as through a haze. She had never been on a train before and when, as it crashed ahead, she clutched Hale's arm in fear and asked how they stopped it, Hale hearing the whistle blow for a station, said:

"I'll show you," and he waved one hand out the window. And he repeated this trick twice before she saw that it was a joke. All day he had soothed her uneasiness in some such way and all day he watched her with an amused smile that was puzzling to her. She remembered sadly watching the mountains dwindle and disappear, and when several of her own people who were on the train were left at way-stations, it seemed as though all links that bound her to her home were broken. The face of the country changed, the people changed in looks, manners and dress, and she shrank closer to Hale with an increasing sense of painful loneliness. These level fields and these farm-houses so strangely built, so varied in colour were the "settlemints," and these people so nicely dressed, so clean and fresh-looking were "furriners." At one station a crowd of school-girls had got on board and she had watched them with keen interest, mystified by their incessant chatter and gayety. And at last had come the big city, with more smoke, more dust, more noise, more confusion—and she was in *his* world. That was the thought that comforted her—it was his world, and now she sat alone in the dismal parlours while Hale was gone to find his sister—waiting and trembling at the ordeal, close upon her, of meeting Helen Hale.

Below, Hale found his sister and her maid registered, and a few minutes later he led Miss Hale into the parlour. As they entered June rose without advancing, and for a moment the two stood facing each other—the still roughly clad, primitive mountain girl and the exquisite modern woman—in an embarrassment equally painful to both.

" June, this is my sister."

At a loss what to do, Helen Hale simply stretched out her hand, but drawn by June's timidity and the quick admiration and fear in her eyes, she leaned suddenly forward and kissed her. A grateful flush overspread the little girl's features and the pallor that instantly succeeded went straightway to the sister's heart.

"You are not well," she said quickly and kindly. "You must go to your room at once. I am going to take care of you—you are *my* little sister now."

June lost the subtlety in Miss Hale's emphasis, but she fell with instant submission under such gentle authority, and though she could say nothing, her eyes glistened and her lips quivered, and without looking to Hale, she followed his sister out of the room. Hale stood still. He had watched the meeting with apprehension and now, surprised and grateful, he went to Helen's parlour and waited with a hopeful heart. When his sister entered, he rose eagerly:

"Well—" he said, stopping suddenly, for there were tears of vexation, dismay and genuine distress on his sister's face.

"Oh, Jack," she cried, "how could you! How could you!"

Hale bit his lips, turned and paced the room. He had hoped too much and yet what else could he have expected? His sister and June knew as little about each other and each other's lives as though they had occupied different planets. He had forgotten that Helen must be shocked by June's inaccuracies of speech and in a hundred other ways to which he had become accustomed. With him, moreover, the process had been gradual and, moreover, he had seen beneath it all. And yet he had foolishly expected Helen to understand everything at once. He was unjust, so very wisely he held himself in silence.

"Where is her baggage, Jack?" Helen had opened her trunk and was lifting out the lid. "She ought to change those dusty clothes at once. You'd better ring and have it sent right up."

"No," said Hale, "I will go down and see about it myself."

He returned presently—his face aflame—with June's carpet-bag.

"I believe this is all she has," he said quietly.

In spite of herself Helen's grief changed to a fit of helpless laughter and, afraid to trust himself further, Hale rose to leave the room. At the door he was met by the negro maid.

"Miss Helen," she said with an open smile, "Miss June say she don't want *nuttin'*." Hale gave her a fiery look and hurried out. June was seated at a window when he went into her room with her face buried in her arms. She lifted her head, dropped it, and he saw that her eyes were red with weeping.

"Are you sick, little girl?" he asked anxiously. June shook her head helplessly.

"You aren't homesick, are you?"

"No." The answer came very faintly.

"Don't you like my sister?" The head bowed an emphatic "Yes—yes."

"Then what is the matter?"

"Oh," she said despairingly, between her sobs, "she—won't—like—me. I never—can—be—like *her*."

Hale smiled, but her grief was so sincere that he leaned over her and with a tender hand soothed her into quiet. Then he went to Helen again and he found her overhauling dresses.

"I brought along several things of different sizes and I am going to try at any rate. Oh," she added hastily, "only of course until she can get some clothes of her own."

"Sure," said Hale, "but—" His sister waved one hand and again Hale kept still.

June had bathed her eyes and was lying down when Helen entered, and she made not the slightest objection to anything the latter proposed. Straightway she fell under as complete subjection to her as she had done to Hale. Without a moment's hesitation she drew off her rudely fashioned dress and stood before Helen with the utmost simplicity—her beautiful arms and throat bare and her hair falling about them with the rich gold of a cloud at an autumn sunset. Dressed, she could

"YOU HAIN'T NEVER GOIN' TO MARRY HIM,"

hardly breathe, but when she looked at herself in the mirror, she trembled. Magic transformation! Apparently the chasm between the two had been bridged in a single instant. Helen herself was astonished and again her heart warmed toward the girl, when a little later, she stood timidly under Hale's scrutiny, eagerly watching his face and flushing rosy with happiness under his brightening look. Her brother had not exaggerated—the little girl was really beautiful. When they went down to the dining-room, there was another surprise for Helen Hale, for June's timidity was gone and to the wonder of the woman, she was clothed with an impassive reserve that in herself would have been little less than haughtiness and was astounding in a child. She saw, too, that the change in the girl's bearing was unconscious and that the presence of strangers had caused it. It was plain that June's timidity sprang from her love of Hale —her fear of not pleasing him and not pleasing her, his sister, and plain, too, that remarkable self-poise was little June's to command. At the table June kept her eyes fastened on Helen Hale. Not a movement escaped her and she did nothing that was not done by one of the others first. She said nothing, but if she had to answer a question, she spoke with such care and precision that she almost seemed to be using a foreign language. Miss Hale smiled but with inward approval, and that night she was in better spirits.

227

"Jack," she said, when he came to bid her good-night, "I think we'd better stay here a few days. I thought of course you were exaggerating, but she is very, very lovely. And that manner of hers—well, it passes my understanding. Just leave everything to me."

Hale was very willing to do that. He had all trust in his sister's judgment, he knew her dislike of interference, her love of autocratic supervision, so he asked no questions, but in grateful relief kissed her good-night.

The sister sat for a long time at her window after he was gone. Her brother had been long away from civilization; he had become infatuated, the girl loved him, he was honourable and in his heart he meant to marry her—that was to her the whole story. She had been mortified by the misstep, but the misstep made, only one thought had occurred to her—to help him all she could. She had been appalled when she first saw the dusty shrinking mountain girl, but the helplessness and the loneliness of the tired little face touched her, and she was straightway responsive to the mute appeal in the dark eyes that were lifted to her own with such modest fear and wonder. Now her surprise at her brother's infatuation was abating rapidly. The girl's adoration of him, her wild beauty, her strange winning personality—as rare and as independent of birth and circumstances as genius—had soon made that phenomenon plain. And now what was to be done? The girl was quick, observant, imitative, docile, and in the presence of strangers, her gravity of manner gave the impression of uncanny self-possession. It really seemed as though anything might be possible. At Helen's suggestion, then, the three stayed where they were for a week, for June's wardrobe was sadly in need of attention. So the week was spent in shopping, driving, and walking, and rapidly as it passed for Helen and Hale it was to June the longest of her life, so filled was it with a thousand sensations unfelt by them. The city had been stirred by the spirit of the new South, but the charm of the old was distinct everywhere. Architectural eccentricities had startled the sleepy maple-shaded rows of comfortable uniform dwellings here and there, and in some streets the life was brisk; but it was still possible to see pedestrians strolling with unconscious good-humour around piles of goods on the sidewalk, business men stopping for a social chat on the streets, street-cars moving independent of time, men invariably giving up their seats to women, and, strangers or not, depositing their fare for them; the drivers at the courteous personal service of each patron of the road—now holding a car and placidly whistling while some lady who had signalled from her doorway went back indoors for some forgotten article, now twisting the reins around the brakes and leaving a parcel in some yard—and no one grumbling! But what was to Hale an atmosphere of amusing leisure was to June bewildering confusion. To her his amusement was unintelligible, but though in constant wonder at everything she saw, no one would ever have suspected that she was making her first acquaintance with city scenes. At first the calm unconcern of her companions had puzzled her. She could not understand how they could walk along, heedless of the wonderful visions that beckoned to her from the shop-windows; fearless of the strange noises about them and scarcely noticing the great crowds of people, or the strange shining vehicles that thronged the streets. But she had quickly concluded that it was one of the demands of that new life to see little and be astonished at nothing, and Helen and Hale surprised in turn at her unconcern, little suspected the effort her self-suppression cost her. And when over some wonder she did lose herself, Hale would say:

"Just wait till you see New York!" and June would turn her dark eyes to Helen for confirmation and to see if Hale could be joking with her.

"It's all true, June," Helen would say. "You must go there some day. It's true." But that town was enough and too much for June. Her head buzzed continuously and she could hardly sleep, and she was glad when one afternoon they took her into the country again—the Bluegrass country—and to the little town near which Hale

230

had been born, and which was a dream-city to June, and to a school of which an old friend of his mother was principal, and in which Helen herself was a temporary teacher. And Rumour had gone ahead of June. Hale had found her dashing about the mountains on the back of a wild bull, said rumour. She was as beautiful as Europa, was of pure English descent and spoke the language of Shakespeare—the Hon. Sam Budd's hand was patent in this. She had saved Hale's life from moonshiners and while he was really in love with her, he was pretending to educate her out of gratitude—and here doubtless was the faint tracery of Miss Anne Saunder's natural suspicions. And there Hale left her under the eye of his sister—left her to absorb another new life like a thirsty plant and come back to the mountains to make his head swim with new witcheries.

XX

THE boom started after its shadow through the hills now, and Hale watched it sweep toward him with grim satisfaction at the fulfilment of his own prophecy and with disgust that, by the irony of fate, it should come from the very quarters where years before he had played the maddening part of lunatic at large. The avalanche was sweeping southward; Pennsylvania was creeping down the Alleghanies, emissaries of New York capital were pouring into the hills, the tide-water of Virginia and the Bluegrass region of Kentucky were sending in their best blood and youth, and friends of the helmeted Englishmen were hurrying over the seas. Eastern companies were taking up principalities, and at Cumberland Gap, those helmeted Englishmen had acquired a kingdom. They were building a town there, too, with huge steel plants, broad avenues and business blocks that would have graced Broadway; and they were pouring out a million for every thousand that it would have cost Hale to acquire the land on which the work was going on. Moreover they were doing it there, as Hale heard, because they were too late to get control of *his* gap through the Cumberland. At his gap, too, the same movement was starting. In stage and wagon, on mule and horse, "riding and tying" sometimes, and even afoot came the rush of madmen. Horses and mules were drowned in the mud holes along the road, such was the traffic and such were the floods. The incomers slept eight in a room, burned oil at one dollar a gallon, and ate potatoes at ten cents apiece. The Grand Central Hotel was a humming Real-Estate Exchange, and, night and day, the occupants of any room could hear, through the thin partitions, lots booming to right, left, behind and in front of them. The labour and capital question was instantly solved, for everybody became a capitalist—carpenter, bricklayer, blacksmith, singing teacher and preacher. There is no difference between the shrewdest business man and a fool in a boom, for the boom levels all grades of intelligence and produces as distinct a form of insanity as you can find within the walls of an asylum. Lots took wings skyward. Hale bought one for June for thirty dollars and sold it for a thousand. Before the autumn was gone, he found himself on the way to ridiculous opulence and, when spring came, he had the world in a sling and, if he wished, he could toss it playfully at the sun and have it drop back into his hand again. And the boom spread down the valley and into the hills. The police guard had little to do and, over in the mountains, the feud miraculously came to a sudden close.

So pervasive, indeed, was the spirit of the times that the Hon. Sam Budd actually got old Buck Falin and old Dave Tolliver to sign a truce, agreeing to a complete cessation of hostilities until he carried through a land deal in which both were interested. And after that was concluded, nobody had time, even the Red Fox, for deviltry and private vengeance—so busy was everybody picking up the manna which was dropping straight from the clouds. Hale bought all of old Judd's land, formed a stock company and in the trade gave June a bonus of the stock. Money was plentiful as grains of sand, and the cashier of the bank in the back of the furniture store at the Gap chuckled to his beardless directors as he locked the wooden door on the day before the great land sale:

"Capital stock paid in—thirteen thousand dollars;

"Deposits—three hundred thousand;

"Loans—two hundred and sixty thousand—interest from eight to twelve per cent." And, beardless though those directors were, that statement made them reel.

A club was formed and the like of it was not below Mason and Dixon's line in the way of furniture, periodicals, liquors and cigars. Poker ceased—it was too tame in competition with this new game of town-lots. On the top of High Knob a kingdom was bought. The young bloods of the town would build a lake up there, run a road up and build a Swiss chalet on the very top for a country club. The "booming" editor was discharged. A new paper was started, and the ex-editor of a New York Daily was got to run it. If anybody wanted anything, he got it from no matter where, nor at what cost. Nor were the arts wholly neglected. One man, who was proud of his voice, thought he would like to take singing lessons. An emissary was sent to Boston to bring back the best teacher he could find. The teacher came with a method of placing the voice by trying to say "Come!" at the base of the nose and between the eyes. This was with the lips closed. He charged two dollars per half hour for this effort, he had each pupil try it twice for half an hour each day, and for six weeks the town was humming like a beehive. At the end of that period, the teacher fell ill and went his way with a fat pocket-book and not a warbling soul had got the chance to open his mouth. The experience dampened nobody. Generosity was limitless. It was equally easy to raise money for a roulette wheel, a cathedral or an expedition to Africa. And even yet the railroad was miles away and even yet in February, the Improvement Company had a great land sale. The day before it, competing purchasers had deposited cheques aggregating three times the sum asked for by the company for the land. So the buyers spent the night organizing a pool to keep down competition and drawing lots for the privilege of bidding. For fairness, the sale was an auction, and one old farmer who had sold some of the land originally for a hundred dollars an acre, bought back some of that land at a thousand dollars a lot.

That sale was the climax and, that early, Hale got a warning word from England, but he paid no heed even though, after the sale, the boom slackened, poised and stayed still; for optimism was unquenchable and another tide would come with another sale in May, and so the spring passed in the same joyous recklessness and the same perfect hope.

In April, the first railroad reached the Gap at last, and families came in rapidly. Money was still plentiful and right royally was it spent, for was not just as much more coming when the second road arrived in May? Life was easier, too—supplies came from New York, eight o'clock dinners were in vogue and everybody was happy. Every man had two or three good horses and nothing to do. The place was full of visiting girls. They rode in parties to High Knob, and the ring of hoof and the laughter of youth and maid made every dusk resonant with joy. On Poplar Hill houses sprang up like magic and weddings came. The passing stranger was stunned to find out in the wilderness such a spot; gayety, prodigal hospitality, a police force of gentlemen—nearly all of whom were college graduates—and a club, where poker flourished in the smoke of Havana cigars, and a barrel of whiskey stood in one corner with a faucet waiting for the turn of any hand. And still the foundation of the new hotel was not started and the coming of the new railroad in May did not make a marked change. For some reason the May sale was postponed by the Improvement Company, but what did it matter? Perhaps it was better to wait for the fall, and so the summer went on unchanged. Every man still had a bank account and in the autumn, the boom would come again. At such a time June came home for her vacation, and Bob Berkley came back from college for his. All through the school year Hale had got the best reports of June. His sister's letters were steadily encouraging. June had been very homesick for the mountains and for Hale at first, but the homesickness had quickly worn off—apparently for both. She had studied hard, had become a favourite among the girls, and had held her own among them in a surprising way. But it was on June's musical talent that Hale's sister always laid most stress, and on her voice which, she said, was really unusual. June wrote, too, at longer and longer intervals and in her letters, Hale could see the progress she was making—the change in her handwriting, the increasing formality of expression, and the increasing shrewdness of her comments on her fellow-pupils, her teachers and the life about her. She did not write home for a reason Hale knew, though June never mentioned it—because there was no one at home who could read her letters—but she always sent messages to her father and Bub and to the old miller and old Hon, and Hale faithfully delivered them when he could.

From her people, as Hale learned from his sister, only one messenger had come during the year to June, and he came but once. One morning, a tall, black-haired, uncouth young man, in a slouch hat and a Prince Albert coat, had strode up to the school with a big paper box under his arm and asked for June. As he handed the box to the maid at the door, it broke and red apples burst from it and rolled down the steps. There was a shriek of laughter from the girls, and the young man, flushing red as the apples, turned, without giving his name, and strode back with no little majesty, looking neither to right nor left. Hale knew and June knew that the visitor was her cousin Dave, but she never mentioned the incident to him, though as the end of the session drew nigh, her letters became more frequent and more full of messages to the people in Lonesome Cove, and she seemed eager to get back home. Over there about this time, old Judd concluded suddenly to go West, taking Bud with him, and when Hale wrote the fact, an answer came from June that showed the blot of tears. However, she seemed none the less in a hurry to get back, and when Hale met her

at the station, he was startled; for she came back
in dresses that were below her shoe-tops, with her
wonderful hair massed in a golden glory on the
top of her head and the little fairy-cross dangling
at a woman's throat. Her figure had rounded, her
voice had softened. She held herself as straight
as a young poplar and she walked the earth as
though she had come straight from Olympus.
And still, in spite of her new feathers and airs and
graces, there was in her eye and in her laugh and
in her moods all the subtle wild charm of the child
in Lonesome Cove. It was fairy-time for June
that summer, though her father and Bud had
gone West, for her step-mother was living with a
sister, the cabin in Lonesome Cove was closed and
June stayed at the Gap, not at the Widow Crane's
boarding-house, but with one of Hale's married
friends on Poplar Hill. And always was she,
young as she was, one of the merry parties of that
happy summer—even at the dances, for the dance,
too, June had learned. Moreover she had picked
up the guitar, and many times when Hale had
been out in the hills, he would hear her silver-
clear voice floating out into the moonlight as he
made his way toward Poplar Hill, and he would
stop under the beeches and listen with ears of
growing love to the wonder of it all. For it was
he who was the ardent one of the two now.

June was no longer the frank, impulsive child
who stood at the foot of the beech, doggedly reck-

less if all the world knew her love for him. She had taken flight to some inner recess where it was difficult for Hale to follow, and right puzzled he was to discover that he must now win again what, unasked, she had once so freely given.

Bob Berkley, too, had developed amazingly. He no longer said "Sir" to Hale—that was bad form at Harvard—he called him by his first name and looked him in the eye as man to man: just as June—Hale observed—no longer seemed in any awe of Miss Anne Saunders and to have lost all jealousy of her, or of anybody else—so swiftly had her instinct taught her she now had nothing to fear. And Bob and June seemed mightily pleased with each other, and sometimes Hale, watching them as they galloped past him on horseback laughing and bantering, felt foolish to think of their perfect fitness—the one for the other—and the incongruity of himself in a relationship that would so naturally be theirs. At one thing he wondered: she had made an extraordinary record at school and it seemed to him that it was partly through the consciousness that her brain would take care of itself that she could pay such heed to what hitherto she had had no chance to learn— dress, manners, deportment and speech. Indeed, it was curious that she seemed to lay most stress on the very things to which he, because of his long rough life in the mountains, was growing more and more indifferent. It was quite plain that Bob, with his extreme gallantry of manner, his smart clothes, his high ways and his unconquerable gayety, had supplanted him on the pedestal where he had been the year before, just as somebody, somewhere—his sister, perhaps—had supplanted Miss Anne. Several times indeed June had corrected Hale's slips of tongue with mischievous triumph, and once when he came back late from a long trip in the mountains and walked in to dinner without changing his clothes, Hale saw her look from himself to the immaculate Bob with an unconscious comparison that half amused, half worried him. The truth was he was building a lovely Frankenstein and from wondering what he was going to do with it, he was beginning to wonder now what it might some day do with him. And though he sometimes joked with Miss Anne, who had withdrawn now to the level plane of friendship with him, about the transformation that was going on, he worried in a way that did neither his heart nor his brain good. Still he fought both to little purpose all that summer, and it was not till the time was nigh when June must go away again, that he spoke both. For Hale's sister was going to marry, and it was her advice that he should take June to New York if only for the sake of her music and her voice. That very day June had for the first time seen her cousin Dave. He was on horseback, he had been drinking and he pulled in and, without an answer to her greeting, stared her over from head to foot. Colouring angrily, she started on and then he spoke thickly and with a sneer:

"'Bout fryin' size, now, ain't ye? I reckon maybe, if you keep on, you'll be good enough fer him in a year or two more."

"I'm much obliged for those apples, Dave," said June quietly—and Dave flushed a darker red and sat still, forgetting to renew the old threat that was on his tongue.

But his taunt rankled in the girl—rankled more now than when Dave first made it, for she better saw the truth of it and the hurt was the greater to her unconquerable pride that kept her from betraying the hurt to Dave long ago, and now, when he was making an old wound bleed afresh. But the pain was with her at dinner that night and through the evening. She avoided Hale's eyes though she knew that he was watching her all the time, and her instinct told her that something was going to happen that night and what that something was. Hale was the last to go and when he called to her from the porch, she went out trembling and stood at the head of the steps in the moonlight.

"I love you, little girl," he said simply, "and I want you to marry me some day—will you, June?" She was unsurprised but she flushed under his hungry eyes, and the little cross throbbed at her throat.

"*Some* day—not *now*," she thought, and then with equal simplicity: "Yes, Jack."

"And if you should love somebody else more, you'll tell me right away—won't you, June?" She shrank a little and her eyes fell, but straightway she raised them steadily:

"Yes, Jack."

"Thank you, little girl—good-night."

"Good-night, Jack."

Hale saw the little shrinking movement she made, and, as he went down the hill, he thought she seemed to be in a hurry to be alone, and that she had caught her breath sharply as she turned away. And brooding he walked the woods long that night.

Only a few days later, they started for New York and, with all her dreaming, June had never dreamed that the world could be so large. Mountains and vast stretches of rolling hills and level land melted away from her wondering eyes; towns and cities sank behind them, swift streams swollen by freshets were outstripped and left behind, darkness came on and, through it, they still sped on. Once during the night she woke from a troubled dream in her berth and for a moment she thought she was at home again. They were running through mountains again and there they lay in the moonlight, the great calm dark faces that she knew and loved, and she seemed to catch the odour of the earth and feel the cool air on her face, but there was no pang of homesickness now—she was too eager for the world into which she was going. Next morning the air was cooler, the skies lower and grayer—the big city was close at hand. Then came the water, shaking and sparkling in the early light like a great cauldron of quicksilver, and the wonderful Brooklyn Bridge—a ribbon of twinkling lights tossed out through the mist from the mighty city that rose from that mist as from a fantastic dream; then the picking of a way through screeching little boats and noiseless big ones and white bird-like floating things and then they disappeared like two tiny grains in a shifting human tide of sand. But Hale was happy now, for on that trip June had come back to herself, and to him, once more—and now, awed but unafraid, eager, bubbling, uplooking, full of quaint questions about everything she saw, she was once more sitting with affectionate reverence at his feet. When he left her in a great low house that fronted on the majestic Hudson, June clung to him with tears and of her own accord kissed him for the first time since she had torn her little playhouse to pieces at the foot of the beech down in the mountains far away. And Hale went back with peace in his heart, but to trouble in the hills.

. . . .

Not suddenly did the boom drop down there, not like a falling star, but on the wings of hope—wings that ever fluttering upward, yet sank inexorably and slowly closed. The first crash came over the waters when certain big men over there went to pieces—men on whose shoulders rested the colossal figure of progress that the English were carving from the hills at Cumberland Gap. Still nobody saw why a hurt to the Lion should make the Eagle sore and so the American spirit at the other gaps and all up the Virginia valleys that skirt the Cumberland held faithful and dauntless—for a while. But in time as the huge steel plants grew noiseless, and the flaming throats of the furnaces were throttled, a sympathetic fire of dissolution spread slowly North and South and it was plain only to the wise outsider as merely a matter of time until, all up and down the Cumberland, the fox and the coon and the quail could come back to their old homes on corner lots, marked each by a pathetic little whitewashed post—a tombstone over the graves of a myriad of buried human hopes. But it was the gap where Hale was that died last and hardest—and of the brave spirits there, his was the last and hardest to die.

In the autumn, while June was in New York, the signs were sure but every soul refused to see them. Slowly, however, the vexed question of labour and capital was born again, for slowly each local capitalist went slowly back to his own trade: the blacksmith to his forge, but the carpenter not to his plane nor the mason to his brick—there was no more building going on. The engineer took up his transit, the preacher-politician was oftener in his pulpit, and the singing teacher started on his round of raucous do-mi-sol-dos through the mountains again. It was curious to see how each man slowly, reluctantly and perforce sank back again to his old occupation—and the town, with the luxuries of electricity, water-works, bath-tubs and a street railway, was having a hard fight for the plain necessities of life. The following spring, notes for the second payment on the lots that had been bought at the great land sale fell due, and but very few were paid. As no suits were brought by the company, however, hope did not quite die. June did not come home for the summer, and Hale did not encourage her to come—she visited some of her school-mates in the North and took a trip West to see her father who had gone out there again and bought a farm. In the early autumn, Devil Judd came back to the mountains and announced his intention to leave them for good. But that autumn, the effects of the dead boom became perceptible in the hills. There were no more coal lands bought, logging ceased, the factions were idle once more, moonshine stills flourished, quarrelling started, and at the county seat, one Court day, Devil Judd whipped three Falins with his bare fists. In the early spring a Tolliver was shot from ambush and old Judd was so furious at the outrage that he openly announced that he would stay at home until he had settled the old scores for good. So that, as the summer came on, matters between the Falins and the Tollivers were worse than they had been for years and everybody knew that, with old Judd at the head of his clan again, the fight would be fought to the finish. At the Gap, one institution only had suffered in spirit not at all and that was the Volunteer Police Guard. Indeed, as the excitement of the boom had died down, the members of that force, as a vent for their energies, went with more enthusiasm than ever into their work. Local lawlessness had been subdued by this time, the Guard had been extending its work into the hills, and it was only a question of time until it must take a part in the Falin-Tolliver troubles. Indeed, that time, Hale believed, was not far away, for Election Day was at hand, and always on that day the feudists came to the Gap in a search for trouble. Meanwhile, not long afterward, there was a pitched battle between the factions at the county seat, and several of each would fight no more. Next day a Falin whistled a bullet through Devil Judd's beard from ambush, and it was at such a crisis of all the warring elements in her mountain life that June's school-days were coming to a close. Hale had had a frank talk with old Judd and the old man agreed that the two had best be married at once and live at the Gap until things were quieter in the mountains, though the old man still clung to his resolution to go West for good when he was done with the Falins. At such a time, then, June was coming home.

XXI

HALE was beyond Black Mountain when her letter reached him. His work over there had to be finished and so he kept in his saddle the greater part of two days and nights and on the third day rode his big black horse forty miles in little more than half a day that he might meet her at the train. The last two years had wrought their change in him. Deterioration is easy in the hills—superficial deterioration in habits, manners, personal appearance and the practices of all the little niceties of life. The morning bath is impossible because of the crowded domestic conditions of a mountain cabin and, if possible, might if practised, excite wonder and comment, if not vague suspicion. Sleeping garments are practically barred for the same reason. Shaving becomes a rare luxury. A lost tooth-brush may not be replaced for a month. In time one may bring himself to eat with a knife for the reason that it is hard for a hungry man to feed himself with a fork that has but two tines. The finger tips cease to be the culminating standard of the gentleman. It is hard to keep a supply of fresh linen when one is constantly in the saddle, and a constant weariness

of body and a ravenous appetite make a man indifferent to things like a bad bed and worse food,
particularly as he must philosophically put up
with them, anyhow. Of all these things the man
himself may be quite unconscious and yet they
affect him more deeply than he knows and show
to a woman even in his voice, his walk, his mouth
—everywhere save in his eyes, which change only
in severity, or in kindliness or when there has been
some serious break-down of soul or character
within. And the woman will not look to his eyes
for the truth—which makes its way slowly—particularly when the woman has striven for the very
things that the man has so recklessly let go. She
would never suffer herself to let down in such a
way and she does not understand how a man can.

Hale's life, since his college doors had closed
behind him, had always been a rough one. He
had dropped from civilization and had gone back
into it many times. And each time he had dropped,
he dropped the deeper, and for that reason had
come back into his own life each time with more
difficulty and with more indifference. The last
had been his roughest year and he had sunk a little
more deeply just at the time when June had been
pluming herself for flight from such depths forever. Moreover, Hale had been dominant in
every matter that his hand or his brain had
touched. His habit had been to say "do this" and
it was done. Though he was no longer acting cap-

tain of the Police Guard, he always acted as captain whenever he was on hand, and always he was the undisputed leader in all questions of business, politics or the maintenance of order and law. The success he had forged had hardened and strengthened his mouth, steeled his eyes and made him more masterful in manner, speech and point of view, and naturally had added nothing to his gentleness, his unselfishness, his refinement or the nice consideration of little things on which women lay such stress. It was an hour by sun when he clattered through the Gap and pushed his tired black horse into a gallop across the valley toward the town. He saw the smoke of the little dummy and, as he thundered over the bridge of the North Fork, he saw that it was just about to pull out and he waved his hat and shouted imperiously for it to wait. With his hand on the bell-rope, the conductor, autocrat that he, too, was, did wait and Hale threw his reins to the man who was nearest, hardly seeing who he was, and climbed aboard. He wore a slouched hat spotted by contact with the roof of the mines which he had hastily visited on his way through Lonesome Cove. The growth of three days' beard was on his face. He wore a gray woollen shirt, and a blue handkerchief—none too clean—was loosely tied about his sun-scorched column of a throat; he was spotted with mud from his waist to the soles of his rough riding boots and his hands were rough and grimy. But his eye was

bright and keen and his heart thumped eagerly.
Again it was the middle of June and the town was
a naked island in a sea of leaves whose breakers
literally had run mountain high and stopped for
all time motionless. Purple lights thick as mist
veiled Powell's Mountain. Below, the valley was
still flooded with yellow sunlight which lay along
the mountain sides and was streaked here and
there with the long shadow of a deep ravine. The
beech trunks on Imboden Hill gleamed in it like
white bodies scantily draped with green, and the
yawning Gap held the yellow light as a bowl holds
wine. He had long ago come to look upon the
hills merely as storehouses for iron and coal, put
there for his special purpose, but now the long
submerged sense of the beauty of it all stirred
within him again, for June was the incarnate spirit
of it all and June was coming back to those
mountains and—to him.

.   .   .   .

And June—June had seen the change in Hale.
The first year he had come often to New York to
see her and they had gone to the theatre and the
opera, and June was pleased to play the part of
heroine in what was such a real romance to the
other girls in school and she was proud of Hale.
But each time he came, he seemed less interested
in the diversions that meant so much to her, more
absorbed in his affairs in the mountains and less

particular about his looks. His visits came at longer intervals, with each visit he stayed less long, and each time he seemed more eager to get away. She had been shy about appearing before him for the first time in evening dress, and when he entered the drawing-room she stood under a chandelier in blushing and resplendent confusion, but he seemed not to recognize that he had never seen her that way before, and for another reason June remained confused, disappointed and hurt, for he was not only unobserving, and seemingly unappreciative, but he was more silent than ever that night and he looked gloomy. But if he had grown accustomed to her beauty, there were others who had not, and smart, dapper college youths gathered about her like bees around a flower—a triumphant fact to which he also seemed indifferent. Moreover, he was not in evening clothes that night and she did not know whether he had forgotten or was indifferent to them, and the contrast that he was made her that night almost ashamed for him. She never guessed what the matter was, for Hale kept his troubles to himself. He was always gentle and kind, he was as lavish with her as though he were a king, and she was as lavish and prodigally generous as though she were a princess. There seemed no limit to the wizard income from the investments that Hale had made for her when, as he said, he sold a part of her stock in the Lonesome Cove mine, and what she wanted Hale always sent her without question. Only, as the end was coming on at the Gap, he wrote once to know if a certain amount would carry her through until she was ready to come home, but even that question aroused no suspicion in thoughtless June. And then that last year he had come no more—always, always he was too busy. Not even on her triumphal night at the end of the session was he there, when she had stood before the guests and patrons of the school like a goddess, and had thrilled them into startling applause, her teachers into open glowing pride, the other girls into bright-eyed envy and herself into still another new world. Now she was going home and she was glad to go.

She had awakened that morning with the keen air of the mountains in her nostrils—the air she had breathed in when she was born, and her eyes shone happily when she saw through her window the loved blue hills along which raced the train. They were only a little way from the town where she must change, the porter said; she had overslept and she had no time even to wash her face and hands, and that worried her a good deal. The porter nearly lost his equilibrium when she gave him half a dollar—for women are not profuse in the way of tipping—and instead of putting her bag down on the station platform, he held it in his hand waiting to do her further service. At the head of the steps she searched about for Hale and her lovely face looked vexed and a little hurt when she did not see him.

"Hotel, Miss?" said the porter.

"Yes, please, Harvey!" she called.

An astonished darky sprang from the line of calling hotel-porters and took her bag. Then every tooth in his head flashed.

"Lordy, Miss June—I never knowed you at all."

June smiled—it was the tribute she was looking for.

"Have you seen Mr. Hale?"

"No'm. Mr. Hale ain't been here for mos' six months. I reckon he aint in this country now. I aint heard nothin' 'bout him for a long time."

June knew better than that—but she said nothing. She would rather have had even Harvey think that he was away. So she hurried to the hotel—she would have four hours to wait—and asked for the one room that had a bath attached— the room to which Hale had sent her when she had passed through on her way to New York. She almost winced when she looked in the mirror and saw the smoke stains about her pretty throat and ears, and she wondered if anybody could have noticed them on her way from the train. Her hands, too, were dreadful to look at and she hurried to take off her things.

In an hour she emerged freshened, immaculate from her crown of lovely hair to her smartly booted feet, and at once she went downstairs. She heard

the man, whom she passed, stop at the head of
them and turn to look down at her, and she saw
necks craned within the hotel office when she
passed the door. On the street not a man and
hardly a woman failed to look at her with wonder
and open admiration, for she was an apparition in
that little town and it all pleased her so much that
she became flushed and conscious and felt like a
queen who, unknown, moved among her subjects
and blessed them just with her gracious presence.
For she was unknown even by several people
whom she knew and that, too, pleased her—to
have bloomed so quite beyond their ken. She was
like a meteor coming back to dazzle the very world
from which it had flown for a while into space.
When she went into the dining-room for the mid-
day dinner, there was a movement in almost every
part of the room as though there were many there
who were on the lookout for her entrance. The
head waiter, a portly darky, lost his imperturbable
majesty for a moment in surprise at the vision
and then with a lordly yet obsequious wave of his
hand, led her to a table over in a corner where no
one was sitting. Four young men came in rather
boisterously and made for her table. She lifted her
calm eyes at them so haughtily that the one in
front halted with sudden embarrassment and
they all swerved to another table from which they
stared at her surreptitiously. Perhaps she was
mistaken for the comic-opera star whose brilliant

picture she had seen on a bill board in front of the "opera house." Well, she had the voice and she might have been and she might yet be—and if she were, this would be the distinction that would be shown her. And, still as it was she was greatly pleased.

At four o'clock she started for the hills. In half an hour she was dropping down a winding ravine along a rock-lashing stream with those hills so close to the car on either side that only now and then could she see the tops of them. Through the window the keen air came from the very lungs of them, freighted with the coolness of shadows, the scent of damp earth and the faint fragrance of wild flowers, and her soul leaped to meet them. The mountain sides were showered with pink and white laurel (she used to call it "ivy") and the rhododendrons (she used to call them "laurel") were just beginning to blossom—they were her old and fast friends—mountain, shadow, the wet earth and its pure breath, and tree, plant and flower; she had not forgotten them, and it was good to come back to them. Once she saw an overshot water-wheel on the bank of the rushing little stream and she thought of Uncle Billy; she smiled and the smile stopped short—she was going back to other things as well. The train had creaked by a log-cabin set in the hillside and then past another and another; and always there were two or three ragged children in the door and a haggard unkempt woman peering over their shoulders. How lonely those cabins looked and how desolate the life they suggested to her now— *now!* The first station she came to after the train had wound down the long ravine to the valley level again was crowded with mountaineers. There a wedding party got aboard with a great deal of laughter, chaffing and noise, and all three went on within and without the train while it was waiting. A sudden thought stunned her like a lightning stroke. They were *her* people out there on the platform and inside the car ahead—those rough men in slouch hats, jeans and cowhide boots, their mouths stained with tobacco juice, their cheeks and eyes on fire with moonshine, and those women in poke-bonnets with their sad, worn, patient faces on which the sympathetic good cheer and joy of the moment sat so strangely. She noticed their rough shoes and their homespun gowns that made their figures all alike and shapeless, with a vivid awakening of early memories. She might have been one of those narrow-lived girls outside, or that bride within had it not been for Jack— Hale. She finished the name in her own mind and she was conscious that she had. Ah, well, that was a long time ago and she was nothing but a child and she had thrown herself at his head. Perhaps it was different with him now and if it was, she would give him the chance to withdraw from everything. It would be right and fair and then life was so full for her now. She was dependent on nobody—on nothing. A rainbow spanned the heaven above her and the other end of it was not in the hills. But one end was and to that end she was on her way. She was going to just such people as she had seen at the station. Her father and her kinsmen were just such men—her step-mother and kinswomen were just such women. Her home was little more than just such a cabin as the desolate ones that stirred her pity when she swept by them. She thought of how she felt when she had first gone to Lonesome Cove after a few months at the Gap, and she shuddered to think how she would feel now. She was getting restless by this time and aimlessly she got up and walked to the front of the car and back again to her seat, hardly noticing that the other occupants were staring at her with some wonder. She sat down for a few minutes and then she went to the rear and stood outside on the platform, clutching a brass rod of the railing and looking back on the dropping darkness in which the hills seemed to be rushing together far behind as the train crashed on with its wake of spark-lit rolling smoke. A cinder stung her face, and when she lifted her hand to the spot, she saw that her glove was black with grime. With a little shiver of disgust she went back to her seat and with her face to the blackness rushing past her window she sat brooding—brooding. Why had Hale not met her? He had said he would and she had written him when she was coming and had telegraphed him at the station in New York when she started. Perhaps he *had* changed. She recalled that even his letters had grown less frequent, shorter, more hurried the past year—well, he should have his chance. Always, however, her mind kept going back to the people at the station and to her people in the mountains. They were the same, she kept repeating to herself—the very same and she was one of them. And always she kept thinking of her first trip to Lonesome Cove after her awakening and of what her next would be. That first time Hale had made her go back as she had left, in home-spun, sun-bonnet and brogans. There was the same reason why she should go back that way now as then—would Hale insist that she should now? She almost laughed aloud at the thought. She knew that she would refuse and she knew that his reason would not appeal to her now—she no longer cared what her neighbours and kinspeople might think and say. The porter paused at her seat.

"How much longer is it?" she asked.

"Half an hour, Miss."

June went to wash her face and hands, and when she came back to her seat a great glare shone through the windows on the other side of the car. It was the furnace, a "run" was on and she could see the streams of white molten metal racing down the narrow channels of sand to their narrow beds on either side. The whistle shrieked ahead for the Gap and she nerved herself with a prophetic sense of vague trouble at hand.

.   .   .   .

At the station Hale had paced the platform. He looked at his watch to see whether he might have time to run up to the furnace, half a mile away, and board the train there. He thought he had and he was about to start when the shriek of the coming engine rose beyond the low hills in Wild Cat Valley, echoed along Powell's Mountain and broke against the wrinkled breast of the Cumberland. On it came, and in plain sight it stopped suddenly to take water, and Hale cursed it silently and recalled viciously that when he was in a hurry to arrive anywhere, the water-tower was always on the wrong side of the station. He got so restless that he started for it on a run and he had gone hardly fifty yards before the train came on again and he had to run back to beat it to the station— where he sprang to the steps of the Pullman before it stopped—pushing the porter aside to find himself checked by the crowded passengers at the door. June was not among them and straightway he ran for the rear of the car.

June had risen. The other occupants of the car had crowded forward and she was the last of them. She had stood, during an irritating wait, at the water-tower, and now as she moved slowly forward again she heard the hurry of feet behind her and she turned to look into the eager, wondering eyes of John Hale.

"June!" he cried in amazement, but his face lighted with joy and he impulsively stretched out his arms as though he meant to take her in them, but as suddenly he dropped them before the startled look in her eyes, which, with one swift glance, searched him from head to foot. They shook hands almost gravely.

XXII

JUNE sat in the little dummy, the focus of curious eyes, while Hale was busy seeing that her baggage was got aboard. The checks that she gave him jingled in his hands like a bunch of keys, and he could hardly help grinning when he saw the huge trunks and the smart bags that were tumbled from the baggage car—all marked with her initials. There had been days when he had laid considerable emphasis on pieces like those, and when he thought of them overwhelming with opulent suggestions that debt-stricken little town, and, later, piled incongruously on the porch of the cabin on Lonesome Cove, he could have laughed aloud but for a nameless something that was gnawing savagely at his heart.

He felt almost shy when he went back into the car, and though June greeted him with a smile, her immaculate daintiness made him unconsciously sit quite far away from her. The little fairy-cross was still at her throat, but a tiny diamond gleamed from each end of it and from the centre, as from a tiny heart, pulsated the light of a little blood-red ruby. To him it meant the loss of June's simplicity and was the symbol of her new estate, but he smiled and forced himself into hearty cheerfulness of manner and asked her questions about her trip. But June answered in halting monosyllables, and talk was not easy between them. All the while he was watching her closely and not a movement of her eye, ear, mouth or hand—not an inflection of her voice—escaped him. He saw her sweep the car and its occupants with a glance, and he saw the results of that glance in her face and the down-dropping of her eyes to the dainty point of one boot. He saw her beautiful mouth close suddenly tight and her thin nostrils quiver disdainfully when a swirl of black smoke, heavy with cinders, came in with an entering passenger through the front door of the car. Two half-drunken men were laughing boisterously near that door and even her ears seemed trying to shut out their half-smothered rough talk. The car started with a bump that swayed her toward him, and when she caught the seat with one hand, it checked as suddenly, throwing her the other way, and then with a leap it sprang ahead again, giving a nagging snap to her head. Her whole face grew red with vexation and shrinking distaste, and all the while, when the little train steadied into its creaking, puffing, jostling way, one gloved hand on the chased silver handle of her smart little umbrella kept nervously swaying it to and fro on its steel-shod point, until she saw that the point was in a tiny pool of tobacco juice, and then she laid it across her lap with shuddering swiftness.

At first Hale thought that she had shrunk from kissing him in the car because other people were around. He knew better now. At that moment he was as rough and dirty as the chain-carrier opposite him, who was just in from a surveying expedition in the mountains, as the sooty brakeman who came through to gather up the fares—as one of those good-natured, profane inebriates up in the corner. No, it was not publicity—she had shrunk from him as she was shrinking now from black smoke, rough men, the shaking of the train —the little pool of tobacco juice at her feet. The truth began to glimmer through his brain. He understood, even when she leaned forward suddenly to look into the mouth of the gap, that was now dark with shadows. Through that gap lay her way and she thought him now more a part of what was beyond than she who had been born of it was, and dazed by the thought, he wondered if he might not really be. At once he straightened in his seat, and his mind made up, as he always made it up—swiftly. He had not explained why he had not met her that morning, nor had he apologized for his rough garb, because he was so glad to see her and because there were so many other things he wanted to say; and when he saw her, conscious and resentful, perhaps, that he had not done these things at once—he deliberately declined to do them now. He became silent, but he grew more courteous, more thoughtful—watchful.

She was very tired, poor child; there were deep shadows under her eyes which looked weary and almost mournful. So, when with a clanging of the engine bell they stopped at the brilliantly lit hotel, he led her at once upstairs to the parlour, and from there sent her up to her room, which was ready for her.

"You must get a good sleep," he said kindly, and with his usual firmness that was wont to preclude argument. "You are worn to death. I'll have your supper sent to your room." The girl felt the subtle change in his manner and her lip quivered for a vague reason that neither knew, but, without a word, she obeyed him like a child. He did not try again to kiss her. He merely took her hand, placed his left over it, and with a gentle pressure, said:

"Good-night, little girl."

"Good-night," she faltered.

．　．　．　．　．　．　．

Resolutely, relentlessly, first, Hale cast up his accounts, liabilities, resources, that night, to see what, under the least favourable outcome, the balance left to him would be. Nearly all was gone. His securities were already sold. His lots would not bring at public sale one-half of the deferred payments yet to be made on them, and if the company brought suit, as it was threatening to do, he would be left fathoms deep in debt. The branch railroad had not come up the river toward Lonesome Cove, and now he meant to build barges and float his cannel coal down to the main line, for his sole hope was in the mine in Lonesome Cove. The means that he could command were meagre, but they would carry his purpose with June for a year at least and then—who knew?—he might, through that mine, be on his feet again.

The little town was dark and asleep when he stepped into the cool night-air and made his way past the old school-house and up Imboden Hill. He could see—all shining silver in the moonlight —the still crest of the big beech at the blessed roots of which his lips had met June's in the first kiss that had passed between them. On he went through the shadowy aisle that the path made between other beech-trunks, harnessed by the moonlight with silver armour and motionless as sentinels on watch till dawn, out past the amphitheatre of darkness from which the dead trees tossed out their crooked arms as though voicing silently now his own soul's torment, and then on to the point of the spur of foot-hills where, with the mighty mountains encircling him and the world, a dreamland lighted only by stars, he stripped his soul before the Maker of it and of him and fought his fight out alone.

His was the responsibility for all—his alone. No one else was to blame—June not at all. He had taken her from her own life—had swerved her from the way to which God pointed when she was born. He had given her everything she wanted, had allowed her to do what she pleased and had let her think that, through his miraculous handling of her resources, she was doing it all herself. And the result was natural. For the past two years he had been harassed with debt, racked with worries, writhing this way and that, concerned only with the soul-tormenting catastrophe that had overtaken him. About all else he had grown careless. He had not been to see her the last year, he had written seldom, and it appalled him to look back now on his own self-absorption and to think how he must have appeared to June. And he had gone on in that self-absorption to the very end. He had got his license to marry, had asked Uncle Billy, who was magistrate as well as miller, to marry them, and, a rough mountaineer himself to the outward eye, he had appeared to lead a child like a lamb to the sacrifice and had found a woman with a mind, heart and purpose of her own. It was all his work. He had sent her away to fit her for his station in life—to make her fit to marry him. She had risen above and now *he was not fit to marry her.* That was the brutal truth—a truth that was enough to make a wise man laugh or a fool weep, and Hale did neither. He simply went on working to make out how he could best discharge the obligations that he had voluntarily, willingly, gladly, selfishly even, assumed. In his mind he treated conditions only as he saw and felt them and believed them at that moment true: and into the problem he went no deeper than to find his simple duty, and that, while the morning stars were sinking, he found. And it was a duty the harder to find because everything had reawakened within him, and the starting-point of that awakening was the proud glow in Uncle Billy's kind old face, when he knew the part he was to play in the happiness of Hale and June. All the way over the mountain that day his heart had gathered fuel from memories at the big Pine, and down the mountain and through the gap, to be set aflame by the yellow sunlight in the valley and the throbbing life in everything that was alive. for the month was June and the spirit of that month was on her way to him. So when he rose now, with back-thrown head, he stretched his arms suddenly out toward those far-seeing stars, and as suddenly dropped them with an angry shake of his head and one quick gritting of his teeth that such a thought should have mastered him even for one swift second—the thought of how lonesome would be the trail that would be his to follow after that day.

XXIII

JUNE, tired though she was, tossed restlessly that night. The one look she had seen in Hale's face when she met him in the car, told her the truth as far as he was concerned. He was unchanged, she could give him no chance to withdraw from their long understanding, for it was plain to her quick instinct that he wanted none. And so she had asked him no question about his failure to meet her, for she knew now that his reason, no matter what, was good. He had startled her in the car, for her mind was heavy with memories of the poor little cabins she had passed on the train, of the mountain men and women in the wedding-party, and Hale himself was to the eye so much like one of them—had so startled her that, though she knew that his instinct, too, was at work, she could not gather herself together to combat her own feelings, for every little happening in the dummy but drew her back to her previous train of painful thought. And in that helplessness she had told Hale good-night. She remembered now how she had looked upon Lonesome Cove after she went to the Gap; how she had looked upon the Gap after her year in the

Bluegrass, and how she had looked back even on the first big city she had seen there from the lofty vantage ground of New York. What was the use of it all? Why laboriously climb a hill merely to see and yearn for things that you cannot have, if you must go back and live in the hollow again? Well, she thought rebelliously, she would not go back to the hollow again—that was all. She knew what was coming and her cousin Dave's perpetual sneer sprang suddenly from the past to cut through her again and the old pride rose within her once more. She was good enough now for Hale, oh, yes, she thought bitterly, good enough *now;* and then, remembering his life-long kindness and thinking what she might have been but for him, she burst into tears at the unworthiness of her own thought. Ah, what should she do—what should she do? Repeating that question over and over again, she fell toward morning into troubled sleep. She did not wake until nearly noon, for already she had formed the habit of sleeping late— late at least, for that part of the world—and she was glad when the negro boy brought her word that Mr. Hale had been called up the valley and would not be back until the afternoon. She dreaded to meet him, for she knew that he had seen the trouble within her and she knew he was not the kind of man to let matters drag vaguely, if they could be cleared up and settled by open frankness of discussion, no matter how blunt he must be. She had to wait until mid-day dinner time for something to eat, so she lay abed, picked a breakfast from the menu, which was spotted, dirty and meagre in offerings, and had it brought to her room. Early in the afternoon she issued forth into the sunlight, and started toward Imboden Hill. It was very beautiful and soul-comforting—the warm air, the luxuriantly wooded hills, with their shades of green that told her where poplar and oak and beech and maple grew, the delicate haze of blue that overlay them and deepened as her eyes followed the still mountain piles north-eastward to meet the big range that shut her in from the outer world. The changes had been many. One part of the town had been wiped out by fire and a few buildings of stone had risen up. On the street she saw strange faces, but now and then she stopped to shake hands with somebody whom she knew, and who recognized her always with surprise and spoke but few words, and then, as she thought, with some embarrassment. Half unconsciously she turned toward the old mill. There it was, dusty and gray, and the dripping old wheel creaked with its weight of shining water, and the muffled roar of the unseen dam started an answering stream of memories surging within her. She could see the window of her room in the old brick boarding-house, and as she passed the gate, she almost stopped to go in, but the face of a strange man who stood in the door with a proprietary air deterred her. There was Hale's little frame cottage and his name, half washed out, was over the wing that was still his office. Past that she went, with a passing temptation to look within, and toward the old school-house. A massive new one was half built, of gray stone, to the left, but the old one, with its shingles on the outside that had once caused her such wonder, still lay warm in the sun, but closed and deserted. There was the play-ground where she had been caught in "Ring around the Rosy," and Hale and that girl teacher had heard her confession. She flushed again when she thought of that day, but the flush was now for another reason. Over the roof of the school-house she could see the beech tree where she had built her playhouse, and memory led her from the path toward it. She had not climbed a hill for a long time and she was panting when she reached it. There was the scattered playhouse—it might have lain there untouched for a quarter of a century—just as her angry feet had kicked it to pieces. On a root of the beech she sat down and the broad rim of her hat scratched the trunk of it and annoyed her, so she took it off and leaned her head against the tree, looking up into the underworld of leaves through which a sunbeam filtered here and there—one striking her hair which had darkened to a duller gold—striking it eagerly, unerringly, as though it had started for just such a shining mark. Below her was outspread the little

273

town—the straggling, wretched little town—crude, lonely, lifeless! She could not be happy in Lonesome Cove after she had known the Gap, and now her horizon had so broadened that she felt now toward the Gap and its people as she had then felt toward the mountaineers: for the standards of living in the Cove—so it seemed—were no farther below the standards in the Gap than they in turn were lower than the new standards to which she had adapted herself while away. Indeed, even that Bluegrass world where she had spent a year was too narrow now for her vaulting ambition, and with that thought she looked down again on the little town, a lonely island in a sea of mountains and as far from the world for which she had been training herself as though it were in mid-ocean. Live down there? She shuddered at the thought and straightway was very miserable. The clear piping of a wood-thrush rose far away, a tear started between her half-closed lashes and she might have gone to weeping silently, had her ear not caught the sound of something moving below her. Some one was coming that way, so she brushed her eyes swiftly with her handkerchief and stood upright against the tree. And there again Hale found her, tense, upright, bareheaded again and her hands behind her; only her face was not uplifted and dreaming—it was turned toward him, unstartled and expectant. He stopped below her and leaned one shoulder against a tree.

274

"I saw you pass the office," he said, "and I thought I should find you here."

His eyes dropped to the scattered playhouse of long ago—and a faint smile that was full of submerged sadness passed over his face. It was his playhouse, after all, that she had kicked to pieces. But he did not mention it—nor her attitude—nor did he try, in any way, to arouse her memories of that other time at this same place.

"I want to talk with you, June—and I want to talk now."

"Yes, Jack," she said tremulously.

For a moment he stood in silence, his face half-turned, his teeth hard on his indrawn lip—thinking. There was nothing of the mountaineer about him now. He was clean-shaven and dressed with care—June saw that—but he looked quite old, his face seemed harried with worries and ravaged by suffering, and June had suddenly to swallow a quick surging of pity for him. He spoke slowly and without looking at her:

"June, if it hadn't been for me, you would be over in Lonesome Cove and happily married by this time, or at least contented with your life, for you wouldn't have known any other."

"I don't know, Jack."

"I took you out—and it rests with you whether I shall be sorry I did—sorry wholly on your account, I mean," he added hastily.

She knew what he meant and she said nothing

—she only turned her head away slightly, with her eyes upturned a little toward the leaves that were shaking like her own heart.

"I think I see it all very clearly," he went on, in a low and perfectly even voice. "You can't be happy over there now—you can't be happy over here now. You've got other wishes, ambitions, dreams, now, and I want you to realize them, and I want to help you to realize them all I can—that's all."

"Jack!—" she helplessly, protestingly spoke his name in a whisper, but that was all she could do, and he went on:

"It isn't so strange. What is strange is that I— that I didn't foresee it all. But if I had," he added firmly, "I'd have done it just the same— unless by doing it I've really done you more harm than good."

"No—no—Jack!"

"I came into your world—you went into mine. What I had grown indifferent about—you grew to care about. You grew sensitive while I was growing callous to certain—" he was about to say "surface things," but he checked himself—"certain things in life that mean more to a woman than to a man. I would not have married you as you were—I've got to be honest now—at least I thought it necessary that you should be otherwise —and now you have gone beyond me, and now you do not want to marry me as I am. And it is

276

all very natural and very just." Very slowly her head had dropped until her chin rested hard above the little jewelled cross on her breast.

"You must tell me if I am wrong. You don't love me now—well enough to be happy with me here"—he waved one hand toward the straggling little town below them and then toward the lonely mountains—"I did not know that we would have to live here—but I know it now—" he checked himself, and afterward she recalled the tone of those last words, but then they had no especial significance.

"Am I wrong?" he repeated, and then he said hurriedly, for her face was so piteous—"No, you needn't give yourself the pain of saying it in words. I want you to know that I understand that there is nothing in the world I blame you for —nothing—nothing. If there is any blame at all, it rests on me alone." She broke toward him with a cry then.

"No—no, Jack," she said brokenly, and she caught his hand in both her own and tried to raise it to her lips, but he held her back and she put her face on his breast and sobbed heart-brokenly. He waited for the paroxysm to pass, stroking her hair gently.

"You mustn't feel that way, little girl. You can't help it—I can't help it—and these things happen all the time, everywhere. You don't have to stay here. You can go away and study, and

277

when I can, I'll come to see you and cheer you up; and when you are a great singer, I'll send you flowers and be so proud of you, and I'll say to myself, 'I helped do that.' Dry your eyes, now. You must go back to the hotel. Your father will be there by this time and you'll have to be starting home pretty soon."

Like a child she obeyed him, but she was so weak and trembling that he put his arm about her to help her down the hill. At the edge of the woods she stopped and turned full toward him.

"You are so good," she said tremulously, "so good. Why, you haven't even asked me if there was another——"

Hale interrupted her, shaking his head.

"If there is, I don't want to know."

"But there isn't, there isn't!" she cried, "I don't know what is the matter with me. I hate——" the tears started again, and again she was on the point of breaking down, but Hale checked her.

"Now, now," he said soothingly, "you mustn't, now—that's all right. You mustn't." Her anger at herself helped now.

"Why, I stood like a silly fool, tongue-tied, and I wanted to say so much. I——"

"You don't need to," Hale said gently, "I understand it all. I understand."

"I believe you do," she said with a sob, "better than I do."

"Well, it's all right, little girl. Come on."

278

They issued forth into the sunlight and Hale walked rapidly. The strain was getting too much for him and he was anxious to be alone. Without a word more they passed the old school-house, the massive new one, and went on, in silence, down the street. Hitched to a post, near the hotel, were two gaunt horses with drooping heads, and on one of them was a side-saddle. Sitting on the steps of the hotel, with a pipe in his mouth, was the mighty figure of Devil Judd Tolliver. He saw them coming—at least he saw Hale coming, and that far away Hale saw his bushy eyebrows lift in wonder at June. A moment later he rose to his great height without a word.

"Dad," said June in a trembling voice, "don't you know me?" The old man stared at her silently and a doubtful smile played about his bearded lips.

"Hardly, but I reckon hit's June."

She knew that the world to which Hale belonged would expect her to kiss him, and she made a movement as though she would, but the habit of a lifetime is not broken so easily. She held out her hand, and with the other patted him on the arm as she looked up into his face.

"Time to be goin', June, if we want to get home afore dark!"

"All right, Dad."

The old man turned to his horse.

"Hurry up, little gal."

In a few mniutes they were ready, and the girl looked long into Hale's face when he took her hand.

"You are coming over soon?"

"Just as soon as I can." Her lips trembled.

"Good-by," she faltered.

"Good-by, June," said Hale.

From the steps he watched them—the giant father slouching in his saddle and the trim figure of the now sadly misplaced girl, erect on the awk-ward-pacing mountain beast—as incongruous, the two, as a fairy on some prehistoric monster. A horseman was coming up the street behind him and a voice called:

"Who's that?" Hale turned—it was the Honourable Samuel Budd, coming home from Court.

"June Tolliver."

"June Taliaferro," corrected the Hon. Sam with emphasis.

"The same." The Hon. Sam silently followed the pair for a moment through his big goggles.

"What do you think of my theory of the latent possibilities of the mountaineer—now?"

"I think I know how true it is better than you do," said Hale calmly, and with a grunt the Hon. Sam rode on. Hale watched them as they rode across the plateau—watched them until the Gap swallowed them up and his heart ached for June. Then he went to his room and there, stretched out on his bed and with his hands clenched behind his head, he lay staring upward.

.   .   .   .

Devil Judd Tolliver had lost none of his taciturnity. Stolidly, silently, he went ahead, as is the custom of lordly man in the mountains— horseback or afoot—asking no questions, answering June's in the fewest words possible. Uncle Billy, the miller, had been complaining a good deal that spring, and old Hon had rheumatism. Uncle Billy's old-maid sister, who lived on Devil's Fork, had been cooking for him at home since the last taking to bed of June's step-mother. Bub had "growed up" like a hickory sapling. Her cousin Loretta hadn't married, and some folks allowed she'd run away some day yet with young Buck Falin. Her cousin Dave had gone off to school that year, had come back a month before, and been shot through the shoulder. He was in Lonesome Cove now.

This fact was mentioned in the same matter-of-fact way as the other happenings. Hale had been raising Cain in Lonesome Cove—"A-cuttin' things down an' tearin' 'em up an' playin' hell ginerally."

The feud had broken out again and maybe June couldn't stay at home long. He didn't want her there with the fighting going on—whereat June's heart gave a start of gladness that the way would be easy for her to leave when she wished to leave. Things over at the Gap "was agoin' to perdition," the old man had been told, while he was waiting for June and Hale that day, and Hale had not only lost a lot of money, but if things didn't take a rise, he would be left head over heels in debt, if that mine over in Lonesome Cove didn't pull him out.

They were approaching the big Pine now, and June was beginning to ache and get sore from the climb. So Hale was in trouble—that was what he meant when he said that, though she could leave the mountains when she pleased, he must stay there, perhaps for good.

"I'm mighty glad you come home, gal," said the old man, "an' that ye air goin' to put an end to all this spendin' o' so much money. Jack says you got some money left, but I don't understand it. He says he made a 'investment' fer ye and tribbled the money. I haint never axed him no questions. Hit was betwixt you an' him, an' 'twant none o' my business long as you an' him air goin' to marry. He said you was goin' to marry this summer an' I wish you'd git tied up right away whilst I'm livin', fer I don't know when a Winchester might take me off an' I'd die a sight easier if I knowed you was tied up with a good man like him."

"Yes, Dad," was all she said, for she had not the heart to tell him the truth, and she knew that Hale never would until the last moment he must, when he learned that she had failed.

Half an hour later, she could see the stone chimney of the little cabin in Lonesome Cove. A little farther down several spirals of smoke were visible—rising from unseen houses which were more miners' shacks, her father said, that Hale had put up while she was gone. The water of the creek was jet black now. A row of rough wooden houses ran along its edge. The geese cackled a doubtful welcome. A new dog leaped barking from the porch and a tall boy sprang after him—both running for the gate.

"Why, Bub," cried June, sliding from her horse and kissing him, and then holding him off at arms' length to look into his steady gray eyes and his blushing face.

"Take the horses, Bub," said old Judd, and June entered the gate while Bub stood with the reins in his hand, still speechlessly staring her over from head to foot. There was her garden, thank God—with all her flowers planted, a new bed of pansies and one of violets and the border of laurel in bloom—unchanged and weedless.

"One o' Jack Hale's men takes keer of it," explained old Judd, and again, with shame, June felt the hurt of her lover's thoughtfulness. When she entered the cabin, the same old rasping petulant voice called her from a bed in one corner, and when June took the shrivelled old hand that was limply thrust from the bed-clothes, the old hag's keen eyes swept her from head to foot with disapproval.

"My, but you air wearin' mighty fine clothes," she croaked enviously. "I ain't had a new dress fer more'n five year;" and that was the welcome she got.

"No?" said June appeasingly. "Well, I'll get one for you myself."

"I'm much obleeged," she whined, "but I reckon I can git along."

A cough came from the bed in the other corner of the room.

"That's Dave," said the old woman, and June walked over to where her cousin's black eyes shone hostile at her from the dark.

"I'm sorry, Dave," she said, but Dave answered nothing but a sullen "howdye" and did not put out a hand—he only stared at her in sulky bewilderment, and June went back to listen to the torrent of the old woman's plaints until Bub came in. Then as she turned, she noticed for the first time that a new door had been cut in one side of the cabin, and Bub was following the direction of her eyes.

"Why, haint nobody told ye?" he said delightedly.

"Told me what, Bub?"

With a whoop Bud leaped for the side of the door and, reaching up, pulled a shining key from between the logs and thrust it into her hands.

"Go ahead," he said. "Hit's yourn."

"Some more o' Jack Hale's fool doin's," said the old woman. "Go on, gal, and see whut he's done."

With eager hands she put the key in the lock and when she pushed open the door, she gasped. Another room had been added to the cabin—and the fragrant smell of cedar made her nostrils dilate. Bub pushed by her and threw open the shutters of a window to the low sunlight, and June stood with both hands to her head. It was a room for her—with a dresser, a long mirror, a modern bed in one corner, a work-table with a student's lamp on it, a wash-stand and a chest of drawers and a piano! On the walls were pictures and over the mantel stood the one she had first learned to love—two lovers clasped in each other's arms and under them the words *"Enfin Seul."*

"Oh-oh," was all she could say, and choking, she motioned Bub from the room. When the door closed, she threw herself sobbing across the bed.

Over at the Gap that night Hale sat in his office with a piece of white paper and a lump of black coal on the table in front of him. His foreman had brought the coal to him that day at dusk. He lifted the lump to the light of his lamp, and from the centre of it a mocking evil eye leered back at him. The eye was a piece of shining black flint and told him that his mine in Lonesome Cove was but a pocket of cannel coal and worth no more than the smouldering lumps in his grate. Then he lifted the piece of white paper—it was his license to marry June.

XXIV

VERY slowly June walked up the little creek to the old log where she had lain so many happy hours. There was no change in leaf, shrub or tree, and not a stone in the brook had been disturbed. The sun dropped the same arrows down through the leaves—blunting their shining points into tremulous circles on the ground, the water sang the same happy tune under her dangling feet and a wood-thrush piped the old lay overhead.

Wood-thrush! June smiled as she suddenly rechristened the bird for herself now. That bird henceforth would be the Magic Flute to musical June—and she leaned back with ears, eyes and soul awake and her brain busy.

All the way over the mountain, on that second home-going, she had thought of the first, and even memories of the memories aroused by that first home-going came back to her—the place where Hale had put his horse into a dead run and had given her that never-to-be-forgotten thrill, and where she had slid from behind to the ground and stormed with tears. When they dropped down into the green gloom of shadow and green leaves toward Lonesome Cove, she had the same feeling that her heart was being clutched by a human hand and that black night had suddenly fallen about her, but this time she knew what it meant. She thought then of the crowded sleeping-room, the rough beds and coarse blankets at home; the oil-cloth, spotted with drippings from a candle, that covered the table; the thick plates and cups; the soggy bread and the thick bacon floating in grease; the absence of napkins, the eating with knives and fingers and the noise Bub and her father made drinking their coffee. But then she knew all these things in advance, and the memories of them on her way over had prepared her for Lonesome Cove. The conditions were definite there: she knew what it would be to face them again—she was facing them all the way, and to her surprise the realities had hurt her less even than they had before. Then had come the same thrill over the garden, and now with that garden and her new room and her piano and her books, with Uncle Billy's sister to help do the work, and with the little changes that June was daily making in the household, she could live her own life even over there as long as she pleased, and then she would go out into the world again.

But all the time when she was coming over from the Gap, the way had bristled with accusing memories of Hale—even from the chattering creeks, the turns in the road, the sun-dappled bushes and trees and flowers; and when she passed the big Pine that rose with such friendly solemnity above her, the pang of it all hurt her heart and kept on hurting her. When she walked in the garden, the flowers seemed not to have the same spirit of gladness. It had been a dry season and they drooped for that reason, but the melancholy of them had a sympathetic human quality that depressed her. If she saw a bass shoot arrow-like into deep water, if she heard a bird or saw a tree or a flower whose name she had to recall, she thought of Hale. Do what she would, she could not escape the ghost that stalked at her side everywhere, so like a human presence that she felt sometimes a strange desire to turn and speak to it. And in her room that presence was all-pervasive. The piano, the furniture, the bits of bric-a-brac, the pictures and books—all were eloquent with his thought of her—and every night before she turned out her light she could not help lifting her eyes to her once-favourite picture—even that Hale had remembered—the lovers clasped in each other's arms—"At Last Alone"—only to see it now as a mocking symbol of his beaten hopes. She had written to thank him for it all, and not yet had he answered her letter. He had said that he was coming over to Lonesome Cove and he had not come—why should he, on her account? Between them all was over—why should he? The question was absurd in her mind, and yet the fact that she had expected him, that she so *wanted*

288

him, was so illogical and incongruous and vividly true that it raised her to a sitting posture on the log, and she ran her fingers over her forehead and down her dazed face until her chin was in the hollow of her hand, and her startled eyes were fixed unwaveringly on the running water and yet not seeing it at all. A call—her step-mother's cry—rang up the ravine and she did not hear it. She did not even hear Bub coming through the underbrush a few minutes later, and when he half angrily shouted her name at the end of the vista, down-stream, whence he could see her, she lifted her head from a dream so deep that in it all her senses had for the moment been wholly lost.

"Come on," he shouted.

She had forgotten—there was a "bean-stringing" at the house that day—and she slipped slowly off the log and went down the path, gathering herself together as she went, and making no answer to the indignant Bub who turned and stalked ahead of her back to the house. At the barnyard gate her father stopped her—he looked worried.

"Jack Hale's jus' been over hyeh." June caught her breath sharply.

"Has he gone?" The old man was watching her and she felt it.

"Yes, he was in a hurry an' nobody knowed whar you was. He jus' come over, he said, to tell

me to tell you that you could go back to New York
and keep on with yo' singin' doin's whenever you
please. He knowed I didn't want you hyeh when
this war starts fer a finish as hit's goin' to, mighty
soon now. He says he ain't quite ready to git married yit. I'm afeerd he's in trouble."

"Trouble?"

"I tol' you t'other day—he's lost all his money;
but he says you've got enough to keep you goin'
fer some time. I don't see why you don't git married right now and live over at the Gap."

June coloured and was silent.

"Oh," said the old man quickly, "you ain't
ready nuther,"—he studied her with narrowing
eyes and through a puzzled frown—"but I reckon
hit's all right, if you air goin' to git married some
time."

"What's all right, Dad?" The old man
checked himself:

"Ever' thing," he said shortly, "but don't you
make a fool of yo'self with a good man like Jack
Hale." And, wondering, June was silent. The
truth was that the old man had wormed out of
Hale an admission of the kindly duplicity the latter had practised on him and on June, and he had
given his word to Hale that he would not tell June.
He did not understand why Hale should have so
insisted on that promise, for it was all right that
Hale should openly do what he pleased for the
girl he was going to marry—but he had given his

word: so he turned away, but his frown stayed where it was.

June went on, puzzled, for she knew that her father was withholding something, and she knew, too, that he would tell her only in his own good time. But she could go away when she pleased—that was the comfort—and with the thought she stopped suddenly at the corner of the garden. She could see Hale on his big black horse climbing the spur. Once it had always been his custom to stop on top of it to rest his horse and turn to look back at her, and she always waited to wave him good-by. She wondered if he would do it now, and while she looked and waited, the beating of her heart quickened nervously; but he rode straight on, without stopping or turning his head, and June felt strangely bereft and resentful, and the comfort of the moment before was suddenly gone. She could hear the voices of the guests in the porch around the corner of the house—there was an ordeal for her around there, and she went on. Loretta and Loretta's mother were there, and old Hon and several wives and daughters of Tolliver adherents from up Deadwood Creek and below Uncle Billy's mill. June knew that the "bean-stringing" was simply an excuse for them to be there, for she could not remember that so many had ever gathered there before—at that function in the spring, at corn-cutting in the autumn, or sorghum-making time or at log-raisings or quilting parties, and she well knew the motive of these many and the curiosity of all save, perhaps, Loretta and the old miller's wife: and June was prepared for them. She had borrowed a gown from her stepmother—a purple creation of home-spun—she had shaken down her beautiful hair and drawn it low over her brows, and arranged it behind after the fashion of mountain women, and when she went up the steps of the porch she was outwardly to the eye one of them except for the leathern belt about her slenderly full waist, her black silk stockings and the little "furrin" shoes on her dainty feet. She smiled inwardly when she saw the same old wave of disappointment sweep across the faces of them all. It was not necessary to shake hands, but unthinkingly she did, and the women sat in their chairs as she went from one to the other and each gave her a limp hand and a grave "howdye," though each paid an unconscious tribute to a vague something about her, by wiping that hand on an apron first. Very quietly and naturally she took a low chair, piled beans in her lap and, as one of them, went to work. Nobody looked at her at first until old Hon broke the silence.

"You haint lost a spec o' yo' good looks, Juny."

June laughed without a flush—she would have reddened to the roots of her hair two years before.

"I'm feelin' right peart, thank ye," she said, dropping consciously into the vernacular; but there was a something in her voice that was vaguely felt by all as a part of the universal strangeness that was in her erect bearing, her proud head, her deep eyes that looked so straight into their own— a strangeness that was in that belt and those stockings and those shoes, inconspicuous as they were, to which she saw every eye in time covertly wandering as to tangible symbols of a mystery that was beyond their ken. Old Hon and the step-mother alone talked at first, and the others, even Loretta, said never a word.

"Jack Hale must have been in a mighty big hurry," quavered the old step-mother. "June ain't goin' to be with us long, I'm afeerd:" and, without looking up, June knew the wireless significance of the speech was going around from eye to eye, but calmly she pulled her thread through a green pod and said calmly, with a little enigmatical shake of her head:

"I—don't know—I don't know."

Young Dave's mother was encouraged and all her efforts at good-humour could not quite draw the sting of a spiteful plaint from her voice.

"I reckon she'd never git away, if my boy Dave had the sayin' of it." There was a subdued titter at this, but Bub had come in from the stable and had dropped on the edge of the porch. He broke in hotly:

"You jest let June alone, Aunt Tilly, you'll have yo' hands full if you keep yo' eye on Loretty thar."

Already when somebody was saying something about the feud, as June came around the corner, her quick eye had seen Loretta bend her head swiftly over her work to hide the flush of her face. Now Loretta turned scarlet as the step-mother spoke severely:

"You hush, Bub," and Bub rose and stalked into the house. Aunt Tilly was leaning back in her chair—gasping—and consternation smote the group. June rose suddenly with her string of dangling beans.

"I haven't shown you my room, Loretty. Don't you want to see it? Come on, all of you," she added to the girls, and they and Loretta with one swift look of gratitude rose shyly and trooped shyly within where they looked in wide-mouthed wonder at the marvellous things that room contained. The older women followed to share sight of the miracle, and all stood looking from one thing to another, some with their hands behind them as though to thwart the temptation to touch, and all saying merely:

"My! My!"

None of them had ever seen a piano before and June must play the "shiny contraption" and sing a song. It was only curiosity and astonishment that she evoked when her swift fingers began running over the keys from one end of the board to the other, astonishment at the gymnastic quality of the performance, and only astonishment when her lovely voice set the very walls of the little room to vibrating with a dramatic love song that was about as intelligible to them as a problem in calculus, and June flushed and then smiled with quick understanding at the dry comment that rose from Aunt Tilly behind:

"She shorely can holler some!"

She couldn't play "Sourwood Mountain" on the piano—nor "Jinny git Aroun'," nor "Soapsuds over the Fence," but with a sudden inspiration she went back to an old hymn that they all knew, and at the end she won the tribute of an awed silence that made them file back to the beans on the porch. Loretta lingered a moment and when June closed the piano and the two girls went into the main room, a tall figure, entering, stopped in the door and stared at June without speaking:

"Why, howdye, Uncle Rufe," said Loretta. "This is June. You didn't know her, did ye?" The man laughed. Something in June's bearing made him take off his hat; he came forward to shake hands, and June looked up into a pair of bold black eyes that stirred within her again the vague fears of her childhood. She had been afraid of him when she was a child, and it was the old fear aroused that made her recall him by his eyes now. His beard was gone and he was much changed. She trembled when she shook hands with him and she did not call him by his name.

Old Judd came in, and a moment later the two men and Bub sat on the porch while the women worked, and when June rose again to go indoors, she felt the newcomer's bold eyes take her slowly in from head to foot and she turned crimson. This was the terror among the Tollivers—Bad Rufe, come back from the West to take part in the feud. *He* saw the belt and the stockings and the shoes, the white column of her throat and the proud set of her gold-crowned head; *he* knew what they meant, he made her feel that he knew, and later he managed to catch her eyes once with an amused, half-contemptuous glance at the simple untravelled folk about them, that said plainly how well he knew they two were set apart from them, and she shrank fearfully from the comradeship that the glance implied and would look at him no more. He knew everything that was going on in the mountains. He had come back "ready for business," he said. When he made ready to go, June went to her room and stayed there, but she heard him say to her father that he was going over to the Gap, and with a laugh that chilled her soul:

"I'm goin' over to kill me a policeman." And her father warned gruffly:

"You better keep away from thar. You don't understand them fellers." And she heard Rufe's brutal laugh again, and as he rode into the creek his horse stumbled and she saw him cut cruelly at the poor beast's ears with the rawhide quirt that he carried. She was glad when all went home, and the only ray of sunlight in the day for her radiated from Uncle Billy's face when, at sunset, he came to take old Hon home. The old miller was the one unchanged soul to her in that he was the one soul that could see no change in June. He called her "baby" in the old way, and he talked to her now as he had talked to her as a child. He took her aside to ask her if she knew that Hale had got his license to marry, and when she shook her head, his round, red face lighted up with the benediction of a rising sun:

"Well, that's what he's done, baby, an' he's axed me to marry ye," he added, with boyish pride, "he's axed *me*."

And June choked, her eyes filled, and she was dumb, but Uncle Billy could not see that it meant distress and not joy. He just put his arm around her and whispered:

"I ain't told a soul, baby—not a soul."

She went to bed and to sleep with Hale's face in the dream-mist of her brain, and Uncle Billy's, and the bold, black eyes of Bad Rufe Tolliver—all fused, blurred, indistinguishable. Then suddenly Rufe's words struck that brain, word by word, like the clanging terror of a frightened bell.

"I'm goin' to kill me a policeman." And with the last word, it seemed, she sprang upright in bed, clutching the coverlid convulsively. Daylight was showing gray through her window. She heard a swift step up the steps, across the porch, the rattle of the door-chain, her father's quick call, then the rumble of two men's voices, and she knew as well what had happened as though she had heard every word they uttered. Rufe had killed him a policeman—perhaps John Hale—and with terror clutching her heart she sprang to the floor, and as she dropped the old purple gown over her shoulders, she heard the scurry of feet across the back porch—feet that ran swiftly but cautiously, and left the sound of them at the edge of the woods. She heard the back door close softly, the creaking of the bed as her father lay down again, and then a sudden splashing in the creek. Kneeling at the window, she saw strange horsemen pushing toward the gate where one threw himself from his saddle, strode swiftly toward the steps, and her lips unconsciously made soft, little, inarticulate cries of joy—for the stern, gray face under the hat of the man was the face of John Hale. After him pushed other men—fully armed—whom he motioned to either side of the cabin to the rear. By his side was Bob Berkley, and behind him was a red-headed Falin whom she well remembered. Within twenty feet, she was looking into that gray face, when the set lips of it opened in a loud command:

"Hello!" She heard her father's bed creak again, again the rattle of the door-chain, and then old Judd stepped on the porch with a revolver in each hand.

"Hello!" he answered sternly.

"Judd," said Hale sharply—and June had never heard that tone from him before—"a man with a black moustache killed one of our men over in the Gap yesterday and we've tracked him over here. There's his horse—and we saw him go into that door. We want him."

"Do you know who the feller is?" asked old Judd calmly.

"No," said Hale quickly. And then, with equal calm:

"Hit was my brother," and the old man's mouth closed like a vise. Had the last word been a stone striking his ear, Hale could hardly have been more stunned. Again he called and almost gently:

"Watch the rear, there," and then gently he turned to Devil Judd.

"Judd, your brother shot a man at the Gap—without excuse or warning. He was an officer and a friend of mine, but if he were a stranger—we want him just the same. Is he here?"

Judd looked at the red-headed man behind Hale.

"So you're turned on the Falin side now, have ye?" he said contemptuously.

"Is he here?" repeated Hale.

"Yes, an' you can't have him." Without a move toward his pistol Hale stepped forward, and June saw her father's big right hand tighten on his huge pistol, and with a low cry she sprang to her feet.

"I'm an officer of the law," Hale said, "stand aside, Judd!" Bub leaped to the door with a Winchester—his eyes wild and his face white.

"Watch out, men!" Hale called, and as the men raised their guns there was a shriek inside the cabin and June stood at Bub's side, barefooted, her hair tumbled about her shoulders, and her hand clutching the little cross at her throat.

"Stop!" she shrieked. "He isn't here. He's— he's gone!" For a moment a sudden sickness smote Hale's face, then Devil Judd's ruse flashed to him and, wheeling, he sprang to the ground.

"Quick!" he shouted, with a sweep of his hand right and left. "Up those hollows! Lead those horses up to the Pine and wait. Quick!"

Already the men were running as he directed and Hale, followed by Bob and the Falin, rushed around the corner of the house. Old Judd's nostrils were quivering, and with his pistols dangling in his hands he walked to the gate, listening to the sounds of the pursuit.

"They'll never ketch him," he said, coming back, and then he dropped into a chair and sat in silence a long time. June reappeared, her face still white and her temples throbbing, for the sun was rising on days of darkness for her. Devil Judd did not even look at her.

"I reckon you ain't goin' to marry John Hale."

"No, Dad," said June.

XXV

THUS Fate did not wait until Election Day for the thing Hale most dreaded—a clash that would involve the guard in the Tolliver-Falin troubles over the hills. There had been simply a preliminary political gathering at the Gap the day before, but it had been a crucial day for the guard from a cloudy sunrise to a tragic sunset. Early that morning, Mockaby, the town-sergeant, had stepped into the street freshly shaven, with polished boots, and in his best clothes for the eyes of his sweetheart, who was to come up that day to the Gap from Lee. Before sunset he died with those boots on, while the sweetheart, unknowing, was bound on her happy way homeward, and Rufe Tolliver, who had shot Mockaby, was clattering through the Gap in flight for Lonesome Cove.

As far as anybody knew, there had been but one Tolliver and one Falin in town that day, though many had noticed the tall Western-looking stranger who, early in the afternoon, had ridden across the bridge over the North Fork, but he was quiet and well-behaved, he merged into the crowd and through the rest of the afternoon was in no way conspicuous, even when the one Tolliver and the one Falin got into a fight in front of the speaker's stand and the riot started which came near ending in a bloody battle. The Falin was clearly blameless and was let go at once. This angered the many friends of the Tolliver, and when he was arrested there was an attempt at rescue, and the Tolliver was dragged to the calaboose behind a slowly retiring line of policemen, who were jabbing the rescuers back with the muzzles of cocked Winchesters. It was just when it was all over, and the Tolliver was safely jailed, that Bad Rufe galloped up to the calaboose, shaking with rage, for he had just learned that the prisoner was a Tolliver. He saw how useless interference was, but he swung from his horse, threw the reins over its head after the Western fashion and strode up to Hale.

"You the captain of this guard?"

"Yes," said Hale; "and you?" Rufe shook his head with angry impatience, and Hale, thinking he had some communication to make, ignored his refusal to answer.

"I hear that a fellow can't blow a whistle or holler, or shoot off his pistol in this town without gittin' arrested."

"That's true—why?" Rufe's black eyes gleamed vindictively.

"Nothin'," he said, and he turned to his horse.

Ten minutes later, as Mockaby was passing

down the dummy track, a whistle was blown on the river bank, a high yell was raised, a pistol shot quickly followed and he started for the sound of them on a run. A few minutes later three more pistol shots rang out, and Hale rushed to the river bank to find Mockaby stretched out on the ground, dying, and a mountaineer lout pointing after a man on horseback, who was making at a swift gallop for the mouth of the gap and the hills.

"He done it," said the lout in a frightened way; "but I don't know who he was."

Within half an hour ten horsemen were clattering after the murderer, headed by Hale, Logan, and the Infant of the Guard. Where the road forked, a woman with a child in her arms said she had seen a tall, black-eyed man with a black moustache gallop up the right fork. She no more knew who he was than any of the pursuers. Three miles up that fork they came upon a red-headed man leading his horse from a mountaineer's yard.

"He went up the mountain," the red-haired man said, pointing to the trail of the Lonesome Pine. "He's gone over the line. Whut's he done—killed somebody?"

"Yes," said Hale shortly, starting up his horse.

"I wish I'd a-knowed you was atter him. I'm sheriff over thar."

Now they were without warrant or requisition, and Hale, pulling in, said sharply:

"We want that fellow. He killed a man at the Gap. If we catch him over the line, we want you to hold him for us. Come along!" The red-headed sheriff sprang on his horse and grinned eagerly:

"I'm your man."

"Who was that fellow?" asked Hale as they galloped. The sheriff denied knowledge with a shake of his head.

"What's your name?" The sheriff looked sharply at him for the effect of his answer.

"Jim Falin." And Hale looked sharply back at him. He was one of the Falins who long, long ago had gone to the Gap for young Dave Tolliver, and now the Falin grinned at Hale.

"I know you—all right." No wonder the Falin chuckled at this Heaven-born chance to get a Tolliver into trouble.

At the Lonesome Pine the traces of the fugitive's horse swerved along the mountain top—the shoe of the right forefoot being broken in half. That swerve was a blind and the sheriff knew it, but he knew where Rufe Tolliver would go and that there would be plenty of time to get him. Moreover, he had a purpose of his own and a secret fear that it might be thwarted, so, without a word, he followed the trail till darkness hid it and they had to wait until the moon rose. Then as they started again, the sheriff said:

"Wait a minute," and plunged down the mountain side on foot. A few minutes later he hallooed for Hale, and down there showed him the tracks doubling backward along a foot-path.

"Regular rabbit, ain't he?" chuckled the sheriff, and back they went to the trail again on which two hundred yards below the Pine they saw the tracks pointing again to Lonesome Cove.

On down the trail they went, and at the top of the spur that overlooked Lonesome Cove, the Falin sheriff pulled in suddenly and got off his horse. There the tracks swerved again into the bushes.

"He's goin' to wait till daylight, fer fear somebody's follered him. He'll come in back o' Devil Judd's."

"How do you know he's going to Devil Judd's?" asked Hale.

"Whar else would he go?" asked the Falin with a sweep of his arm toward the moonlit wilderness. "Thar ain't but one house that way fer ten miles —and nobody lives thar."

"How do you know that he's going to any house?" asked Hale impatiently. "He may be getting out of the mountains."

"D'you ever know a feller to leave these mountains jus' because he'd killed a man? How'd you foller him at night? How'd you ever ketch him with his start? What'd he turn that way fer, if he wasn't goin' to Judd's—why d'n't he keep on down the river? If he's gone, he's gone. If he ain't, he'll be at Devil Judd's at daybreak if he ain't thar now."

"What do you want to do?"

"Go on down with the hosses, hide 'em in the bushes an' wait."

"Maybe he's already heard us coming down the mountain."

"That's the only thing I'm afeerd of," said the Falin calmly. "But whut I'm tellin' you's our only chance."

"How do you know he won't hear us going down? Why not leave the horses?"

"We might need the hosses, and hit's mud and sand all the way—you ought to know that."

Hale did know that; so on they went quietly and hid their horses aside from the road near the place where Hale had fished when he first went to Lonesome Cove. There the Falin disappeared on foot.

"Do you trust him?" asked Hale, turning to Budd, and Budd laughed.

"I reckon you can trust a Falin against a friend of a Tolliver, or t'other way round—any time."

Within half an hour the Falin came back with the news that there were no signs that the fugitive had yet come in.

"No use surrounding the house now," he said, "he might see one of us first when he comes in an' git away. We'll do that atter daylight."

And at daylight they saw the fugitive ride out

of the woods at the back of the house and boldly around to the front of the house, where he left his horse in the yard and disappeared.

"Now send three men to ketch him if he runs out the back way—quick!" said the Falin. "Hit'll take 'em twenty minutes to git thar through the woods. Soon's they git thar, let one of 'em shoot his pistol off an' that'll be the signal fer us."

The three men started swiftly, but the pistol shot came before they had gone a hundred yards, for one of the three—a new man and unaccustomed to the use of fire-arms, stumbled over a root while he was seeing that his pistol was in order and let it go off accidentally.

"No time to waste now," the Falin called sharply. "Git on yo' hosses and git!" Then the rush was made and when they gave up the chase at noon that day, the sheriff looked Hale squarely in the eye when Hale sharply asked him a question:

"Why didn't you tell me who that man was?"

"Because I was afeerd you wouldn't go to Devil Judd's atter him. I know better now," and he shook his head, for he did not understand. And so Hale at the head of the disappointed Guard went back to the Gap, and when, next day, they laid Mockaby away in the thinly populated little graveyard that rested in the hollow of the river's arm, the spirit of law and order in the heart of every guard gave way to the spirit of revenge, and the grass would grow under the feet of none until

Rufe Tolliver was caught and the death-debt of the law was paid with death.

That purpose was no less firm in the heart of Hale, and he turned away from the grave, sick with the trick that Fate had lost no time in playing him; for he was a Falin now in the eyes of both factions and an enemy—even to June.

The weeks dragged slowly along, and June sank slowly toward the depths with every fresh realization of the trap of circumstance into which she had fallen. She had dim memories of just such a state of affairs when she was a child, for the feud was on now and the three things that governed the life of the cabin in Lonesome Cove were hate, caution, and fear.

Bub and her father worked in the fields with their Winchesters close at hand, and June was never easy if they were outside the house. If somebody shouted "hello"—that universal hail of friend or enemy in the mountains—from the gate after dark, one or the other would go out the back door and answer from the shelter of the corner of the house. Neither sat by the light of the fire where he could be seen through the window nor carried a candle from one room to the other. And when either rode down the river, June must ride behind him to prevent ambush from the bushes, for no Kentucky mountaineer, even to kill his worst enemy, will risk harming a woman. Sometimes Loretta would come and spend the day, and she seemed little less distressed than June. Dave was constantly in and out, and several times June had seen the Red Fox hanging around. Always the talk was of the feud. The killing of this Tolliver and of that long ago was rehearsed over and over; all the wrongs the family had suffered at the hands of the Falins were retold, and in spite of herself June felt the old hatred of her childhood reawakening against them so fiercely that she was startled: and she knew that if she were a man she would be as ready now to take up a Winchester against the Falins as though she had known no other life.

Loretta got no comfort from her in her tentative efforts to talk of Buck Falin, and once, indeed, June gave her a scathing rebuke. With every day her feeling for her father and Bub was knit a little more closely, and toward Dave grew a little more kindly. She had her moods even against Hale, but they always ended in a storm of helpless tears. Her father said little of Hale, but that little was enough. Young Dave was openly exultant when he heard of the favouritism shown a Falin by the Guard at the Gap, the effort Hale had made to catch Rufe Tolliver and his well-known purpose yet to capture him; for the Guard maintained a fund for the arrest and prosecution of criminals, and the reward it offered for Rufe, dead or alive, was known by everybody on both sides of the State line. For nearly a week no word was heard of the fugitive, and then one night, after supper, while June was sitting at the fire, the back door was opened, Rufe slid like a snake within, and when June sprang to her feet with a sharp cry of terror, he gave his brutal laugh:

"Don't take much to skeer you—does it?" Shuddering she felt his evil eyes sweep her from head to foot, for the beast within was always unleashed and ever ready to spring, and she dropped back into her seat, speechless. Young Dave, entering from the kitchen, saw Rufe's look and the hostile lightning of his own eyes flashed at his foster-uncle, who knew straightway that he must not for his own safety strain the boy's jealousy too far.

"You oughtn't to 'a' done it, Rufe," said old Judd a little later, and he shook his head. Again Rufe laughed:

"No—" he said with a quick pacificatory look to young Dave, "not to *him!*" The swift gritting of Dave's teeth showed that he knew what was meant, and without warning the instinct of a protecting tigress leaped within June. She had seen and had been grateful for the look Dave gave the outlaw, but without a word she rose now and went to her own room. While she sat at her window, her step-mother came out the back door and left it open for a moment. Through it June could hear the talk:

"No," said her father, "she ain't goin' to marry

him." Dave grunted and Rufe's voice came again:

"Ain't no danger, I reckon, of her tellin' on me?"

"No," said her father gruffly, and the door banged.

No, thought June, she wouldn't, even without her father's trust, though she loathed the man, and he was the only thing on earth of which she was afraid—that was the miracle of it and June wondered. She was a Tolliver and the clan loyalty of a century forbade—that was all. As she rose she saw a figure skulking past the edge of the woods. She called Bub in and told him about it, and Rufe stayed at the cabin all night, but June did not see him next morning, and she kept out of his way whenever he came again. A few nights later the Red Fox slouched up to the cabin with some herbs for the step-mother. Old Judd eyed him askance.

"Lookin' fer that reward, Red?" The old man had no time for the meek reply that was on his lips, for the old woman spoke up sharply:

"You let Red alone, Judd—I tol' him to come." And the Red Fox stayed to supper, and when Rufe left the cabin that night, a bent figure with a big rifle and in moccasins sneaked after him.

The next night there was a tap on Hale's window just at his bedside, and when he looked out he saw the Red Fox's big rifle, telescope, moccasins and all in the moonlight. The Red Fox had discovered the whereabouts of Rufe Tolliver, and that very night he guided Hale and six of the guard to the edge of a little clearing where the Red Fox pointed to a one-roomed cabin, quiet in the moonlight. Hale had his requisition now.

"Ain't no trouble ketchin' Rufe, if you bait him with a woman," he snarled. "There mought be several Tollivers in thar. Wait till daybreak and git the drap on him, when he comes out." And then he disappeared.

Surrounding the cabin, Hale waited, and on top of the mountain, above Lonesome Cove, the Red Fox sat waiting and watching through his big telescope. Through it he saw Bad Rufe step outside the door at daybreak and stretch his arms with a yawn, and he saw three men spring with levelled Winchesters from behind a clump of bushes. The woman shot from the door behind Rufe with a pistol in each hand, but Rufe kept his hands in the air and turned his head to the woman who lowered the half-raised weapons slowly. When he saw the cavalcade start for the county seat with Rufe manacled in the midst of them, he dropped swiftly down into Lonesome Cove to tell Judd that Rufe was a prisoner and to retake him on the way to jail. And, as the Red Fox well knew would happen, old Judd and young Dave and two other Tollivers who were at the cabin galloped into the county seat to find Rufe in jail, and that jail guarded by seven grim young men armed with Winchesters and shot-guns.

Hale faced the old man quietly—eye to eye.

"It's no use, Judd," he said, "you'd better let the law take its course." The old man was scornful.

"Thar's never been a Tolliver convicted of killin' nobody, much less hung—an' thar ain't goin' to be."

"I'm glad you warned me," said Hale still quietly, "though it wasn't necessary. But if he's convicted, he'll hang."

The giant's face worked in convulsive helplessness and he turned away.

"You hold the cyards now, but my deal is comin'."

"All right, Judd—you're getting a square one from me."

Back rode the Tollivers and Devil Judd never opened his lips again until he was at home in Lonesome Cove. June was sitting on the porch when he walked heavy-headed through the gate.

"They've ketched Rufe," he said, and after a moment he added gruffly:

"Thar's goin' to be sure enough trouble now. The Falins'll think all them police fellers air on their side now. This ain't no place fer you—you must git away."

June shook her head and her eyes turned to the flowers at the edge of the garden:

"I'm not goin' away, Dad," she said.

313

XXVI

BACK to the passing of Boone and the landing of Columbus no man, in that region, had ever been hanged. And as old Judd said, no Tolliver had ever been sentenced and no jury of mountain men, he well knew, could be found who would convict a Tolliver, for there were no twelve men in the mountains who would dare. And so the Tollivers decided to await the outcome of the trial and rest easy. But they did not count on the mettle and intelligence of the grim young "furriners" who were a flying wedge of civilization at the Gap. Straightway, they gave up the practice of law and banking and trading and store-keeping and cut port-holes in the brick walls of the Court House and guarded town and jail night and day. They brought their own fearless judge, their own fearless jury and their own fearless guard. Such an abstract regard for law and order the mountaineer finds a hard thing to understand. It looked as though the motive of the Guard was vindictive and personal, and old Judd was almost stifled by the volcanic rage that daily grew within him as the toils daily tightened about Rufe Tolliver. Every happening the old man learned through

314

the Red Fox, who, with his huge pistols, was one of
the men who escorted Rufe to and from Court
House and jail—a volunteer, Hale supposed, because he hated Rufe; and, as the Tollivers supposed, so that he could keep them advised of
everything that went on, which he did with se-
crecy and his own peculiar faith. And steadily and
to the growing uneasiness of the Tollivers, the
law went its way. Rufe had proven that he was
at the Gap all day and had taken no part in the
trouble. He produced a witness—the mountain
lout whom Hale remembered—who admitted that
he had blown the whistle, given the yell, and fired
the pistol shot. When asked his reason, the witness, who was stupid, had none ready, looked
helplessly at Rufe and finally mumbled—"fer
fun." But it was plain from the questions that
Rufe had put to Hale only a few minutes before
the shooting, and from the hesitation of the witness,
that Rufe had used him for a tool. So the testimony of the latter that Mockaby without even
summoning Rufe to surrender had fired first, carried no conviction. And yet Rufe had no trouble
making it almost sure that he had never seen the
dead man before—so what was his motive? It
was then that word reached the ear of the prosecuting attorney of the only testimony that could
establish a motive and make the crime a hanging
offence, and Court was adjourned for a day, while
he sent for the witness who could give it. That

afternoon one of the Falins, who had grown bolder, and in twos and threes were always at the trial, shot at a Tolliver on the edge of town and there was an immediate turmoil between the factions that the Red Fox had been waiting for and that suited his dark purposes well.

That very night, with his big rifle, he slipped through the woods to a turn of the road, over which old Dave Tolliver was to pass next morning, and built a "blind" behind some rocks and lay there smoking peacefully and dreaming his Swedenborgian dreams. And when a wagon came round the turn, driven by a boy, and with the gaunt frame of old Dave Tolliver lying on straw in the bed of it, his big rifle thundered and the frightened horses dashed on with the Red Fox's last enemy, lifeless. Coolly he slipped back to the woods, threw the shell from his gun, tirelessly he went by short cuts through the hills, and at noon, benevolent and smiling, he was on guard again.

The little Court Room was crowded for the afternoon session. Inside the railing sat Rufe Tolliver, white and defiant—manacled. Leaning on the railing, to one side, was the Red Fox with his big pistols, his good profile calm, dreamy, kind —to the other, similarly armed, was Hale. At each of the gaping port-holes, and on each side of the door, stood a guard with a Winchester, and around the railing outside were several more. In spite of window and port-hole the air was close and heavy

with the smell of tobacco and the sweat of men.
Here and there in the crowd was a red Falin, but
not a Tolliver was in sight, and Rufe Tolliver sat
alone. The clerk called the Court to order after
the fashion since the days before Edward the Con-
fessor—except that he asked God to save a com-
monwealth instead of a king—and the prosecuting
attorney rose:

"Next witness, may it please your Honour":
and as the clerk got to his feet with a slip of paper
in his hand and bawled out a name, Hale wheeled
with a thumping heart. The crowd vibrated,
turned heads, gave way, and through the human
aisle walked June Tolliver with the sheriff following meekly behind. At the railing-gate she stopped, head uplifted, face pale and indignant; and
her eyes swept past Hale as if he were no more
than a wooden image, and were fixed with proud
inquiry on the Judge's face. She was bareheaded, her bronze hair was drawn low over her
white brow, her gown was of purple home-spun,
and her right hand was clenched tight about the
chased silver handle of a riding whip, and in eyes,
mouth, and in every line of her tense figure was the
mute question: "Why have you brought *me*
here?"

"Here, please," said the Judge gently, as though
he were about to answer that question, and as she
passed Hale she seemed to swerve her skirts aside
that they might not touch him.

"Swear her."

June lifted her right hand, put her lips to the soiled, old, black Bible and faced the jury and Hale and Bad Rufe Tolliver whose black eyes never left her face.

"What is your name?" asked a deep voice that struck her ears as familiar, and before she answered she swiftly recalled that she had heard that voice speaking when she entered the door.

"June Tolliver."

"Your age?"

"Eighteen."

"You live——"

"In Lonesome Cove."

"You are the daughter of——"

"Judd Tolliver."

"Do you know the prisoner?"

"He is my foster-uncle."

"Were you at home on the night of August the tenth?"

"I was."

"Have you ever heard the prisoner express any enmity against this volunteer Police Guard?" He waved his hand toward the men at the portholes and about the railing—unconsciously leaving his hand directly pointed at Hale. June hesitated and Rufe leaned one elbow on the table, and the light in his eyes beat with fierce intensity into the girl's eyes into which came a curious frightened look that Hale remembered—the same look she had shown long ago when Rufe's name was mentioned in the old miller's cabin, and when going up the river road she had put her childish trust in him to see that her bad uncle bothered her no more. Hale had never forgot that, and if it had not been absurd he would have stopped the prisoner from staring at her now. An anxious look had come into Rufe's eyes—would she lie for him?

"Never," said June. Ah, she would—she was a Tolliver and Rufe took a breath of deep content.

"You never heard him express any enmity toward the Police Guard—before that night?"

"I have answered that question," said June with dignity and Rufe's lawyer was on his feet.

"Your Honour, I object," he said indignantly.

"I apologize," said the deep voice—"sincerely," and he bowed to June. Then very quietly:

"What was the last thing you heard the prisoner say that afternoon when he left your father's house?"

It had come—how well she remembered just what he had said and how, that night, even when she was asleep, Rufe's words had clanged like a bell in her brain—what her awakening terror was when she knew that the deed was done and the stifling fear that the victim might be Hale. Swiftly her mind worked—somebody had blabbed, her step-mother, perhaps, and what Rufe had said had reached a Falin ear and come to the relentless man in front of her. She remembered, too,

now, what the deep voice was saying as she came
into the door:

"There must be deliberation, a malicious purpose proven to make the prisoner's crime a capital
offence—I admit that, of course, your Honour.
Very well, we propose to prove that now," and
then she had heard her·name called. The proof
that was to send Rufe Tolliver to the scaffold was
to come from her—that was why she was there.
Her lips opened and Rufe's eyes, like a snake's,
caught her own again and held them.

"He said he was going over to the Gap——"

There was a commotion at the door, again the
crowd parted, and in towered giant Judd Tolliver,
pushing people aside as though they were straws,
his bushy hair wild and his great frame shaking
from head to foot with rage.

"You went to my house," he rumbled hoarsely
—glaring at Hale—"an' took my gal thar when I
wasn't at home—you——"

"Order in the Court," said the Judge sternly,
but already at a signal from Hale several guards
were pushing through the crowd and old Judd saw
them coming and saw the Falins about him and
the Winchesters at the port-holes, and he stopped
with a hard gulp and stood looking at June.

"Repeat his exact words," said the deep voice
again as calmly as though nothing had happened.

"He said, 'I'm goin' over to the Gap—'" and
still Rufe's black eyes held her with mesmeric

320

power—would she lie for him—would she lie for him?

It was a terrible struggle for June. Her father was there, her uncle Dave was dead, her foster-uncle's life hung on her next words and she was a Tolliver. Yet she had given her oath, she had kissed the sacred Book in which she believed from cover to cover with her whole heart, and she could feel upon her the blue eyes of a man for whom a lie was impossible and to whom she had never stained her white soul with a word of untruth.

"Yes," encouraged the deep voice kindly.

Not a soul in the room knew where the struggle lay—not even the girl—for it lay between the black eyes of Rufe Tolliver and the blue eyes of John Hale.

"Yes," repeated the deep voice again. Again, with her eyes on Rufe, she repeated:

"'I'm goin' over to the Gap—'" her face turned deadly white, she shivered, her dark eyes swerved suddenly full on Hale and she said slowly and distinctly, yet hardly above a whisper:

"'*To kill me a policeman.*'"

"That will do," said the deep voice gently, and Hale started toward her—she looked so deadly sick and she trembled so when she tried to rise; but she saw him, her mouth steadied, she rose, and without looking at him, passed by his out-stretched hand and walked slowly out of the Court Room.

XXVII

THE miracle had happened. The Tollivers, following the Red Fox's advice to make no attempt at rescue just then, had waited, expecting the old immunity from the law and getting instead the swift sentence that Rufe Tolliver should be hanged by the neck until he was dead. Astounding and convincing though the news was, no mountaineer believed he would ever hang, and Rufe himself faced the sentence defiant. He laughed when he was led back to his cell:

"I'll never hang," he said scornfully. They were the first words that came from his lips, and the first words that came from old Judd's when the news reached him in Lonesome Cove, and that night old Judd gathered his clan for the rescue—to learn next morning that during the night Rufe had been spirited away to the capital for safe-keeping until the fatal day. And so there was quiet for a while—old Judd making ready for the day when Rufe should be brought back, and trying to find out who it was that had slain his brother Dave. The Falins denied the deed, but old Judd never questioned that one of them was the murderer, and he came out openly now and made no

"'WHY HAVE YOU BROUGHT ME HERE?'"

secret of the fact that he meant to have revenge. And so the two factions went armed, watchful and wary—especially the Falins, who were lying low and waiting to fulfil a deadly purpose of their own. They well knew that old Judd would not open hostilities on them until Rufe Tolliver was dead or at liberty. They knew that the old man meant to try to rescue Rufe when he was brought back to jail or taken from it to the scaffold, and when either day came they themselves would take a hand, thus giving the Tollivers at one and the same time two sets of foes. And so through the golden September days the two clans waited, and June Tolliver went with dull determination back to her old life, for Uncle Billy's sister had left the house in fear and she could get no help—milking cows at cold dawns, helping in the kitchen, spinning flax and wool, and weaving them into rough garments for her father and step-mother and Bub, and in time, she thought grimly—for herself: for not another cent for her maintenance could now come from John Hale, even though he claimed it was hers—even though it was in truth her own. Never, but once, had Hale's name been mentioned in the cabin—never, but once, had her father referred to the testimony that she had given against Rufe Tolliver, for the old man put upon Hale the fact that the sheriff had sneaked into his house when he was away and had taken June to Court, and that was the crowning touch of bitterness in his growing hatred for the captain of the guard of whom he had once been so fond.

"Course you had to tell the truth, baby, when they got you there," he said kindly; "but kidnappin' you that-a-way—" He shook his great bushy head from side to side and dropped it into his hands.

"I reckon that damn Hale was the man who found out that you heard Rufe say that. I'd like to know how—I'd like to git my hands on the feller as told him."

June opened her lips in simple justice to clear Hale of that charge, but she saw such a terrified appeal in her step-mother's face that she kept her peace, let Hale suffer for that, too, and walked out into her garden. Never once had her piano been opened, her books had lain unread, and from her lips, during those days, came no song. When she was not at work, she was brooding in her room, or she would walk down to Uncle Billy's and sit at the mill with him while the old man would talk in tender helplessness, or under the honeysuckle vines with old Hon, whose brusque kindness was of as little avail. And then, still silent, she would get wearily up and as quietly go away while the two old friends, worried to the heart, followed her sadly with their eyes. At other times she was brooding in her room or sitting in her garden, where she was now, and where she found most comfort—the garden that Hale had planted for her—

324

where purple asters leaned against lilac shrubs that would flower for the first time the coming spring; where a late rose bloomed, and marigolds drooped, and great sunflowers nodded and giant castor-plants stretched out their hands of Christ. And while June thus waited the passing of the days, many things became clear to her: for the grim finger of reality had torn the veil from her eyes and let her see herself but little changed, at the depths, by contact with John Hale's world, as she now saw him but little changed, at the depths, by contact with hers. Slowly she came to see, too, that it was his presence in the Court Room that made her tell the truth, reckless of the consequences, and she came to realize that she was not leaving the mountains because she would go to no place where she could not know of any danger that, in the present crisis, might threaten John Hale.

And Hale saw only that in the Court Room she had drawn her skirts aside, that she had looked at him once and then had brushed past his helping hand. It put him in torment to think of what her life must be now, and of how she must be suffering. He knew that she would not leave her father in the crisis that was at hand, and after it was all over —what then? His hands would still be tied and he would be even more helpless than he had ever dreamed possible. To be sure, an old land deal had come to life, just after the discovery of the worthlessness of the mine in Lonesome Cove, and was holding out another hope. But if that, too, should fail—or if it should succeed—what then? Old Judd had sent back, with a curt refusal, the last "allowance" he forwarded to June and he knew the old man was himself in straits. So June must stay in the mountains, and what would become of her? She had gone back to her mountain garb—would she lapse into her old life and ever again be content? Yes, she would lapse, but never enough to keep her from being unhappy all her life, and at that thought he groaned. Thus far he was responsible and the paramount duty with him had been that she should have the means to follow the career she had planned for herself outside of those hills. And now if he had the means, he was helpless. There was nothing for him to do now but to see that the law had its way with Rufe Tolliver, and meanwhile he let the reawakened land deal go hang and set himself the task of finding out who it was that had ambushed old Dave Tolliver. So even when he was thinking of June his brain was busy on that mystery, and one night, as he sat brooding, a suspicion flashed that made him grip his chair with both hands and rise to pace the porch. Old Dave had been shot at dawn, and the night before the Red Fox had been absent from the guard and had not turned up until nearly noon next day. He had told Hale that he was going home. Two days later, Hale

326

heard by accident that the old man had been seen near the place of the ambush about sunset of the day before the tragedy, which was on his way home, and he now learned straightway for himself that the Red Fox had not been home for a month —which was only one of his ways of mistreating the patient little old woman in black.

A little later, the Red Fox gave it out that he was trying to ferret out the murderer himself, and several times he was seen near the place of ambush, looking, as he said, for evidence. But this did not halt Hale's suspicions, for he recalled that the night he had spent with the Red Fox, long ago, the old man had burst out against old Dave and had quickly covered up his indiscretion with a pious characterization of himself as a man that kept peace with both factions. And then why had he been so suspicious and fearful when Hale told him that night that he had seen him talking with a Falin in town the Court day before, and had he disclosed the whereabouts of Rufe Tolliver and guided the guard to his hiding-place simply for the reward? He had not yet come to claim it, and his indifference to money was notorious through the hills. Apparently there was some general enmity in the old man toward the whole Tolliver clan, and maybe he had used the reward to fool Hale as to his real motive. And then Hale quietly learned that long ago the Tollivers bitterly opposed the Red Fox's marriage to a Tolliver—

that Rufe, when a boy, was always teasing the Red
Fox and had once made him dance in his moccasins to the tune of bullets spitting about his feet,
and that the Red Fox had been heard to say that
old Dave had cheated his wife out of her just inheritance of wild land; but all that was long, long
ago, and apparently had been mutually forgiven
and forgotten. But it was enough for Hale, and
one night he mounted his horse, and at dawn he
was at the place of ambush with his horse hidden
in the bushes. The rocks for the ambush were
waist high, and the twigs that had been thrust in
the crevices between them were withered. And
there, on the hypothesis that the Red Fox was the
assassin, Hale tried to put himself, after the deed,
into the Red Fox's shoes. The old man had
turned up on guard before noon—then he must
have gone somewhere first or have killed considerable time in the woods. He would not have
crossed the road, for there were two houses on the
other side; there would have been no object in
going on over the mountain unless he meant to
escape, and if he had gone over there for another
reason he would hardly have had time to get to
the Court House before noon: nor would he have
gone back along the road on that side, for on that
side, too, was a cabin not far away. So Hale
turned and walked straight away from the road
where the walking was easiest—down a ravine,
and pushing this way and that through the bushes

where the way looked easiest. Half a mile down the ravine he came to a little brook, and there in the black earth was the faint print of a man's left foot and in the hard crust across was the deeper print of his right, where his weight in leaping had come down hard. But the prints were made by a shoe and not by a moccasin, and then Hale recalled exultantly that the Red Fox did not have his moccasins on the morning he turned up on guard. All the while he kept a sharp lookout, right and left, on the ground—the Red Fox must have thrown his cartridge shell somewhere, and for that Hale was looking. Across the brook he could see the tracks no farther, for he was too little of a woodsman to follow so old a trail, but as he stood behind a clump of rhododendron, wondering what he could do, he heard the crack of a dead stick down the stream, and noiselessly he moved farther into the bushes. His heart thumped in the silence—the long silence that followed—for it might be a hostile Tolliver that was coming, so he pulled his pistol from his holster, made ready, and then, noiseless as a shadow, the Red Fox slipped past him along the path, in his moccasins now, and with his big Winchester in his left hand. The Red Fox, too, was looking for that cartridge shell, for only the night before had he heard for the first time of the whispered suspicions against him. He was making for the blind and Hale trembled at his luck. There was no path on the other side of the stream, and Hale could barely hear him moving through the bushes. So he pulled off his boots and, carrying them in one hand, slipped after him, watching for dead twigs, stooping under the branches, or sliding sidewise through them when he had to brush between their extremities, and pausing every now and then to listen for an occasional faint sound from the Red Fox ahead. Up the ravine the old man went to a little ledge of rocks, beyond which was the blind, and when Hale saw his stooped figure slip over that and disappear, he ran noiselessly toward it, crept noiselessly to the top and peeped carefully over to see the Red Fox with his back to him and peering into a clump of bushes—hardly ten yards away. While Hale looked, the old man thrust his hand into the bushes and drew out something that twinkled in the sun. At the moment Hale's horse nickered from the bushes, and the Red Fox slipped his hand into his pocket, crouched listening a moment, and then, step by step, backed toward the ledge. Hale rose:

"I want you, Red!"

The old man wheeled, the wolf's snarl came, but the big rifle was too slow—Hale's pistol had flashed in his face.

"Drop your gun!" Paralyzed, but the picture of white fury, the old man hesitated.

"Drop—your—gun!" Slowly the big rifle was loosed and fell to the ground.

"Back away—turn around and hands up!"

With his foot on the Winchester, Hale felt in the old man's pockets and fished out an empty cartridge shell. Then he picked up the rifle and threw the slide.

"It fits all right. March—toward that horse!"

Without a word the old man slouched ahead to where the big black horse was restlessly waiting in the bushes.

"Climb up," said Hale. "We won't 'ride and tie' back to town—but I'll take turns with you on the horse."

The Red Fox was making ready to leave the mountains, for he had been falsely informed that Rufe was to be brought back to the county seat next day, and he was searching again for the sole bit of evidence that was out against him. And when Rufe was spirited back to jail and was on his way to his cell, an old freckled hand was thrust between the bars of an iron door to greet him and a voice called him by name. Rufe stopped in amazement; then he burst out laughing; he struck then at the pallid face through the bars with his manacles and cursed the old man bitterly; then he laughed again horribly. The two slept in adjoining cells of the same cage that night—the one waiting for the scaffold and the other waiting for the trial that was to send him there. And away over the blue mountains a little old woman in black sat on the porch of her cabin as she had sat patiently many and many a long day. It was time, she thought, that the Red Fox was coming home.

XXVIII

AND so while Bad Rufe Tolliver was waiting for death, the trial of the Red Fox went on, and when he was not swinging in a hammock, reading his Bible, telling his visions to his guards and singing hymns, he was in the Court House giving shrewd answers to questions, or none at all, with the benevolent half of his mask turned to the jury and the wolfish snarl of the other half showing only now and then to some hostile witness for whom his hate was stronger than his fear for his own life. And in jail Bad Rufe worried his enemy with the malicious humour of Satan. Now he would say:

"Oh, there ain't nothin' betwixt old Red and me, nothin' at all—'cept this iron wall," and he would drum a vicious tattoo on the thin wall with the heel of his boot. Or when he heard the creak of the Red Fox's hammock as he droned his Bible aloud, he would say to his guard outside:

"Course I don't read the Bible an' preach the word, nor talk with sperits, but thar's worse men than me in the world—old Red in thar' for instance"; and then he would cackle like a fiend and the Red Fox would writhe in torment and

333

beg to be sent to another cell. And always he would daily ask the Red Fox about his trial and ask him questions in the night, and his devilish instinct told him the day that the Red Fox, too, was sentenced to death—he saw it in the gray pallour of the old man's face, and he cackled his glee like a demon. For the evidence against the Red Fox was too strong. Where June sat as chief witness against Rufe Tolliver—John Hale sat as chief witness against the Red Fox. He could not swear it was a cartridge shell that he saw the old man pick up, but it was something that glistened in the sun, and a moment later he had found the shell in the old man's pocket—and if it had been fired innocently, why was it there and why was the old man searching for it? He was looking, he said, for evidence of the murderer himself. That claim made, the Red Fox's lawyer picked up the big rifle and the shell.

"You say, Mr. Hale, the prisoner told you the night you spent at his home that this rifle was rim-fire?"

"He did." The lawyer held up the shell.

"You see this was exploded in such a rifle." That was plain, and the lawyer shoved the shell into the rifle, pulled the trigger, took it out, and held it up again. The plunger had struck below the rim and near the centre, but not quite on the centre, and Hale asked for the rifle and examined it closely.

"It's been tampered with," he said quietly, and he handed it to the prosecuting attorney. The fact was plain; it was a bungling job and better proved the Red Fox's guilt. Moreover, there were only two such big rifles in all the hills, and it was proven that the man who owned the other was at the time of the murder far away. The days of brain-storms had not come then. There were no eminent Alienists to prove insanity for the prisoner. Apparently, he had no friends—none save the little old woman in black who sat by his side, hour by hour and day by day.

And the Red Fox was doomed.

In the hush of the Court Room the Judge solemnly put to the gray face before him the usual question:

"Have you anything to say whereby sentence of death should not be pronounced on you?"

The Red Fox rose:

"No," he said in a shaking voice; "but I have a friend here who I would like to speak for me." The Judge bent his head a moment over his bench and lifted it:

"It is unusual," he said; "but under the circumstances I will grant your request. Who is your friend?" And the Red Fox made the souls of his listeners leap.

"Jesus Christ," he said.

The Judge reverently bowed his head and the hush of the Court Room grew deeper when the

335

old man fished his Bible from his pocket and calmly read such passages as might be interpreted as sure damnation for his enemies and sure glory for himself—read them until the Judge lifted his hand for a halt.

And so another sensation spread through the hills and a superstitious awe of this strange new power that had come into the hills went with it hand in hand. Only while the doubting ones knew that nothing could save the Red Fox they would wait to see if that power could really avail against the Tolliver clan. The day set for Rufe's execution was the following Monday, and for the Red Fox the Friday following—for it was well to have the whole wretched business over while the guard was there. Old Judd Tolliver, so Hale learned, had come himself to offer the little old woman in black the refuge of his roof as long as she lived, and had tried to get her to go back with him to Lonesome Cove; but it pleased the Red Fox that he should stand on the scaffold in a suit of white— cap and all—as emblems of the purple and fine linen he was to put on above, and the little old woman stayed where she was, silently and without question, cutting the garments, as Hale pityingly learned, from a white table-cloth and measuring them piece by piece with the clothes the old man wore in jail. It pleased him, too, that his body should be kept unburied three days—saying that he would then arise and go about preaching, and that duty, too, she would as silently and with as little question perform. Moreover, he would preach his own funeral sermon on the Sunday before Rufe's day, and a curious crowd gathered to hear him. The Red Fox was led from jail. He stood on the porch of the jailer's house with a little table in front of him. On it lay a Bible, on the other side of the table sat a little pale-faced old woman in black with a black sun-bonnet drawn close to her face. By the side of the Bible lay a few pieces of bread. It was the Red Fox's last communion—a communion which he administered to himself and in which there was no other soul on earth to join save that little old woman in black. And when the old fellow lifted the bread and asked the crowd to come forward to partake with him in the last sacrament, not a soul moved. Only the old woman who had been ill-treated by the Red Fox for so many years—only she, of all the crowd, gave any answer, and she for one instant turned her face toward him. With a churlish gesture the old man pushed the bread over toward her and with hesitating, trembling fingers she reached for it.

Bob Berkley was on the death-watch that night, and as he passed Rufe's cell a wiry hand shot through the grating of his door, and as the boy sprang away the condemned man's fingers tipped the butt of the big pistol that dangled on the lad's hip.

337

"Not this time," said Bob with a cool little laugh, and Rufe laughed, too.

"I was only foolin'," he said, "I ain't goin' to hang. You hear that, Red? I ain't goin' to hang —but you are, Red—sure. Nobody'd risk his little finger for your old carcass, 'cept maybe that little old woman o' yours who you've treated like a hound—but my folks ain't goin' to see me hang."

Rufe spoke with some reason. That night the Tollivers climbed the mountain, and before day-break were waiting in the woods a mile on the north side of the town. And the Falins climbed, too, farther along the mountains, and at the same hour were waiting in the woods a mile to the south.

Back in Lonesome Cove June Tolliver sat alone—her soul shaken and terror-stricken to the depths—and the misery that matched hers was in the heart of Hale as he paced to and fro at the county seat, on guard and forging out his plans for that day under the morning stars.

XXIX

DAY broke on the old Court House with its black port-holes, on the graystone jail, and on a tall topless wooden box to one side, from which projected a cross-beam of green oak. From the centre of this beam dangled a rope that swung gently to and fro when the wind moved. And with the day a flock of little birds lighted on the bars of the condemned man's cell window, chirping through them, and when the jailer brought breakfast he found Bad Rufe cowering in the corner of his cell and wet with the sweat of fear.

"Them damn birds ag'in," he growled sullenly.

"Don't lose yo' nerve, Rufe," said the jailer, and the old laugh of defiance came, but from lips that were dry.

"Not much," he answered grimly, but the jailer noticed that while he ate, his eyes kept turning again and again to the bars; and the turnkey went away shaking his head. Rufe had told the jailer, his one friend through whom he had kept in constant communication with the Tollivers, how on the night after the shooting of Mockaby, when he lay down to sleep high on the mountain side and under some rhododendron bushes, a flock of little birds flew in on him like a gust of rain and perched over and around him, twittering at him until he had to get up and pace the woods, and how, throughout the next day, when he sat in the sun planning his escape, those birds would sweep chattering over his head and sweep chattering back again, and in that mood of despair he had said once, and only once: "Somehow I knowed this time my name was Dennis"—a phrase of evil prophecy he had picked up outside the hills. And now those same birds of evil omen had come again, he believed, right on the heels of the last sworn oath old Judd had sent him that he would never hang.

With the day, through mountain and valley, came in converging lines mountain humanity— men and women, boys and girls, children and babes in arms; all in their Sunday best—the men in jeans, slouched hats, and high boots, the women in gay ribbons and brilliant home-spun; in wagons, on foot and on horses and mules, carrying man and man, man and boy, lover and sweetheart, or husband and wife and child—all moving through the crisp autumn air, past woods of russet and crimson and along brown dirt roads, to the straggling little mountain town. A stranger would have thought that a county fair, a camp-meeting, or a circus was their goal, but they were on their way to look upon the Court House with its black port-holes, the graystone jail, the tall wooden box, the projecting beam, and that dangling rope which, when the wind moved, swayed gently to and fro. And Hale had forged his plan. He knew that there would be no attempt at rescue until Rufe was led to the scaffold, and he knew that neither Falins nor Tollivers would come in a band, so the incoming tide found on the outskirts of the town and along every road boyish policemen who halted and disarmed every man who carried a weapon in sight, for thus John Hale would have against the pistols of the factions his own Winchesters and repeating shot-guns. And the wondering people saw at the back windows of the Court House and at the threatening port-holes more youngsters manning Winchesters, more at the windows of the jailer's frame house, which joined and fronted the jail, and more still—a line of them—running all around the jail; and the old men wagged their heads in amazement and wondered if, after all, a Tolliver was not really going to be hanged.

So they waited—the neighbouring hills were black with people waiting; the housetops were black with men and boys waiting; the trees in the streets were bending under the weight of human bodies; and the jail-yard fence was three feet deep with people hanging to it and hanging about one another's necks—all waiting. All morning they waited silently and patiently, and now the fatal noon was hardly an hour away and not a Falin nor a Tolliver had been seen. Every Falin had been

341

disarmed of his Winchester as he came in, and as yet no Tolliver had entered the town, for wily old Judd had learned of Hale's tactics and had stayed outside the town for his own keen purpose. As the minutes passed, Hale was beginning to wonder whether, after all, old Judd had come to believe that the odds against him were too great, and had told the truth when he set afoot the rumour that the law should have its way; and it was just when his load of anxiety was beginning to lighten that there was a little commotion at the edge of the Court House and a great red-headed figure pushed through the crowd, followed by another of like build, and as the people rapidly gave way and fell back, a line of Falins slipped along the wall and stood under the port-holes—quiet, watchful, and determined. Almost at the same time the crowd fell back the other way up the street, there was the hurried tramping of feet and on came the Tollivers, headed by giant Judd, all armed with Winchesters—for old Judd had sent his guns in ahead —and as the crowd swept like water into any channel of alley or doorway that was open to it, Hale saw the yard emptied of everybody but the line of Falins against the wall and the Tollivers in a body but ten yards in front of them. The people on the roofs and in the trees had not moved at all, for they were out of range. For a moment old Judd's eyes swept the windows and port-holes of the Court House, the windows of the jailer's house, the line

342

of guards about the jail, and then they dropped to the line of Falins and glared with contemptuous hate into the leaping blue eyes of old Buck Falin, and for that moment there was silence. In that silence and as silently as the silence itself issued swiftly from the line of guards twelve youngsters with Winchesters, repeating shot-guns, and in a minute six were facing the Falins and six facing the Tollivers, each with his shot-gun at his hip. At the head of them stood Hale, his face a pale image, as hard as though cut from stone, his head bare, and his hand and his hip weaponless. In all that crowd there was not a man or a woman who had not seen or heard of him, for the power of the guard that was at his back had radiated through that wild region like ripples of water from a dropped stone and, unarmed even, he had a personal power that belonged to no other man in all those hills, though armed to the teeth. His voice rose clear, steady, commanding:

"The law has come here and it has come to stay." He faced the beetling eyebrows and angrily working beard of old Judd now:

"The Falins are here to get revenge on you Tollivers, if you attack us. I know that. But"— he wheeled on the Falins—"understand! We don't want your help! If the Tollivers try to take that man in there, and one of you Falins draws a pistol, those guns there"—waving his hand toward the jail windows—"will be turned loose on *you*.

343

We'll fight you both!" The last words shot like bullets through his gritted teeth, then the flash of his eyes was gone, his face was calm, and as though the whole matter had been settled beyond possible interruption, he finished quietly:

"The condemned man wishes to make a confession and to say good-by. In five minutes he will be at that window to say what he pleases. Ten minutes later he will be hanged." And he turned and walked calmly into the jailer's door. Not a Tolliver nor a Falin made a movement or a sound. Young Dave's eyes had glared savagely when he first saw Hale, for he had marked Hale for his own and he knew that the fact was known to Hale. Had the battle begun then and there, Hale's death was sure, and Dave knew that Hale must know that as well as he: and yet with magnificent audacity, there he was—unarmed, personally helpless, and invested with an insulting certainty that not a shot would be fired. Not a Falin or a Tolliver even reached for a weapon, and the fact was the subtle tribute that ignorance pays intelligence when the latter is forced to deadly weapons as a last resort; for ignorance faced now belching shot-guns and was commanded by rifles on every side. Old Judd was trapped and the Falins were stunned. Old Buck Falin turned his eyes down the line of his men with one warning glance. Old Judd whispered something to a Tolliver behind him and a moment later the man slipped from the band and disappeared. Young Dave followed Hale's figure with a look of baffled malignant hatred and Bub's eyes were filled with angry tears. Between the factions, the grim young men stood with their guns like statues.

At once a big man with a red face appeared at one of the jailer's windows and then came the sheriff, who began to take out the sash. Already the frightened crowd had gathered closer again and now a hush came over it, followed by a rustling and a murmur. Something was going to happen. Faces and gun-muzzles thickened at the portholes and at the windows; the line of guards turned their faces sidewise and upward; the crowd on the fence scuffled for better positions; the people in the trees craned their necks from the branches or climbed higher, and there was a great scraping on all the roofs. Even the black crowd out on the hills seemed to catch the excitement and to sway, while spots of intense blue and vivid crimson came out here and there from the blackness when the women rose from their seats on the ground. Then —sharply—there was silence. The sheriff disappeared, and shut in by the sashless window as by a picture frame and blinking in the strong light, stood a man with black hair, cropped close, face pale and worn, and hands that looked white and thin—stood bad Rufe Tolliver.

He was going to confess—that was the rumour. His lawyers wanted him to confess; the preacher

345

who had been singing hymns with him all morning
wanted him to confess; the man himself said he
wanted to confess; and now he was going to confess. What deadly mysteries he might clear up if
he would! No wonder the crowd was eager, for
there was no soul there but knew his record—and
what a record! His best friends put his victims no
lower than thirteen, and there looking up at him
were three women whom he had widowed or or-
phaned, while at one corner of the jail-yard stood
a girl in black—the sweetheart of Mockaby, for
whose death Rufe was standing where he stood
now. But his lips did not open. Instead he took
hold of the side of the window and looked behind
him. The sheriff brought him a chair and he sat
down. Apparently he was weak and he was going
to wait a while. Would he tell how he had killed
one Falin in the presence of the latter's wife at a
wild bee tree; how he had killed a sheriff by dropping to the ground when the sheriff fired, in this
way dodging the bullet and then shooting the
officer from where he lay supposedly dead; how
he had thrown another Falin out of the Court
House window and broken his neck—the Falin
was drunk, Rufe always said, and fell out; why,
when he was constable, he had killed another—
because, Rufe said, he resisted arrest; how and
where he had killed Red-necked Johnson, who
was found out in the woods? Would he tell all
that and more? If he meant to tell there was no

346

sign. His lips kept closed and his bright black eyes were studying the situation; the little squad of youngsters, back to back, with their repeating shot-guns, the line of Falins along the wall toward whom protruded six shining barrels, the huddled crowd of Tollivers toward whom protruded six more—old Judd towering in front with young Dave on one side, tense as a leopard about to spring, and on the other Bub, with tears streaming down his face. In a flash he understood, and in that flash his face looked as though he had been suddenly struck a heavy blow by some one from behind, and then his elbows dropped on the sill of the window, his chin dropped into his hands and a murmur arose. Maybe he was too weak to stand and talk—perhaps he was going to talk from his chair. Yes, he was leaning forward and his lips were opening, but no sound came. Slowly his eyes wandered around at the waiting people—in the trees, on the roofs and the fence—and then they dropped to old Judd's and blazed their appeal for a sign. With one heave of his mighty chest old Judd took off his slouch hat, pressed one big hand to the back of his head and, despite that blazing appeal, kept it there. At that movement Rufe threw his head up as though his breath had suddenly failed him, his face turned sickening white, and slowly again his chin dropped into his trembling hands, and still unbelieving he stared his appeal, but old Judd dropped his big hand and

347

turned his head away. The condemned man's mouth twitched once, settled into defiant calm, and then he did one kindly thing. He turned in his seat and motioned Bob Berkley, who was just behind him, away from the window, and the boy, to humour him, stepped aside. Then he rose to his feet and stretched his arms wide. Simultaneously came the far-away crack of a rifle, and as a jet of smoke spurted above a clump of bushes on a little hill, three hundred yards away, Bad Rufe wheeled half-way round and fell back out of sight into the sheriff's arms. Every Falin made a nervous reach for his pistol, the line of gun-muzzles covering them wavered slightly, but the Tollivers stood still and unsurprised, and when Hale dashed from the door again, there was a grim smile of triumph on old Judd's face. He had kept his promise that Rufe should never hang.

"Steady there," said Hale quietly. His pistol was on his hip now and a Winchester was in his left hand.

"Stand where you are—everybody!"

There was the sound of hurrying feet within the jail. There was the clang of an iron door, the bang of a wooden one, and in five minutes from within the tall wooden box came the sharp click of a hatchet and then—dully:

"*T-h-o-o-mp!*" The dangling rope had tightened with a snap and the wind swayed it no more.

At his cell door the Red Fox stood with his

watch in his hand and his eyes glued to the second-hand. When it had gone three times around its circuit, he snapped the lid with a sigh of relief and turned to his hammock and his Bible.

"He's gone now," said the Red Fox.

Outside Hale still waited, and as his eyes turned from the Tollivers to the Falins, seven of the faces among them came back to him with startling distinctness, and his mind went back to the opening trouble in the county-seat over the Kentucky line, years before—when eight men held one another at the points of their pistols. One face was missing, and that face belonged to Rufe Tolliver. Hale pulled out his watch.

"Keep those men there," he said, pointing to the Falins, and he turned to the bewildered Tollivers.

"Come on, Judd," he said kindly—"all of you."

Dazed and mystified, they followed him in a body around the corner of the jail, where in a coffin, that old Judd had sent as a blind to his real purpose, lay the remains of Bad Rufe Tolliver with a harmless bullet hole through one shoulder. Near by was a wagon and hitched to it were two mules that Hale himself had provided. Hale pointed to it:

"I've done all I could, Judd. Take him away. I'll keep the Falins under guard until you reach the Kentucky line, so that they can't waylay you."

If old Judd heard, he gave no sign. He was

349

looking down at the face of his foster-brother—his shoulder drooped, his great frame shrunken, and his iron face beaten and helpless. Again Hale spoke:

"I'm sorry for all this. I'm even sorry that your man was not a better shot."

The old man straightened then and with a gesture he motioned young Dave to the foot of the coffin and stooped himself at the head. Past the wagon they went, the crowd giving way before them, and with the dead Tolliver on their shoulders, old Judd and young Dave passed with their followers out of sight.

XXX

THE longest of her life was that day to June.
The anxiety in times of war for the women
who wait at home is vague because they are mer-
cifully ignorant of the dangers their loved ones
run, but a specific issue that involves death to those
loved ones has a special and poignant terror of its
own. June knew her father's plan, the precise
time the fight would take place, and the especial
danger that was Hale's, for she knew that young
Dave Tolliver had marked him with the first shot
fired. Dry-eyed and white and dumb, she watched
them make ready for the start that morning while
it was yet dark; dully she heard the horses snorting from the cold, the low curt orders of her father,
and the exciting mutterings of Bub and young
Dave; dully she watched the saddles thrown on,
the pistols buckled, the Winchesters caught up,
and dully she watched them file out the gate and
ride away, single file, into the cold, damp mist like
ghostly figures in a dream. Once only did she
open her lips and that was to plead with her father
to leave Bub at home, but her father gave her no
answer and Bub snorted his indignation—he was
a man now, and his now was the privilege of a

man. For a while she stood listening to the ring of metal against stone that came to her more and more faintly out of the mist, and she wondered if it was really June Tolliver standing there, while father and brother and cousin were on their way to fight the law—how differently she saw these things now—for a man who deserved death, and to fight a man who was ready to die for his duty to that law—the law that guarded them and her and might not perhaps guard him: the man who had planted for her the dew-drenched garden that was waiting for the sun, and had built the little room behind her for her comfort and seclusion; who had sent her to school, had never been anything but kind and just to her and to everybody— who had taught her life and, thank God, love. Was she really the June Tolliver who had gone out into the world and had held her place there; who had conquered birth and speech and customs and environment so that none could tell what they all once were; who had become the lady, the woman of the world, in manner, dress, and education: who had a gift of music and a voice that might enrich her life beyond any dream that had ever sprung from her own brain or any that she had ever caught from Hale's? Was *she* June Tolliver who had been and done all that, and now had come back and was slowly sinking back into the narrow grave from which Hale had lifted her? It was all too strange and bitter, but if she wanted proof there was her step-mother's voice now—the same old, querulous, nerve-racking voice that had embittered all her childhood—calling her down into the old mean round of drudgery that had bound forever the horizon of her narrow life just as now it was shutting down like a sky of brass around her own. And when the voice came, instead of bursting into tears as she was about to do, she gave a hard little laugh and she lifted a defiant face to the rising sun. There was a limit to the sacrifice for kindred, brother, father, home, and that limit was the eternal sacrifice—the eternal undoing of herself: when this wretched terrible business was over she would set her feet where that sun could rise on her, busy with the work that she could do in that world for which she felt she was born. Swiftly she did the morning chores and then she sat on the porch thinking and waiting. Spinning wheel, loom, and darning needle were to lie idle that day. The old step-mother had gotten from bed and was dressing herself—miraculously cured of a sudden, miraculously active. She began to talk of what she needed in town, and June said nothing. She went out to the stable and led out the old sorrel-mare. She was going to the hanging.

"Don't you want to go to town, June?"

"No," said June fiercely.

"Well, you needn't git mad about it—I got to go some day this week, and I reckon I might as well go ter-day." June answered nothing, but in silence watched her get ready and in silence watched her ride away. She was glad to be left alone. The sun had flooded Lonesome Cove now with a light as rich and yellow as though it were late afternoon, and she could yet tell every tree by the different colour of the banner that each yet defiantly flung into the face of death. The yard fence was festooned with dewy cobwebs, and every weed in the field was hung with them as with flashing jewels of exquisitely delicate design: Hale had once told her that they meant rain. Far away the mountains were overhung with purple so deep that the very air looked like mist, and a peace that seemed motherlike in tenderness brooded over the earth. Peace! Peace—with a man on his way to a scaffold only a few miles away, and two bodies of men, one led by her father, the other by the man she loved, ready to fly at each other's throats —the one to get the condemned man alive, the other to see that he died. She got up with a groan. She walked into the garden. The grass was tall, tangled, and withering, and in it dead leaves lay everywhere, stems up, stems down, in reckless confusion. The scarlet sage-pods were brown and seeds were dropping from their tiny gaping mouths. The marigolds were frost-nipped and one lonely black-winged butterfly was vainly searching them one by one for the lost sweets of summer. The gorgeous crowns of the sun-flowers were nothing but grotesque black mummy-heads set on lean, dead bodies, and the clump of big castor-plants, buffeted by the wind, leaned this way and that like giants in a drunken orgy trying to keep one another from falling down. The blight that was on the garden was the blight that was in her heart, and two bits of cheer only she found— one yellow nasturtium, scarlet-flecked, whose fragrance was a memory of the spring that was long gone, and one little cedar tree that had caught some dead leaves in its green arms and was firmly holding them as though to promise that another spring would surely come. With the flower in her hand, she started up the ravine to her dreaming place, but it was so lonely up there and she turned back. She went into her room and tried to read. Mechanically, she half opened the lid of the piano and shut it, horrified by her own act. As she passed out on the porch again she noticed that it was only nine o'clock. She turned and watched the long hand—how long a minute was! Three hours more! She shivered and went inside and got her bonnet—she could not be alone when the hour came, and she started down the road toward Uncle Billy's mill. Hale! Hale! Hale!—the name began to ring in her ears like a bell. The little shacks he had built up the creek were deserted and gone to ruin, and she began to wonder in the light of what her father had said how much of a tragedy that meant to him. Here was the spot where he was

355

fishing that day, when she had slipped down behind him and he had turned and seen her for the first time. She could recall his smile and the very tone of his kind voice:

"Howdye, little girl!" And the cat had got her tongue. She remembered when she had written her name, after she had first kissed him at the foot of the beech—"June *Hail*," and by a grotesque mental leap the beating of his name in her brain now made her think of the beating of hailstones on her father's roof one night when as a child she had lain and listened to them. Then she noticed that the autumn shadows seemed to make the river darker than the shadows of spring—or was it already the stain of dead leaves? Hale could have told her. Those leaves were floating through the shadows and when the wind moved, others zigzagged softly down to join them. The wind was helping them on the water, too, and along came one brown leaf that was shaped like a tiny trireme —its stem acting like a rudder and keeping it straight before the breeze—so that it swept past the rest as a yacht that she was once on had swept past a fleet of fishing sloops. She was not unlike that swift little ship and thirty yards ahead were rocks and shallows where it and the whole fleet would turn topsy-turvy—would her own triumph be as short and the same fate be hers? There was no question as to that, unless she took the wheel of her fate in her own hands and with them steered the ship. Thinking hard, she walked on slowly, with her hands behind her and her eyes bent on the road. What should she do? She had no money, her father had none to spare, and she could accept no more from Hale. Once she stopped and stared with unseeing eyes at the blue sky, and once under the heavy helplessness of it all she dropped on the side of the road and sat with her head buried in her arms—sat so long that she rose with a start and, with an apprehensive look at the mounting sun, hurried on. She would go to the Gap and teach; and then she knew that if she went there it would be on Hale's account. Very well, she would not blind herself to that fact; she would go and perhaps all would be made up between them, and then she knew that if that but happened, nothing else could matter. . . .

When she reached the miller's cabin, she went to the porch without noticing that the door was closed. Nobody was at home and she turned listlessly. When she reached the gate, she heard the clock beginning to strike, and with one hand on her breast she breathlessly listened, counting—"eight, nine, ten, eleven"—and her heart seemed to stop in the fraction of time that she waited for it to strike once more. But it was only eleven, and she went on down the road slowly, still thinking hard. The old miller was leaning back in a chair against the log side of the mill, with his dusty slouched hat down over his eyes. He did not hear her coming and she thought he must be asleep, but he looked up with a start when she spoke and she knew of what he, too, had been thinking. Keenly his old eyes searched her white face and without a word he got up and reached for another chair within the mill.

"You set right down now, baby," he said, and he made a pretence of having something to do inside the mill, while June watched the creaking old wheel dropping the sun-shot sparkling water into the swift sluice, but hardly seeing it at all. By and by Uncle Billy came outside and sat down and neither spoke a word. Once June saw him covertly looking at his watch and she put both hands to her throat—stifled.

"What time is it, Uncle Billy?" She tried to ask the question calmly, but she had to try twice before she could speak at all and when she did get the question out, her voice was only a broken whisper.

"Five minutes to twelve, baby," said the old man, and his voice had a gulp in it that broke June down. She sprang to her feet wringing her hands:

"I can't stand it, Uncle Billy," she cried madly, and with a sob that almost broke the old man's heart. "I tell you I can't stand it."

.   .   .   .

And yet for three hours more she had to stand it, while the cavalcade of Tollivers, with Rufe's body, made its slow way to the Kentucky line

358

where Judd and Dave and Bub left them to go home for the night and be on hand for the funeral next day. But Uncle Billy led her back to his cabin, and on the porch the two, with old Hon, waited while the three hours dragged along. It was June who was first to hear the galloping of horses' hoofs up the road and she ran to the gate, followed by Uncle Billy and old Hon to see young Dave Tolliver coming in a run. At the gate he threw himself from his horse:

"Git up thar, June, and go home," he panted sharply. June flashed out the gate.

"Have you done it?" she asked with deadly quiet.

"Hurry up an' go home, I tell ye! Uncle Judd wants ye!"

She came quite close to him now.

"You said you'd do it—I know what you've done—you—" she looked as if she would fly at his throat, and Dave, amazed, shrank back a step.

"Go home, I tell ye—Uncle Judd's shot. Git on the hoss!"

"No, no, no! I wouldn't *touch* anything that was yours"—she put her hands to her head as though she were crazed, and then she turned and broke into a swift run up the road.

Panting, June reached the gate. The front door was closed and there she gave a tremulous cry for Bub. The door opened a few inches and through it Bub shouted for her to come on. The back door, too, was closed, and not a ray of daylight entered the room except at the port-hole where Bub, with a Winchester, had been standing on guard. By the light of the fire she saw her father's giant frame stretched out on the bed and she heard his laboured breathing. Swiftly she went to the bed and dropped on her knees beside it.

"Dad!" she said. The old man's eyes opened and turned heavily toward her.

"All right, Juny. They shot me from the laurel and they might nigh got Bub. I reckon they've got me this time."

"No—no!" He saw her eyes fixed on the matted blood on his chest.

"Hit's stopped. I'm afeared hit's bleedin' inside." His voice had dropped to a whisper and his eyes closed again. There was another cautious "Hello" outside, and when Bub again opened the door Dave ran swiftly within. He paid no attention to June.

"I follered June back an' left my hoss in the bushes. There was three of 'em." He showed Bub a bullet hole through one sleeve and then he turned half contemptuously to June:

"I hain't done it"—adding grimly—"not yit. He's as safe as you air. I hope you're satisfied that hit hain't him 'stid o' yo' daddy thar."

"Are you going to the Gap for a doctor?"

"I reckon I can't leave Bub here alone agin all the Falins—not even to git a doctor or to carry a love-message fer you."

"Then I'll go myself."

A thick protest came from the bed, and then an appeal that might have come from a child.

"Don't leave me, Juny." Without a word June went into the kitchen and got the old bark horn.

"Uncle Billy will go," she said, and she stepped out on the porch. But Uncle Billy was already on his way and she heard him coming just as she was raising the horn to her lips. She met him at the gate, and without even taking the time to come into the house the old miller hurried upward toward the Lonesome Pine. The rain came then—the rain that the tiny cobwebs had heralded at dawn that morning. The old step-mother had not come home, and June told Bub she had gone over the mountain to see her sister, and when, as darkness fell, she did not appear they knew that she must have been caught by the rain and would spend the night with a neighbour. June asked no question, but from the low talk of Bub and Dave she made out what had happened in town that day and a wild elation settled in her heart that John Hale was alive and unhurt—though Rufe was dead, her father wounded, and Bub and Dave both had but narrowly escaped the Falin assassins that afternoon. Bub took the first turn at watching while Dave slept, and when it was Dave's turn she saw him drop quickly asleep in his chair, and she was left alone with the breathing of the wounded man and the beating of rain on the roof.

And through the long night June thought her
brain weary over herself, her life, her people, and
Hale. They were not to blame—her people, they
but did as their fathers had done before them.
They had their own code and they lived up to it
as best they could, and they had had no chance to
learn another. She felt the vindictive hatred that
had prolonged the feud. Had she been a man, she
could not have rested until she had slain the man
who had ambushed her father. She expected Bub
to do that now, and if the spirit was so strong in
her with the training she had had, how helpless
they must be against it. Even Dave was not to
blame—not to blame for loving her—he had always
done that. For that reason he could not help ha-
ting Hale, and how great a reason he had now, for
he could not understand as she could the absence
of any personal motive that had governed him in
the prosecution of the law, no matter if he hurt
friend or foe. But for Hale, she would have loved
Dave and now be married to him and happier
than she was. Dave saw that—no wonder he hated
Hale. And as she slowly realized all these things,
she grew calm and gentle and determined to stick
to her people and do the best she could with her
life.

And now and then through the night old Judd
would open his eyes and stare at the ceiling, and
at these times it was not the pain in his face that
distressed her as much as the drawn beaten look

that she had noticed growing in it for a long time. It was terrible—that helpless look in the face of a man, so big in body, so strong of mind, so iron-like in will; and whenever he did speak she knew what he was going to say:

"It's all over, Juny. They've beat us on every turn. They've got us one by one. Thar ain't but a few of us left now and when I git up, if I ever do, I'm goin' to gether 'em all together, pull up stakes and take 'em all West. You won't ever leave me, Juny?"

"No, Dad," she would say gently. He had asked the question at first quite sanely, but as the night wore on and the fever grew and his mind wandered, he would repeat the question over and over like a child, and over and over, while Bub and Dave slept and the rain poured, June would repeat her answer:

"I'll never leave you, Dad."

XXXI

BEFORE dawn Hale and the doctor and the old miller had reached the Pine, and there Hale stopped. Any farther, the old man told him, he would go only at the risk of his life from Dave or Bub, or even from any Falin who happened to be hanging around in the bushes, for Hale was hated equally by both factions now.

"I'll wait up here until noon, Uncle Billy," said Hale. "Ask her, for God's sake, to come up here and see me. '

"All righ . I'll axe her, but—" the old miller shook his head. Breakfastless, except for the munching of a piece of chocolate, Hale waited all the morning with his black horse in the bushes some thirty yards from the Lonesome Pine. Every now and then he would go to the tree and look down the path, and once he slipped far down the trail and aside to a spur whence he could see the cabin in the cove. Once his hungry eyes caught sight of a woman's figure walking through the little garden, and for an hour after it disappeared into the house he watched for it to come out again. But nothing more was visible, and he turned back to the trail to see Uncle Billy labori-

364

ously climbing up the slope. Hale waited and ran down to meet him, his face and eyes eager and his lips trembling, but again Uncle Billy was shaking his head.

"No use, John," he said sadly. "I got her out on the porch and axed her, but she won't come."

"She won't come at all?"

"John, when one o' them Tollivers gits white about the mouth, an' thar eyes gits to blazin' and they *keeps quiet*—they're plumb out o' reach o' the Almighty hisself. June skeered me. But you mustn't blame her jes' now. You see, you got up that guard. You ketched Rufe and hung him, and she can't help thinkin' if you hadn't done that, her old daddy wouldn't be in thar on his back nigh to death. You mustn't blame her, John— she's most out o' her head now."

"All right, Uncle Billy. Good-by." Hale turned, climbed sadly back to his horse and sadly dropped down the other side of the mountain and on through the rocky gap—home.

A week later he learned from the doctor that the chances were even that old Judd would get well, but the days went by with no word of June. Through those days June wrestled with her love for Hale and her loyalty to her father, who, sick as he was, seemed to have a vague sense of the trouble within her and shrewdly fought it by making her daily promise that she would never leave him. For as old Judd got better, June's fierceness against

365

Hale melted and her love came out the stronger, because of the passing injustice that she had done him. Many times she was on the point of sending him word that she would meet him at the Pine, but she was afraid of her own strength if she should see him face to face, and she feared she would be risking his life if she allowed him to come. There were times when she would have gone to him herself, had her father been well and strong, but he was old, beaten and helpless, and she had given her sacred word that she would never leave him. So once more she grew calmer, gentler still, and more determined to follow her own way with her own kin, though that way led through a breaking heart. She never mentioned Hale's name, she never spoke of going West, and in time Dave began to wonder not only if she had not gotten over her feeling for Hale, but if that feeling had not turned into permanent hate. To him, June was kinder than ever, because she understood him better and because she was sorry for the hunted, hounded life he led, not knowing, when on his trips to see her or to do some service for her father, he might be picked off by some Falin from the bushes. So Dave stopped his sneering remarks against Hale and began to dream his old dreams, though he never opened his lips to June, and she was unconscious of what was going on within him. By and by, as old Judd began to mend, overtures of peace came, singularly enough, from the Falins, and while the old man snorted with contemptuous disbelief at them as a pretence to throw him off his guard, Dave began actually to believe that they were sincere, and straightway forged a plan of his own, even if the Tollivers did persist in going West. So one morning as he mounted his horse at old Judd's gate, he called to June in the garden:

"I'm a-goin' over to the Gap." June paled, but Dave was not looking at her.

"What for?" she asked, steadying her voice.

"Business," he answered, and he laughed curiously and, still without looking at her, rode away.

.   .   .   .   .   .

Hale sat in the porch of his little office that morning, and the Hon. Sam Budd, who had risen to leave, stood with his hands deep in his pockets, his hat tilted far over his big goggles, looking down at the dead leaves that floated like lost hopes on the placid mill-pond. Hale had agreed to go to England once more on the sole chance left him before he went back to chain and compass—the old land deal that had come to life—and between them they had about enough money for the trip.

"You'll keep an eye on things over there?" said Hale with a backward motion of his head toward Lonesome Cove, and the Hon. Sam nodded his head:

"All I can."

"Those big trunks of hers are still here." The

Hon. Sam smiled. "She won't need 'em. I'll keep an eye on 'em and she can come over and get what she wants—every year or two," he added grimly, and Hale groaned.

"Stop it, Sam."

"All right. You ain't goin' to try to see her before you leave?" And then at the look on Hale's face he said hurriedly: "All right—all right," and with a toss of his hands turned away, while Hale sat thinking where he was.

Rufe Tolliver had been quite right as to the Red Fox. Nobody would risk his life for him—there was no one to attempt a rescue, and but a few of the guards were on hand this time to carry out the law. On the last day he had appeared in his white suit of tablecloth. The little old woman in black had made even the cap that was to be drawn over his face, and that, too, she had made of white. Moreover, she would have his body kept unburied for three days, because the Red Fox said that on the third day he would arise and go about preaching. So that even in death the Red Fox was consistently inconsistent, and how he reconciled such a dual life at one and the same time over and under the stars was, except to his twisted brain, never known. He walked firmly up the scaffold steps and stood there blinking in the sunlight. With one hand he tested the rope. For a moment he looked at the sky and the trees with a face that was white and absolutely expressionless.

368

Then he sang one hymn of two verses and quietly dropped into that world in which he believed so firmly and toward which he had trod so strange a way on earth. As he wished, the little old woman in black had the body kept unburied for the three days—but the Red Fox never rose. With his passing, law and order had become supreme. Neither Tolliver nor Falin came on the Virginia side for mischief, and the desperadoes of two sister States, whose skirts are stitched together with pine and pin-oak along the crest of the Cumberland, confined their deviltries with great care to places long distant from the Gap. John Hale had done a great work, but the limit of his activities was that State line and the Falins, ever threatening that they would not leave a Tolliver alive, could carry out those threats and Hale not be able to lift a hand. It was his helplessness that was making him writhe now.

Old Judd had often said he meant to leave the mountains—why didn't he go now and take June for whose safety his heart was always in his mouth? As an officer, he was now helpless where he was; and if he went away he could give no personal aid —he would not even know what was happening— and he had promised Budd to go. An open letter was clutched in his hand, and again he read it. His coal company had accepted his last proposition. They would take his stock—worthless as they thought it—and surrender the cabin and two hundred acres of field and woodland in Lonesome Cove. That much at least would be intact, but if he failed in his last project now, it would be subject to judgments against him that were sure to come. So there was one thing more to do for June before he left for the final effort in England—to give back her home to her—and as he rose to do it now, somebody shouted at his gate:

"Hello!" Hale stopped short at the head of the steps, his right hand shot like a shaft of light to the butt of his pistol, stayed there—and he stood astounded. It was Dave Tolliver on horseback, and Dave's right hand had kept hold of his bridle-reins.

"Hold on!" he said, lifting the other with a wide gesture of peace. "I want to talk with you a bit." Still Hale watched him closely as he swung from his horse.

"Come in—won't you?" The mountaineer hitched his horse and slouched within the gate.

"Have a seat." Dave dropped to the steps.

"I'll set here," he said, and there was an embarrassed silence for a while between the two. Hale studied young Dave's face from narrowed eyes. He knew all the threats the Tolliver had made against him, the bitter enmity that he felt, and that it would last until one or the other was dead. This was a queer move. The mountaineer took off his slouched hat and ran one hand through his thick black hair.

"I reckon you've heard as how all our folks air sellin' out over the mountains."

"No," said Hale quickly.

"Well, they air, an' all of 'em are going West—Uncle Judd, Loretty and June, and all our kinfolks. You didn't know that?"

"No," repeated Hale.

"Well, they hain't closed all the trades yit," he said, "an' they mought not go mebbe afore spring. The Falins say they air done now. Uncle Judd don't believe 'em, but I do, an' I'm thinkin' I won't go. I've got a leetle money, an' I want to know if I can't buy back Uncle Judd's house an' a leetle ground around it. Our folks is tired o' fightin' and I couldn't live on t'other side of the mountain, after they air gone, an' keep as healthy as on this side—so I thought I'd see if I couldn't buy back June's old home, mebbe, an' live thar."

Hale watched him keenly, wondering what his game was—and he went on: "I know the house an' land ain't wuth much to your company, an' as the coal-vein has petered out, I reckon they might not axe much fer it." It was all out now, and he stopped without looking at Hale. "I ain't axin' any favours, leastwise not o' you, an' I thought my share o' Mam's farm mought be enough to git me the house an' some o' the land."

"You mean to live there, yourself?"

"Yes."

371

"Alone?" Dave frowned.

"I reckon that's my business."

"So it is—excuse me." Hale lighted his pipe and the mountaineer waited—he was a little sullen now.

"Well, the company has parted with the land." Dave started.

"Sold it?"

"In a way—yes."

"Well, would you mind tellin' me who bought it—maybe I can git it from him."

"It's mine now," said Hale quietly.

"*Yourn!*" The mountaineer looked incredulous and then he let loose a scornful laugh.

"*You* goin' to live thar?"

"Maybe."

"Alone?"

"That's my business." The mountaineer's face darkened and his fingers began to twitch.

"Well, if you're talkin' 'bout June, hit's *my* business. Hit always has been and hit always will be."

"Well, if I was talking about June, I wouldn't consult you."

"No, but I'd consult you like hell."

"I wish you had the chance," said Hale coolly; "but I wasn't talking about June." Again Dave laughed harshly, and for a moment his angry eyes rested on the quiet mill-pond. He went backward suddenly.

"You went over thar in Lonesome with your high notions an' your slick tongue, an' you took June away from me. But she wusn't good enough fer you *then*—so you filled her up with yo' fool notions an' sent her away to git her po' little head filled with furrin' ways, so she could be fitten to marry you. You took her away from her daddy, her family, her kinfolks and her home, an' you took her away from me; an' now she's been over thar eatin' her heart out just as she et it out over here when she fust left home. An' in the end she got so highfalutin that *she* wouldn't marry *you*." He laughed again and Hale winced under the laugh and the lashing words. "An' I know you air eatin' yo' heart out, too, because you can't git June, an' I'm hopin' you'll suffer the torment o' hell as long as you live. God, she hates ye now! To think o' your knowin' the world and women and books"—he spoke with vindictive and insulting slowness—"You bein' such a —— fool!"

"That may all be true, but I think you can talk better outside that gate." The mountaineer, deceived by Hale's calm voice, sprang to his feet in a fury, but he was too late. Hale's hand was on the butt of his revolver, his blue eyes were glittering and a dangerous smile was at his lips. Silently he sat and silently he pointed his other hand at the gate. Dave laughed:

"D'ye think I'd fight you hyeh? If you killed me, you'd be elected County Jedge; if I killed you,

373

what chance would I have o' gittin' away? I'd swing fer it." He was outside the gate now and unhitching his horse. He started to turn the beast, but Hale stopped him.

"Get on from this side, please."

With one foot in the stirrup, Dave turned savagely: "Why don't you go up in the Gap with me now an' fight it out like a man?"

"I don't trust you."

"I'll git ye over in the mountains some day."

"I've no doubt you will, if you have the chance from the bush." Hale was getting roused now.

"Look here," he said suddenly, "you've been threatening me for a long time now. I've never had any feeling against you. I've never done anything to you that I hadn't to do. But you've gone a little too far now and I'm tired. If you can't get over your grudge against me, suppose we go across the river outside the town-limits, put our guns down and fight it out—fist and skull."

"I'm your man," said Dave eagerly. Looking across the street Hale saw two men on the porch.

"Come on!" he said. The two men were Budd and the new town-sergeant. "Sam," he said, "this gentleman and I are going across the river to have a little friendly bout, and I wish you'd come along—and you, too, Bill, to see that Dave here gets fair play."

The sergeant spoke to Dave. "You don't need

nobody to see that you git fair play with them two —but I'll go 'long just the same." Hardly a word was said as the four walked across the bridge and toward a thicket to the right. Neither Budd nor the sergeant asked the nature of the trouble, for either could have guessed what it was. Dave tied his horse and, like Hale, stripped off his coat. The sergeant took charge of Dave's pistol and Budd of Hale's.

"All you've got to do is to keep him away from you," said Budd. "If he gets his hands on you— you're gone. You know how they fight rough-and-tumble."

Hale nodded—he knew all that himself, and when he looked at Dave's sturdy neck, and gigantic shoulders, he knew further that if the mountaineer got him in his grasp he would have to gasp "enough" in a hurry, or be saved by Budd from being throttled to death.

"Are you ready?" Again Hale nodded.

"Go ahead, Dave," growled the sergeant, for the job was not to his liking. Dave did not plunge toward Hale, as the three others expected. On the contrary, he assumed the conventional attitude of the boxer and advanced warily, using his head as a diagnostician for Hale's points—and Hale remembered suddenly that Dave had been away at school for a year. Dave knew something of the game and the Hon. Sam straightway was anxious, when the mountaineer ducked and swung his left.

Budd's heart thumped and he almost shrank himself from the terrific sweep of the big fist.

"God!" he muttered, for had the fist caught Hale's head it must, it seemed, have crushed it like an egg-shell. Hale coolly withdrew his head not more than an inch, it seemed to Budd's practised eye, and jabbed his right with a lightning uppercut into Dave's jaw, that made the mountaineer reel backward with a grunt of rage and pain, and when he followed it up with a swing of his left on Dave's right eye and another terrific jolt with his right on the left jaw, and Budd saw the crazy rage in the mountaineer's face, he felt easy. In that rage Dave forgot his science as the Hon. Sam expected, and with a bellow he started at Hale like a cave-dweller to bite, tear, and throttle, but the lithe figure before him swayed this way and that like a shadow, and with every side-step a fist crushed on the mountaineer's nose, chin or jaw, until, blinded with blood and fury, Dave staggered aside toward the sergeant with the cry of a madman:

"Gimme my gun! I'll kill him! Gimme my gun!" And when the sergeant sprang forward and caught the mountaineer, he dropped weeping with rage and shame to the ground.

"You two just go back to town," said the sergeant. "I'll take keer of him. Quick!" and he shook his head as Hale advanced. "He ain't goin' to shake hands with you."

The two turned back across the bridge and Hale went on to Budd's office to do what he was setting out to do when young Dave came. There he had the lawyer make out a deed in which the cabin in Lonesome Cove and the acres about it were conveyed in fee simple to June—her heirs and assigns forever; but the girl must not know until, Hale said, "her father dies, or I die, or she marries." When he came out the sergeant was passing the door.

"Ain't no use fightin' with one o' them fellers thataway," he said, shaking his head. "If he whoops you, he'll crow over you as long as he lives, and if you whoop him, he'll kill ye the fust chance he gets. You'll have to watch that feller as long as you live—'specially when he's drinking. He'll remember that lickin' and want revenge fer it till the grave. One of you has got to die some day—shore."

And the sergeant was right. Dave was going through the Gap at that moment, cursing, swaying like a drunken man, firing his pistol and shouting his revenge to the echoing gray walls that took up his cries and sent them shrieking on the wind up every dark ravine. All the way up the mountain he was cursing. Under the gentle voice of the big Pine he was cursing still, and when his lips stopped, his heart was beating curses as he dropped down the other side of the mountain.

When he reached the river, he got off his horse

and bathed his mouth and his eyes again, and he cursed afresh when the blood started afresh at his lips again. For a while he sat there in his black mood, undecided whether he should go to his uncle's cabin or go on home. But he had seen a woman's figure in the garden as he came down the spur, and the thought of June drew him to the cabin in spite of his shame and the questions that were sure to be asked. When he passed around the clump of rhododendrons at the creek, June was in the garden still. She was pruning a rose-bush with Bub's penknife, and when she heard him coming she wheeled, quivering. She had been waiting for him all day, and, like an angry goddess, she swept fiercely toward him. Dave pretended not to see her, but when he swung from his horse and lifted his sullen eyes, he shrank as though she had lashed him across them with a whip. Her eyes blazed with murderous fire from her white face, the penknife in her hand was clenched as though for a deadly purpose, and on her trembling lips was the same question that she had asked him at the mill:

"Have you done it this time?" she whispered, and then she saw his swollen mouth and his bat-tered eye. Her fingers relaxed about the handle of the knife, the fire in her eyes went swiftly down, and with a smile that was half pity, half contempt, she turned away. She could not have told the whole truth better in words, even to Dave, and as he looked after her his every pulse-beat was a new curse, and if at that minute he could have had Hale's heart he would have eaten it like a savage— raw. For a minute he hesitated with reins in hand as to whether he should turn now and go back to the Gap to settle with Hale, and then he threw the reins over a post. He could bide his time yet a little longer, for a crafty purpose suddenly entered his brain. Bub met him at the door of the cabin and his eyes opened.

"What's the matter, Dave?"

"Oh, nothin'," he said carelessly. "My hoss stumbled comin' down the mountain an' I went clean over his head." He raised one hand to his mouth and still Bub was suspicious.

"Looks like you been in a fight." The boy began to laugh, but Dave ignored him and went on into the cabin. Within, he sat where he could see through the open door.

"Whar you been, Dave?" asked old Judd from the corner. Just then he saw June coming and, pretending to draw on his pipe, he waited until she had sat down within ear-shot on the edge of the porch.

"Who do you reckon owns this house and two hundred acres o' land roundabouts?"

The girl's heart waited apprehensively and she heard her father's deep voice.

"The company owns it." Dave laughed harshly.

"Not much—John Hale." The heart out on the porch leaped with gladness now.

379

"He bought it from the company. It's just as well you're goin' away, Uncle Judd. He'd put you out."

"I reckon not. I got writin' from the company which 'lows me to stay here two year or more—if I want to."

"I don't know. He's a slick one."

"I heerd him say," put in Bub stoutly, "that he'd see that we stayed here jus' as long as we pleased."

"Well," said old Judd shortly, "ef we stay here by his favour, we won't stay long."

There was silence for a while. Then Dave spoke again for the listening ears outside—maliciously:

"I went over to the Gap to see if I couldn't git the place myself from the company. I believe the Falins ain't goin' to bother us an' I ain't hankerin' to go West. But I told him that you-all was goin' to leave the mountains and goin' out thar fer good." There was another silence.

"He never said a word." Nobody had asked the question, but he was answering the unspoken one in the heart of June, and that heart sank like a stone.

"He's goin' away hisself—goin' ter-morrow—goin' to that same place he went before—England, some feller called it."

Dave had done his work well. June rose unsteadily, and with one hand on her heart and the other clutching the railing of the porch, she crept noiselessly along it, staggered like a wounded thing around the chimney, through the garden and on, still clutching her heart, to the woods—there to sob it out on the breast of the only mother she had ever known.

Dave was gone when she came back from the woods—calm, dry-eyed, pale. Her step-mother had kept her dinner for her, and when she said she wanted nothing to eat, the old woman answered something querulous to which June made no answer, but went quietly to cleaning away the dishes. For a while she sat on the porch, and presently she went into her room and for a few moments she rocked quietly at her window. Hale was going away next day, and when he came back she would be gone and she would never see him again. A dry sob shook her body of a sudden, she put both hands to her head and with wild eyes she sprang to her feet and, catching up her bonnet, slipped noiselessly out the back door. With hands clenched tight she forced herself to walk slowly across the foot-bridge, but when the bushes hid her, she broke into a run as though she were crazed and escaping a madhouse. At the foot of the spur she turned swiftly up the mountain and climbed madly, with one hand tight against the little cross at her throat. He was going away and she must tell him—she must tell him—what? Behind her a voice was calling, the voice that pleaded all one night for her not to leave him, that had made that plea a daily prayer, and it had come from an old man—wounded, broken in health and heart, and her father. Hale's face was before her, but that voice was behind, and as she climbed, the face that she was nearing grew fainter, the voice she was leaving sounded the louder in her ears, and when she reached the big Pine she dropped helplessly at the base of it, sobbing. With her tears the madness slowly left her, the old determination came back again and at last the old sad peace. The sunlight was slanting at a low angle when she rose to her feet and stood on the cliff overlooking the valley—her lips parted as when she stood there first, and the tiny drops drying along the roots of her dull gold hair. And being there for the last time she thought of that time when she was first there—ages ago. The great glare of light that she looked for then had come and gone. There was the smoking monster rushing into the valley and sending echoing shrieks through the hills—but there was no booted stranger and no horse issuing from the covert of maple where the path disappeared. A long time she stood there, with a wandering look of farewell to every familiar thing before her, but not a tear came now. Only as she turned away at last her breast heaved and fell with one long breath—that was all. Passing the Pine slowly, she stopped and turned back to it, unclasping the necklace from her throat. With trembling fingers she detached from it the little luck-piece that Hale had given her—the tear of a fairy that had turned into a tiny cross of stone when a strange messenger brought to the Virginia valley the story of the crucifixion. The penknife was still in her pocket, and, opening it, she went behind the Pine and dug a niche as high and as deep as she could toward its soft old heart. In there she thrust the tiny symbol, whispering:

"I want all the luck you could ever give me, little cross—for *him*." Then she pulled the fibres down to cover it from sight and, crossing her hands over the opening, she put her forehead against them and touched her lips to the tree.

"Keep it safe, old Pine." Then she lifted her face—looking upward along its trunk to the blue sky. "And bless him, dear God, and guard him evermore." She clutched her heart as she turned, and she was clutching it when she passed into the shadows below, leaving the old Pine to whisper, when he passed, her love.

. . . . . .

Next day the word went round to the clan that the Tollivers would start in a body one week later for the West. At daybreak, that morning, Uncle Billy and his wife mounted the old gray horse and rode up the river to say good-by. They found the cabin in Lonesome Cove deserted. Many things were left piled in the porch; the Tollivers had left apparently in a great hurry and the two old people were much mystified. Not until noon did they learn what the matter was. Only the night before a Tolliver had shot a Falin and the Falins had gathered to get revenge on Judd that night. The warning word had been brought to Lonesome Cove by Loretta Tolliver, and it had come straight from young Buck Falin himself. So June and old Judd and Bub had fled in the night. At that hour they were on their way to the railroad—old Judd at the head of his clan—his right arm still bound to his side, his bushy beard low on his breast, June and Bub on horseback behind him, the rest strung out behind them, and in a wagon at the end, with all her household effects, the little old woman in black who would wait no longer for the Red Fox to arise from the dead. Loretta alone was missing. She was on her way with young Buck Falin to the railroad on the other side of the mountains. Between them not a living soul disturbed the dead stillness of Lonesome Cove.

XXXII

ALL winter the cabin in Lonesome Cove slept through rain and sleet and snow, and no foot passed its threshold. Winter broke, floods came and warm sunshine. A pale green light stole through the trees, shy, ethereal and so like a mist that it seemed at any moment on the point of floating upward. Colour came with the wild flowers and song with the wood-thrush. Squirrels played on the tree-trunks like mischievous children, the brooks sang like happy human voices through the tremulous underworld and woodpeckers hammered out the joy of spring, but the awakening only made the desolate cabin lonelier still. After three warm days in March, Uncle Billy, the miller, rode up the creek with a hoe over his shoulder—he had promised this to Hale—for his labour of love in June's garden. Weeping April passed, May came with rosy face uplifted, and with the birth of June the laurel emptied its pink-flecked cups and the rhododendron blazed the way for the summer's coming with white stars.

Back to the hills came Hale then, and with all their rich beauty they were as desolate as when he left them bare with winter, for his mission had miserably failed.

His train creaked and twisted around the benches of the mountains, and up and down ravines into the hills. The smoke rolled in as usual through the windows and doors. There was the same crowd of children, slatternly women and tobacco-spitting men in the dirty day-coaches, and Hale sat among them—for a Pullman was no longer attached to the train that ran to the Gap. As he neared the bulk of Powell's mountain and ran along its mighty flank, he passed the ore-mines. At each one the commissary was closed, the cheap, dingy little houses stood empty on the hillsides, and every now and then he would see a tipple and an empty car, left as it was after dumping its last load of red ore. On the right, as he approached the station, the big furnace stood like a dead giant, still and smokeless, and the piles of pig iron were red with rust. The same little dummy wheezed him into the dead little town. Even the face of the Gap was a little changed by the gray scar that man had slashed across its mouth, getting limestone for the groaning monster of a furnace that was now at peace. The streets were deserted. A new face fronted him at the desk of the hotel and the eyes of the clerk showed no knowledge of him when he wrote his name. His supper was coarse, greasy and miserable, his room was cold (steam heat, it seemed, had been given up), the sheets were ill-smelling, the mouth of the pitcher was broken, and the one towel had seen much previous use. But the water was the same, as was the cool, pungent night-air—both blessed of God—and they were the sole comforts that were his that night.

The next day it was as though he were arranging his own funeral, with but little hope of a resurrection. The tax-collector met him when he came downstairs—having seen his name on the register.

"You know," he said, "I'll have to add 5 per cent. next month." Hale smiled.

"That won't be much more," he said, and the collector, a new one, laughed good-naturedly and with understanding turned away. Mechanically he walked to the Club, but there was no club—then on to the office of *The Progress*—the paper that was the boast of the town. *The Progress* was defunct and the brilliant editor had left the hills. A boy with an ink-smeared face was setting type and a pallid gentleman with glasses was languidly working a hand-press. A pile of fresh-smelling papers lay on a table, and after a question or two he picked up one. Two of its four pages were covered with announcements of suits and sales to satisfy judgments—the printing of which was the *raison d'être* of the noble sheet. Down the column his eye caught John Hale *et al.* John Hale *et al.*, and he wondered why "the others" should be so persistently anonymous. There was a cloud of them—thicker than the smoke of coke-ovens. He had breathed that thickness for a long time, but he got a fresh sense of suffocation now. Toward the post-office he moved. Around the corner he came upon one of two brothers whom he remembered as carpenters. He recalled his inability once to get that gentleman to hang a door for him. He was a carpenter again now and he carried a saw and a plane. There was grim humour in the situation. The carpenter's brother had gone—and he himself could hardly get enough work, he said, to support his family.

"Goin' to start that house of yours?"

"I think not," said Hale.

"Well, I'd like to get a contract for a chicken-coop just to keep my hand in."

There was more. A two-horse wagon was coming with two cottage-organs aboard. In the mouth of the slouch-hatted, unshaven driver was a corn-cob pipe. He pulled in when he saw Hale.

"Hello!" he shouted grinning. Good Heavens, was that uncouth figure the voluble, buoyant, flashy magnate of the old days? It was.

"Sellin' organs agin," he said briefly.

"And teaching singing-school?"

The dethroned king of finance grinned.

"Sure! What you doin'?"

"Nothing."

"Goin' to stay long?"

"No."

"Well, see you again. So long. Git up!"

Wheel-spokes whirred in the air and he saw a

388

buggy, with the top down, rattling down another street in a cloud of dust. It was the same buggy in which he had first seen the black-bearded Senator seven years before. It was the same horse, too, and the Arab-like face and the bushy black whiskers, save for streaks of gray, were the same. This was the man who used to buy watches and pianos by the dozen, who one Xmas gave a present to every living man, woman and child in the town, and under whose colossal schemes the pillars of the church throughout the State stood as supports. That far away the eagle-nosed face looked haggard, haunted and all but spent, and even now he struck Hale as being driven downward like a madman by the same relentless energy that once had driven him upward. It was the same story everywhere. Nearly everybody who could get away was gone. Some of these were young enough to profit by the lesson and take surer root elsewhere —others were too old for transplanting, and of them would be heard no more. Others stayed for the reason that getting away was impossible. These were living, visible tragedies—still hopeful, pathetically unaware of the leading parts they were playing, and still weakly waiting for a better day or sinking, as by gravity, back to the old trades they had practised before the boom. A few sturdy souls, the fittest, survived—undismayed. Logan was there—lawyer for the railroad and the coal-company. MacFarlan was a judge, and two or three others, too, had come through unscathed in spirit and undaunted in resolution—but gone were the young Bluegrass Kentuckians, the young Tide-water Virginians, the New England school-teachers, the bankers, real-estate agents, engineers; gone the gamblers, the wily Jews and the vagrant women that fringe the incoming tide of a new prosperity—gone—all gone!

Beyond the post-office he turned toward the red-brick house that sat above the mill-pond. Eagerly he looked for the old mill, and he stopped in physical pain. The dam had been torn away, the old wheel was gone and a caved-in roof and supporting walls, drunkenly aslant, were the only remnants left. A red-haired child stood at the gate before the red-brick house and Hale asked her a question. The little girl had never heard of the Widow Crane. Then he walked toward his old office and bedroom. There was a voice inside his old office when he approached, a tall figure filled the doorway, a pair of great goggles beamed on him like beacon lights in a storm, and the Hon. Sam Budd's hand and his were clasped over the gate.

"It's all over, Sam."

"Don't you worry—come on in."

The two sat on the porch. Below it the dimpled river shone through the rhododendrons and with his eyes fixed on it, the Hon. Sam slowly approached the thought of each.

"The old cabin in Lonesome Cove is just as the Tollivers left it."

"None of them ever come back?" Budd shook his head.

"No, but one's comin'—Dave."

"Dave!"

"Yes, an' you know what for."

"I suppose so," said Hale carelessly. "Did you send old Judd the deed?"

"Sure—along with that fool condition of yours that June shouldn't know until he was dead or she married. I've never heard a word."

"Do you suppose he'll stick to the condition?"

"He has stuck," said the Hon. Sam shortly; "otherwise you would have heard from June."

"I'm not going to be here long," said Hale.

"Where you goin'?"

"I don't know." Budd puffed his pipe.

"Well, while you are here, you want to keep your eye peeled for Dave Tolliver. I told you that the mountaineer hates as long as he remembers, and that he never forgets. Do you know that Dave sent his horse back to the stable here to be hired out for his keep, and told it right and left that when you came back he was comin', too, and he was goin' to straddle that horse until he found you, and then one of you had to die? How he found out you were comin' about this time I don't know, but he has sent word that he'll be here. Looks like he hasn't made much headway with June."

"I'm not worried."

"Well, you better be," said Budd sharply.

"Did Uncle Billy plant the garden?"

"Flowers and all, just as June always had 'em. He's always had the idea that June would come back."

"Maybe she will."

"Not on your life. She might if you went out there for her."

Hale looked up quickly and slowly shook his head.

"Look here, Jack, you're seein' things wrong. You can't blame that girl for losing her head after you spoiled and pampered her the way you did. And with all her sense it was mighty hard for her to understand your being arrayed against her flesh and blood—law or no law. That's mountain nature pure and simple, and it comes mighty near bein' human nature the world over. You never gave her a square chance."

"You know what Uncle Billy said?"

"Yes, an' I know Uncle Billy changed his mind. Go after her."

"No," said Hale firmly. "It'll take me ten years to get out of debt. I wouldn't now if I could—on her account."

"Nonsense." Hale rose.

"I'm going over to take a look around and get some things I left at Uncle Billy's and then—me for the wide, wide world again."

392

The Hon. Sam took off his spectacles to wipe them, but when Hale's back was turned, his handkerchief went to his eyes:

"Don't you worry, Jack."

"All right, Sam."

An hour later Hale was at the livery stable for a horse to ride to Lonesome Cove, for he had sold his big black to help out expenses for the trip to England. Old Dan Harris, the stableman, stood in the door and silently he pointed to a gray horse in the barn-yard.

"You know that hoss?"

"Yes."

"You know whut's he here fer?"

"I've heard."

"Well, I'm lookin' fer Dave every day now."

"Well, maybe I'd better ride Dave's horse now," said Hale jestingly.

"I wish you would," said old Dan.

"No," said Hale, "if he's coming, I'll leave the horse so that he can get to me as quickly as possible. You might send me word, Uncle Dan, ahead, so that he can't waylay me."

"I'll do that very thing," said the old man seriously.

"I was joking, Uncle Dan."

"But I ain't."

The matter was out of Hale's head before he got through the great Gap. How the memories thronged of June—June—June!

393

"You didn't give her a chance."

That was what Budd said. Well, had he given her a chance? Why shouldn't he go to her and give her the chance now? He shook his shoulders at the thought and laughed with some bitterness. He hadn't the car-fare for half-way across the continent—and even if he had, he was a promising candidate for matrimony!—and again he shook his shoulders and settled his soul for his purpose. He would get his things together and leave those hills forever.

How lonely had been his trip—how lonely was the God-forsaken little town behind him! How lonely the road and hills and the little white clouds in the zenith straight above him—and how unspeakably lonely the green dome of the great Pine that shot into view from the north as he turned a clump of rhododendron with uplifted eyes. Not a breath of air moved. The green expanse about him swept upward like a wave—but unflecked, motionless, except for the big Pine which, that far away, looked like a bit of green spray, spouting on its very crest.

"Old man," he muttered, "you know—you know." And as to a brother he climbed toward it.

"No wonder they call you Lonesome," he said as he went upward into the bright stillness, and when he dropped into the dark stillness of shadow and forest gloom on the other side he said again:

"My God, no wonder they call you Lonesome."

And still the memories of June thronged—at the brook—at the river—and when he saw the smokeless chimney of the old cabin, he all but groaned aloud. But he turned away from it, unable to look again, and went down the river toward Uncle Billy's mill.

.   .   .   .   .   .

Old Hon threw her arms around him and kissed him.

"John," said Uncle Billy, "I've got three hundred dollars in a old yarn sock under one of them hearthstones and its yourn. Ole Hon says so too."

Hale choked.

"I want ye to go to June. Dave'll worry her down and git her if you don't go, and if he don't worry her down, he'll come back an' try to kill ye. I've always thought one of ye would have to die fer that gal, an' I want it to be Dave. You two have got to fight it out some day, and you mought as well meet him out thar as here. You didn't give that little gal a fair chance, John, an' I want you to go to June."

"No, I can't take your money, Uncle Billy— God bless you and old Hon—I'm going—I don't know where—and I'm going now."

XXXIII

CLOUDS were gathering as Hale rode up the river after telling old Hon and Uncle Billy good-by. He had meant not to go to the cabin in Lonesome Cove, but when he reached the forks of the road, he stopped his horse and sat in indecision with his hands folded on the pommel of his saddle and his eyes on the smokeless chimney. The memories tugging at his heart drew him irresistibly on, for it was the last time. At a slow walk he went noiselessly through the deep sand around the clump of rhododendron. The creek was clear as crytsal once more, but no geese cackled and no dog barked. The door of the spring-house gaped wide, the barn-door sagged on its hinges, the yard-fence swayed drunkenly, and the cabin was still as a gravestone. But the garden was alive, and he swung from his horse at the gate, and with his hands clasped behind his back walked slowly through it. June's garden! The garden he had planned and planted for June—that they had tended together and apart and that, thanks to the old miller's care, was the one thing, save the sky above, left in spirit unchanged. The periwinkles, pink and white, were almost gone. The flags were at half-mast and sinking fast. The annunciation lilies were bending their white foreheads to the near kiss of death, but the pinks were fragrant, the poppies were poised on slender stalks like brilliant butterflies at rest, the hollyhocks shook soundless pink bells to the wind, roses as scarlet as June's lips bloomed everywhere and the richness of mid-summer was at hand.

Quietly Hale walked the paths, taking a last farewell of plant and flower, and only the sudden patter of raindrops made him lift his eyes to the angry sky. The storm was coming now in earnest and he had hardly time to lead his horse to the barn and dash to the porch when the very heavens, with a crash of thunder, broke loose. Sheet after sheet swept down the mountains like wind-driven clouds of mist thickening into water as they came. The shingles rattled as though with the heavy slapping of hands, the pines creaked and the sudden dusk outside made the cabin, when he pushed the door open, as dark as night. Kindling a fire, he lit his pipe and waited. The room was damp and musty, but the presence of June almost smothered him. Once he turned his face. June's door was ajar and the key was in the lock. He rose to go to it and look within and then dropped heavily back into his chair. He was anxious to get away now—to get to work. Several times he rose restlessly and looked out the window. Once he went outside and crept along the wall of the cabin to the east and the west, but there was no break of light in the murky sky and he went back to pipe and fire. By and by the wind died and the rain steadied into a dogged downpour. He knew what that meant—there would be no letting up now in the storm, and for another night he was a prisoner. So he went to his saddle-pockets and pulled out a cake of chocolate, a can of potted ham and some crackers, munched his supper, went to bed, and lay there with sleepless eyes, while the lights and shadows from the wind-swayed fire flicked about him. After a while his body dozed but his racked brain went seething on in an endless march of fantastic dreams in which June was the central figure always, until of a sudden young Dave leaped into the centre of the stage in the dream-tragedy forming in his brain. They were meeting face to face at last—and the place was the big Pine. Dave's pistol flashed and his own stuck in the holster as he tried to draw. There was a crashing report and he sprang upright in bed—but it was a crash of thunder that wakened him and that in that swift instant perhaps had caused his dream. The wind had come again and was driving the rain like soft bullets against the wall of the cabin next which he lay. He got up, threw another stick of wood on the fire and sat before the leaping blaze, curiously disturbed but not by the dream. Somehow he was again in doubt—was he going to stick it out in the mountains after all, and if he should, was not the reason, deep down in his soul, the foolish hope that June would come back again. No, he thought, searching himself fiercely, that was not the reason. He honestly did not know what his duty to her was—what even was his inmost wish, and almost with a groan he paced the floor to and fro. Meantime the storm raged. A tree crashed on the mountainside and the lightning that smote it winked into the cabin so like a mocking, malignant eye that he stopped in his tracks, threw open the door and stepped outside as though to face an enemy. The storm was majestic and his soul went into the mighty conflict of earth and air, whose beginning and end were in eternity. The very mountain tops were rimmed with zigzag fire, which shot upward, splitting a sky that was as black as a nether world, and under it the great trees swayed like willows under rolling clouds of gray rain. One fiery streak lit up for an instant the big Pine and seemed to dart straight down upon its proud, tossing crest. For a moment the beat of the watcher's heart and the flight of his soul stopped still. A thunderous crash came slowly to his waiting ears, another flash came, and Hale stumbled, with a sob, back into the cabin. God's finger was pointing the way now—the big Pine was no more.

XXXIV

THE big Pine was gone. He had seen it first, one morning at daybreak, when the valley on the other side was a sea of mist that threw soft, clinging spray to the very mountain tops—for even above the mists, that morning, its mighty head arose, sole visible proof that the earth still slept beneath. He had seen it at noon—but little less majestic, among the oaks that stood about it; had seen it catching the last light at sunset, clean-cut against the after-glow, and like a dark, silent, mysterious sentinel guarding the mountain pass under the moon. He had seen it giving place with sombre dignity to the passing burst of spring, had seen it green among dying autumn leaves, green in the gray of winter trees and still green in a shroud of snow—a changeless promise that the earth must wake to life again. It had been the beacon that led him into Lonesome Cove—the beacon that led June into the outer world. From it her flying feet had carried her into his life—past it, the same feet had carried her out again. It had been their trysting place—had kept their secrets like a faithful friend and had stood to him as the changeless symbol of their love. It had stood a mute but sympathetic witness of his hopes, his despairs and the struggles that lay between them. In dark hours it had been a silent comforter, and in the last year it had almost come to symbolize his better self as to that self he came slowly back. And in the darkest hour it was the last friend to whom he had meant to say good-by. Now it was gone. Always he had lifted his eyes to it every morning when he rose, but now, next morning, he hung back consciously as one might shrink from looking at the face of a dead friend, and when at last he raised his head to look upward to it, an impenetrable shroud of mist lay between them—and he was glad.

And still he could not leave. The little creek was a lashing yellow torrent, and his horse, heavily laden as he must be, could hardly swim with his weight, too, across so swift a stream. But mountain streams were like June's temper—up quickly and quickly down—so it was noon before he plunged into the tide with his saddle-pockets over one shoulder and his heavy transit under one arm. Even then his snorting horse had to swim a few yards, and he reached the other bank soaked to his waist line. But the warm sun came out just as he entered the woods, and as he climbed, the mists broke about him and scudded upward like white sails before a driving wind. Once he looked back from a "fire-scald" in the woods at the lonely cabin in the cove, but it gave him so

keen a pain that he would not look again. The
trail was slippery and several times he had to stop
to let his horse rest and to slow the beating of his
own heart. But the sunlight leaped gladly from
wet leaf to wet leaf until the trees looked decked
out for unseen fairies, and the birds sang as though
there was nothing on earth but joy for all its
creatures, and the blue sky smiled above as though
it had never bred a lightning flash or a storm.
Hale dreaded the last spur before the little Gap
was visible, but he hurried up the steep, and when
he lifted his apprehensive eyes, the gladness of the
earth was as nothing to the sudden joy in his own
heart. The big Pine stood majestic, still unscathed, as full of divinity and hope to him as a
rainbow in an eastern sky. Hale dropped his
reins, lifted one hand to his dizzy head, let his
transit to the ground, and started for it on a run.
Across the path lay a great oak with a white wound
running the length of its mighty body, from crest
to shattered trunk, and over it he leaped, and like
a child caught his old friend in both arms. After
all, he was not alone. One friend would be with
him till death, on that border-line between the
world in which he was born and the world he had
tried to make his own, and he could face now the
old one again with a stouter heart. There it lay
before him with its smoke and fire and noise and
slumbering activities just awakening to life again.
He lifted his clenched fist toward it:

"You got *me* once," he muttered, "but this time I'll get *you*." He turned quickly and decisively—there would be no more delay. And he went back and climbed over the big oak that, instead of his friend, had fallen victim to the lightning's kindly whim and led his horse out into the underbrush. As he approached within ten yards of the path, a metallic note rang faintly on the still air the other side of the Pine and down the mountain. Something was coming up the path, so he swiftly knotted his bridle-reins around a sapling, stepped noiselessly into the path and noiselessly slipped past the big tree where he dropped to his knees, crawled forward and lay flat, peering over the cliff and down the winding trail. He had not long to wait. A riderless horse filled the opening in the covert of leaves that swallowed up the path. It was gray and he knew it as he knew the saddle as his old enemy's—Dave. Dave had kept his promise—he had come back. The dream was coming true, and they were to meet at last face to face. One of them was to strike a trail more lonesome than the Trail of the Lonesome Pine, and that man would not be John Hale. One detail of the dream was going to be left out, he thought grimly, and very quietly he drew his pistol, cocked it, sighted it on the opening—it was an easy shot —and waited. He would give that enemy no more chance than he would a mad dog—or would he? The horse stopped to browse. He waited so

long that he began to suspect a trap. He withdrew his head and looked about him on either side
and behind—listening intently for the cracking of
a twig or a footfall. He was about to push backward to avoid possible attack from the rear, when
a shadow shot from the opening. His face paled
and looked sick of a sudden, his clenched fingers
relaxed about the handle of his pistol and he drew
it back, still cocked, turned on his knees, walked
past the Pine, and by the fallen oak stood upright,
waiting. He heard a low whistle calling to the
horse below and a shudder ran through him. He
heard the horse coming up the path, he clenched
his pistol convulsively, and his eyes, lit by an un-
earthly fire and fixed on the edge of the bowlder
around which they must come, burned an instant
later on—June. At the cry she gave, he flashed a
hunted look right and left, stepped swiftly to one
side and stared past her—still at the bowlder. She
had dropped the reins and started toward him,
but at the Pine she stopped short.

"Where is he?"

Her lips opened to answer, but no sound came.
Hale pointed at the horse behind her.

"That's his. He sent me word. He left that
horse in the valley, to ride over here, when he came
back, to kill me. Are *you* with him?" For a moment she thought from his wild face that he had
gone crazy and she stared silently. Then she
seemed to understand, and with a moan she cov-

ered her face with her hands and sank weeping in a heap at the foot of the Pine.

The forgotten pistol dropped, full cocked to the soft earth, and Hale with bewildered eyes went slowly to her.

"Don't cry,"—he said gently, starting to call her name. "Don't cry," he repeated, and he waited helplessly.

"He's dead. Dave was shot—out—West," she sobbed. "I told him I was coming back. He gave me his horse. Oh, how could you?"

"Why did you come back?" he asked, and she shrank as though he had struck her—but her sobs stopped and she rose to her feet.

"Wait," she said, and she turned from him to wipe her eyes with her handerchief. Then she faced him.

"When dad died, I learned everything. You made him swear never to tell me and he kept his word until he was on his death-bed. *You* did everything for me. It was *your* money. *You* gave me back the old cabin in the Cove. It was always you, you, *you*, and there was never anybody else but you." She stopped for Hale's face was as though graven from stone.

"And you came back to tell me that?"

"Yes."

"You could have written that."

"Yes," she faltered, "but I had to tell you face to face."

"Is that all?"

Again the tears were in her eyes.

"No," she said tremulously.

"Then I'll say the rest for you. You wanted to come to tell me of the shame you felt when you knew," she nodded violently—"but you could have written that, too, and I could have written that you mustn't feel that way—that" he spoke slowly—"you mustn't rob me of the dearest happiness I ever knew in my whole life."

"I knew you would say that," she said like a submissive child. The sternness left his face and he was smiling now.

"And you wanted to say that the only return you could make was to come back and be my wife."

"Yes," she faltered again, "I did feel that—I did."

"You could have written that, too, but you thought you had to *prove* it by coming back yourself."

This time she nodded no assent and her eyes were streaming. He turned away—stretching out his arms to the woods.

"God! Not that—no—no!"

"Listen, Jack!" As suddenly his arms dropped. She had controlled her tears but her lips were quivering.

"No, Jack, not that—thank God. I came because I wanted to come," she said steadily. "I loved you when I went away. I've loved you every minute since—" her arms were stealing about his neck, her face was upturned to his and her eyes, moist with gladness, were looking into his wondering eyes—"and I love you now—Jack."

"June!" The leaves about them caught his cry and quivered with the joy of it, and above their heads the old Pine breathed its blessing with the name—June—June—June.

XXXV

WITH a mystified smile but with no question, Hale silently handed his penknife to June and when, smiling but without a word, she walked behind the old Pine, he followed her. There he saw her reach up and dig the point of the knife into the trunk, and when, as he wonderingly watched her, she gave a sudden cry, Hale sprang toward her. In the hole she was digging he saw the gleam of gold and then her trembling fingers brought out before his astonished eyes the little fairy stone that he had given her long ago. She had left it there for him, she said, through tears, and through his own tears Hale pointed to the stricken oak:

"It saved the Pine," he said.

"And you," said June.

"And you," repeated Hale solemnly, and while he looked long at her, her arms dropped slowly to her sides and he said simply:

"Come!"

.   .   .   .   .   .

Leading the horses, they walked noiselessly through the deep sand around the clump of rhododendron, and there sat the little cabin of Lonesome Cove. The holy hush of a cathedral seemed to shut it in from the world, so still it was below the great trees that stood like sentinels on eternal guard. Both stopped, and June laid her head on Hale's shoulder and they simply looked in silence.

"Dear old home," she said, with a little sob, and Hale, still silent, drew her to him.

"You were *never* coming back again?"

"I was never coming back again." She clutched his arm fiercely as though even now something might spirit him away, and she clung to him, while he hitched the horses and while they walked up the path.

"Why, the garden is just as I left it! The very same flowers in the very same places!" Hale smiled.

"Why not? I had Uncle Billy do that."

"Oh, you dear—you dear!"

Her little room was shuttered tight as it always had been when she was away, and, as usual, the front door was simply chained on the outside. The girl turned with a happy sigh and looked about at the nodding flowers and the woods and the gleaming pool of the river below and up the shimmering mountain to the big Pine topping it with sombre majesty.

"Dear old Pine," she murmured, and almost unconsciously she unchained the door as she had so often done before, stepped into the dark room, pulling Hale with one hand after her, and almost unconsciously reaching upward with the other to the right of the door. Then she cried aloud:

"My key—my key is there!"

"That was in case you should come back some day."

"Oh, I might—I might! and think if I had come too late—think if I hadn't come *now!*" Again her voice broke and still holding Hale's arm, she moved to her own door. She had to use both hands there, but before she let go, she said almost hysterically:

"It's so dark! You won't leave me, dear, if I let you go?"

For answer Hale locked his arms around her, and when the door opened, he went in ahead of her and pushed open the shutters. The low sun flooded the room and when Hale turned, June was looking with wild eyes from one thing to another in the room—her rocking-chair at a window, her sewing close by, a book on the table, her bed made up in the corner, her washstand of curly maple—the pitcher full of water and clean towels hanging from the rack. Hale had gotten out the things she had packed away and the room was just as she had always kept it. She rushed to him, weeping.

"It would have killed me," she sobbed. "It would have killed me." She strained him tightly to her—her wet face against his cheek: "Think—*think*—if I hadn't come now!" Then loosening

410

herself she went all about the room with a caressing touch to everything, as though it were alive. The book was the volume of Keats he had given her—which had been loaned to Loretta before June went away.

"Oh, I wrote for it and wrote for it," she said.

"I found it in the post-office," said Hale, "and I understood."

She went over to the bed.

"Oh," she said with a happy laugh. "You've got one slip inside out," and she whipped the pillow from its place, changed it, and turned down the edge of the covers in a triangle.

"That's the way I used to leave it," she said shyly. Hale smiled.

"I never noticed that!" She turned to the bureau and pulled open a drawer. In there were white things with frills and blue ribbons—and she flushed.

"Oh," she said, "these haven't even been touched." Again Hale smiled but he said nothing. One glance had told him there were things in that drawer too sacred for his big hands.

"I'm so happy—so happy."

Suddenly she looked him over from head to foot—his rough riding boots, old riding breeches and blue flannel shirt.

"I am pretty rough," he said. She flushed, shook her head and looked down at her smart cloth suit of black.

"Oh, *you* are all right—but you must go out now, just for a little while."

"What are you up to, little girl?"

"How I love to hear that again!"

"Aren't you afraid I'll run away?" he said at the door.

"I'm not afraid of anything else in this world any more."

"Well, I won't."

He heard her moving around as he sat planning in the porch.

"To-morrow," he thought, and then an idea struck him that made him dizzy. From within June cried:

"Here I am," and out she ran in the last crimson gown of her young girlhood—her sleeves rolled up and her hair braided down her back as she used to wear it.

"You've made up my bed and I'm going to make yours—and I'm going to cook your supper—why, what's the matter?" Hale's face was radiant with the heaven-born idea that lighted it, and he seemed hardly to notice the change she had made. He came over and took her in his arms:

"Ah, sweetheart, *my* sweetheart!" A spasm of anxiety tightened her throat, but Hale laughed from sheer delight.

"Never you mind. It's a secret," and he stood back to look at her. She blushed as his eyes went downward to her perfect ankles.

"It *is* too short," she said.

"No, no, no! Not for me! You're mine now, little girl, *mine*—do you understand that?"

"Yes," she whispered, her mouth trembling. Again he laughed joyously.

"Come on!" he cried, and he went into the kitchen and brought out an axe:

"I'll cut wood for you." She followed him out to the wood-pile and then she turned and went into the house. Presently the sound of his axe rang through the woods, and as he stooped to gather up the wood, he heard a creaking sound. June was drawing water at the well, and he rushed toward her:

"Here, you mustn't do that."

She flashed a happy smile at him.

"You just go back and get that wood. I reckon," she used the word purposely, "I've done this afore." Her strong bare arms were pulling the leaking moss-covered old bucket swiftly up, hand under hand—so he got the wood while she emptied the bucket into a pail, and together they went laughing into the kitchen, and while he built the fire, June got out the coffee-grinder and the meal to mix, and settled herself with the grinder in her lap.

"Oh, isn't it fun?" She stopped grinding suddenly.

"What would the neighbours say?"

"We haven't any."

413

"But if we had!"

"Terrible!" said Hale with mock solemnity.

"I wonder if Uncle Billy is at home," Hale trembled at his luck. "That's a good idea. I'll ride down for him while you're getting supper."

"No, you won't," said June, "I can't spare you. Is that old horn here yet?"

Hale brought it out from behind the cupboard.

"I can get him—if he is at home."

Hale followed her out to the porch where she put her red mouth to the old trumpet. One long, mellow hoot rang down the river—and up the hills. Then there were three short ones and a single long blast again.

"That's the old signal," she said. "And he'll know I want him *bad*." Then she laughed.

"He may think he's dreaming, so I'll blow for him again." And she did.

"There, now," she said. "He'll come."

It was well she did blow again, for the old miller was not at home and old Hon, down at the cabin, dropped her iron when she heard the horn and walked to the door, dazed and listening. Even when it came again she could hardly believe her ears, and but for her rheumatism, she would herself have started at once for Lonesome Cove. As it was, she ironed no more, but sat in the doorway almost beside herself with anxiety and bewilderment, looking down the road for the old miller to come home.

Back the two went into the kitchen and Hale sat at the door watching June as she fixed the table and made the coffee and corn bread. Once only he disappeared and that was when suddenly a hen cackled, and with a shout of laughter he ran out to come back with a fresh egg.

"Now, my lord!" said June, her hair falling over her eyes and her face flushed from the heat.

"No," said Hale. "I'm going to wait on you."

"For the last time," she pleaded, and to please her he did sit down, and every time she came to his side with something he bent to kiss the hand that served him.

"You're nothing but a big, nice boy," she said. Hale held out a lock of his hair near the temples and with one finger silently followed the track of wrinkles in his face.

"It's premature," she said, "and I love every one of them." And she stooped to kiss him on the hair. "And those are nothing but troubles. I'm going to smooth every one of *them* away."

"If they're troubles, they'll go—now," said Hale.

All the time they talked of what they would do with Lonesome Cove.

"Even if we do go away, we'll come back once a year," said Hale.

"Yes," nodded June, "once a year."

"I'll tear down those mining shacks, float them down the river and sell them as lumber."

"Yes."

"And I'll stock the river with bass again."

"Yes."

"And I'll plant young poplars to cover the sight of every bit of uptorn earth along the mountain there. I'll bury every bottle and tin can in the Cove. I'll take away every sign of civilization, every sign of the outside world."

"And leave old Mother Nature to cover up the scars," said June.

"So that Lonesome Cove will be just as it was."

"Just as it was in the beginning," echoed June.

"And shall be to the end," said Hale.

"And there will never be anybody here but you."

"And you," said June.

While she cleared the table and washed the dishes Hale fed the horses and cut more wood, and it was dusk when he came to the porch. Through the door he saw that she had made his bed in one corner. And through her door he saw one of the white things, that had lain untouched in her drawer, now stretched out on her bed.

The stars were peeping through the blue spaces of a white-clouded sky and the moon would be coming by and by. In the garden the flowers were dim, quiet and restful. A kingfisher screamed from the river. An owl hooted in the woods and crickets chirped about them, but every passing sound seemed only to accentuate the stillness in which they were engulfed. Close together they sat on the old porch and she made him tell of everything that had happened since she left the mountains, and she told him of her flight from the mountains and her life in the West—of her father's death and the homesickness of the ones who still were there.

"Bub is a cowboy and wouldn't come back for the world, but I could never have been happy there," she said, "even if it hadn't been for you—here."

"I'm just a plain civil engineer, now," said Hale, "an engineer without even a job and—" his face darkened.

"It's a shame, sweetheart, for you—" She put one hand over his lips and with the other turned his face so that she could look into his eyes. In the mood of bitterness, they did show worn, hollow and sad, and around them the wrinkles were deep.

"Silly," she said, tracing them gently with her finger tips, "I love every one of them, too," and she leaned over and kissed them.

"We're going to be happy each and every day, and all day long! We'll live at the Gap in winter and I'll teach."

"No, you won't."

"Then I'll teach *you* to be patient and how little I care for anything else in the world while I've got you, and I'll teach you to care for nothing else while you've got me. And you'll have me, dear, forever and ever——"

"Amen," said Hale.

Something rang out in the darkness, far down the river, and both sprang to their feet. "It's Uncle Billy!" cried June, and she lifted the old horn to her lips. With the first blare of it, a cheery halloo answered, and a moment later they could see a gray horse coming up the road—coming at a gallop, and they went down to the gate and waited.

"Hello, Uncle Billy!" cried June. The old man answered with a fox-hunting yell and Hale stepped behind a bush.

"Jumping Jehosophat—is that you, June? Air ye all right?"

"Yes, Uncle Billy!" The old man climbed off his horse with a groan.

"Lordy, Lordy, Lordy, but I was skeered!" He had his hands on June's shoulders and was looking at her with a bewildered face.

"What air ye doin' here alone, baby?"

June's eyes shone: "Nothin', Uncle Billy." Hale stepped into sight.

"Oh, ho! I see! You back an' he ain't gone! Well, bless my soul, if this ain't the beatenest—" he looked from the one to the other and his kind old face beamed with a joy that was but little less than their own.

"You come back to stay?"

June nodded.

"My—where's that horn? I want it right now. Ole Hon down thar is a-thinkin' she's gone crazy and I thought she shorely was when she said she heard you blow that horn. An' she tol' me the minute I got here, if hit was you—to blow three times." And straightway three blasts rang down the river.

"Now she's all right, if she don't die o' curiosity afore I git back and tell her why you come. Why did you come back, baby? Gimme a drink o' water, son. I reckon me an' that ole hoss hain't travelled sech a gait in five year."

June was whispering something to the old man when Hale came back, and what it was the old man's face told plainly.

"Yes, Uncle Billy—right away," said Hale.

"Just as soon as you can git yo' license?" Hale nodded.

"An' June says I'm goin' to do it."

"Yes," said Hale, "right away."

Again June had to tell the story to Uncle Billy that she had told to Hale and to answer his questions, and it was an hour before the old miller rose to go. Hale called him then into June's room and showed him a piece of paper.

"Is it good now?" he asked.

The old man put on his spectacles, looked at it and chuckled:

"Just as good as the day you got hit."

"Well, can't you——"

419

"Right now! Does June know?"

"Not yet. I'm going to tell her now. June!" he called.

"Yes, dear." Uncle Billy moved hurriedly to the door.

"You just wait till I git out o' here." He met June in the outer room.

"Where are you going, Uncle Billy?"

"Go on, baby," he said, hurrying by her, "I'll be back in a minute."

She stopped in the doorway—her eyes wide again with sudden anxiety, but Hale was smiling.

"You remember what you said at the Pine, dear?" The girl nodded and she was smiling now, when with sweet seriousness she said again: "Your least wish is now law to me, my lord."

"Well, I'm going to test it now. I've laid a trap for you." She shook her head.

"And you've walked right into it."

"I'm glad." She noticed now the crumpled piece of paper in his hand and she thought it was some matter of business.

"Oh," she said, reproachfully. "You aren't going to bother with anything of that kind *now?*"

"Yes," he said. "I want you to look over this."

"Very well," she said resignedly. He was holding the paper out to her and she took it and held it to the light of the candle. Her face flamed and she turned remorseful eyes upon him.

420

"And you've kept that, too, you had it when I——"

"When you were wiser maybe than you are now."

"God save me from ever being such a fool again." Tears started in her eyes.

"You haven't forgiven me!" she cried.

"Uncle Billy says it's as good now as it was then."

He was looking at her queerly now and his smile was gone. Slowly his meaning came to her like the flush that spread over her face and throat. She drew in one long quivering breath and, with parted lips and her great shining eyes wide, she looked at him.

"Now?" she whispered.

"Now!" he said.

Her eyes dropped to the coarse gown, she lifted both hands for a moment to her hair and unconsciously she began to roll one crimson sleeve down her round, white arm.

"No," said Hale, "just as you are."

She went to him then, put her arms about his neck, and with head thrown back she looked at him long with steady eyes.

"Yes," she breathed out—"just as you are—and now."

Uncle Billy was waiting for them on the porch and when they came out, he rose to his feet and they faced him, hand in hand. The moon had risen. The big Pine stood guard on high against the outer world. Nature was their church and stars were their candles. And as if to give them even a better light, the moon had sent a luminous sheen down the dark mountainside to the very garden in which the flowers whispered like waiting happy friends. Uncle Billy lifted his hand and a hush of expectancy seemed to come even from the farthest star.

For your reading pleasure ...